KITCHENER PUBLIC LIBRARY
3 9098 01182005 6

D1396860

MISSING MAN

MICHAEL CASSUTT

MISSING MAN

A TOM DOHERTY ASSOCIATES BOOK

NEW YORK

This is a work of fiction. All the characters and events portrayed in this novel are either fictitious or are used fictitiously.

MISSING MAN

Copyright © 1998 by St. Croix Productions, Inc.

All rights reserved, including the right to reproduce this book, or portions thereof, in any form.

This book is printed on acid-free paper.

A Forge Book
Published by Tom Doherty Associates, Inc.
175 Fifth Avenue
New York, NY 10010

Forge® is a registered trademark of Tom Doherty Associates, Inc.

Design by Ann Gold

Diagram by Mark Stein Studios

Library of Congress Cataloging-in-Publication Data

Cassutt, Michael.
    Missing man / Michael Cassutt. — 1st ed.
        p.   cm.
    "A Tom Doherty Associates book."
    ISBN 0–312–86620–8 (alk. paper)
    I. Title
PS3553.A812M5   1998
813'.54—dc21   98–22541

First Edition: September 1998

Printed in the United States of America

0   9   8   7   6   5   4   3   2   1

FOR MY PARENTS

PART I

THE COMMANDMENTS

THE ASTRONAUT CANDIDATE'S TEN COMMANDMENTS

1. Thou shalt smile, but not grin.
2. Thou shalt keep thy humor harmless, pure and perfect, without irony.
3. Thou shalt keep thy weaknesses to thyself; others may thus fail to notice.
4. Thou shalt not complain; maketh survival look easy.
5. Thou shalt make compliments after each flight, class or simulation.
6. If thou canst not say something nice, thou shalt lie.
7. Thou shalt practice saying "Thanks for pointing that out, sir! I'll really work on that!" all the days of thy life.
8. Thou shalt be aggressively humble and dynamically inconspicuous.
9. That which is encouraged is mandatory; that which is discouraged is forbidden.
10. When in doubt, say thou nothing.

REVIEW THIS LIST DAILY!

CHAPTER 1

Twelve miles south of Galveston, strapped into the rear cockpit of NASA T-38 number 911, Mark Koskinen began to wonder if he really had the Right Stuff after all.

It wasn't an admission that came easily to him. He was thirty-three years old and had wanted to be an astronaut for at least twenty of those years. He had built Estes model rockets and dragged his parents to all the IMAX movies about the Space Shuttle. He had majored in aerospace engineering and spent seven years in the Air Force. He had worked hard to qualify for selection—not only getting the right training but keeping himself in good physical condition (the new astronauts were going to be doing a lot of space walks on the International Space Station) and broadening himself: he had learned to fly gliders and taken a Dale Carnegie course in public speaking.

With all that, NASA had *still* turned him down on his first application, selecting him only on his second try, after he'd finished his master's degree. He had persisted; he had earned his place.

On this bright October morning he had been an astronaut candidate—ASCAN—for six months. He had undergone a week of NASA orientation. He had attended college-level classes in astronomy, geology, and aerospace medicine. He had started to learn the systems and architecture of the Shuttle orbiter and the ISS. And, like all mission specialist astronaut candidates, Mark had attended Air Force flight school, to qualify as a backseater in the T-38. So far Mark had logged exactly 127 hours of time in the bird—a meager amount for an operational air crew member but enough to make him feel at home in the aircraft. He had probably flown with twenty different pilots, ranging from the ones who flew slow and steady to the hot dogs who lived to make the guy in the backseat throw up.

None of this had prepared him for the Joe Buerhle experience.

Colonel Joseph Buerhle, USAF, a veteran test pilot and astronaut with over 4,500 flying hours and four Shuttle missions, was the guy in the front seat. And what a ride he had given Mark so far!

It started with the rotation at Ellington Field. The supersonic T-38 wasn't much more than a set of stubby wings mounted in front of two huge Pratt and Whitney engines. That and a pair of seats. Pilots called it the white rocket, and taking off left you with no illusions about its lift over drag . . . when a T-38 rotated, you were going *up*, and straight up was where NASA 911 had gone, so straight that Mark was sure he felt the beginnings of a stall burble. It was hard to tell, flat on his back, pulling four Gs and staring at the blue sky in front of him.

Then the bird had whipped through a series of turns before leveling out for the streak toward the operating area over the Gulf of Mexico, fifty miles south.

All these gymnastics had taken place within a few miles of the runway, uncomfortably close to the houses, apartments (including Mark's own) and malls of Clear Lake, Seabrook and League City. Mark was sure he saw the sprawling campus of the Johnson Space Center during one of those turns. Had there been such a thing as an air traffic patrolman, he would have expected to hear sirens, too.

Mark was amazed that he, the plane and Buerhle had lived through the maneuvers. What was more miraculous was the apparent ease with which Buerhle had done things. The only words he had said to Mark after receiving clearance to take off were: "Ready to rumble?"

When he had wound up slotted to Buerhle's plane, luck of the draw after Steve Goslin, the Marine who was his original pilot, turned out to be a last-minute scratch, Mark had expected something out of the ordinary. Buerhle, after all, was the chief of the astronaut office. Mark had seen him presiding over the weekly pilots' meetings for six months. Buerhle was handsome, popular and charismatic.

But he had never struck Mark as a silk scarf guy, a kick-the-wheels, strap-on-the-bird, light-this-candle kind of flier. He was known to be quite the opposite, a tough, demanding, by-the-book pilot who was all too ready to land on those who broke the rules. (And there were several habitual offenders in the astronaut office.)

And here he was, hot-rodding all over south Texas, and now the Gulf of Mexico, like a teenager with his first license. Every maneuver was harsher than it really needed to be, and as Mark struggled to hold on to his breakfast, he felt a little like the man being ridden out of town on a rail: if not for the honor of the experience, he would just as soon have missed it.

Then Joe Buerhle suddenly said, "Hey, Mark, take the stick."

The response was automatic. When the pilot offered you control, you took it. "Got it."

Feet on the rudders, hands on the stick. Try to fly it straight, Mark told himself. Nice and easy does it. Here he was, flying Joe Buerhle's airplane—

"Okay, Mark, why don't you give me a two-minute turn to the right?"

Now, this was something new. Doing a two-minute turn meant putting the snub-nosed T-38 into a bank and taking it through a full circle. Joe Buerhle could do it with his eyes closed. So could any of the pilots and a few of the mission specialists in the astronaut office. Mark had done such turns in small planes—well, at least twice—and in gliders. He eased the stick to the right . . . gently, gently . . . and then waited maybe fifteen seconds before moving the stick back to neutral.

"Nice touch, for a scope dope," Buerhle said. The term was hardly a compliment coming from a pilot, but Mark was proud of his time as a satellite controller. It was one of the jobs that had gotten him hired by NASA, after all.

"Copy that." Give him a little scope dope lingo.

The Gulf of Mexico shone through the clouds above and around them. *Whoosh*, they punched through. There was a chance of rain—this time of year along the Gulf there was always a chance of rain—but the sun was bright and the sky was blue.

"Sorry about the bumps on the way up," Buerhle said. "I just started feeling a little light-headed. Remind me never to have a Le-Roy's special late at night again."

Le-Roy's was the Cajun restaurant right outside the main gate at Ellington Field. "I always thought Le-Roy overdid the jalapeños," Mark said. Buerhle laughed, and Mark began to relax. He was acutely aware that his every move was being performed under surveillance, but had no fear of screwing up. People who were insecure didn't get selected as astronauts. People who didn't get a little insecure after selection weren't paying attention, but Mark honored the ASCAN Commandments, especially the third one, about keeping your weaknesses to yourself. And he knew how to keep a T-38 straight and level.

Joe Buerhle was still laughing. Mark knew he could be funny from time to time, but not that funny. Something wasn't right here.

For an instant Mark felt a sickening chill. Suppose this was a bizarre initiation rite? Break in the new ASCAN. Or worse yet, a test! Would he be too intimidated by his commander's reputation to do his job? It didn't matter anymore—

"Colonel, I think we ought to turn back."

"Not yet." He heard Buerhle laugh. "I don't want them to know it was us falling all over the sky back there. I don't need my ticket yanked."

"Me, neither."

"Well, then, let's give it a few minutes. I'm feeling better." Before Mark could say anything, the stick smacked against his right knee, and Buerhle announced, "I've got it now."

And then Mark was lying on his back with nothing but the sky in front of him. He watched the altimeter numbers going up, then suddenly felt thrown to his left as Buerhle put the plane into a turn.

"That seem like a guy in trouble, Mark?"

Well, yes, actually, it did.

"Have it your way, Colonel . . . I'm not feeling good." There, he'd said it. If this was some screwy test, he had just flunked it.

But Buerhle ignored him. The T-38 was snapped into a quick roll. Then a second. A third.

That third roll made Mark's stomach a lot more queasy. He was suddenly aware of his own breath hissing in the face mask. "Colonel Buerhle?"

There was no answer. Buerhle put the bird in a steep climb, then nosed over into a flat spin. Mark knew that this was the kind of thing that your ordinary pilot never wanted to see . . . wouldn't know how to avert. But he also knew that Joe Buerhle had taught spin recovery at Edwards.

The real Joe Buerhle, that is. Not this impostor in the front seat.

The bird was well south in the bay now, with Galveston and the Bolivar Peninsula far behind them. "Now, listen, Mark, this is worse than anything you'll encounter on an ascent or entry. If you can hack this, you can hack anything." Mark appreciated the sentiment, but Buerhle sounded strange, manic.

They rolled right again and nosed down. Mark waited for the crushing six-G pullout at the bottom. Concentrate on the instruments. Think about the fact that Joe Buerhle just thought of you on a Shuttle crew—

At fifty-four hundred feet Mark saw the engine warning light. He looked

at it with a surprising sense of detachment, even though he knew they were
in a pretty steep dive to be messing with an engine out. "Warning light,"
Mark said, waiting for Buerhle to deal with it.

"Nolo problemo."

Sure enough, they began to level out . . . and Mark found that he had
been holding his breath. Buerhle tried starting the engine. *Bang.* Nothing.
Bang again . . . still nothing. Mark tried to remember how well a T-38 would
fly on one engine—

"Oh, man. . . ."

Suddenly they were in clouds, and Mark wasn't sure he'd heard
Buerhle's words. "Colonel?"

"You know what?" Buerhle's voice was suddenly calm. "I can't see."
The bird stayed in an ungodly bank. It started to buffet. Mark could hear
Buerhle's labored breathing in the helmet phone.

"Let me take it!" Without waiting for confirmation, Mark grabbed at
the stick just as the plane broke free of the clouds. Now Mark saw that they
were nose down, rolled to the left, and getting very goddamn close to the
water. And, oh God, the bird wasn't responding! They were stalled!

"Get out!"

Those weeks of training paid off. Without thinking, Mark forced himself
back into his seat and squeezed the handles.

There was a bang and a puff of smoke as the canopy blew off, then a
wrenching jolt as the rockets beneath the seat fired. He felt a blast of wind
on his chest and face. Before he could even orient himself, the seat fell away
and his parachute jerked open.

He looked around wildly for another chute—nothing. Then he heard a
muffled smash. Wrenching himself around, he saw a plume of black smoke
on the water. The plane had gone in.

Still no sign of Joe Buerhle.

Mark Koskinen braced himself as the waters of the Gulf rose all too
quickly to meet him.

CHAPTER 2

For an astronaut, the first four or six weeks after a space flight were usually a time of misery. Forget about the parades and speeches to the hometown folks. That sort of acclaim was reserved for the heroes of Mercury or Apollo, not to the latest run-of-the-mill Shuttle crew. The postflight experience for an astronaut in the 1990s consisted of endless debriefs with the folks in the Mission Operations Directorate (MOD).

What made it worse was the fact that almost every astronaut went through this tedious round of second-guessing and memo writing feeling listless, grouchy, easily bored, satisfied by nothing. There was even a name for the syndrome: postorbital remorse (POR).

Knowing what it was didn't make it any easier to endure. Expecting POR, to Kelly Gessner's surprise, only seemed to have made it worse, like premenstrual unpleasantness, doubled. Otherwise there was no explanation for the violent way she had squealed her Volvo out of the parking lot at Ellington and headed straight for Joe Buerhle's house in Clear Lake. She hadn't intended to make that trip; she had planned to head for the astronaut office after dropping Joe off at ops. She had yet to look at her desk after returning from sixteen days in space and was afraid of the stack of messages she would find.

But they had had an argument. Make that an out-and-out fight, with raised voices on both sides. It was thirty minutes in the past, and already she'd forgotten how it had started. Some innocent remark of hers, probably, that Joe, being especially sensitive, had taken as criticism.

It wasn't as though they had been living together, though Kelly had spent many nights at Joe's place. It wasn't as though they had even slept together in something like six weeks. But whatever it was, their relationship had somehow come to a definite end.

Maybe it was the sight of Joe's T-38 roaring off the runway at Ellington that caused Kelly to wave off, as Joe liked to say, and head for his house. He was in the air, where he belonged. He would simply land and hope to find the whole Kelly business settled, without having to have one of *those* conversations.

Kelly realized she had not visited his house in a month, and even that had been in the company of the STS-93 flight crew, for the chief astronaut's traditional barbecue. The house was a relatively tiny, one-story place with a yard that had not, in Kelly's time with Joe, been touched by a mower or a gardener. He was a believer in the natural look. "People drive themselves nuts trying to make a swamp look like Iowa," he had told her once. "It's south Texas . . . let it grow wild." Growing wild wasn't actually an option: the front yard consisted of a gravel driveway and a sidewalk. The backyard was mostly bare earth, though some years past Joe had acquired a small storage bin. Inside it were spare pieces of the homebuilt airplane he kept over at Houston Gulf Airport. One weekend Kelly had brought a couple of rosebushes around and stuck them in the back, but Joe failed to water them, and they had died.

Kelly let herself in with the key and immediately began looking for her belongings.

Unlike the houses of the other men in Kelly's life, this one looked lived in. Maybe too lived in. It wasn't sloppy—the matter of the yard aside. Joe had been single for ten years when Kelly met him, and had acquired some of the habits of a perpetual bachelor. He really did know a Randall's Supermarket over in League City that had the best prices on steaks. He had a wonderful CD player and big-screen TV with blessedly undersized speakers. There were even some expensive silk sheets for the bed. And there was always food in the refrigerator. (Never beer; Joe drank vodka when he drank at all.) It might have been your basic meat, salad and potatoes, but it was, in fact, more food than Kelly had ever managed to lodge in her own refrigerator at any point in her unmarried life.

But even as chief astronaut Joe traveled a lot. Clothes piled up. Paperwork got scattered. And in the last year Joe had started upgrading his home computer system, so there were diskettes, magazines and Internet guides piled on all available surfaces as well as the floor. A couple of dust bunnies in the corner.

The sweep didn't take long. Kelly had one nice dress—worn exactly once with Joe—in the closet, along with a couple of shirts. Some underwear and jeans in the drawer. That would all fit under one arm.

She found a cardboard box in the closet, went into the bathroom and scooped up her backup toothbrush, her spare diaphragm, and a whole array of conditioners, shampoos and makeup. Good God, she had more of this stuff at Joe's place than she did at her own! Of course, Joe liked his women to look like women. That didn't necessarily mean vamp it up like a runway model; the dress code for women around JSC was strictly soccer mom. But he liked her to wear lipstick and mascara from time to time. Even high heels.

Their relationship had never been about love or commitment, just companionship. Play. Honesty. But Joe had simply dropped her. Stopped wanting her. Maybe it was because she was in training—flying the Shuttle—and he was behind a desk. Whatever . . . she really wished he was standing here so she could tell him what an asshole he was.

Maybe she was just disgusted with the whole business. Here she was, thirty-four years old, sneaking her belongings out of an ex-boyfriend's place. Her best friend from high school had a great husband and two children now. Kelly? Well, gee, Kelly had flown in space twice. Like three hundred and eighty other people. It wasn't a very exclusive club anymore. And was she having fun? The longer mission had been less fun than the first. All she faced in the future were longer missions aboard the International Space Station. Or a series of dreary technical assignments, like being chief of the computer support branch.

Maybe it was time to look around for a new job, too.

Kelly had the clothes under one arm and the box under the other as she went back to the living room for one last look. Where she wound up was at Joe's look-at-me wall, the one with all the pictures of Joe's airplanes . . . Joe's Shuttle missions.

Their Shuttle mission, STS-76. There was a picture of the two of them floating on the mid-deck . . . Oh my God, that inscription: "To Joe, the best stick a girl astronaut could find!" She must have been drunk when she wrote that. She took it off the wall and stuck it in the box, too.

The sky had clouded over when she reached the car. It seemed colder.

"Hey, Kelly!"

She closed the trunk and looked up to see one of the neighbor kids.

"Hi." Greg, that was his name. Maybe twelve years old, a slim boy wearing glasses. "Shouldn't you be in school today?"

"Teachers' conferences." The kid was practically bursting with the need to say *something*. Kelly waited. "Uh . . . how was your flight?"

Had it been anybody over the age of twenty, she would have said, *It was awful. Too long and too smelly and too much broken equipment.* Instead: "It was terrific. Sixteen days, sixteen sunrises and sunsets every day." Well, that was why she had been selected: roll Kelly Gessner out of a warm bed in the middle of the night and she could sling that space cadet stuff like no one else.

"Oh, man." Greg was almost speechless. "I'd love to do that someday."

"Study hard. Maybe you'll get selected." Maybe you'll be the one in a hundred.

He pointed to his glasses. "My eyes."

"You don't have to have perfect eyesight. I wear contacts myself."

"You do?"

"Yeah. You can't be legally blind, of course. But as long as you're not a pilot . . ."

Rain was starting to fall.

"I'd like to be a pilot. Like Colonel Buerhle." He nodded toward the house with a gesture of what could only have been reverence.

"Well, I don't know what to tell you, except"—she leaned over and almost whispered to Greg—"*his* eyes aren't perfect either."

"No fooling?"

"It happens. It really bothers him, too." Among other failings. "Don't tell anyone."

"Oh, no."

"You'd better get inside." He still seemed anxious, somehow. Kelly forced herself to give him a warm smile. "You want to ask me something, don't you?"

He let out a breath. "Could I get an autographed picture? From your flight?"

Sometimes the body was just a little ahead of the brain. Probably all that training. The autographed "stick" picture of Kelly and Joe seemed to appear in Greg's hands. "Why don't you take this one? It's from my first flight, but . . ."

From the look on the kid's face, it wasn't going to be a problem. "Yeah, wow. Thanks, Miss Gessner."

"Kelly."

She got in her car, started it up and drove off, waving. The sky opened as Kelly hit the autodialer on her car phone and heard Shannon, one of the secretaries, answer. "Astronaut office."

Funny. She seemed to be crying.

CHAPTER 3

How are you feeling?''

Mark opened his eyes and saw Lester Fehrenkamp standing in front of him. He had not heard him enter, which was not surprising. Fehrenkamp was a slim, short man in his late fifties who looked and moved like a jockey. His supernaturally light tread allowed him to sneak up on people, which he did frequently.

''I'll live,'' Mark said. That much was true. He was lying on a bed in the infirmary of the U.S. Coast Guard facility on Galveston Channel, a little bruised and sore, but otherwise all right. His worst injury had been swallowing seawater, which had made him sick to his stomach, and still left his mouth with a briny aftertaste. Not bad for punching out over the water and having to float for over an hour until being picked up by a shrimp boat. ''What about Joe?''

''I'm not anticipating any good news on that front,'' Fehrenkamp said. ''You saw the bird go in . . . you didn't see another chute, and neither did anyone else.'' Fehrenkamp sighed. Mark saw that he was glancing over some papers, probably notes on Mark's first debrief. Fehrenkamp was the director of flight crew operations at JSC. His directorate included the astronaut office, meaning he was the man who had hired Joe Buerhle to be chief astronaut, as well as aircraft operations, meaning the airplane Joe and Mark had just wrecked was his. ''We're still searching, but . . .'' He shrugged.

''I'm sorry.'' The words were out of Mark's mouth before he could stop them. But the thought had been nagging at him, in between relief at being alive and amazement that Joe Buerhle probably wasn't: would they blame him?

''You don't have anything to apologize for. Joe Buerhle was a good stick, one of the best I've ever known. He was in charge of that aircraft, and if he told you to get out, that was your job." Mark saw the ghost of a smile on Fehrenkamp's face. "The only really bad trait all our hotshot test pilots have is that they think they can work their way out of any problem. Given the very dangerous nature of what we do, they only need to be wrong once. Yes?" Fehrenkamp turned toward the door a full second before a Coast Guard lieutenant, junior grade, appeared there. In addition to being able to creep up on people, Fehrenkamp apparently also had hearing like Batman.

"Phone call from JSC," the j.g. said. "A Mr. Hutchins."

"Dr. Hutchins," Fehrenkamp said, correcting the j.g. Dr. Maynard Hutchins was the director of the Johnson Space Center. "I'll take it." To Mark he said: "We have two more items to discuss, as soon as I'm off the phone." To the j.g.: "Can we feed this young man?" Then he was gone.

The j.g. turned to Mark. "I can run over to the commissary for you. . . ."

Mark was shocked to realize it was only lunchtime. Not even three hours had passed since the accident! He was even more shocked to realize that he was hungry. "How about a peanut butter sandwich and a Diet Coke?"

"Will do."

The j.g. left Mark alone. He closed his eyes and put himself back in the cockpit of that T-38. Yes, here was the Plexiglas cockpit, here was the back of Joe Buerhle's ejection seat, here were the instruments. Mark could still read them: heading 185, altitude 2,400 and dropping. All his life he'd possessed a trick memory, one that allowed him to retrieve snapshots of scenes, book pages, faces. Not that it was going to do him any good now.

He swung his legs off the bed and stood up. He still seemed to be in one piece. The only thing he wanted to do now was get home—get into some real clothes instead of a hospital robe—and figure out just what this was going to mean to his chances of flying in space. He tried to imagine the scene in Building 4-South right now. That was where the astronauts had their offices, up on the sixth floor, where the eighteen other members of his group would be, too. The Worms, they called themselves. Every ASCAN group invented a degrading team name to remind its members of their place in the NASA hierarchy.

This week the Worms' schedules would contain their future technical assignment. All of them now, except Mark, would have received their printouts from the schedulers . . . were they jumping up and down with joy?

Were some of them sitting in their offices looking glum and feeling depressed?

Were any of them thinking about Mark? It was killing him to be here and not there, sharing the experience. The six months of ASCAN training had made them a family, of sorts, sometimes quarreling, often jockeying for favor from Dad, but looking out for each other.

Of course, now Dad was gone. . . .

This time Mark was watching the door as Fehrenkamp glided in carrying a bundle that turned out to be a set of Coast Guard overalls. "Dr. Hutchins sends his best." Fehrenkamp hesitated for a moment, then gently closed the door. The gesture made Mark feel uneasy. "I said there were two other items to discuss. The first is that we may need your help over the next couple of weeks."

"I'll do whatever I can," Mark said, wondering just what Fehrenkamp meant.

"We've formed an accident board. Since we're a government agency, we have complete jurisdiction. We can, in effect, investigate ourselves. We don't need to turn to the National Transportation Safety Board.

"But," he added, smiling that ghost smile again, "since we *are* a government agency, we'd be asking for trouble if we didn't invite the NTSB to send a representative. In addition to the Air Force, the plane's manufacturers, aircraft ops."

"Do you want me to represent CB?" CB was the administrative code for the astronaut office within NASA.

Fehrenkamp's smile froze ever so slightly. "I have someone else in mind for that. Remember, you are a participant. We could even say a witness. You've already given a very thorough statement, and I doubt that you'll have to do anything but repeat that for the board. What I'm talking about is making yourself available to serve as an adviser or consultant for the next two weeks to a month, until there's a preliminary report."

That seemed fair. Of course, it would put Mark two weeks to a month behind his fellow Worms. "I'm sure I can be wherever I have to be," he said, thinking of the fourth Commandment, the one about not complaining.

"I felt sure you would," Fehrenkamp said, with all the calm sincerity Mark could have wanted. He slapped Mark's bed, as if to end the meeting. "Let's get you home. There's an ambulance outside—no sirens or lights," he said, anticipating Mark's protest. "We're just going to take you back to

JSC and let one of our doctors sign you out. If you'll give me your keys, I'll have your car brought over from ops."

"I rode my bike this morning."

"Then I guess we don't need to worry about that right now." He nodded at the clothing on the bed. "Get those on and we'll get you out of here."

As Fehrenkamp reached for the door, Mark said, "Les? What was the second item?"

"Hmm? Oh, your technical assignment. Joe and I were putting you in flight support, as you requested. With the support team at the Cape effective with STS-96."

Exactly what he wanted. STS-95 was scheduled for launch on Friday, too late for any personnel changes. But 96 would launch in six weeks. And here Fehrenkamp was telling Mark that he would be part of the team! He would be the guy crawling around inside the orbiter, helping the crew get strapped in. The last one to shake their hands prior to ignition. If not for the grim business of the day, and the closeness of the room, Mark would have jumped for joy.

"You understand, of course," Fehrenkamp continued, "that the board has priority over your technical assignment."

"I understand perfectly," Mark said.

The moment Fehrenkamp was gone, he added, too softly to be heard by anyone, "Thanks for pointing that out, sir. I'll really work on that."

Then he began to get dressed.

CHAPTER 4

"**C**olonel Buerhle's plane is missing."

That was the tearful message Kelly received on her car phone from Shannon the secretary. "What do you mean?"

"We had a call from Mr. Akin's office about an hour ago that his plane was overdue. . . ."

Oh my God, *oh my God*. Kelly suddenly felt sick. "Have they called around the area? He could have landed somewhere else. . . ."

"I don't know," Shannon said, as if pleading with Kelly not to ask her questions like this.

"I'm sorry," Kelly said. "I'll call Ellington direct." She hung up and tried to think. Joe's plane missing! He *couldn't* have crashed! She had flown with him enough to know he was a truly great pilot—cautious, in tune with the bird, and never stupid. And he'd been flying T-38s off and on for almost twenty years.

No, this was a mistake. A rumor. She told herself to think of something else. How had she sounded on the phone with Shannon? Calm and businesslike? Kelly had never been quite sure exactly who knew about her relationship with Joe. They had tried to be discreet, if only because Kelly didn't need people whispering that she was sleeping with their boss. He hadn't been her boss when the relationship started, but anyone who was troubled by the situation wasn't likely to be soothed by that fact.

She was due at a debrief in an hour. Should she go? One of the flight directors who would take part in the debrief was Scott McDowell, Joe's best friend! She wasn't sure she could sit there and pretend nothing had happened, especially knowing she was, in effect, putting on an act for McDowell.

And now she was crying. She blinked back tears and fumbled for a tissue.

She had to get out of this. But the debrief would be full of coldhearted flight operations people, each one trying harder than the next to prove that he couldn't be rattled. Joe Buerhle's plane is missing? Bad news. Next problem.

It was the brutal nature of their business, people dying, and not just in some *Challenger*-style accident. One astronaut Kelly knew had died in a commercial plane crash a few years back. Another had wracked up an old prop plane while doing acrobatics.

The T-38 itself had a fairly spotty record, if you went back far enough. During one bad three-year patch in the 1960s *five* astronauts had gotten killed in the thing. When Kelly flew the Shuttle Training Aircraft before joining CB she'd had a couple of close calls herself.

The rule was that you never gave up hope—never gave in to the feeling that yes, the guy was gone. But she couldn't help feeling that Joe was. Certainly she had sensed that all morning. Why else would she have been possessed by that sudden impulse to get her things out of Joe's house?

Why else would she have acted on it?

Poor Joe! He always said he wanted to die in an aircraft. "Say that loudly enough and no one's going to fly with you," she had told him once. But Joe's father had been eaten away by throat cancer—it had taken him months to die—and Kelly could understand the sentiment.

Still. It was one thing to say it, and quite another to have it happen. Joe Buerhle, dead at age forty-three. No, it was still too hard to believe.

She realized she was approaching JSC on NASA Road One. Instead of pulling in and heading for the astronaut office, she elected to keep going, turning right into what used to be a Lockheed site across the road from Space Center Houston. Sitting there in the rain, calmer than she had been, she dialed ops. "Boyd Akin, please. It's Kelly Gessner." Given what was going on, most people wouldn't be able to get through to Akin, who was the head of aircraft ops. But Kelly had worked for him. And Akin, unlike most people, knew about Joe and Kelly.

"We're doing everything we can, honey." Those were the first words out of Akin's mouth.

"Good God, Boyd. Suppose it wasn't me on the phone?" Boyd Akin was one of those old military gentlemen who believed that a woman's place was at home, in school, maybe on a stool in a smoky bar, but never in a cockpit. He tried not to show it, though.

"I'd just pretend to be someone else," he said. He quickly briefed her. "There was one of your ASCANs in the backseat. He punched out and got picked up by a boat."

"They sure as shit aren't *my* ASCANs," she snapped. "Which one?"

"Koskinen."

"I don't know him at all." That wasn't surprising. The nineteen new ASCANs had arrived at JSC just as Kelly's crew had started full-time training for STS-93. She had barely shown her face in the office for six months. "Is he a pilot?"

"No. Ex–Air Force, not rated. He seems pretty levelheaded, though."

"Is he all right?"

"Shaken up, I guess, but fine." Akin paused. "I'm putting up some of the birds to look for a chute. If Joe's out there, we'll find him."

"I know you will," Kelly said. "There are no reports he landed somewhere else?" That was Kelly's best hope, that Joe had put down somewhere along the Gulf Coast and was just out of touch.

"Not so far." Akin hesitated. "How are you, you know, doing?" Bless him, he meant emotionally.

"Fine, Boyd. Thank you. Hoping for the best." Here was Kelly the space cadet again. "I'd rather be helping out than sitting around waiting for the phone to ring." Besides, she wanted to add, Joe and I were yesterday's news, officially having ended an unofficial relationship. "I wish there was something else I could do."

Akin hesitated, then said, "The Coast Guard's going to be sending out a ship to take part in the search. . . ."

Perfect. *Perfect.* She could help out and stay away from people at the same time. "Tell me where, and let them know I'm coming. And, oh, could you call the MOD and tell them I won't be making that debrief after all?"

CHAPTER 5

Before he even made it out of Galveston's sluggish traffic and across the bridge, Les Fehrenkamp had made his assistant cry on the telephone, and for the second time this week!

Poor Valerie. She had worked for Fehrenkamp for four years now, and for three-point-seven of them had been terrific at her job. But her father had died a year back, and she had started seeing a therapist, who now had Valerie convinced that her late father had abused her. That is, if Fehrenkamp was reading Valerie's vague hints correctly; they certainly never discussed it openly. It was bad enough that Fehrenkamp was allowing her to duck out of the office early twice a week in order to see this clown. Her ability to deal with stress had vanished.

She had started blubbering on the phone over a mild Fehrenkamp re-buke. Well, she had failed to tell Fehrenkamp that Melinda Pruett had called from NASA Headquarters this morning. Melinda was one of Les's women—a former astronaut who, with a little help from Fehrenkamp, had found glory as an associate administrator. She was an incredibly valuable source of HQ gossip for Fehrenkamp, and never called without a reason. Fehrenkamp prided himself on being totally accessible to all his women, and most of his men, but especially for his feisty women, like Melinda, who would quit calling if they didn't get through.

Yes, Fehrenkamp had left the office. Yes, he had a bit of a crisis on his hands. But with the International Space Station program having to fight for its financial life every year in Washington, with the Russian participation in the program serving as a constant headache, with power over the Shuttle program and the ISS being shifted from HQ to Johnson—everything was a crisis.

Oh, yes. He had a mission launching in two days. He had been at Ellington this morning to say good-bye to the crew of STS-95. The six astronauts were flying down to the Cape in a trio of T-38s. Fehrenkamp would follow tomorrow.

Depending on how the rest of today went.

There was never a convenient time for an accident, much less a fatal crash involving his chief astronaut, but some times were better than others. As far as Les Fehrenkamp was concerned, Joe Buerhle's death couldn't have been more inconvenient. True, Buerhle wasn't in actual flight training— what a problem that would have caused! But now Fehrenkamp had to re-evaluate his senior pilot astronauts, to find someone who could take over the day-to-day running of the madhouse that was CB. He carried a lot of the training matrix in his head. . . . Not only did he know all the current flight crews—seven of them, forty different astronauts—but he could tell you which astronauts were assigned to which of the seven branches inside CB. The dozen others assigned outside the office. And how long each had served in his or her job. And where he or she should go next. And which ones had indicated that they would like to take a break from flight training (the travel and hours were absolute hell on people trying to raise young children). And which ones were scheduled to be rotated back to their parent military service. For years the Department of Defense had basically let NASA have some of its top people indefinitely. Not anymore: military astronauts were detailed to NASA for seven years, and now, with few exceptions, they were going back.

And which astronauts had screwed up and were in Les Fehrenkamp's doghouse. There were currently about five names on that list.

All this was in his head. *There was no room today for the business of forming an accident board and making funeral arrangements and reassuring HQ! None! He was sick and fucking tired of having to run everything! To make every goddamn decision!*

He realized he was shouting. Worse than that . . . the driver next to him, some Latino gentleman in a pickup, was looking at him as if he were de-ranged.

Well, for a moment he had been. His breathing returned to normal. He wondered how close he'd come to running off the road. . . .

As he passed the dog track, headed north on I-45, he realized just what to do. There was a person he could call for help! Someone who understood exactly what the pressures were! His subconscious had come through for him. He dialed his car phone.

"Valerie, it's me."

"Standing by."

"Find Don Drury for me. He's in my personal Rolodex."

"I'll call you back in five." Valerie sounded as though she'd pulled herself together. So had Fehrenkamp. Crisis averted, for now.

NASA N E W S
National Aeronautics and
Space Administration
Lyndon B. Johnson Space Center
Houston TX 77058
281 483-5111

October 12, 1998
Sam Wirth
Johnson Space Center

RELEASE 98-104

ASTRONAUT CANDIDATES COMPLETE FIRST PHASE OF TRAINING

Members of the newest group of astronaut candidates (ASCANs) have reached the six-month point in their training. By now the 19 members of the group, which includes candidates from Russia and Europe, have completed a syllabus which includes general NASA orientation and visits to NASA centers, introduction to Shuttle systems, flight operations and mission operations. They have attended classes on astronomy, geology, oceanography, and space physiology and medicine. Pilots have qualified on the T-38 trainer while nonpilots have also become familiar with the aircraft and have undergone survival training.

At this point the candidates are assigned to technical duties within the astronaut office (CB). Branches of the astronaut office include flight support, spacecraft systems EVA, robotics, operations, operations planning, computer support and payload/habitation. The candidates will spend approximately six months in on-the-job training before being evaluated. Only at that point will they be qualified Shuttle pilots or mission specialists.

There will be no opportunities for interviews until the candidates are certified as astronauts in May 1999.

1998 Astronaut Candidates (ASCANs)

NAME	CLASSIFICATION	SERVICE
Cmdr. Jeffrey Betts	Pilot	USN
Lt. Cmdr. Jason Borders	Pilot	USN
Maj. Anton Craig	Pilot	USAF
Capt. Karl Dennet	Pilot	USAF
Gunter Diemer	Mission Specialist	civilian
John Essington	Mission Specialist	civilian
Vardon Hall	Pilot	civilian
Capt. Diana Herron	Mission Specialist	USAF

Melanie Juin	Mission Specialist	ESA
Lt. Col. Viktor Kondratko	Mission Specialist	Russian AF
Mark Koskinen	Mission Specialist	civilian
Cmdr. Thomas Moad	Mission Specialist	USN
Capt. Ray Murdaugh	Pilot	USMC
Miguel Raquena	Mission Specialist	civilian
Maj. Daniel Raybourne	Pilot	USAF
Geraldine Reed	Mission Specialist	civilian
Lt. Cmdr. Donald Schuetz	Pilot	USN
Wayne Shelton	Mission Specialist	civilian
Capt. Gregory Yakubik	Mission Specialist	USA

Astronaut candidate selections are conducted approximately every two years. The number of candidates depends on Space Shuttle flight rates, overall program requirements and attrition.

CHAPTER 6

Mark Koskinen, it's time you got your ass home.''

Startled, Mark looked up from his desk. When he realized it was Viktor Kondratko standing in the doorway, he relaxed. Viktor was a Russian cosmonaut who had come to JSC to train as a Shuttle mission specialist with the Worms. He was a heavyset guy in his late thirties who, after eight months in Texas, could do a better shit-kicker accent than any of his American-born colleagues. "Damn it, Viktor, you scared me."

Kondratko presented Mark with a covered Styrofoam cup, then plopped down behind the next desk. There were five in the room; the other three belonged to real astronauts, who were rarely to be found at them. "I was very sorry to hear about your accident. About Colonel Buerhle. Everyone says you are fine?"

"Got a bad case of telephone ear, yeah. Other than that, just fine." The hidden penalty for being in an aircraft accident was that you had to make a lot of phone calls reassuring people that you weren't dead. Thank God he had reached his parents in Iowa before they had heard. Then there was Allyson, in Los Angeles, who promised to inform interested parties at the Aerospace Corporation. A couple of Air Force buddies. And, finally, Mark's sister in Portland. All this while undergoing exams at the JSC clinic in Building 37. He had had to get firm to be allowed to stop by the astronaut office.

"Telephone ear?" Kondratko said. "I get it." He nodded at the cup. "Drink up."

"What is it?" Mark opened the lid and sniffed.

"Brandy. Something to steady your nerves. An old Russian recipe."

"Uh-huh." Mark could not remember seeing booze of any kind here on the sixth floor. Well, not belonging to anyone but Kondratko. He took a sip, and almost immediately felt soothed.

"Drink half of that, and I will drive you home. It's after seven."

"Is it that late already?" Mark realized he had been talking as the sun went down. The office was on the east side of Building 4-South, in the shade on a sunny day. When it was cloudy or rainy, night could sneak up on you. Especially if you never bothered to look out the window.

The whole sixth floor of 4-South was taken up by CB, 115 astronauts and ASCANs deployed in offices all around the perimeter, five or six to an office. Seven of the offices currently held flight crews, the others, like Mark's, a mixture of ASCANs and veterans working technical assignments. In the middle of the floor were the desks for secretaries, and a conference room. On the floors below were Boeing support staff, the crew equipment division, and some ISS people. There wasn't a foot of extra room.

Even though it was already overcrowded, Building 4-South at the NASA Johnson Space Center was relatively new, completed only in the last five years. For twenty years CB had been located on the third floor of Building 4, located directly to the north. A freeze on new federal construction should have made it impossible to throw up a new building, but 4-South was connected to 4 by a series of walkways, making it an "addition," and thus exempt.

Mark took a sip from the cup, then another. Whoa. "We better get going." He had nothing to take with him: his backpack with his workbooks was still in a locker at Ellington.

As he and Kondratko emerged from the office, Mark asked, "What tech assignment did you wind up with?" He felt bad that he hadn't bothered to ask, but, then, he had hardly thought about his own since hearing the news from Fehrenkamp.

"Flight support branch. Capcom."

"Outstanding." It was; working as a capcom had the highest visibility of any of the technical assignments. You were sitting right there in Mission Control next to the flight director during your shift. It was a chance to shine.

Of course, it was also a chance to fail big time, but Kondratko was tough, a former test pilot in the Soviet Buran shuttle program who had hung in, waiting seven years for a flight that never came. He had then managed to get himself assigned to NASA, which wasn't the easiest trick in the world, either. With several Shuttle-Mir docking flights still on the manifest, providing the Russian station held out, having Kondratko as a capcom was a smart move.

"In fact," Kondratko said, "I need to pick up some documents on the third floor. I'll meet you in the parking lot."

He headed toward the elevator while Mark headed toward the back stairs. Mark couldn't help smiling. Kondratko was the only astronaut who ever used that elevator. And he was shameless about it, too. Everyone else made a point to walk.

The office was still busy. Several secretaries were at desks. The lights were always on in the offices, and Mark could hear voices working the phones as he passed.

Knowing that Kondratko was likely to spend a few minutes chatting down on the third floor, Mark figured he could stop in the men's room. He was in a stall with his pants around his ankles when he heard voices.

"...can't ditch a T-38 in the water any more than you can ditch the orbiter. You're just going too fast."

"I'd still take a shot at it." It had to be a couple of astronauts who were pilots. All Mark knew was that they didn't sound like Worms.

Now he heard water running. They were washing their hands. And the voices got a little quieter. "Well, whatever the reason, if it had to be somebody—"

"I didn't like him any more than you did, but—"

"Do you have any idea how many people hated that guy?"

"I have a very good idea—"

"When are people going to admit that Buerhle was a son of a bitch?"

"Not until after the funeral. . . ." The voices trailed off as the speakers left the men's room. Mark blinked as he pulled himself together. Nobody ever really liked a boss, especially a chief astronaut. But . . . *wow.*

Mark emerged from the bathroom and saw that half a dozen astronauts were gathered around Shannon the secretary, who was telling them about plans for a missing man formation. Mark immediately tried to see if his two Buerhle fans were among them, but the only person talking was Shannon. "Boyd thinks he ought to have two from aircraft ops and two from CB. One of them should probably be you, Steve," she said, nodding at one of the pilots, who happened to be Steve Goslin, the same Marine Mark had originally been scheduled to fly with instead of Buerhle.

"I'd be honored," Goslin said. He was tall, thin and a bit stooped. With his trim blond mustache he reminded Mark of a young minister, perhaps because he was, like some of the astronauts, openly religious.

As the group broke up, Goslin spied Mark. "Hey," he said, clearing his throat as if he was having trouble speaking. "I think I owe you an apology."

Mark remembered that Goslin was the astronaut office safety officer for the T-38! No wonder he was nervous. "How's your daughter?" Mark asked, not knowing what else he could possibly say.

"She's fine. A little fever. In fact, I should be getting home to see how she is. You're looking good—"

"For a guy in Coast Guard fatigues." Cal Stipe, the bearded wonder, had come out of his office. A veteran of five Shuttle flights in his twenty years as a mission specialist, fifty-one years old, Stipe was nevertheless among the freer spirits in CB.

Goslin cleared his throat. Stipe's jollity seemed to bother him. "We were just finalizing the funeral arrangements."

"What's going to happen?" Mark asked.

Stipe said, "They'll have a memorial on Saturday, assuming they find the body. Play the 'Wild Blue Yonder' and do the missing man formation. The ex-wife or ex-widow gets a pension, and I think he had a daughter. She'll get a flag. Joe wasn't assigned to a mission, so nothing changes."

"There'll be a new chief," Goslin said.

"There always is." Stipe was already walking off, with Mark and Goslin staring after him.

Goslin finally hefted his briefcase. "Glad to see you made it." Then he left, too.

Mark looked around the office, and felt as though he were in the midst of strangers. Those things he had heard about Joe Buerhle had bothered him. Or was it just postaccident trauma?

Oh, hell, he'd forgotten all about Kondratko, waiting down in the parking lot.

CHAPTER 7

Following the call with Akin, Kelly aimed her Volvo down Highway 45 toward Galveston, past the racetrack, over the bridge. Since it was still midday, well before even the early JSC rush hour, she made the trip in little more than half an hour. She got stuck in some traffic mess in front of the AME Church on Broadway, which is what I-45 became, but eventually made a left onto Seawall, then another one to Second Street and presented herself at the gate to Old Fort San Jacinto. She was directed to the Coast Guard dock just as the salvage ship *Halverson* was about to put out. She was saved from having to open her wallet and start showing ID when a man recognized her and helped her aboard.

As the *Halverson* moved away from the pier the man said he was Walter Thompson from the NTSB. He sure didn't look like a member of the Coast Guard: he wore slacks, a white shirt and a tie, in contrast to the jeans or vaguely nautical blue of the rest of the crew.

Thompson was around thirty, tall, curly-haired and thick through the middle. "The people at Ellington told me what you looked like."

Kelly wondered what they had said. "Look for a slim woman about five-foot-five, with short reddish brown hair and brown eyes"? Had they said she was usually considered quite pretty, if not exactly beautiful? Or had they just told Thompson to look out for a tomboy in a flannel shirt and jeans? "That's me. So, you're in charge?"

He grunted. "Hardly. I'm some kind of adviser thing."

"Does that bother you?"

"It's new, that's all."

"You've done this before."

"Oh, yeah. With a couple of thousand crashes a year, you keep pretty busy."

Thompson's role as an "adviser thing" worried Kelly a bit. NASA had a habit of investigating itself that went back to the Apollo days. When it came to spacecraft there had been some justification for the idea that you needed a space expert to judge liability, and where were you going to get them if not inside NASA? While that might have been true twenty-five years back, it wasn't true now. There were dozens of independent satellite engineers, for one thing, not to mention all those people who had worked on the many Air Force space programs. Her father had joked that NASA stood for Never A Straight Answer, but he had other reasons to dislike the agency.

"Did you talk to the captain? What are the chances we're going to make the recovery?"

"Pretty good, I think," Thompson said, grateful for the chance to provide some small bit of expertise. "The water's shallow at the crash site. . . . I guess there's a buoy out there already. And it's only been a few hours. We've got to hurry, though."

Kelly suddenly realized, "Oh, shit. It's salt water!"

"And the magnesium in the plane will start to combine." The T-38 could literally crumble to pieces.

Thompson paused. "I suppose we might also find a body."

Kelly wanted to change the subject. "How do you relate to the FAA, Walter?"

"Different organization completely. They only get involved if we find a serious mechanical error that would require this type of plane to be modified. Or negligence or criminality, in which case someone might get arrested."

A gull swooped by overhead. The ship began to roll as it moved out beyond the breakwater. Kelly took one look at Walter Thompson and said, "Let's go inside and get you some Dramamine. This may take a while."

And, she added to herself, it won't be pleasant.

They motored right out to the apparent crash location, less than an hour south of Galveston proper. The water here was shallow—drafts ran to no more than forty feet, and didn't begin to drop off until hundreds of miles farther into the Gulf. The bottom was sandy and relatively flat.

There were two divers on the ship, Pollack and McHugh. Pollack was a bearded guy with a gut, while McHugh was younger and, except for some tattoos on his forearms, kind of cute. Both of the men went about suiting up with a casualness that almost offended her, remembering how deadly serious Carlos Rivera and Christy Nasvik had been while getting ready for their EVA on STS-76. Diving gear was simpler, of course, and the penalty for a mistake in water this shallow wasn't likely to be immediately fatal, but still . . . She wanted them to be more dignified. She wanted the cute one to be less cute.

She realized she was basically just filled with simmering anger. She knew from experience that at times like this she had to be careful or she would be in a sudden screaming fight with someone—probably harmless Walter Thompson from the NTSB—for no good reason.

The divers went off the tail, one splash after another, and Walter told her the captain said it might be a while before they found anything, even though they had been able to motor almost directly to the crash site, where the shrimp boat that had picked up Mark Koskinen had dropped a buoy. Water flowed, of course, so the possible footprint surrounding the location of the T-38 was still several hundred feet across. The search would begin at the buoy itself and move upstream, back toward the expected point of impact. If that didn't produce results, they would go downstream from the buoy. Then into wider circles.

Kelly tried to nap in one of the cabins, which smelled of diesel and possibly something worse. It was better than trying to sleep on orbit—at least in the first few days of a mission—but not much. After forty minutes or so she gave up, splashed some water on her face and went on deck.

Walter Thompson was there, now without his tie and wearing a McCauley Marine baseball cap, nursing a can of 7Up. He looked as though he was already starting to burn. "You'd better stay inside," Kelly told him.

"I *should* have stayed on shore."

Kelly looked at him for a moment. Yes, he was turning red and green at the same time. Christmas colors. "Here." She pulled a tab of two pink pills out of her pocket. "This is scop-dex. We use it on orbit for motion sickness."

Thompson swallowed both of them with his 7Up.

"Did I mention that these are prescription drugs?" she added.

"Don't worry," he said, belching slightly. "I won't report you."

"Well . . . we're in international waters, anyway. You'll find that the stuff gives fast, effective relief. Just don't go into your nearest Sav-On looking for it."

He nodded. "How many times have you been into space?"

"Twice." Ordinarily she avoided conversations that started with that question. But today there were other subjects higher on the to-be-avoided list. "Four hundred and seventy-three hours, to be precise. Just about twenty days."

"What's it like?"

"I guess I would say it's the most interesting job in the world. It's hard work. You spent all these hours getting ready for it. Then you finally get a chance, and half the time it's *nothing* like the training. You're in microgravity . . . floating around. Your head kind of swells up and your toes get cold and you look Chinese. But you've practiced all the moves and you're dealing with all this equipment you could take apart in the dark. . . .

"And every once in a while you go up on the flight deck and look out one of those big windows, and there's, I don't know, Italy below you, looking like a boot! Just like the maps you saw when you were a kid. Only there aren't any lines, and it's never, you know, straight up and down on a page.

"And you go flying by. Five minutes later you're over the Middle East. All that in a matter of minutes. Then it's back to work."

More gulls swooped over them, calling. Kelly realized she was saying things she had spent years hiding—in front of her colleagues, reporters, schoolchildren. But it felt good to talk out here on the ocean . . . and, if nothing else, she could see that she was taking Thompson's mind off his condition.

"Are you ever scared?"

The official answer was that you were always cautious but that you wouldn't do the job if it wasn't safe. But that was bullshit: looking at the mortality rates, being an astronaut was one of the most dangerous jobs in the world, worse than being a coal miner. Not just flying into space itself, but the career. You could get killed traveling to work, like Joe Buerhle. "Sometimes."

"Then why do you do it?"

"Because most people can't." She had to laugh at herself. "I guess it was a challenge. I also—I always wanted to live in space . . . you know, up there away from noise and crowds."

"Why not move to Idaho?"

"Well, that's one way to do it. But to me moving to Idaho would be like going *backward*. People did that two hundred years ago. I'd like to go someplace new. . . ."

"To conquer a new frontier?"

"Yeah. It sounds a little like high school civics, but yeah. I mean, if nothing else, it gives the human race more options. You remember when those comet chunks hit Jupiter? What if that had been Earth? Two or three of those babies and the human race is right there with the dinosaurs. Extinct."

"So you must like the human race . . . even though you want to get away from it."

He had a good point. "People are inconsistent," she said. "Why do *you* do what you do?"

He shrugged. "I guess I like solving puzzles."

"And it doesn't have anything to do with making airplanes safer." She waited.

"Well . . . people are inconsistent." They both laughed. Thompson belched one more time. "Excuse me. That stuff really works." Now he merely looked sunburned. "What do you do after this? The investigation?"

"I'm hoping I get a third flight. Most of them over the next five years are to assemble the ISS. I really want to be part of that."

"It's not automatic . . . getting another flight?"

"Nothing is automatic."

"What will you do then? After the station is built, I mean."

She never got the chance to frame an answer—had never, in fact, looked that far ahead. The station *built*? Let's get it *started* first—when there was a shout from the wheelhouse. "They found something!"

The fat diver, Pollack, had surfaced. "It's a little cloudy down there, but it's an airplane, all right."

Kelly crossed her arms on her chest, hugging herself. "Did you see the tail number?"

"NASA 911," he said. "Easy to read. I mean, it's a little beat up, but it's intact."

The question she didn't want to ask: "Did you get a look at the cockpit area? Was it open?" Meaning, had the pilot ejected?

"The plane is on its side, a little dug into the sand," Pollack continued, turning his hand so that it looked as if he were about to clasp Kelly's, and giving her a brief moment of hope before saying, "but the front seat is still in there. So is the pilot."

So Joe Buehrle hadn't been able to eject. He was officially dead. Kelly turned to face Walter Thompson, who had the gall to ask, "Are you feeling all right?"

"I'm fine," she snapped, walking toward the bridge. "I just want to make sure there's a coroner on hand when we get in."

An hour later they had a wire down to the wreck. McHugh managed to get it hooked up. By now, of course, it was after 4:00 P.M. They had another sixty minutes of sunlight. The captain, after consulting with Kelly, was anxious to finish the job. "It's not gonna be any easier tomorrow. We'll just have to start all over." Kelly agreed.

There was some discussion of having McHugh and Pollack try to remove the remains from the cockpit before the plane was lifted—broken airplanes had the nasty habit of falling apart when moved, and Kelly didn't want to come back here tomorrow to get the cockpit if it separated. But both divers balked: they were salvage divers, not morgue assistants. Kelly wanted to punch both of them, but let it pass.

She went to the fantail and watched as the motor started to grind and the wires pulled taut. Pollack and McHugh were down there somewhere, adding a tug if necessary. Within minutes the bent tail appeared near the surface, the yellow NASA banner still easily readable. The back of the plane, in fact, only looked mildly scratched. A little paint and it would be as good as new.

But as the rest of the bird emerged from its sandy nest it was easy to see how violently it had hit the water. The right side inlet was crushed and bent and the right wing had broken off at the root. The nose had been flattened and twisted—in fact, the whole plane was clearly several feet shorter than it used to be.

The mates grabbed for it as the crane swung it toward the deck, and only then did Kelly and Thompson get a look at the cockpit. "Oh, Jesus," Thompson said.

The cockpit had been crushed. Joe Buehrle was still strapped in . . . wedged in . . . wearing his NASA flight helmet and blue flight suit. The body was twisted . . . embedded somehow in all the metal. Only a few hours in the water and the body had already started to turn white. "All right," one of the mates said, "somebody get a fucking bag."

Kelly caught a whiff of the worst odor she had ever encountered in her life, and had to leave the deck.

NASA N E W S
National Aeronautics and
Space Administration
Lyndon B. Johnson Space Center
Houston TX 77058
218 481-5111

October 14, 1998
Sam Wirth
Johnson Space Center

RELEASE 98-105

ASTRONAUT BUERHLE KILLED IN CRASH; KOSKINEN EJECTS SAFELY

Chief astronaut Joseph Buerhle was killed today in an aircraft accident over the Gulf of Mexico. The 43-year-old Air Force colonel's T-38 jet crashed at approximately 8:30 A.M. while on a routine training flight that originated at Ellington Field.

Mark Koskinen, 33, a member of the astronaut candidate group selected in March 1998, was a passenger in Buerhle's jet. He ejected safely and without serious injury.

"Joe Buerhle was a terrific pilot and an outstanding astronaut," said director of flight crew operations Lester Fehrenkamp. "We will all miss him."

Buerhle was born in Manhattan Beach, California, and attended the U.S. Air Force Academy, graduating in 1975. He completed undergraduate pilot training at Williams Air Force Base, Arizona, in 1976, then served as an F-111F fighter pilot at Cannon AFB, New Mexico, and RAF Lakenheath, England. In 1982, following an assignment at the Pentagon, he served as an instructor pilot with the 549th Combat Training Squadron at Nellis AFB, Nevada. He attended the USAF Test Pilot School at Edwards AFB in 1985, and was assigned to the F-15 upgrade program when selected by NASA in 1986.

As an astronaut Buerhle served as technical assistant to the director of flight crew operations and in the mission support branch. He made four Shuttle flights, two as a pilot, and most recently served as commander of STS-91, which carried the Spartan 201-5 and the third Shuttle Radar Laboratory. He was named chief of the astronaut office in July 1998.

Buerhle is survived by his daughter, Grace, and his parents, Harold and Margaret Buerhle, of Lancaster, California.

An investigative panel will be formed.

43

CHAPTER 8

It was almost nine-thirty when Mark got back to his apartment, carrying a bag of takeout from Le-Roy's. Given what Joe Buerhle had said before the event this morning, it wouldn't have been Mark's first choice, but he had let Kondratko drop him at home before remembering that his backpack, bike and workbooks were still at the hangar where he'd left them before the flight. So he'd jumped in his Explorer and driven to Ellington to get them. Coming out, he had seen Le-Roy's right in front of him just as he realized how famished he was.

He hadn't seen anyone he knew around the Air Patch, which was probably a good thing. A couple of the DynCor crew guys were working late on one of the birds. One of them had stared in his direction but ultimately kept working. He might have recognized Mark as the survivor of that morning's crash, but maybe not: the DynCor crews had seen about two hundred different astronauts come and go over the years.

Mark's books were in the locker room on the ground floor of Hangar 276. Along with all the other astronauts, ASCANs, and the twenty aircraft ops pilots, Mark had his own cage with his name on it; his parachute and helmet were stored there. Of course, the helmet was probably still sitting on a shrimp boat down in Galveston. What did people do with used parachutes, anyway?

He found that memories of the ejection were returning, not that there were many. Being catapulted out of the T-38 had taken only a few seconds. It was wrenching—Mark's back, neck and butt still ached—but brief.

What he remembered was the sudden sense of falling as the seat separated and he waited for the chute to open. Then the cold water and the struggle to lose the chute. He was very glad he'd paid attention during survival school back in June. It had all been almost automatic, like driving home after a hard day at work. He'd only been in the water for a few minutes before he spotted the shrimp boat, so he'd never really gotten too concerned about how long his life vest would actually keep him afloat.

It had given him time to think about Joe Buerhle, though. What had happened to him? He'd sounded crazy—or sick. Why hadn't he ejected, too?

Nobody knew the answer. Mark certainly wasn't going to discover it standing around the Air Patch. He threw his backpack into his car, then went to get his bike.

Mark lived on the second floor and never relished the thought of making two trips to the car, so he had the takeout bag balanced atop his workbooks when he reached the door. He was about to dig out his key when he noticed that the door was open.

This was a secure building in a low-crime neighborhood. Mark was skeptical about crime rates in general, believing that they generally stayed the same over the years, rising or falling a percent or two depending on the number of young people in the population. Still . . . he knew a potentially dangerous situation when he saw it. He had locked the door; the landlord had no reason to visit, and would certainly have relocked the door if he had.

Mark gently opened the door with his foot. No sound from inside . . . the lights were off. He let his eyes adjust as he carefully set the workbooks and takeout bag on the counter. The TV, the CD player, the computer. These were the logical targets for any thief, and they were still in place. There was no cash in the place, nothing of value other than personal mementos. Even the NASA materials scattered on most flat surfaces were readily available elsewhere. For a brief moment he wondered if the intruder was some space fan. There were hundreds, a good number in foreign countries, who besieged astronauts with autograph requests. Some were even prone to just showing up on one's front door without warning.

A quick tour of the kitchen, living room and downstairs bedroom-office convinced him no one was on the first floor. He did note a record-high number of messages on his telephone answering machine.

He moved up the stairs, quietly, checking the hall bathroom—clear—then his bedroom.

There was a woman on the bed. In the bed, actually, like a *Playboy* magazine version of Goldilocks. She seemed to be of average height, even lying down. Olive-skinned, long sandy hair curled on the pillow. Mark sighed and turned on the light. "Allyson."

She rolled over, her left breast spilling out of a silk camisole, and looked at him sleepily. "Surprise, surprise."

Weren't you in L.A. about four hours ago?"

"They have these big metal birds called jets, you know. I managed to get one to bring me here."

"I'm glad."

"I didn't think you should be alone after what happened."

They were downstairs now. Allyson had wrapped herself in Mark's robe, but not too carefully. They had been together for almost two years, in their fashion, and Mark found the sight of her thigh and knee peeking out of the robe to be intensely distracting.

Mark had donated his Cajun takeout to Allyson—she was the junk food junkie of the pair—and scraped together dinner for himself from the remains of some salad in a bag. "You scared the shit out of me," he told her.

"Come on, a big, brave astronaut like you?" She smiled. "You used to like it when I'd leave the door open for you."

Mark had to laugh. It wasn't as though sex was all their relationship was about—nor had there been a lot of fantasy role-playing. But, yes, on two or three occasions when both were working at their project at Hughes she had called him at the office and told him to get to her apartment. He could no more have explained Allyson's mind than he could have stopped himself from going. "That was your place. That was Los Angeles. That was after you . . . lured me."

"I thought you were ready for a totally spontaneous event. I guess you're not as adventurous as I thought."

"You'd be right. But, hey, don't let that keep you from trying." She made a face at him.

They had met on his first day at the Aerospace Corporation, in Mark's first meeting with the Hughes Aircraft team building his satellite. Allyson Morin had a degree in chemistry, but she wasn't a scientist or engineer; she was a program element monitor, an accountant who had enough technical training to know when an engineer was trying to pull a fast one. Mark's specialty was integration: he was the guy who had to fit all the systems together, which impacted directly on budgets and schedules, and he and Allyson had found themselves in heated discussions from the outset.

She was certainly attractive and dressed to show it, but their early conversations were strictly professional. Allyson was one of the few women Mark had met who were both feminine and completely at ease around men.

It was only after they'd been working together for a month, and their particular dispute was resolved, that they went out for a drink to celebrate. Maybe it was three drinks. Mark wound up telling her that he wanted to be an astronaut. At which point Allyson had leaned over, put her hand on his thigh and said, "Can I be the first woman to fuck you when you come back from space?"

Mark had never been one for bar pickups. By the age of thirty-one he had been through two long-term relationships . . . in his whole life he had slept with perhaps ten different women. But from somewhere within what he later realized was his darker side came the words "Why wait?"

Which launched the strangest relationship Mark had ever experienced. Allyson's frankness startled him at first. She would talk about oral sex as easily as she could discuss the combustible properties of fuming nitric acid. She went out of her way during their first few dates to make sure he understood that they would be sleeping together. For two years he and Allyson dated as regularly as any couple . . . Mark found it easy to be monogamous and Allyson claimed she was. "I've slept with a lot of different men, but I never overlap them," she said. They took vacations together and even visited each other's families.

But they never spoke of love or marriage.

Well, not never. One night after Mark got his first turndown from NASA, when he was looking around at his life and not liking it much, he asked Allyson the question "Where is this relationship going?"

As plainly as she approached her sexual activities, Allyson told him that she didn't know whether she would ever get married. She had a career; she had a busy life. She had had a number of relationships, usually with someone in the aerospace business, usually but not always older, sometimes married, though she wasn't anxious to repeat that particular mistake. She couldn't remember whether she had ever been in love. She knew that one day she would think about children—she had a younger sister who was the mother of twin girls—but not yet.

When Mark was finally selected and moved to Houston it was understood that he and Allyson were going their separate ways. She told Mark she had found a much younger engineer. Yet they had continued to see each other about every six weeks, either in Houston or in Los Angeles. It had been Allyson, in fact, who monitored the selection of Mark's apartment and was trying to get him to buy a condo. Mark wouldn't consider it until after he completed Worm training.

Now she slid off the stool and put her hands on his chest. "This shirt. We really need to take you shopping." Mark didn't protest that it belonged to the Coast Guard. Allyson kissed him, her lips moving gently against his, then stepped back and tugged the shirt out of his pants.

Mark slipped it over his head and reached for her, his arms circling her as she pushed back the robe and dropped it. His hands slid up the back of her camisole, cupping her and pulling her to him. Mark and Allyson were almost exactly the same height. Mark had always liked that about her. Among other things.

She went to work on his pants. "I'm not crazy about this belt, either," she said.

"Then get rid of it." Which she did; the buckle hit the floor with a bang. His khakis went next, followed by his boxers.

"I hope this is all right," she said. Without waiting for an answer, her mouth moved onto his cock, which was rising without any assistance. This was an activity that Allyson excelled at—in fact, she seemed to like it more than Mark did. She kept her head absolutely still, letting him grow to his fullest, then, without pulling back, began to move her tongue.

Mark was happy to come under these circumstances, but he usually wanted to be a full participant—which Allyson knew. After a few achingly tender moments, she raised her head and smiled as she let him draw her up. "You're always such a quick starter. Sometimes I think you don't even need a little suck."

"I don't." He took her hand and led her half a dozen steps to the living room couch. With the easy confidence of lovers who know each other, they kissed again. Mark sat on the couch first, and Allyson straddled him, her knees up under his arms, a breast in his mouth. She began her wonderful, rhythmic moaning.

CHAPTER 9

Don Drury's deal with Harriman Astro only required him to consult and be on-site for the final flight readiness reviews of the X-39 Spacelifter. Interfacing with suppliers and the government had been excluded from his agreement by choice: he'd done enough of that in thirty-five years with NASA.

But he had flown down to the Cape for a reunion of the Gemini launch team, and had scheduled a layover in Houston on his way back to California because of that little problem with Unisys, some goddamn software that was supposed to come right off the shelf.

In the cab from Houston Hobby to the hotel he heard about the T-38 crash and the death of chief astronaut Joe Buerhle. And there, at the hotel, was a message from Lester Fehrenkamp asking him to get in touch. Drury knew without asking that it was about the crash.

Nobody at Unisys was talking about Joe Buerhle, of course. In the first place, they were systems people, and the small unit inside the Houston office which dealt with Harriman's little rocket had nothing to do with manned space systems. Drury would have bet money that not one of the people he met with that Wednesday afternoon could have picked Joe Buerhle out of a police lineup.

Well, to be perfectly fair, Drury wasn't sure he could have, either. Astronauts were *supposed* to be interchangeable. "Any man can do whatever job we have, or he wouldn't be here." That was what Deke Slayton used to say when he was the boss. When astronauts were all men.

But that hadn't really been true in the good old days, in 1969, when you had men like Frank Borman and Jim McDivitt and Pete Conrad and

Tom Stafford, who tended to stand out. If old Deke hadn't been able to admit it, plenty of others, including Drury, had known it.

Astronauts in those days were pioneers. They were doing things that had never been done—without realizing that, in some cases, they would never be done again! The whole deal now, with the Space Shuttle, was to do the same thing over and over again without screwing up. You didn't want some hot-rodder like Pete Conrad running around . . . you wanted people who were steady, predictable. You wanted team players.

The fact that he was in Houston on the exact day Buerhle crashed was typical, however. Drury had a knack for bad timing which went back years. He was doing some Sunday work out at what was then Ellington Air Force Base the day in October 1964 when Ted Freeman's T-38 flew through a flock of geese, then into the ground. He was at Lambert Field in St. Louis in 1966 when Elliott See and Charlie Bassett tried to land their T-38 on a snowy day and hit the roof of the McDonnell Aircraft plant there, killing both men.

He had managed not to be in Florida eleven months later when Gus Grissom, Ed White and Roger Chaffee burned to death inside their Apollo spacecraft. But he got caught again seven months after that when C. C. Williams tried to eject from a diving T-38 over a Florida swamp—and didn't get out in time. That was a tough one, because no one could understand why that plane had crashed. One minute it was flying along nicely at ten thousand feet . . . C.C. turning to make the run directly west to Houston . . . the next it had nosed over and plunged straight into the ground.

For years after that Drury thought he'd met his quota, and it seemed that he had, until early 1986. He still didn't like to think about 1986.

He caught up with Les Fehrenkamp in Building 2 at 6:00 P.M., just as the place was starting to empty. They shook hands and exchanged the ritual condolences. "I thought you were spending all your free time out at White Sands," Fehrenkamp said.

"Sometimes I show my face on enemy territory. You should come out sometime and see how we're doing things. Get out of this humidity."

"There are days when I think that might not be the worst idea in the world." Drury smiled at the thought of Les Fehrenkamp clumping around White Sands at the base of the Spacelifter, a cheap, reusable prototype rocket built out of existing materials and systems. It was about as far from the Shuttle and the NASA way of doing things as you could get and still be in roughly the same business.

Drury and Fehrenkamp had overlapped at NASA in the early 1980s, as the Shuttle was making its first test flights. Drury was dividing his time between Houston and NASA Headquarters in Washington, working for the Shuttle program manager, while Fehrenkamp was one of the chief flight controllers in mission operations. It had been a difficult time for Drury. He found himself losing battles for the second or third time, and one of the guys he kept losing to was Fehrenkamp. Nevertheless, they had been friends, of a sort.

"What happened with Buerhle?"

"We still don't know. It was just a routine flight—forty-five minutes out and back. You know these guys."

Drury knew exactly. In the Apollo days the astronauts had been a mixture of some of the most talented pilots in the world and a bunch who were a little above average. The only thing they shared was the *belief* that they were the best. "I was on the board for the Williams accident. Never did find out what the problem was, other than a bum airplane."

"There was another guy with Buerhle who managed to punch out."

"Pilot?"

"No. One of our mission specialists. Air Force background, but not a pilot."

Drury tried to read Fehrenkmap's expression, knowing it was a waste of time. "Do you think this guy screwed up somehow?"

"You never know, do you? That's what I wanted to talk to you about. The agency needs a favor."

Drury almost laughed. "I can't sabotage the Spacelifter even for you, Les."

Fehrenkamp ignored the joke; he was famous for not having a sense of humor. "I'm having a tough time putting together a board. I've managed to line up people inside and contractor types from outside, but I really need somebody everybody respects." Now he did force a smile. "Somebody who won't roll over for the agency."

Drury sighed. In the old days this wouldn't have been a question. When you were given the chance to do more work, you just did it. What the hell . . . you were trying to beat the Russians to the Moon! But here he was over seventy, with a nice life in Las Cruces and enough work at White Sands to keep him interested. Did he want to spend a few weeks of his remaining time—hell, did he want to spend five *minutes*—working for NASA again?

He wanted to tell Fehrenkamp he would think about it . . . let Lester take the hint and find somebody else.

Still, Buerhle was a man who had gone into space four times. To Drury that still set him apart from the rest of dirt-bound humanity. After all, hadn't Drury worked all his life to make something like the Space Shuttle possible? Anybody who was willing to go ride that thing into orbit time after time was braver than he was.

Drury told Les Fehrenkamp yes, he'd head the board.

So here he was again, at a lonely pier after dark, waiting for a boat carrying a body. A Galveston County ambulance waited with him. Fehrenkamp had briefed Drury on Kelly Gessner's role on the board, and he recognized her and what he took to be the young man from the NTSB, Thompson. Both looked tired as Drury approached them and introduced himself. "Where are they taking the plane?" Thompson asked.

"A hangar at Ellington," Drury answered. "We'll start going over it in the morning. You should go get some sleep."

Thompson left then, leaving Drury alone with Kelly. He wondered what it was like, being part of what was jokingly known as the "faceless mob" of astronauts. There were a lot of them on any given mission, true, but they were faceless only when you compared them to Neil Armstrong and Buzz Aldrin, and possibly John Glenn, those being the only three astronauts an American adult could be counted upon to recognize. Make that four astronauts, since the younger generation knew Sally Ride. "How did the recovery go?" he asked, sensing that she would welcome professional small talk.

"It was very straightforward. We got the body, and just about all the plane itself."

Drury realized that they were watching the ambulance driver and one of the mates hustling aboard the *Halverson* with a stretcher. Kelly Gessner didn't seem concerned, but Drury had a flash of anger. If this had been a proper military ship there would have been a flag and a salute. "How well did you know him?" he asked quietly, meaning Buerhle.

She blinked for a moment and seemed lost in thought. Finally she said, with a sigh, "I did a mission with him." From her tone Drury gathered that they had become friends. This wasn't always true; it sure hadn't been true in the Gemini and Apollo days. Nor was it necessary. People who became astronauts were sufficiently motivated to overlook personality differences in order to get the mission accomplished. "I suppose it's finally over," she said.

"Almost." He nodded toward the boat, where the guys from the meat wagon were bagging the body. "Where are they going with him?"

"Thompson said it would be the Galveston County morgue. I guess an autopsy is required by the state of Texas. Once the coroner's through, the death certificate can be signed and the body released to the family."

"Well, I'm not so sure about that. The accident took place in international waters." He pulled a business card out of his pocket—the product of a stop he had made in League City following his conversation with Fehrenkamp. "I want you to do me a favor, Kelly. Tell these men that Buerhle's body goes to this funeral home."

Kelly stared at the card as if it were written in a foreign language. "Why?"

"This is agency business, not Galveston County or Harris County."

"They won't listen to me—"

"You're an astronaut, Kelly. They'll listen to you."

"Okay." She wiggled the card in her hand while she gathered her thoughts.

Drury asked quietly, "Is there family?"

"His ex-wife in California. I should call her and tell her we found him."

She didn't look as though she wanted to. Drury patted her on the shoulder, finding it surprisingly well muscled through the fabric of the shirt. "Why don't you give me the number and let me do it? I have all the information. You should go home."

She nodded. "I'll take you up on that." She told him the phone number of Buerhle's ex-wife, then headed for the boat to deliver the news to the drivers of the meat wagon.

Drury waited long enough to be sure that the astronaut magic had, indeed, worked.

It wasn't until he was across the bridge and back on the mainland that he realized that Kelly knew that phone number, the one belonging to Joe Buerhle's ex-wife, by heart.

NASA N E W S
National Aeronautics and
Space Administration
John F. Kennedy Space Center
Kennedy Space Center FL 32899
407 867-2468

For Release: October 15, 1998
Brad Orloff
(Phone 407/867-2468)

KSC RELEASE 116-98

ATLANTIS CLEARED FOR
FRIDAY LAUNCH OF STS-95

The Space Shuttle *Atlantis* was cleared for launch at 4:13 P.M. EST Friday, October 16, program managers said today. The STS-95 mission will carry the U.S. Microgravity Payload and also dock with the Russian space station Mir. The KSC launch team will conduct the countdown from Firing Room 1 of the Launch Control Center.

Problems with orbiter auxiliary power units had threatened to delay the flight, but the units have been repaired and are now cleared for use. The countdown includes 26 hours and 13 minutes of planned holds.

STS-95 is the sixth Space Shuttle mission of 1998, the 94th flight overall. It will carry into orbit a crew of five, returning with six, including mission specialist Gary McMinn, who has been on Mir since late July.

The STS-95 crew are: commander, Ronald Kubiak (Captain, USN); pilot, Sandra Rhodes (Major, USAF); and mission specialists Brian Monteleone (Commander, USN); Dolores McCoy (civilian) and Norman Sakmar (Colonel, USAF).

The crew members arrived at KSC at about 2 P.M. Wednesday, October 14. Their activities prior to launch include equipment fit checks, medical examinations and opportunities to fly in the Shuttle Training Aircraft.

CHAPTER 10

Mark came wide awake sometime around one, which was highly unusual for him. Maybe it was the presence of another: Allyson was next to him in the bed, back toward him. But, no. They had spent the night with each other dozens of times, even several times here in Houston.

He was awake because of what had happened the day before. He found himself running through it all again. Not the ejection and the accident, but the takeoff. The switch from Goslin to Buerhle.

He also thought about his new assignment as a member of the astronaut support team—good God, he hadn't even bothered to pick up his schedule! Not that it meant anything anymore. Les Fehrenkamp had told him he was on call for the accident board.

He thought about Joe Buerhle. A good-looking, charming guy. Not someone he'd ever gotten to know, just one of the senior guys. *Boom*; here one minute, gone the next.

He thought about how, if things had gone slightly differently, this bedroom would be empty and he would have joined Buerhle on the sandy bottom of the Gulf. His parents and Allyson would be in the middle of funeral arrangements. Where would they be burying the crushed body? Not Houston. L.A.? Probably back in Marshalltown, Iowa.

No. Don't dwell on that. He was allowing himself to get all worked up because he never woke up in the middle of the night. It didn't matter whether it was taking a big test, leaving home for college, or going on active duty, he never tossed and turned. In fact, he could clearly remember the last time he had had this much trouble sleeping—it was just about three years ago, when he and twenty-four other prospective astronaut candidates had spent their first night in the King's Inn Ramada on the other side of the center, just west of the main gate.

They were the fifth group of finalists for the 1994 astronaut selection—the agency would collect up to a couple of thousand applications during the previous two years, throwing out the obviously nonqualified, like those from fourth graders, reducing the group to about 120 finalists, who would then be invited to JSC in groups of twenty-five for a week of medical tests and interviews.

Mark's flight from Los Angeles had been long delayed on that hot, muggy night in July 1994. If there had been any kind of official welcome, he had missed it; by the time he reached the motel the place was like a tomb. He saw no one who struck him as another potential candidate. Saw no one at all, other than the desk clerk. In his room was a package welcoming him to Houston and giving an itinerary that began with a briefing in one of the motel conference rooms at nine the next morning.

He hadn't slept more than an hour or two that night. Meeting his fellow applicants for the first time at breakfast the next morning, he was relieved to note that he obviously hadn't been the only light sleeper.

But he never had caught his stride during that week. And he learned, two months after the visit, that he hadn't been selected, either. Not that first time.

So here he was, awake, vaguely unsettled and apprehensive, and with much more reason. He didn't think of himself as superstitious, but the bad night felt an awful lot like an omen. Had he done the right thing by ejecting? People were bound to be wondering. He wondered himself. Had he imagined Joe Buerhle's order? Had he imagined the ten minutes of insanity prior to the order?

If so, had he possibly, somehow, caused the T-38 to crash by ejecting when he did? Had he accidentally killed the chief astronaut?

No, no. A third time, no. He'd heard what he heard. He had followed procedures, done what he'd been taught.

Of course, none of that meant other people had to see it that way. What about Kondratko? His attitude hadn't changed. But what about the other seventeen Worms? What were they thinking? Seven of them had called and left messages for Mark; that was encouraging. But what about the real astronauts? Were they having doubts about flying with Mark? He didn't have to screw up . . . he just had to be unlucky. Those strained encounters in the office earlier this evening with Stipe and Goslin. Was that how it started?

What about the flight directors? Would they trust him?

Since NASA had started selecting ASCANs for the Shuttle program in 1978, there hadn't been a single person who failed to qualify. One pilot had been killed in an off-duty plane crash just as he was becoming eligible for assignment to crews, but everyone else who had been selected—over two hundred ASCANs—had gone on to fly at least *once*.

But no other ASCAN had had the bad luck to be riding with the chief astronaut when he got killed.

It would be hell to get selected, go through a year of ASCAN training, then be told that they were going to find a job somewhere else in NASA for you because of some stupid accident—

He sat up in bed. This wasn't doing him any good at all. Allyson lay next to him, looking inviting. He put his hand on her hip, found it warm and firm. He knew from past experience that she wouldn't mind being awakened. . . .

The phone rang before 6:00 A.M. "Mark? Les Fehrenkamp. Sorry it's so early, but I'm on my way to the Cape." Mark was instantly awake. Fehrenkamp. The Cape. Oh, yes . . . the STS-95 mission was supposed to launch tomorrow, which was Friday. Meaning today was Thursday.

The day *after* the accident. "No problem," Mark said. "I was already up." Well, he was half awake. He grabbed the phone and moved to the hallway, to give Allyson a little more sleep.

"I've been doing a little thinking since our chat yesterday," Fehrenkamp said in a tone of voice that made Mark's heart stop. It was the voice people used when they were giving you bad news. "I know I said you could start your tech assignment and just be on call for the board, but in looking at the situation at the Cape, it's clear that we can spare you for a few weeks.

"I'd like you to be full-time on the board until it delivers its preliminary report."

"I understand," Mark said, his mouth going dry. "How long will that take?"

"It might be as little as two weeks." Or months. Or to the end of your ASCAN career.

"I'll do whatever I can." Did Fehrenkamp enjoy this? Mark wondered. Was it all a game with him, screwing with people's lives and making them smile about it?

"I know you will. The first meeting will be at Ellington this morning at eight. You should probably be there."

"I'll be there." Mark hoped he was being aggressively humble. The eighth ASCAN Commandment. "Good luck with the launch."

"Hmm? Thank you, Mark." Fehrenkamp hung up without even a slightly conciliatory Don't worry, Mark. You won't be left behind, Mark. If they were going to ease him out, this would be the first step. Full-time on the board!

At least Mark had surprised him by mentioning the launch.

Running her hands through her hair to bring some order to it, Allyson came downstairs. "What was that all about?"

"The end of my astronaut career," Mark said.

CHAPTER 11

Mark Koskinen was the main topic of conversation on the sixth floor Thursday morning. The only way Cal Stipe could have missed hearing about it was to have stayed home. But he had to finish his presentation for Monday's pilots' meeting, so he needed to be in.

The first bit of dish was that Koskinen had panicked, hit the ejection handles and somehow forced Joe Buerhle to fly into the ocean. That came from a senior mission specialist astronaut with a Navy background.

Another senior pilot, this one from the Air Force, had come to Mark's defense. ''Bullshit. They weren't on approach, where, okay, a bomb going off in the seat behind you might put you in a bad situation. But they were still in the operating area. Buerhle could recover from *anything* at that altitude, except maybe the wings falling off.''

Eventually there were ten astronauts in the conversation—Stipe counted them before retreating to the conference room to get some peace. Sometimes the astronaut office wasn't a very nice place. It was true that every office since the construction of the Pyramids had had interpersonal conflicts and rivalries, but astronauts took those battles to new levels of intensity, dividing themselves in many varied ways. Pilots versus mission specialists. People with doctorates versus everyone else. Veteran astronauts versus ASCANs. Americans versus foreigners. Military versus civilian. Believers versus atheists and agnostics. Republicans versus Democrats.

The only thing the entire group agreed on was that everybody outside it was somehow even worse.

An anthropologist could have built a career out of such a study, and Cal Stipe, who considered himself a worthy amateur on most subjects, knew why: take one hundred supremely healthy, accomplished, self-motivated adults, and throw them together in a situation where they are, in essence, back in grade school, forced to compete for the attentions of a teacher, and they're going to eat each other alive.

On Monday morning Cal Stipe, in his capacity as the latest in a long line of directors, operations—Russia, was going to be the featured speaker at the weekly pilots' meeting. The subject would be training questions for the International Space Station. This had become another area of contention within the astronaut office. The Russians wanted every ISS crew member to spend some time training at the Gagarin Center, outside Moscow, not only to learn about the Russian module that was the core of the station but also the Soyuz rescue vehicle. And for language and cultural lessons, which Stipe felt was even more important.

About two thirds of the astronaut office—including most of the senior pilots, and most especially the late Joseph Buerhle—thought any time spent in Russia was time wasted. They had gotten friends in Congress to budget some money to build a Soyuz simulator right there at JSC.

Stipe was either the best person in the world to handle the briefing, or the worst. The best because he had spent most of the past year training in Russia for a trip aboard Mir. The worst because he was Cal Stipe.

Stipe had knocked around a lot before becoming an astronaut in 1978. He had dropped out of Brown in 1968 to join the Marines and wound up doing two combat tours in Vietnam as a Marine, first as a grunt, then as a second lieutenant flying F-4 Phantoms.

Then it was on to grad school in physics. He was working on his doctorate when he learned NASA was selecting its first group of Shuttle astronauts. With his combat background, military flying and scientific credentials, he was as close to a shoo-in choice for mission specialist as there was.

He had flown five Shuttle missions. He had spent a thousand hours in orbit aboard all five Shuttles—a record no other person would ever be able to claim. He had done three EVAs, eighteen hours of floating free above the blue Earth, protected from death by a few layers of fabric.

He had also managed to log ten thousand hours in aircraft and dozens of parachute jumps. He had gone deep-sea diving; he had taken a leave and climbed K2 in the Himalayas.

He even used the *Challenger* hiatus to finish his dissertation, the only time an active astronaut ever managed that trick. He had gone on to publish scientific papers, though his research time was more limited than he liked.

Along the way he had gathered a fistful of aerospace awards and decorations. He had five children from his marriages. When Cal Stipe faced obstacles, he simply wore them down. Including the senior heads in CB.

"Oh, sorry, Cal. Didn't realize you were in here."

He looked up from his viewgraphs to find Jinx Seamans coming into the conference room. Seamans was the deputy chief of the astronaut office. He immediately started helping Stipe gather up his presentation materials. He was the kind of guy who picked up stray wrappers on a city sidewalk.

"Too bad about Joe," Stipe said.

"I'm still in shock."

"What are they going to do about replacing him?"

"No one's said a thing to me." Both men knew that Seamans wouldn't be the next chief astronaut; Seamans was a mission specialist. The chief of CB was always a pilot.

"How about Koskinen?" Stipe asked casually.

"Looks like somebody made a mistake there."

"Who?"

"The selection board. I know he's Air Force, but, Jesus, he wasn't rated." Not being rated meant that Mark was not a pilot or air crew member, and clearly, to Seamans, therefore suspect.

"What's going to happen to him?"

"I don't know. If it were my decision, I'd just let him finish training and then ship him off to some other center. He's probably not a bad kid, but clearly he doesn't belong in the cockpit." Stipe knew that the official NASA policy was that civilian ASCANs who failed to qualify as Shuttle crew members had to be placed within NASA.

"Sounds harsh."

"So is smacking the Gulf at five hundred miles an hour." Stipe accepted the last of his viewgraphs from Seamans. "Cal? I hope this Star Town stuff isn't your presentation for Monday."

"What if it is?"

"I thought you were going to talk about when and how we get our own Soyuz up and running. . . ."

"I'm still not convinced that's going to happen—"

"Bullshit, Cal. Didn't you and Joe have a discussion about this earlier? I got the clear impression that this Soyuz simulator issue was a done deal."

"Maybe I was misinformed." Stipe knew that Seamans didn't really have an opinion on this issue. He was merely following orders.

"I can tell you, I'm going to be real disappointed if I hear you talk about this on Monday."

Stipe put the papers and graphs in a folder. "We'll just have to see, then."

Stipe let the door close behind him. Had he expected Buerhle's death to change anything? The office was still split on how to deal with the Russians, and Stipe was on the side that had no power or authority.

Well, he would fight that in his way. In the meantime, someone should warn young Mark Koskinen what fate awaited him.

CHAPTER 12

Kelly collapsed in bed around midnight, then awakened as usual at five-thirty because Thursday was usually her day to fly. She knew Fehren-kamp and Akin had ordered a temporary stand-down, so here she was, with free time.

She thought of some unfinished business at Ellington. Then realized she had unfinished business at Joe's house.

She would have skipped it, but she knew that Joe's ex or widow or whatever the hell she was now, Donna, would be coming to town for the funeral and would certainly go to the house. Joe had a will—anybody who flew on the Shuttle usually got around to that sometime shortly before launch—that left everything to his daughter, but the girl was still a minor. Donna would be handling things, and Kelly was just picky enough to want her to see Joe's place at its best.

Going there again had been a huge mistake. The house was just him—the clothes still smelled of him. Yes, he had treated her badly, but he was dead. There was no chance for redemption. And all she thought about was the fact that Joe had been smart, he'd been funny, he had been . . . alive.

Kelly was amazed when she realized how long she had known Joe Buerhle before they went out on a date. She had come to NASA at almost the same time he had, in 1986, though she was a new engineer in aircraft ops while he was already an astronaut.

She remembered being introduced to him at a meeting about, of all things, Shuttle brakes and rollout matters. Here was this man of average height with short black hair and blue eyes and, she learned, a quick smile. Even at first glance she thought he was the most handsome man she had seen in her life—and you didn't have to look hard around JSC and Ellington to find handsome men. But they hardly exchanged a word for almost two years. She was busy learning the Shuttle Training Aircraft, cycling from Ellington to El Paso to the Cape with the bird, since it was being flown almost exclusively by commanders and pilots in their last weeks before a launch. Joe Buerhle wasn't at that stage of his career yet; his work kept him in a slightly different orbit of JSC, especially the avionics lab.

Without making any effort to gather the information, she also heard that Joe was active with a large number of the single women around JSC, some of them overlapping. She had a fling in there herself, with a doctor from the Life Sciences Division.

The first time she saw Joe's name on the schedule for STA checkout (he had been assigned to his first mission) she realized she was nervous, something that had never happened before. When Joe showed up early the next morning and found her alone he seemed happy to see her, and mentioned their original meeting years past. "Why didn't I call you? I must be some kind of idiot." She had found this more than moderately charming, but laughed it off as merely the first step in a well-tested astronaut pickup routine.

They flew a dozen STA missions together over the next few weeks, and she was forced to admit that Buerhle was a fast learner and a good pilot—quicker through the syllabus than his more experienced commander. She told herself this was probably the second step of the pickup.

The entanglement with Kelly's doctor had not officially ended by that time—would not officially end for the better part of a year—so as Joe went off to fly his mission, not to be seen on the STA schedule for a few months at least, Kelly filed him as one that was going to get away.

Then she got selected as an ASCAN herself, and they were in the same office.

Put a hundred unusually healthy, successful, certified outgoing, well-rounded and above-average-looking men and women together in an incredibly pressured, even dangerous environment for weeks at a time, and they're going to get involved. The only thing that kept CB from turning into a soap opera was the ratio of four men to each woman. That and the fact that several of the women were happily married—some of them to other astronauts.

But there were enough active singles left over, not to mention married people who lived as if they were single, to fill a tabloid with spicy goings-on. Kelly was pretty sure no one was actually having sex in the office itself—it was just too crowded. But, my God, there were trips to the Cape, trips to

California, trips to Washington, trips to Alabama! There was one motel near the Marshall Spaceflight Center in Huntsville that became a notorious love nest. It was known around CB as "the honeymoon suite."

And it wasn't just men preying on women, either. There was one female astronaut who had a higher body count than any two of her male counterparts—and that was even if you limited the candidates to CB itself, which she most certainly did not. At one point she was having passionate affairs with a married astronaut assigned to a crew . . . a flight controller at Marshall . . . and a guy from Lockheed. Kelly never knew how that had all worked out, or if it had. The woman was still around, still flying.

Kelly got caught up in a pair of serious flirtations herself. Aside from the doctor, there had been an earlier heartbreaker with a Navy pilot in her own group of ASCANs. They slept together twice during a tour at the Cape, then both recognized the affair for what it was—heat of battle—and went their separate ways.

Kelly didn't actually fall in love with Joe Buerhle until after she was assigned to her first Shuttle crew. Joe was the pilot in the same crew.

He never came on to her; quite the opposite. During their eight months of training he treated her like a smart kid sister. He seemed to have forgotten that he'd ever flirted with her at all. At first Kelly was annoyed, but soon she grew to understand the wisdom of that choice. For one thing, there was a lot of work to do. An in-crew romance would have been a big distraction.

It was only when they flew to the Cape at launch minus two days that anything changed.

Their launch was scheduled for early morning, so together with Jackson Willett, the commander, they had shot a couple of landings in the STA. It went well, and Willet, who had a family problem to attend to in Cocoa Beach, left them alone at crew quarters. Neither of them had even changed out of their flight suits when Kelly decided it was now or never. As Joe dropped a clipboard on a desk and turned to face her, she put a hand on his shoulder. "Are you going to kiss me?" he said.

"Yes."

"It's about goddamn time."

Kelly would have sworn under oath that it was entirely spontaneous, that she had planned nothing, yet she had taken the trouble to add her diaphragm to her personal hygiene kit.

It turned out to be the best and the strangest first time she had ever had.

Best in the sense that their long "courtship" made them as uninhibited as a couple of drunken teenagers on prom night. Strangest in the sense that the same association, including hours in the cockpit, meant things could be discussed. The business of safe sex was handled quickly. "Blood test in April," she said.

"Blood test in May," he said.

"Not that it's going to stop me," she told him, "but I really ought to know if you're sleeping with anyone else."

"I've been saving myself for you," he said.

"Ha ha."

"Is four months enough of a cushion for you?"

"It will just barely do." She wondered briefly who this ghost of four months past was, realized even more briefly that she probably did know, then slid into bed next to him—

Enough memories. Stick to the job at hand.

Kelly got all Joe's clothes washed and dried, folded and bagged and in her car for the Salvation Army. Food had either been put in the garbage or in her car. Sheets were washed and put away.

A bucket of dirty water and some rags in hand, she looked around the place for one last time . . . she had had some good times here, and some that were far from good. Poor Joe, she thought. So charming . . . and such a goddamn prick.

Suddenly there was a noise at the door, keys in the lock. Kelly held her breath. For some irrational reason, she had a vision of mysterious NASA-related goons coming to do a sweep for . . . what, exactly? The only thing around Joe's house that might have made someone at NASA nervous was a series of draft memos about how the association with the Russians on the ISS was going to doom America's space program. You could have probably found the same thing in half the NASA homes in the area.

There was only one intruder, a pretty woman of about twenty. She had big eyes and large breasts. Of course, the same could have been said of all of Joe's women—except Kelly.

"Oh," she said, seeing Kelly and the bucket, a look of confusion on her face.

"Can I help you with something?"

"I was just . . ."

"Coming over to clean up? Don't bother. I think I did most of it." She turned her back and headed for the kitchen.

Thank God that next-door neighbor kid hadn't seen her. Otherwise he would have seen an astronaut cry.

She had finished cleaning out Joe's locker at the Air Patch and was making coffee upstairs when Les Fehrenkamp sneaked up on her.

"I was afraid I'd find you here." Kelly turned slowly at the sound of Les Fehrenkamp's voice. After six years as an astronaut, she was almost used to Fehrenkamp's ability to sneak up on people.

"Hello to you, too."

Fehrenkamp put his arm around her. "I heard you found him," he said.

"Yes."

"How was it?"

"Well, it won't be an open casket."

Fehrenkamp blinked at that. Kelly wondered why she was so snippy. Could it have anything to do with the fact that she had gone from breaking up with Joe Buerhle to finding his body in the Gulf? "Where is he now?"

"Mayer's Funeral Home on El Dorado," she said. "Last I heard, anyway. It was all in Mr. Drury's hands."

"He'll take care of everything."

"I'm sure he will."

"You aren't here to fly this morning?"

"How can I? The birds are grounded." She smiled. "Maybe I came to wish you bon voyage."

Fehrenkamp forced a smile. He had absolutely no sense of irony, like most of the men in the space business Kelly knew, and never knew how to take her. "Well, then, thank you. In fact, I should get downstairs." One of the NASA Gulfstreams sat on the apron, ready to carry Fehrenkamp and several other Level C types down to the Cape for the STS-95 launch. Just as Kelly was about to judge the conversation ended, Fehrenkamp took her arm. "I need a favor."

"Sure, Les."

"I'd like you to be the CB rep on the accident board," he said quietly.

Kelly couldn't believe what she was hearing. She supposed it was just possible that Fehrenkamp didn't know about them. Then she realized it was just as possible that he did, and wanted her on the board, anyway. "If you need me."

"I'm shorthanded right now, what with flight crews and a bunch of people over in Russia. The ASCANs aren't fully on-line yet. You're the only one I've got who knows her way around the Air Patch.'' Kelly had spent four years working in aircraft ops prior to becoming an astronaut. So, yeah, choosing her made some sense, but still . . .

Fehrenkamp seemed to sense her agitation. ''Look, if you'd rather not, I'll get somebody else.''

That was out of the question. It was even one of the ASCAN Commandments: that which is suggested is mandatory. This was a regular god-damn order from Les Fehrenkamp. You didn't refuse an order from the chief of flight crew operations, not if you ever wanted to fly in space again.

''I do whatever it takes, Les,'' Kelly said. ''I'm just a little tired.''

He punched her in the shoulder, lightly. A playground move. ''You're strong. And I've got to go.'' He headed for the door, then turned back. ''Oh, Drury is the chair. I hope you can hook up with him before the end of the day.''

For a moment Kelly wondered just how much she wanted to fly in space again.

PART II

MEETING AT OPS

NASA N E W S
National Aeronautics and
Space Administration
Lyndon B. Johnson Space Center
Houston TX 77058
281 483-5111

October 16, 1998
Sam Wirth
Johnson Space Center

RELEASE 98-107

ACCIDENT BOARD NAMED

Seven people have been named to the board investigating the T-38 crash which killed chief astronaut Joseph Buerhle, flight crew operations director Lester Fehrenkamp said today.

The board is headed by former NASA chief engineer Donald Drury, now a consultant with Harriman Astro. Other members include Tyrone Timmins of Northrop-Grumman, builders of the T-38A; Stanley Smith of Collins Aviation; Neil A. Armitrage of Pratt and Whitney; Walter Thompson of the National Transportation Safety Board; and two members of the astronaut office, two-time Shuttle veteran Kelly Gessner and astronaut candidate Mark Koskinen.

The board is expected to produce its findings within three weeks.

The USCG salvage vessel *Halverson* has completed recovery operations in the Gulf of Mexico just south of Point Bolivar.

CHAPTER 13

"There are so many ways to die in a T-38 it's not funny," Boyd Akin told Mark as a pair of NASA security personnel unlocked the door to Hangar 275 at Ellington Field.

The collection of broken airplane pieces that had been NASA T-38A tail number 911 were now laid out on the floor. Since the wreckage had been brought in a few hours before, Mark knew, a whole series of events had occurred. Maintenance records on 911 had been impounded and were being examined. Radar and air-to-ground data from Houston Intercontinental had been secured. Dozens of photographs had been taken. Now the wreckage was being disassembled in the first step toward a search for a cause, which meant each piece of it was being washed in a tub of fresh water to retard the effects of salt water on the metal.

"I thought it was supposed to be safe," Mark said, amazed to be having this kind of conversation with Akin. "Hasn't it been used as a trainer for thirty-five years?"

"It has a great record because it's mostly flown in daylight over flat ground with experienced instructors around. And no other traffic. But it's a supersonic jet! It's designed to go very fast, which means it doesn't fly well when it goes very slow. It also has a limited range. I'm continually amazed that we haven't wracked one up just by running it out of gas."

Prior to the accident Mark had a user's familiarity with the T-38. That is, he knew as much as you could learn by being a passenger with 127 hours of flying time. Perhaps slightly more; he was the kind of person who read the owner's manual on his Ford Explorer the first night he had it home. He knew that the 38 weighed less than six tons; three of that was fuel. With its powerful twin engines it would climb from zero altitude to thirty thousand feet in a minute, practically straight up. But a design that permitted that kind of performance had its price: if you let the 38 fly too slow, it would fall like a goddamn brick. With its small wings it needed lots of altitude to recover, and altitude was something Joe Buerhle had run out of.

If his initial ASCAN training and time in the cockpit gave him a bachelor's degree in the airplane, the next few days were likely to push him beyond a master's.

Piece by piece the team would go through the various systems looking for potential problems, a job complicated almost beyond belief by the fact that they weren't dealing with a whole airplane, but one that had been smashed up. Mark had been impressed by the documentation available on a single airplane—by the thoroughness of the ground crew in preparing it for a routine flight. If there was a mechanical failure, he was sure it wouldn't be traced to any kind of lapse on the part of DynCor's ground team. No, it was going to be blamed on the pilot—or his mission specialist passenger.

"We've got good troops here," Akin continued, a bit nervously, as if he felt that whatever he said to Mark was going to come back later to haunt him. "The system has proven itself. But good maintenance can't prevent pilot error or acts of God." He forced a smile. "You didn't happen to see a bird, did you?"

Bird strikes were always a concern. The coastal area was home to geese, owls, ducks, millions of big birds. Mark had heard the story about the T-38 crew which had speared a goose at ten thousand feet, covering their windshield in blood. They'd landed safely, but suppose the bird had been sucked into an engine, causing a flameout? That was a whole different type of problem. "No, I didn't see a bird, but I'm not sure I would have," Mark said.

"Your report said there was an engine out."

"There was."

Akin made a face. "A guy like Buerhle should have been able to fly a long way with an engine out."

"We were in a dive at the time." He kept his voice even, but what he wanted to say was, The plane wasn't hit by lightning. The plane, in fact, seemed to be fine. *What happened is that my goddamn pilot just freaked out!*

"Well," Akin said finally, "this is where I leave you."

Without another word, he walked off, leaving Mark to twist in the wind. His whole manner made it clear that he considered Mark guilty until proven innocent. Guilty of not being a fighter jock. Guilty of having survived when Joe Buerhle didn't.

For a moment Mark wanted nothing more than to turn on his heel and walk out of the hangar. These people were simply not worth it. He was fairly certain that Fehrenkamp and Buerhle had never considered him the pick of the Worms; there were too many people with first-rate operational flying backgrounds and test work.

But Mark knew that he had worked his way into the top half, and maybe even the top third. And it wasn't as though he had come to NASA out of the cradle. In fact, looked at on paper, his career was a regular goddamn straight line to the astronaut office. A degree in aeronautical engineering, ROTC to the Air Force. His eyes were never good enough for flying or even the backseat, but he'd done the next best thing, flying an important group of satellites in an actual war! He knew spacecraft and how they worked. He had something to contribute. And he wasn't getting the chance.

Mark tried to calm himself by watching the work being performed by some of the DynCor crew members under the eyes of two men from Northrop, the company that originally built the T-38A. Mark didn't feel he could or should intrude. What was he going to say? "You missed a piece over there!"

"I'm thinking pilot error." Mark turned and saw a tall guy approaching out of the darkness.

"Walt Thompson, NTSB."

They shook hands. "Mark Koskinen."

"The guy who punched out?" Thompson's eyes went wide. "They're moving fast."

"Why do you say that?"

"Usually the board has a meeting before a witness is called."

"I'm advising the board."

Thompson seemed to find that hard to believe. "Get out of here."

"I'm serious."

Now Thompson shook his head. "I guess I shouldn't be surprised. Nothing about this fucking deal has made any sense so far. You astronauts . . . you've really got this town dicked." He was clearly ready for a fight.

But Mark was trying hard to keep from smiling. "First of all, I'm not officially an astronaut, just a candidate. An ASCAN. You can think of me as a half-astronaut, if that'll make you feel better."

"You're not part of this?"

"I'm just as far out of the loop as you are. I want to get this thing resolved more than anyone for miles around. Maybe I can help."

Thompson was wary. "I've heard about astronauts. Individually you're great. As a group, you're a bunch of bastards."

"Come on. That's not fair."

"You haven't seen the crap I've seen in the past couple of days. Take the plane back to NASA? Sure. Skip the autopsy? Who needs an autopsy? I've been investigating plane crashes for five years, and I've never seen anything like it. It feels as though the accident report is already written."

"What can I do?"

"Tell me how that plane flown by that guy could crash. You were there."

"You read my report?" Thompson nodded. "That's all I know."

"Then your pilot just screwed up."

"Why do you say that?"

"Look, I've spent the morning going over the maintenance logs on this plane. There was nothing wrong with it. No discrepancies. The crew chief has been babying it for ten years. The Air Force sends people around to ask *him* questions."

Thompson took a small package out of his pocket—a roll of Tums, Mark saw.

"Are you feeling okay?"

"The smell in here. My stomach."

Mark had to admit, there was a stench of some kind in the hangar, a mixture of J-4 fumes, burnt metal and . . . fish. "Look," Mark said to Thompson, "I'm sorry about all that stuff. I'm just here to get the answers."

"You'd be the only one." Thompson crumpled the Tums wrapper and tossed it toward a garbage can, missing it. "It's already too late." Then he walked away.

As Mark retrieved the errant wrapper, he heard: "Oh, Jesus." The voice came from the team of three who were disassembling the T-38's cockpit.

Mark went over as one of the mechanics wriggled his way backwards out of the bent fuselage. One of the Northrop guys said, "What's your problem?"

The mechanic was completely out now. "There's something in there."

"Yeah, parts of smashed airplane," the second Northrop guy said.

The mechanic shook his head. "This isn't airplane. It's body parts."

Mark realized what the source of that mystery odor was. Neither one of the Northrop men was in a hurry to take a look. "Let me see," Mark heard himself say.

He had never been one of those kids who was fascinated by smashed body parts. When he was eleven years old he and his best friend, Kevin Brennan, had had the chance to look inside a wrecked Mustang at a Standard station. It had been towed there following a horrific highway accident that had killed its two occupants. Kevin had heard there was still blood—maybe worse—in that car. Mark had let himself be drawn close to it but had not been able to look inside. Neither, for that matter, had Kevin.

But here he was, twisting himself through a hole in the crumpled nose of a T-38. Well, he was a Worm, the lowest of the low.

In spite of the fact that most of the landing gear mechanism and avionics had been removed, there wasn't much room inside the fuselage. The only light came from a single bulb hooked there by the mechanic.

It was clear that Joe Buerhle had essentially merged with the control panel of his aircraft. Removing the body underwater would have been impossible. It would have been difficult enough on the deck of a rolling ship, in the darkness. They had gotten most of him. But not all. Some dark tissue—and a fragment of blue cloth—had been driven into the shattered panel, coming free only when the mechanic had started pulling it apart.

"Get me some gloves and a plastic bag. A couple of bags," Mark said, and had the pleasure of hearing the request repeated like an order by Northrop Number One.

A few thick moments later he emerged with two bags, which, in deference to the sensitivities of the others, he declined to display. He felt as though he was carrying a couple of pounds of hamburger.

"No wonder they cremated the guy," Northrop Number Two said.

"There's still some blood in there. Can you wash it?" Mark asked the mechanic.

"Yeah."

"How do we report this?" Northrop Number One said.

"We don't," Mark said. "I don't think his family would appreciate it." He didn't anticipate any argument, and didn't get any.

"What are you gonna do with it?" Number Two asked.

"I'm going to dispose of the remains."

He knew just where they belonged.

CHAPTER 14

Les Fehrenkamp had certain rituals he was required to perform before each Shuttle launch.

First he sat in on the weather briefings with Chad Connors, the astronaut who was doing the chief astronaut jobs Joe Buerhle would have done. Three hours before liftoff Connors would take the Shuttle Training Aircraft up to run approaches—just in case *Atlantis* had to turn around and come back to the Cape.

Then Fehrenkamp visited the white room where the crew's personal gear was being stowed—traditionally the last thing aboard, except for the crew itself. That was being handled by the Cape Crusaders, the very team poor young Koskinen should have been observing.

Fehrenkamp personally tended to some of the grimmer details that went with a Shuttle countdown: making sure the astronauts' wills were routed to the proper attorneys, that last letters were stored, that family escorts were thoroughly briefed on their duties—just in case. That he had a direct phone line to the Shuttle program manager and NASA administrator—just in case.

He returned to the crew quarters near the Vehicle Assembly Building to make sure the cake with the STS-95 patch was ready; so was the traditional launch meal, which was always breakfast no matter the time of day. He made sure that, yes, all five crew members had returned from their beach house frolic and were now in their rooms.

Then he called Valerie. No tears this time. She had already received a report from Boyd Akin that the disassembly of Joe Buerhle's plane was proceeding and that Don Drury had formally convened his accident board this morning. He tried to picture the situation at aircraft ops—had Kelly shown up? What was her mood?

And what about Koskinen? It was terrible to put the young man through this process, but it had to be done! If he had a problem, all he had to do was open his mouth and say something.

But so far he hadn't. So Les Fehrenkamp assumed everything was going according to plan.

At 1:30 P.M. he knocked on five doors. Four of the crew were already up; the fifth, a former Navy radar-intercept officer named Monteleone, was sacked out. Sometimes that was a bad sign; it meant the astronaut was exhausted. But Monteleone had flown two-hundred carrier landings and had maintained an even strain during the last weeks of endless sims. He happened to be one of those people who could put fear aside. Fehrenkamp made a mental note.

Kubiak and his crew sat at their breakfast table and posed for pictures. "I want Lester in here. Goddamn it," Kubiak called to the photographer. "He's the boss and no one ever sees him. Lester!"

But Fehrenkamp had already ducked out of the room. The flight crew ops director stays in the background. Another tradition.

The suiting was routine, and Fehrenkamp stayed out of the way, checking in with the launch director to assure himself that everything was all right. Then it was time to get in the bus and ride out to the pad.

Fehrenkamp hated the walkout. Every photographer for miles around was there, and for one reason: it was the death watch. He had lost count of the times he'd seen Scobee's crew walking out on that cold morning, waving gamely at these same photographers. But you couldn't sneak the crew to the pad. It was just another thing that had to be endured. Fortunately the crew was in that almost hyper mode—all of them gave the thumbs-up.

They were loose and joking around in the bus, another good sign. No point in going over flight data files now: if you didn't know the vehicle and the timeline after a thousand hours of sims, you never would.

The drive to Launch Complex 39, which Fehrenkamp had made twelve previous times, seemed to get shorter each time. As the other crew members got up and staggered their way out, Kubiak lingered. "Any last words, Coach?"

"Bring 'em back alive, Captain."

Kubiak laughed as he shook hands, then made his way out. Fehrenkamp rapped on the glass of the driver's compartment, his signal to go back to the crew quarters. Fehrenkamp never got out of the bus.

It was on the drive back, and the walk into the firing room with its cathedral-like windows, and plugging his headset into the console, that Feh-renkamp thought of Joe Buerhle. Too bad Joe hadn't been content to play squadron commander. No, he wanted to act like a program manager, sending memos on everything from safety and press relations to EVA plans for the International Space Station and the English-versus-metric argument.

Still, for all their differences, Buerhle had gone through these rituals with him for the past four missions. He was surprised to realize that he missed him.

The countdown ticked past a planned hold. There was a brief question about weather at Banjul, one of the transatlantic abort sites, but it turned out to be within margins. Go.

Five minutes. Fehrenkamp could only hear the air-to-ground commu-nications loop, but he had observed enough sims to know what was going on up on the *Atlantis* flight deck. Kubiak would be telling the crew to "close those lids"—the faceplates on their helmets. The four on the flight deck would squirm, searching for comfort on the hard metal couches. The one on the mid-deck would be seeing a sudden burst of late-afternoon sunlight through the hatch window as the access arm moved away.

The auxiliary power units would start with a whine. They were a never-ending source of trouble, but so far the systems monitors said they were looking good.

One minute. The cap atop the big rust-colored external tank popped up and slid aside. Fehrenkamp could see wisps of supercold steam on the video monitor.

Thirty seconds. Guidance went internal. That big three-barreled bird was on its own now. . . . Twenty . . . fifteen . . . ten . . . main engine start! One, two, three, all looking good. One of Fehrenkamp's many nightmares saw one of those engines fail just as—

—the solids ignited and the whole goddamn five-million-pound thing started rising.

Up into the sky she went, all five motors looking good. Inside the orbiter there would be a sharp, clattering noise like staccato thunder . . . everything would be shaking, any loose pieces of metal or equipment clanging off the walls.

"*Atlantis*, you're go at throttle up," said Arnaldo Rivera from Mission Control in Houston.

"Roger," Kubiak said. "Go at throttle up."

This was always the bad patch . . . the shuttle thundering through fifty thousand feet, still in a relatively thick part of the atmosphere with its buffeting and wind shear, still accelerating, still heavy and sluggish. This was where *Challenger* had come apart. This was the time where you could *do nothing*. The voices came to Fehrenkamp no matter what he wanted: "Uh-oh." "We've got a problem—" "Burn through." "Discreting sources." He saw the inside of the orbiter as the crew was thrown around horribly in sudden darkness—

No, this time things were all right. Coming up on two minutes and thirty-five seconds, solid rocket motor separation. There they went, pretty as a sunset.

From this point on there were still many things to worry about . . . but most of them had been simmed, worked through. You had a chance. Fehrenkamp let himself breathe freely again. He wiped a tear from his eye and looked around.

Four years back his best friend, Mitch Naugle, left NASA for Loral, making three times the money for about half the workload. Every six months he would call Fehrenkamp to offer him a job. Something with real authority.

Authority? Les Fehrenkamp, the closest thing on this earth to a thunder god, would just laugh and laugh.

NASA N E W S

National Aeronautics and
Space Administration
Lyndon B. Johnson Space Center
Houston TX 77058
281 483-5111

October 17, 1998
Sam Wirth
Johnson Space Center

STS-95 MISSION CONTROL STATUS REPORT #3

The Space Shuttle *Atlantis* continued its flight today with the first full day of operations of the U.S. Microgravity Payload.

Commander Ron Kubiak and pilot Sandra Rhodes performed the last shaping burn of the *Atlantis*'s orbital maneuvering engines, raising the orbiter's apogee to 211 miles, the current altitude of Mir. A final burn tomorrow will allow *Atlantis* to rendezvous with Mir shortly after 8:00 A.M., Central Standard Time. Docking should follow at approximately 8:20.

Atlantis is scheduled to spend six days linked with Mir, during which time several pounds of experimental materials will be transferred to the Shuttle for return to earth.

NASA astronaut Gary McMinn has completed his three-month stay aboard Mir. He is to be replaced by astronaut Calvin Stipe, who is scheduled to launch aboard a Russian *Soyuz TM* spacecraft in early November.

CHAPTER 15

Don Drury was getting tired of the funerals. He had once joked, somewhat bitterly, to his wife that for a guy who rarely wore a dark suit, his was being put to a lot of use. First there had been Deke Slayton's memorial on that rainy day back in '93, then one for Karl Henize—died on Mount Everest, of all the goddamn places, and been buried there, too!—and Stu Roosa. Bob Overmyer. The old gang was thinning out. Of course, demographics demanded it. Most of the Apollo-era astronauts had been born in the 1930s, meaning they were all in their sixties now. When you reached sixty a funeral was much more likely than a wedding.

And these were just the astronauts, the people known outside the business. Drury had spent thirty years behind the scenes, starting as an engineer with the Space Task Group at Langley Field in Virginia, when the idea of putting a man in a can and shooting him into space seemed like a fairly radical concept. Good people had come out of that group, like Bob Gilruth and Chris Kraft and George Low. They were the ones who made the big decisions, like going to the Moon with Apollo 8. They fought the big fights. They were dying, too. Jim Webb a few years back. Harrison Storms. Walt Williams.

Drury remembered Stormy's funeral as much for the people who hadn't showed as for those who had. Storms had been the head of North American Aviation, the company that built the Apollo spacecraft that burned on the launchpad and killed three astronauts. Drury had always thought Stormy had been blamed unfairly—and he was in a position to know. At that time he was one of those NASA program managers who was driving Stormy and North American crazy with continuing "improvements" in the spacecraft.

But this was a beautiful morning, even for Joe Buerhle's funeral. A few puffy clouds slid up from the Gulf, otherwise the sky was blue and clear. There was even a slight southerly breeze to stir the air. People were starting to gather, and Drury realized he would like to sit down.

"Don!"

Drury heard his name called, as much a question as a statement. He turned and saw Les Fehrenkamp coming out of Building 4-South. "I thought you were down at the Cape," Drury said.

"I just flew back in an hour ago."

"Things going all right?"

Fehrenkamp nodded. "Came to pay your respects?"

"Yes." Drury squinted at the sky. "Looks like you'll have a good flyby."

"Yeah. It won't be like Deke's service." It had poured the day Deke Slayton, the original chief astronaut, was memorialized, and the whole service had to be taken inside. The flyby of a NASA T-38 formation and a vintage B-25 bomber had had to be canceled.

"How's the board coming along?" Fehrenkamp meant with the investigation.

"They're examining the plane now. We'll get down to business first thing Monday."

"Everything else all right?" That meant the body, the press, anything which could cause a problem.

"Under control."

"Thank you." Fehrenkamp clapped him on the shoulder. "If you need me in the next couple of days, you've got my home number."

Drury figured he must have Fehrenkamp's home number somewhere on his person, not that he had the slightest intention of calling it. He did wonder what Fehrenkamp's home life was like. The director had been married—no children—in the years when he and Drury had knocked heads on a weekly basis, though Drury could only remember meeting the woman once. She had walked out or maybe died some years back, before Les had become head of flight crew ops, in fact, and since then all Drury had heard was that if Les was ever in love, it was with his lady astronauts.

Drury found himself swept away as a tide of mourners flowed out to the square. The band was already playing somber music. It seemed there was some kind of assigned seating. Drury figured to grab the first open chair and dare anyone to kick him out of it. But he was slowing down: as he worked his way back from the podium, he saw there wasn't going to be a place to sit down. Worse yet, though he knew he must have some old friends in the crowd, he couldn't find them. He stepped back, fuming, as the director of the center, Maynard Hutchins, moved to the podium and said, "On behalf of the government and contractor family of JSC, I thank you all for coming."

"Excuse me, sir?" Drury looked into the face of a young man of average height, with dark hair and blue eyes. At first Drury thought he was a page or an usher. But the lines around the young man's eyes suggested he was at least thirty. He moved with the air of a fair athlete, too. "I think you need a seat."

"You'd be right."

"Take mine."

He was on the end of a row. A couple of others nearby were looking at the two of them, clearly hoping by their glances to urge them to be quiet. Never one to turn away from a gesture, Drury sat down. "Where will you sit?"

"I'll stand."

And he did, though, in fact, he squatted down next to Drury as Hutchins introduced Buerhle's ex-wife and daughter and turned the proceedings over to another astronaut, who was saying how Joe Buerhle never talked about dying except once, before his first Shuttle flight . . . and how if anything happened he wanted a party, not a goddamn bunch of long faces—

"Excuse me, sir?" It was the young man again. "Aren't you Don Drury?"

This was a surprise. "Yes, although I can't imagine why you would know."

"You worked on Gemini and Apollo. Didn't you testify before the Rogers Commission about *Challenger*, too?" He most certainly had, which was one of the reasons he had been so happy to leave NASA behind.

"What's your name, young man?"

"Koskinen, sir. Mark Koskinen."

"And what do you do here?"

The young man looked both pleased and uncomfortable. "I'm an astronaut candidate."

"Congratulations. And good luck."

"Thank you, sir."

It wasn't until a full five minutes later that Drury remembered that there was a *second* astronaut assigned to the board, in addition to Kelly Gessner. The young man who had ejected from the plane before Buerhle was killed. That was Koskinen?

He seemed smart and likable. Drury wondered just how many other astronauts would have known who he was. Or given up their seats.

It was never easy to ruin some young man's career. Now it was going to be even harder.

CHAPTER 16

As he sat on the grass next to Don Drury, Mark was amazed at the number of astronauts here in one place. The regular Monday morning pilots' meetings still brought most of the group together, of course, but that was limited to the currently active astronauts. Looking around, Mark realized that he was seeing a lot of recent American space history. John Young, of course. Crippen. Brandenstein. Thagard. Stipe. People who had been in space four, five, six times; on Gemini, Apollo, Skylab, Shuttle, even Soyuz and Mir. Not to mention the people who had sent them there, like Drury.

For Drury's generation, and Neil Armstrong's, space flight had been, at best, a giant leap beyond aviation and, at worst, something out of the funny pages. For people Mark's age space flight had always been there, like baseball or the Statue of Liberty or Tony Bennett. Mark was born in June 1965, the week Ed White walked in space. The Apollo lunar landings started when he was in preschool. The only Apollo mission he actually remembered was the last one, with the nighttime launch and the geologist on the Moon finding orange soil. He had been able to stay up late and watch the TV coverage because he was home from second grade with bronchitis. Everybody in the country *thought* he or she remembered Apollo 13, but that was because it got turned into a Tom Hanks movie.

There hadn't been many American-manned space flights for several years after the last landing. The Russians were going up and down constantly, of course, but no one paid any attention. What really got Mark interested in space were two things: seeing *Star Wars* at the age of twelve; and watching the *Voyager* missions to Jupiter and Saturn at the same time. *Voyager*'s color pictures of pizza moons, of swirling red clouds the size of the planet Earth, of previously unknown rings around entire worlds were just as exciting as Luke Skywalker's confrontation with the Death Star. Maybe even more so: Jupiter and Saturn were real. You could walk outside in a cold winter night and see them in the sky. For all its virtues, *Star Wars* took place a long time ago in a galaxy far, far away . . . a galaxy in which the sound of exploding spaceships somehow traveled through vacuum.

The first Space Shuttle flew in the spring of 1981, when Mark was a sophomore in high school. He hadn't seen the launch—which took place on a Sunday morning—but on Tuesday Mr. Parfit, his physics teacher, let them watch the landing live.

What a spectacle! Mr. Parfit had been careful to point out that some of the protective tiles on the orbiter had been knocked off during the launch. No one knew whether the Shuttle would survive reentry.

The minutes dragged on. The TV commentators fell silent. Suddenly there it was . . . an arrowhead-shaped dot in the sky over California. And there was John Young's voice saying, "We're doing Mach 24 at 295,000 feet." The classroom erupted in cheers. All that Mark wanted was for people to *sit down!* *Columbia* hadn't landed yet! But, sure enough, it got bigger and bigger. You could see it banking as it turned . . . see occasional wisps of vapor from the wingtips. . . . Finally it was over the desert, plummeting toward the runway, chase plane edging closer. "Twenty feet," the chase pilot said. "Fifteen . . . ten . . . five. . . ." *Bang!* Wheels down, dust on the runway. They'd made it.

From that moment on Mark followed Space Shuttle missions with the same intensity his best friend applied to following the Cubs. He collected mission patches and crew portraits, bought every book on the subject there was, and even began to pay attention to various congressional debates about the development of a space station.

But it was only at the age of twenty, when he saw the *Challenger* blow up, that Mark decided maybe it would be worth trying to *become* an astronaut.

He never examined the decision too closely; he felt it too deeply. It wasn't as though he was a daredevil. He didn't drive fast or drive drunk; he'd passed up any number of chances to take up skydiving. In Colorado he'd learned to fly sailplanes, but that wasn't particularly dangerous. Maybe it was that flying in space suddenly became a challenge. It was not routine; it wasn't going to be routine any time soon.

There was nothing he could do immediately about it, not at the age of twenty. He had already enrolled in ROTC in order to help pay for his schooling, so he was committed to five years in the Air Force after graduation. The Air Force had a bigger space program than NASA did—

The last eulogy had finished. Mark suddenly became aware of an approaching roar just as an F-111 erupted into view over the center at probably five hundred feet. A few moments later a smaller, propeller-powered job zipped by. There was a scattering of applause . . . then a long moment of anticipation. Mark followed the eyes of the more experienced military funeral-goers in the crowd to the west.

There, in the bright sunlight of late morning, came four NASA T-38s, low and level. As they got closer, one of the middle pair peeled off and disappeared from view. A moment later the other three flashed overhead. Maybe it was ridiculously sentimental, but when you thought of all the ways people died . . . and Mark was perfectly aware that someday, somehow, it would be him, either from cancer or in a car crash or keeling over on the tennis court . . . there was something noble about falling from the sky and being remembered by a flyover. Mark found that he had tears in his eyes, and so, he noticed, did most of the people around him.

That ended the service. The band played the Navy hymn as Mark found Kondratko. "This formation," the Russian said. "What do they call that?"

"The missing man."

"I loved that. A friend of mine got killed a couple of years ago—drowned. But he was a pilot and he should have had this. A missing man." He shrugged. "But we couldn't afford the fuel."

Mark was about to leave with Kondratko when he saw a woman looking directly at the two of them. "Do you know her?" Mark asked.

Kondratko was already saying "Hello, Kelly." He shot Mark a smug look that said, in essence, So much for your wonderful memory.

To be fair, Kelly Gessner wasn't wearing her customary torn jeans and flannel shirt. She wore a dark jacket and a skirt with a white silk blouse. Even though she wore sunglasses, she appeared to be made up. She didn't look much at all like the woman Mark had seen around the office precisely twice, and then from across a room. "Hello, Viktor," she said to the Russian. "You must be Mark."

They shook hands. "You and I need to talk."

Kondratko gave them a little wave. "See you Monday." And disappeared into the crowd.

"I'm the CB representative on the board," Kelly said. "I guess that means we're going to be working together."

"So I hear."

"I'm willing to bet that you're less happy than anyone about this, but trust me: I'm a close second." Mark had to laugh. Thank God she seemed to have a sense of humor. Most people in CB didn't. "How are you feeling?"

"Fine, physically. Starting to wonder if I did the right thing."

"Given that the plane was going in, yeah, you did the right thing." There was a brief, distant smile on her face. "I know you were just following Joe's orders."

"I hope everyone else agrees with you."

What Mark wanted was reassurance. What he got, instead, was: "That may be a challenge." And nothing else. Gee, thanks.

Mark and Kelly drifted toward the duck pond behind the podium, where the efficient custodial members of the NASA family were already in disassembly mode. "Look," Kelly said, "we just met, but we're going to have to watch out for each other. Will you promise to call me if you find out anything?"

"Sure"

"And I promise to watch out for you. I have some idea what you're going through." She stopped and changed direction. "I've got to be in the MOD in ten minutes. I guess I'll see you Monday."

Mark watched Kelly go. What was that? Just a say hello? Or a warning of some kind? If she was warning him, why? They didn't know each other. For all Kelly Gessner knew, Mark could *be* a screwup.

Maybe this was some kind of test . . . another Fehrenkamp mindfuck. Kelly Gessner was cute, no doubt about it. Was she one of Fehrenkamp's pets? Following his orders? Keeping the kid off balance?

Mark realized he wasn't going to answer any of these questions here and now. If ever. All he knew was that it was going to be a very long weekend.

CHAPTER 17

Steve Goslin knew why he had wound up being everybody's choice to be the missing man in Joe Buerhle's memorial flyover. It was because he had been Joe's pilot on STS-90. People hear your name tied to another one long enough, they start to believe they belong together. Buerhle and Goslin. Like beer and pretzels. Oil and filter. Lennon and McCartney.

The first problem was that Goslin knew Joe was never comfortable with him; he probably didn't even like him. Goslin had tried to figure out why. Yes, they had different views on life: Goslin was an evangelical Christian and had been married to the same woman since the age of twenty-two. He had two daughters, and hoped for a son. Yes, he loved flying, but if you made him choose between spending time with Diane and the kids and flying off to, say, Colorado at, say, the height of ski season for a little, uh, training—well, that wasn't even a decision.

Joe always seemed to be juggling women. Goslin just never understood that. . . . Yes, there were beautiful women all around, all the time, women you would love to screw. But then what? If you kept screwing them you were in a relationship, and relationships either led to a big fight or to marriage and children. Steve Goslin didn't need the big fight, and he already had a good marriage and wonderful kids. He had told himself that someday Joe Buerhle was going to wind up old and alone.

Well, he had been wrong about that.

Having a straight arrow as a pilot shouldn't have been a crisis for Joe. Goslin wasn't the only straight arrow in CB, and Joe had to have had a veto over his assignment. And it wasn't as though Goslin ever said anything . . . ever allowed himself to disapprove. At most he just shook his head when telling Diane about Joe's problems. . . .

Of course, there was the combat thing. Joe Buerhle had come to NASA ten years back, so he had missed Operation Desert Storm, the attacks on Iraq. But Steve Goslin had been right in there, flying F/A-18s out of Bahrain. Thirty-three combat missions; he'd been shot at. It must have eaten Joe Buerhle alive.

Goslin was sure he had never alluded to his combat experience, but you never knew. Buerhle would have known about it, that was certain.

The STS-90 mission itself had gone pretty well, on the theory that any mission you survived was a good one. True, there had been a moderate screwup in the deployment and retrieval of a Spartan pallet satellite because Joe had ordered Goslin to skip over large chunks of the checklist. But eventually they'd gotten the Spartan settled down and grappled on the remote manipulator arm, even though the science take was a fraction of what it should have been.

The problem was the landing.

The prime landing site for all Shuttle missions was the big runway at the Cape. Every time a mission had to use the backup site out at Edwards, NASA had to spend a million dollars because then the orbiter would have to be hauled into the air and bolted onto the back of a modified 747 for a flight across the country.

But the Cape simply wasn't an ideal prime landing site because of the weather. It was on the Florida coast, and at certain times of the year you were likely to get sudden squalls. The orbiter wasn't designed to fly through rain. No one wanted to see what sort of pelting the fragile thermal tiles on its skin would take from raindrops smacking into them at several hundred miles an hour. So when the weather in Florida was bad, and not expected to improve, it was necessary to go to Edwards.

Which happened to Joe Buerhle and Steve Goslin.

Out there in the high desert of California you usually had terrific flying conditions. But now and then the winds kicked up, which they did rather late in the game, after the de-orbit burn, when the orbiter was already committed to coming home.

Shuttle commanders and pilots were trained to deal with a crosswind landing, and if you had to face that, Edwards was the place. Nevertheless, as they fell below two hundred feet . . . as Goslin dropped the gear on Joe's order as they had in probably two hundred separate sims . . . they caught a gust of wind or some damn thing that made the orbiter literally bank to the left. Joe was at the controls . . . he quickly corrected and set *Discovery* down on the runway safely, although a lot farther to the left of the centerline than he wanted. It was hairy, but everything turned out fine.

But Goslin got the clear impression over the next few days and weeks that their colleagues, the other astronauts, and not a few people in mission operations, thought mistakes had been made.

Goslin wanted to talk to Joe about it, but never seemed to find the time. In fact, he had had exactly one conversation with Joe after the end of their debriefs, which came when Joe, now the chief astronaut, called him in to say he was going to be doing a turn as the T-38 safety officer. It was a flying job, sure, but not exactly what Goslin expected, which was his own Shuttle command. The T-38 job was for an ASCAN.

Well, that was one of the reasons Goslin had made recent inquiries to USMC HQ about whether the service had a place for an ex-astronaut. He wasn't entirely sure that was what he wanted to do: going back to the Marines meant relocating again, and Diane and the kids loved being in Houston, loved their schools, their church. There weren't a whole lot of jobs for a lieutenant colonel who had never done a Pentagon tour or served as a director of operations, either. Goslin's six years at NASA had effectively ruined his chance at commanding a Marine air squadron.

He had also begun to think about going into church work when he retired. The Nazarene church here was growing and would be a great place to bear witness.

But he was still a pilot, and an astronaut, and what he really wanted was to do what he'd been trained for—fly another mission, preferably as commander. He wondered how much longer he would have to suffer on the sidelines.

He was the last of the missing man formation to reach the hangar at Ellington. There was one other plane on the apron as Goslin taxied in and shut down, a NASA Gulfstream 3. The tail number was 1, which was the administrator's bird. Of course, the head of the agency had showed up for the Buerhle memorial. Now he would be flying back to Washington. As Goslin did his walkaround—thinking again what a shame it would be if the ground crew at Ellington got blamed for Buerhle—he saw the administrator and a few staff types drive up and get out. One of them nodded in Goslin's direction, someone who probably had no idea who Goslin was. Fair enough: he didn't know anybody at HQ, either, other than a couple of people from CB who were there on detached assignments.

The Gulfstream seemed to be waiting, and as Goslin finished his walkaround he saw why: Les Fehrenkamp hurried down the stairs from the duty office. This would be a test. Would the director even see him?

"Good job on the flyby," Fehrenkamp said, smiling. "Joe would have approved."

How about that? "I'd like to think so," Goslin said. Not wanting to give up this chance to be one-on-one with Fehrenkamp so quickly, Goslin asked, "When is the actual burial?"

"There isn't going to be one. The body went to a funeral home and was cremated yesterday. That's what his ex wanted."

"No autopsy?"

"No. Not required, so . . ." Fehrenkamp shrugged. It struck Goslin as a little odd, but what, really, would anyone learn from that? The cause of the accident would either be the plane itself, another plane, the weather, or that nebulous thing called pilot error.

It wasn't as though Joe Buerhle had had a heart attack.

"Looks like you're off to Washington."

"Yeah. There are some ISS management issues we need to get resolved. For the third time." Fehrenkamp turned away, then, surprisingly, turned back. "We'll talk when I get back Monday, Steve."

Goslin found himself lifted by this innocuous exchange. If you were on Fehrenkamp's blacklist—and Goslin had been on *somebody's* blacklist—he never saw you, much less talked to you. But he had smiled warmly; he had said words to Goslin. He had mentioned the ISS, then said they would talk. The only thing that could mean was that Goslin was somehow linked in Fehrenkamp's mind with future Shuttle missions, since 90 percent of those manifested for the next five years were going to carry station hardware.

Maybe he wasn't completely forgotten after all. Joe Buerhle's death *had* meant something for Steve Goslin.

NASA N E W S

National Aeronautics and
Space Administration
Lyndon B. Johnson Space Center
Houston TX 77058
281 483-5111

October 18, 1998
Sam Wirth
Johnson Space Center

Following a flawless rendezvous, the orbiter *Atlantis* successfully docked with the Russian space station Mir at 8:22 A.M. Central Daylight Time this morning.

Within two hours mission specialist Dolores McCoy completed the safing and pressurization process for the docking module carried by *Atlantis*, and the hatches were opened between the two spacecraft. STS-95 commander Ron Kubiak was greeted by Mir-29 commander Nikolai Dolgov and flight engineer Nikolai Kazantsev as well as astronaut Gary McMinn.

The crews exchanged the traditional gifts during a short welcoming ceremony in the Mir's core docking module. Following the ceremony and safety briefings, the astronauts and cosmonauts began transferring hundreds of pounds of water, supplies, science equipment and other gear from the *Atlantis* to Mir.

The 230-ton *Atlantis*-Mir complex orbits the earth every ninety minutes at an altitude of 238 statute miles. All systems aboard both vehicles are operating normally.

CHAPTER 18

On Sunday mornings the good people of JSC, including astronauts and flight controllers, joined with their brothers and sisters of the surrounding communities—the real estate agents, the store owners, the computer salespeople, the waiters in the restaurants—in attending church. For Scott McDowell, however, working on the plane he owned with Joe Buerhle was all he needed in the way of religious refreshment. What the hell: you had the potential for a transcendent experience any time you took off, not to mention a constant reminder about the closeness of death. For McDowell, going to church meant spending three or sometimes four Sundays a month at the hangar working on the Pitts, a homebuilt two-seater. Most Sundays he and Joe would put her in the air, then have lunch.

During that time they never spoke a word about JSC or the Shuttle. Mostly they talked sports and fishing and the airplane. Sometimes women. It was like a regular beer commercial.

It suddenly struck McDowell, as he parked his car and unlocked the hangar, that he and Joe Buerhle went back twenty years, to Cannon Air Force Base and the 45th Tactical Fighter Wing, to one day in January 1978 when McDowell heard something on the radio that wound him up so much he literally had to pull over and take some deep breaths. "NASA has just announced the selection of thirty-five new astronauts, including six women and three blacks."

New astronauts? The reason McDowell got interested in flying in the first place was because all the astronauts of Mercury, Gemini and Apollo had been pilots. He had since grown to love flying for its own joys and freedoms, but he had never quite given up the idea of being an astronaut himself. He knew there was a Space Shuttle in the works. If he thought much about that, he assumed that someday it would require new astronauts.

But in the first two weeks of 1978 it never occurred to him that he could be one of them.

He'd gone into the squadron room in search of the *Albuquerque Journal* . . . and couldn't find the news section. Asking around, he managed to locate the section in a trash can behind the bar . . . with one article on page 3 cut out. He glanced at the front page and saw a news brief about the astronauts directing him to page 3.

Someone had clipped the article.

Butter bars—new second lieutenants—were supposed to show up when told, try not to break their airplanes, and otherwise keep their mouths shut. But McDowell couldn't help it. He snapped at the airman first class who was cleaning up the lounge, "Who's cutting up the goddamn paper before anyone gets a chance to read it?"

The airman told him he didn't know who did any clipping, but the guy who threw the paper in the trash was Lieutenant Buerhle . . .

Who was sitting at a desk in the ready room with the article tacked on the bulletin board above him. McDowell tried not to look angry—though he was a little peeved—when he got there. He nodded toward the clipping. "Mind if I read that?"

Buerhle smiled, plucked the clipping off the board and handed it to him. McDowell scanned the article quickly. It seemed to be mostly about the women astronauts who had been picked, all of them civilian scientists or physicians. "So . . . you're interested in space?" McDowell decided to be honest. He knew Buerhle well enough by that point to know he wasn't setting himself up for a hard time.

"Yeah."

Buerhle actually sighed. "Me, too." He accepted the article from Mc-Dowell and stuck it back on the wall.

They had gone their separate ways within the year, McDowell to the Air Force Institute of Technology, then an instructor's job at Davis-Monthan, then the radical move, leaving the USAF to become a civilian flight controller with NASA. All the while Joe was slogging through a typical fighter jock career, a tour at the Pentagon, then back to the cockpit and then to Edwards for test pilot school.

Scott McDowell's first astronaut application failed because he didn't have a test pilot background. True, test flying wasn't a *requirement*; the application merely said such experience was "helpful." The problem was that McDowell was competing with two hundred other pilots who *did* have test pilot backgrounds for half a dozen jobs. He didn't even get called for an interview.

Two years later he applied as a mission specialist. This time he was interviewed and tested, and didn't make the cut. Well, that was the year NASA picked a lot of its civilians from outside JSC. Some congressman had complained that the civilian astronaut candidates were being selected from too small a pool. . . .

It was also the year they selected Major Joe Buerhle.

McDowell's third application failed because NASA selected more pilots than usual. And McDowell had committed the cardinal sin of the astronaut applicant: he had done nothing to add to his résumé over the intervening two years. The fact that he had been busy making the transition to lead flight director—a job at least twice as pressured as being a mission specialist—didn't make any difference.

Then there was last year's application, his fourth. . . . Well, he was still looking for an explanation on *that* one.

McDowell looked at the Pitts and, for the first time he could remember, didn't know what to do with it. Shit, the plane was always in fine shape. It was Joe who set the agenda. Today we're going to repaint it. Today we're going to take the wings off and then put them back on. Today we're going to tune this baby—

The hangar door opened as McDowell was standing there looking at the Pitts. It was Kelly Gessner in shorts and a T-shirt, looking a little grubby. With her was a girl about fourteen, tall and gangly, with long blond hair, wearing the same. McDowell knew about Joe and Kelly, of course. Knew they were spending time together. But Kelly had never come to the hangar, at least not when McDowell was around.

"Hi. What are you doing here?"

"This is where I usually am on Sunday mornings."

"I hope we're not bothering you. I just wanted to show Grace her father's plane."

So this tall girl was the baby Scott had once met—it felt as though it was about two weeks ago. "I was a good friend of your dad. I'm very sorry."

"Thank you," she said.

"Look around," Kelly said, encouraging the girl. "You own part of it now." As she said that, she smiled at McDowell.

Grace walked around to the other side as Kelly ran her hand along the trailing edge of a wing. "I heard you found him," McDowell said to her.

"Yes."

"How was it?"

"Pretty bad."

You got hardened to that sort of thing in the military. Face it, when airplanes hit the ground, there's usually not a lot left. One of McDowell's classmates had splashed an F-117 a few years back. The plane itself disintegrated into a collection of toothpick-sized plastic shards imbedded in a crater about as big as a backyard swimming pool. The only actual remains of the pilot were a few fragments of bone.

"Any idea what happened?"

"Not so far. We've got the plane, though, so . . ." She trailed off. She seemed tired.

"Yeah." It was inconceivable to McDowell that they would find some major malfunction on that plane. He suspected that Kelly believed the same. "What about Koskinen?"

"Looks like he got away clean. Physically. God only knows what this board is going to do with him."

That exhausted McDowell's store of small talk. He wasn't big on warm, personal conversations with people, but even he couldn't ignore the bitterness in Kelly's voice.

"Joe really . . . loved you."

Kelly glanced around to be sure Grace wasn't in earshot. "Bullshit, Scott. Bull *shit*. Yeah, he liked having me around, because I'm a girl who could talk airplanes and fuck. Fine. We had a pretty good thing going, but then he had to start—" She stopped. "Well, he could have been better about a lot of things, but who cares now?"

"I'm sorry." He really was. He had figured out that Joe started dating another woman while Kelly was in her final training, and thought it a bad idea for a variety of reasons. Hell, it was just rude. She was a grown-up: all he had to do was tell her things were over.

"Thank you." She smiled—was it sadly?—then said, "Grace, honey? Seen enough?" Clearly the girl had. She gave the Pitts one last pat, then headed for the door. Kelly was a step behind her, but stopped suddenly and turned back to McDowell. "Scott? You were supposed to fly with him Wednesday, weren't you?"

He'd been trying not to think about that. "Is that what they're saying?"

"Well, that was what Joe was saying when I dropped him off at ops. He said you guys were having some kind of disagreement."

"I don't know about that. We'd talked about me taking a ride with him. I was out there for a Fehrenkamp meeting and . . ." He was having trouble explaining this for some reason. "But they wound up with an ASCAN who needed a ride, and I had a sim coming up. . . ."

"I'm sorry, Scott," she said. She actually stepped up and kissed him on the cheek. "I was just asking."

And she went out, leaving McDowell with two thoughts: Kelly Gessner was pretty; and Kelly Gessner was dangerous.

CHAPTER 19

For the first time in his career as a Worm, Mark missed the Monday morning pilots' meeting. It made him feel quite uncomfortable, like skipping school. He knew it was silly: the meetings weren't in any way mandatory. But he remembered the ASCAN Commandments . . . and attendance was certainly *encouraged*. Nevertheless, Mark's presence at the first meeting of the board investigating the Buerhle accident had priority.

The day hadn't started well. He had driven Allyson out to Hobby so she could catch an early Southwest flight back to L.A. "You don't have to drive me," she had said. "I'll call a cab."

"I want to. I've hardly seen you this weekend."

"It's still more than you've seen me for the past few *months*."

It turned out that Allyson was behind the wheel of Mark's Explorer when they took off. Allyson had passed through Hobby several times a year for the past six years, so Mark was happy to let her be the pilot. This was becoming his role in life, anyway.

Most of their chat on the trip up the freeway concerned plans for their next rendezvous. "Of course," she said, "you might be in Florida."

"I wish I knew." He had no idea how long this assignment to the board would keep him from moving on to that Cape Crusader job.

"Do you still want to see me?" she asked suddenly.

"Sure." The word sounded unconvincing, which surprised Mark. He wasn't thinking of marrying Allyson—anymore—but he still wanted to see her, especially at times like this, when they had just spent time together. He remembered again how much he enjoyed being with her. Sleeping with her.

"I don't think you've thought much about it."

"I haven't thought about *not* seeing you anymore, if that's what you mean."

She smiled and glanced at him. "Don't get cute." It was said lightly, but Mark knew that she meant it.

"Look, are you worried that there's someone else? Because there isn't." That was the truth. He had flirted with a few of the many interesting women he'd met since moving to Houston but had refused to make any serious moves. In fact, he'd turned down a couple of invitations. This was his style, or his weakness, to let the woman make the moves. The truth was that he was just too damned busy. He would think about the love and companionship part of the syllabus *after* he made it through the ASCAN training. As if it were another part of the syllabus.

"I've convinced myself that we're honest with each other. If you found someone else, you'd tell me." Her statement didn't invite agreement or anything else.

"Have *you* found someone else?"

Allyson was shaking her head before she said the word. "No." They were turning south into the main terminal at Hobby. "I just . . ." She frowned. "I'm asking myself a lot of questions, too. I'm not getting any younger . . . I see my sister with her kids . . . Don't panic."

"Sir, no, sir." She laughed. But he *had* started to panic.

"This job is changing you. You always worked hard, but now you're obsessive. It feels strange."

"I think it'll be better in a few months. And this accident hasn't made things any easier."

"I understand. I'm not trying to make things more complicated." She drove in silence for several minutes. "Maybe we should just hold these thoughts for a few months."

"Unless we're going to have a big conversation in the white zone. . . ."

"You're right." Allyson put the car in park as Mark climbed out. He grabbed her bag from the back and handed it to her. "You're not coming in. You're going to give me a good kiss good-bye." Which he did. "And I'm going to see you again in a couple of weeks . . . whether I ought to or not."

With a wave, she was off. As Mark turned back onto Airport Boulevard and headed east toward the freeway, he asked himself what he really wanted. It would be easier on both of them if they split up as they had originally planned. But he didn't like the thought of Allyson's falling in love with some other guy—marrying him—being out of his life forever. Which made

Mark feel even more cold-blooded. It wasn't as if he wanted her . . . he just didn't want someone else to have her. Great!

Then he just got angry, first at himself, then at Allyson. She had initiated this whole thing, the whole relationship! She had chosen to end it—then not end it. Now she wanted to change it again. Didn't she realize what kind of pressure he was under? How little time he had to *think*, much less live a normal life?

Calm down, he told himself. It's not fair. Do what Allyson said—table it. Worry about it later.

Maybe the problem would solve itself.

Well,'' Don Drury said, ''I hope the rest of the day goes better than this.'' He had just spilled a cup of coffee in his lap as he sat down to start their meeting. One of the men Mark took to be from Northrop handed Drury a napkin.

They were just off the hangar floor where NASA 911 was being taken apart, Mark and Kelly, Northrops One and Two, another man from Pratt and Whitney, and yet another one from Collins, plus Drury. The only person missing was Thompson, who showed up just as Drury was about to begin again. ''Sorry,'' he said, looking a little flushed.

''No problem,'' Drury said. ''We had a technical malfunction.'' The guy from Pratt and Whitney laughed.

Mark rarely looked back on his time in the Air Force and certainly never cited it except when desperate for credibility around CB. He knew that for people on deployments or at remote installations—not to mention combat or operational flying—military life could mean living in foreign countries or in ratty base housing, working long hours under extreme conditions and risking injury or death. But for Mark, having gone from college to Falcon Air Force Base in Colorado Springs and then to Los Angeles, working for the Air Force was a lot like working for an aerospace company, except that he wore a uniform with a blue shirt and pants and military insignia instead of a uniform with a white shirt and gray pants and no insignia. At Falcon they called it the ''Corporate Air Force'' as opposed to the RAF, or ''Real Air Force.''

He had appreciated the theater and practical value of most of his Air Force briefings, especially during the Gulf War, when a senior officer walked into the room to deliver the day's package and conversation ceased. Every person knew where to sit and how to respond if queried. A ton of useful information would be presented in the optimum fashion. Wham, bam, thank you, gentlemen. Everyone would stand, and it would be over.

Mark couldn't help feeling that the military style was just a bit more impressive than seeing Don Drury shamble into a tiny office where six people waited and spill coffee on himself.

There was only one desk, an old gray metal General Services model that dated back to World War II. On it were a yellow pad and pencils, and, looking alien to its surroundings, a Toshiba laptop. Drury sat down and arranged these items as he spoke. "We've had a couple of informal meetings on this, of course, while we all gathered here. I don't know how many of you have ever been on a board before. . . ."

"I have." That was Thompson.

"Anyone else?" No one responded. "Well, then, here's the drill. Given the, well, unique status of this aircraft, I will serve as the president. If this were a civil aircraft, it would be Mr. Thompson here. But a NASA aircraft is classed as 'public,' which means not military but not civil. In fact, most of you are here in an advisory capacity.

"But that doesn't make any difference to me. We're going to pitch in and do this job together, and do it quickly. If there was a mechanical problem, we need to know about it. Whatever the cause—if we can determine a cause—we need to issue a preliminary report within two weeks." He smiled. "Astronauts are still flying these things every day.

"Now, since this was not a commercial aircraft, there was no cockpit voice recorder . . ."

As Drury rambled on, Mark realized that Thompson was trying to catch his eye. *We need to talk*, he mouthed. Mark turned away, trying to be casual, even though his heart rate had just shot up.

He found himself looking right at Kelly Gessner and feeling bad that he had not, as promised, been in touch with her. That he hadn't told her about finding tissue from Joe Buerhle's body, or that he had given it to Thompson. By the time they had met Mark was already having second thoughts about that . . . frankly, he had been afraid she would blow up.

Which of the Commandments applied to a potential screwup? When in doubt, say thou nothing?

"We don't have a support staff. The aircraft ops people have been kind enough to give us some room and"—he tapped the Toshiba—"equipment. You're all going to have to keep your own notes and photos. I will handle the final coordination and, with Mr. Thompson's help here, the preliminary report.

"As of this morning the vehicle has been disassembled. The engines are off in the shop being torn down, which the gentlemen from Pratt and Whitney will be observing with one of our Northrop representatives. Miss Gessner, I'd like you to observe that as well."

"Okay," Kelly said. Mark couldn't tell whether she was happy about it or not.

"The cockpit instruments are still being . . . reconstructed. The avionics will be shipped back to Collins today. Mark, why don't you and Mr. Timmins"—that must be the name of Northrop Two—"observe that."

Well, he knew what he was going to be doing all day.

"Mr. Thompson and I will continue to review the maintenance records and Colonel Buerhle's fitness reports, check rides, that sort of thing. We will meet here tonight at six."

Just like that the board meeting was over. Drury asked Thompson to wait for a moment, which meant that Mark wound up alone with Kelly on the hangar floor. "Are you feeling all right?" she asked.

"Fine."

"You looked pale in there."

Mark debated the wisdom of telling Kelly what he had done, and instantly rejected it. He hadn't talked to Thompson yet: there might be nothing to worry about.

"I'm always pale on Monday mornings."

"I was an ASCAN once. I know what you're going through. But Drury seems to have this thing under control. We'll get a preliminary report out in two weeks, and then you can go on to being a Cape Crusader." She shook her head. "We might even be working together."

Mark knew that there was always one veteran astronaut in the support team at the Cape. "They're not going to turn you around on a third flight?"

"I'm not that sure I want one."

Mark wasn't sure he'd heard that. If there were Ten Commandments for real astronauts, two of the top three would be "Thou shalt always be eager to fly." He said, "Well, it leaves more room for the rest of us."

She smiled slightly and moved off. Looking back at her, Mark couldn't help noticing how she stood, just staring at the wreckage. He felt as though he was intruding on a private moment, and was actually relieved when

Thompson appeared behind him and tapped him on the shoulder. "Just the man I wanted to talk to." He seemed cheerful.

Mark tried to be casual. "What's up?"

"Got some good news for you."

"Then don't wait." Mark doubted that the news was actually going to be good.

"I gave that tissue to a guy I know in the Harris County coroner's office. We worked together on this rice rocket that crashed a year ago. He sent your tissue off to a buddy of his at the FBI Crime Lab, who ran some tests. Took a while."

"And?"

"He found something pretty interesting." Mark wondered what a coroner would find from that handful of tissue. "It was full of cocaine."

Cocaine? *Joe Buerhle?* Mark began to feel sick. He could already imagine the questions he would have to answer now. He could see that waiting job at the Cape going to someone else. "And how is this good news for me?"

"Your pilot was flipping out. I mean, you did say he seemed to be in distress . . . losing control of the plane."

It all sounded good. "So, as we say, we've got a preliminary cause already. Not bad for a Monday."

Mark had been around NASA long enough to see another problem. "Explaining how we got the tissue and had it tested outside channels may be a little tricky."

"Yeah. But you've got truth on your side. Truth still counts around NASA, doesn't it?"

"Don't bet on it."

Mark wasn't that cynical. He could just throw himself on the mercy of the court. Maybe he'd get out of this after all.

Then Thompson said, "You've got a much bigger problem, though. Figuring out how or why Joe Buerhle got that stuff in him in the first place."

"I suppose he wouldn't have just . . . taken it. Wouldn't coke screw up your perceptions? It would be like flying drunk."

"I'm not saying *he* did it."

"Then what are you saying?"

"Your chief astronaut didn't have an accident," Thompson said with what appeared to be nervous satisfaction. "Somebody wanted him dead."

CHAPTER 20

When Kelly heard the phone ring at what?—a little before six in the morning—she thought of Clark. Something must be wrong with Clark, and this is Mom calling to tell me.

Before she had a chance to get truly wound up, or sad, she had answered the phone and discovered that it wasn't Mom at all but Melinda Pruett. "I know you were probably asleep," Melinda said. "Believe me, I really tried to wait, but I just found out my plane doesn't have a phone."

Melinda Pruett was a former astronaut, one of the first women selected by NASA. She had flown four missions, then moved on to HQ. Kelly had shared an office with her when she was an ASCAN, and they had gotten to be friends. "Where are you?"

"New Orleans, on my way to Houston. I expect to be in your neighborhood by nine. Can you meet me for breakfast at your Coco's?"

"I'm supposed to be at Ellington at eight—"

"Oh, just tell them you're meeting an AA." AA meant associate administrator. "I'll sign your excuse."

Typical Melinda. Half hard-nosed bureaucrat, half suburban mom. "I think I can buy an extra hour, if it's important."

"It's only about your life, girlfriend." This began to sound intriguing, but the next thing Melinda said was, "They're calling me. See you in a couple of hours."

Kelly had hung up the phone and was well into her shower before she began to wonder seriously about the reason for Melinda's sudden call. Sure, they were professional acquaintances. If women had mentors or mentoresses in the space program (God knew they needed them!), Melinda might have qualified as Kelly's. But why now? And about her life?

Had someone talked about her relationship with Joe? Was it something she had done on her mission? Was it something she had said in the debriefs? Or was there something else going on?

In any case, as she dried off and looked with dismay at her hair Kelly realized she was feeling a little better than she had last week. Except for the Joe business, of course, but that would be a long time healing, if ever. She felt as though she had some energy today. Why not have breakfast with Melinda Pruett? Make an appointment to get your hair cut, too!

And empty the box you took out of Joe Buerhle's house.

As soon as she was dressed she went to the den to get it. When she had finished dumping the dirty clothes into the laundry basket and sticking the extra toiletries under the sink, she realized there were still some items in the box. A pair of computer diskettes.

She picked them up. They were Joe's, all right. The labels had his meticulous draftsman's printing. One said "NOFORN" and the other "TIK," both terms from the world of military secrets. One last little joke from Joe Buerhle. Kelly knew she hadn't picked them up deliberately. Maybe they had been lying in the box in the first place. She put them on her own desk next to her computer.

Before she left, she called home and learned that Clark was fine. Everybody there was fine.

I hear you're feeling a little burned out," Melinda said the moment they sat down. She looked very corporate in a dark gray suit from Anne Klein II. Her hair seemed darker than Kelly remembered, too. This from the woman who used to wear overalls to sims.

For almost a second Kelly planned to deny the charge. But what she said was, "Everybody's burned out after a mission. Especially a long mission."

"Especially a moderately screwed-up mission."

"Is that what they're saying at HQ?"

"Let's just say a lot of people feel the work could have gone better. That's your judgment, too, isn't it?"

So Melinda did have a wire into the debrief. "I'll take my share of the blame."

"No one's suggesting that you deserve any of the blame, Kelly. I'm just trying to find out where your head is at." That phrase reminded Kelly that Melinda had been a college student in the 1960s.

"I guess I'm still trying to dig out from under this thing, then."

"I know what it's like." She paused as the waiter brought them coffee and took their orders, then said: "What kind of career do you want, Kelly? Do you want to be like Cal Stipe, going endlessly from flight to flight for the next ten years? You'll be lucky to get one more flight, if it's a long one. The medical stuff we're seeing is making us nervous, mostly because we don't know what prolonged exposure does to you."

"It hasn't hurt the Russians."

"Hasn't it?" Nobody really knew what the long-term effects of space-flight were on a human body. There hadn't been nearly enough subjects exposed to it—four-hundred people were not enough for a true medical study—for nearly long enough. That didn't even begin to address the needs for standard tests. Besides . . . the list of four-hundred space travelers went all the way back to Yuri Gagarin, who had been in space for less than two hours and had been in the grave for twenty years. "We could probably tough it out, but we're violating OSHA standards every time we fly as it is."

It wasn't generally known, but astronauts were exposed to horribly toxic chemicals in the routine course of a mission. As civil servants, they had to sign waivers to allow launches to proceed. "So what if you decided to hang up your helmet tomorrow? Would it be back to aircraft ops?"

Kelly smiled. "Nope." She had really enjoyed flying with STA and working with the pilots, but that would be like going back to high school as a coach after having played professional sports.

"There could be a place for you at HQ. Even for a year or so, a detached assignment."

Kelly was getting impatient. "Come on, Melinda. For the last few years the flow of power has been *away* from HQ and back to the centers. Look at Hutchins." Hutchins was the director of JSC; more than that, he was now one of the senior managers of the Shuttle program, more powerful on paper than just about anyone at HQ, and in reality, the boss of the program.

"Well, then," Melinda said, flushing a little at the directness of Kelly's challenge, "how about here? Hutchins is always looking for cute little astronauts to serve as his technical assistants."

"How am I supposed to react to a statement like that?"

"Sorry. I was getting back at you for what you said about the flow of power. You were right—but moving there cost me a marriage and at least one other relationship."

Kelly wanted to ask, Well, then, Melinda, why did you take the job? But didn't. It was just Melinda's way of showing that, hey, she had problems, too. "Anyway," Kelly said, "I can't do anything while I'm still on this board."

"Oh, yes. I should have asked how you were doing." Melinda actually arched an eyebrow, looking for all the world like some socialite in a prime time soap.

"Joe and I were officially broken up, if that's what you mean."

"Sorry to hear it. And that's only part of what I meant. How is the work on the board going?"

"We're charging right ahead."

"Anything an AA would like to know about ahead of time?"

It suddenly struck Kelly that Melinda had ordered her to breakfast to get a wire into the accident board!

"I don't think so," she said, trying to sound as helpful as she could. "We're just going through all the steps. There's no sign of any mechanical problem that would be a showstopper."

"Promise to let me know if anything . . . unpredicted turns up?"

Kelly chose not to directly answer the question. "What could possibly turn up?"

"Every time something goes wrong, we look bad. Even if one of our contractors screws up, NASA always gets the blame."

"Everything is going just fine. I think we're going to have a preliminary report in two weeks." That was all she really wanted to tell Melinda. There was no reason to tell her how frustrated she'd gotten in just two full days with the lack of any real cause for the accident. Or with her general sense that there were too many people asking questions.

Melinda smiled. "Good. Very good."

CHAPTER 21

Mark Koskinen spent most of Monday being ticked off.

He started with Thompson. After dropping his bombshell, the NTSB investigator had given Mark a time and place to meet his "buddy" in the coroner's office, then gone off to his own meeting at Ellington with the avionics people, leaving Mark to sit through a long, dreary afternoon of T-38 disassembly. The wrecked plane had been reduced to components now, all of it bagged and tagged.

Then Don Drury had taken Mark aside and told him that Tuesday they would start drafting the preliminary report. "It's not as daunting as it sounds. We already have a Form 6120 from the NTSB. We just fill in the blanks."

"And what are we saying?" Mark asked.

"We should have a better idea when the reports from Pratt and Collins come in. They're supposed to be ready the end of the week."

"What if they don't tell us anything?"

Drury barely blinked. "Then we'll be looking at pilot error. Case closed. Unless you have something unusual to tell us."

It was meant as a joke, but it still left Mark angry with Drury. Why hadn't he allowed the Harris or Galveston County medical examiners to get hold of Joe Buerhle's body? Then this whole business of the cocaine would be the board's problem, not Mark's alone.

Mark's real anger, as he headed the Explorer up the Gulf Freeway toward the towers of downtown Houston, was directed at Les Fehrenkamp in particular, and NASA and possibly the whole aerospace community in general. If Fehrenkamp had assigned one astronaut with some clout to this board instead of a lowly Worm and a bitchy woman, this wouldn't be happening.

A real pilot or commander would have taken charge of this thing from Drury, and Mark would be home packing to go to the Cape.

Poison. Murder. It was hard to believe they had any place in the space program.

It wasn't as though sabotage was a real possibility. Yes, there were people in the world who would blow up the Space Shuttle just to see it go boom. But would that kind of nut be satisfied with an invisible crash off in the Gulf of Mexico? Put aside for the moment the sheer difficulty of a terrorist's or saboteur's getting into Ellington and doing real damage. . . .

The idea of some stalker's going after Buerhle was just as unlikely. Astronauts just weren't famous enough.

That left the usual pool of potential murderers . . . that is, people who knew the victim. Some of the guys in CB were womanizers out of the old school. One astronaut in particular had been through three wives during his tenure there, and from what Mark knew, Buerhle wasn't sitting home nights. Maybe some jealous husband gimmicked the plane. But he would have to know which plane and how. . . .

Maybe it wasn't even a husband. How about a jilted lover? Suddenly the whole idea got twice as difficult.

Nevertheless, one thing was clear. If Joe Buerhle had been poisoned somehow, it was wrong to blame the accident on him, especially if it meant ignoring a murder. The trick was going to be finding out the unpleasant truth without screwing up his astronaut career. People hated to be told bad news. People at NASA hated it worse than most.

Mark saw that he had passed the Harris County Law Enforcement and Criminal Justice Complex and was now winding his way through some goddamn park or country club. He'd managed to make the tricky transition from I-45 to Memorial Drive, right in the heart of downtown, then missed the clearly marked exit for Shepherd Drive. He began to search for a way to get turned around, but this was parkland now, with few cross streets. Living in the city for six months, Mark barely knew this even existed. When he thought of Houston at all it was the area around JSC, not these gleaming skyscrapers, expensive old homes, and country clubs. Of course there would be country clubs. This was Texas, where they bred golfers the way Kentuckians bred horses.

Just like that, his anger was gone. Here was the reason he was in this mess . . . ruining his career, making everyone's life difficult. Forget his memory: that was really just a *Rain Man*–like trick. He just wasn't as smart as he needed to be. NASA had made a big fucking mistake selecting him, because he was a screwup.

Mark, this is Todd.'' Thompson had been waiting at the Dickson Street entrance to the complex. With him was an overweight guy in a wispy mustache, maybe twenty-five years old. At this late hour Mark had simply been able to park on the street and jaywalk. He shook hands with Todd, who seemed full of attitude. "I've got fifteen minutes," he said.

For a moment Mark thought they were going inside the complex, but Todd marched them down toward Shepherd Drive. "I hope you guys understand, there wasn't a whole lot of tissue and the FBI ran this thing as a favor to me.''

"What did they do, exactly?'' Mark said, knowing he was in danger of further antagonizing Todd and not much caring.

Todd glanced at Thompson as he spoke. "The usual pathologies, plus a neutron backscatter analysis.''

Thompson stepped in at that point. "They just got all this equipment up there. My office uses it all the time.''

"The sample showed traces—more than traces—of a fairly pure strain of coke, something called White Smoke.''

"Never heard of it.''

"Unless you're a cop, you wouldn't have. I've seen it here before, though. It's a street hype—you get these stupid gangbangers in here who've been shot, and they're usually full of it.'' Todd gave a mean laugh. "And they wonder why they're slow.''

"So it screws up your reactions.''

"Oh, yeah. It'd be like having four or five beers. You'd be legally drunk.''

"And if you were flying, you could get yourself in trouble.''

"I don't see how anyone could fly or drive with a load of that.''

Thompson interrupted. "How would you get dosed with this White Smoke without knowing it?''

Mark thought he knew already. He could easily remember Joe Buerhle downing a cup of coffee and making a face that morning. He could picture the setting: the second floor of Hangar 276, at the top of the stairway that led down to the flight line.

He had even seen Joe pouring some white powder into the coffee! Sweetener, yes, but—

"It's not exactly tasteless, but the taste can be, uh, overwhelmed. Most of my patients just dump it in their Colt malt liquor." Todd glanced at his watch again. "Now, you guys can explain something for me. . . . Where did this tissue come from? I'm happy to run some tests for a friend, but I want to be covered if this winds up on *60 Minutes*."

"I, ah, told Todd the tissue was from an accident that took place outside his jurisdiction—"

"I think we can do better than that," Mark said suddenly. "Todd, what Walter here has told you is true. I would add that this is—well, I don't like to use the term 'national security.' "

Before Mark could add to this, Todd said, "What do you do?"

It was Mark's turn to glance at Thompson, as if to say, Watch this. "I work with NASA. I'm an astronaut." To drive home the point, he hauled out his white JSC badge. It didn't say he was an astronaut, but it looked impressive.

It was as if someone had thrown a switch inside Todd. The superior, put-upon attitude disappeared like a soap bubble popping. "God! Have you been in space?"

"Not yet. Still working on that."

"I wanted to become an astronaut. They take doctors, don't they?"

"We've got quite a few of them," Mark said, without adding that none of the physicians in CB were overweight junior coroners with nasty attitudes. "In any case, I'm sure you can understand the need for discretion here . . . NASA . . . tissue from a mysterious source . . . narcotics."

Todd was nodding enthusiastically before Mark could even finish. "I understand completely."

Mark squeezed Todd's shoulder, surprising himself. He was not a toucher. Was this what working for NASA had done to him? "Thank you, from all of us. Now . . . where is the tissue?"

Todd nodded back toward the complex. "In a freezer in the basement. . . ."

"Will you do me a favor? Now that you've run the tests—and I want you to make sure your records are complete and secure—would you let me have the tissue back? I want to see that it's . . ."

"Properly honored," Thompson finished.

Todd said, "If you guys will wait here, I'll go get it right now."

"That's not too much trouble?" Todd was already heading back down the street, waving a no.

"I'll send you an application package. You can't get in until you try, you know," Mark called after him.

The moment Todd was out of earshot, Thompson said, "I don't fucking believe it."

"Astro suckups. The world's full of them."

"Why did you tell him? I thought you guys were worried about people knowing."

"Maybe I'm not," Mark heard himself say. "Besides . . . you saw the look on his face. He's thinking this is *X-Files*.

"Todd's on our side now."

CHAPTER 22

Bad writers on the fringe of the space program persisted in the belief that somewhere in Houston or at the Cape there existed an astronaut hangout, some quaint little bar or restaurant where one could find, say, Neil Armstrong knocking back a few bourbons with John Glenn. Maybe there were in the good old days; in fact, Scott McDowell knew they had existed then, because in the good old days the areas around JSC and KSC were so damned undeveloped that the nearest bar was usually the *only* bar, a hangout by default.

But astronauts these days, by and large, didn't drink the way the Apollo crews did. And the JSC community was too big and diverse. There were restaurants in the Bay Area that were frequented by astronauts and flight controllers, but there was nothing you could consider a hangout. You would be lucky to spend a whole evening in any one of them and see a single face you would recognize.

Which is why McDowell was so surprised to see Les Fehrenkamp walk in the door of Le-Roy's. Fehrenkamp gave McDowell his ghost smile. "Drowning your sorrows, Scottie?" He must have suddenly remembered McDowell's partnership with the late Joe Buerhle, because he quickly added, "Or a bit of a wake?"

McDowell was nursing a beer and waiting for Stephanie Bonhoff, a woman who worked for Raytheon—and whose husband happened to be out of town tonight. They usually met here because it was just a drive around the block to her place. "I thought you were in Washington."

"Only for the day. I just got back, and figured I might as well take dinner home with me. If they ever get the order ready." McDowell wondered, not for the first or even thirty-first time, just what or who awaited

Fehrenkamp at home. The man worked constantly. He was like some kind of priest—always on call for the church of NASA. "No matter how early you call ahead . . ." Fehrenkamp leaned against the railing by the counter and prepared to wait.

"They never start until you show up. Been burned too many times."

Fehrenkamp smiled almost to himself. Apparently he realized he was going to have to make some conversation. "So how are you doing?"

"Fine, why?"

Fehrenkamp pursed his lips. "Joe Buerhle was your best friend. If there hadn't been a last-minute switch, you'd have been in that cockpit with him."

"Don't remind me." He shrugged. "He went the way he would have wanted."

"Not quite so soon."

"Well . . . it's *always* too soon." He decided he needed another beer.

McDowell sort of hoped that Stephanie would come walking through the door. Just to see the look on Fehrenkamp's face. Then he got an idea. "Les, what happened to my application?"

He had the pleasure of seeing the unflappable Fehrenkamp get ever so slightly nervous. "Applications are confidential, Scottie. And it isn't as though I have final say over who gets in—"

"I understand perfectly. I know there are lots of people who have to sign off on the final selection—even the goddamn minority affairs people."

"Especially the minority affairs people."

"Does everybody on the board get a veto?"

Fehrenkamp sighed and McDowell felt he'd won a small victory just to get that much response. "If somebody feels strongly that an applicant is wrong . . ."

"Who felt that I was wrong? I mean, I know I was in the final list of twenty, Les." One of McDowell's many former girlfriends worked in flight crew ops and "happened" across a preliminary list of finalists.

"I can tell you, Scottie, that . . . concern was expressed over how . . . willing you'd be to take a step back. You're a lead; you've done a good job as a lead. It's nothing like being a mission specialist, working for me or Joe Buerhle."

"Goddamn it, Les, don't you think I know that? I came to NASA because I wanted to work on spacecraft. I became a flight director because I was good at it. But being a lead isn't like flying and never will be. You guys should have looked at it the other way around: *none* of your other applicants knows what it's like, not the way I do. If I'm willing to fill out a goddamn piece of paper and sit through a bunch of interviews—Christ, isn't that motivation?''

Fehrenkamp's order was ready. He excused himself to go to the window. As he was counting out some bills, he said to McDowell, ''If it makes any difference to you, I would have been happy to hire you.''

''I think I know who blackballed me, Les—''

''I've said all I'm going to say—''

''—Joe never understood why I quit the Air Force when I did—'' Mc-Dowell stopped. Maybe he had read it all wrong. All the time they spent together . . . The hell of it was Joe had always been Scott's choice for the second-best pilot in the world. But he'd never been Joe Buerhle's.

''Do you think you could have saved him?'' Fehrenkamp asked suddenly.

''Who? *Joe?*''

''Yeah. Suppose you had been in the backseat of that bird . . .''

McDowell was already shaking his head. This was dangerous ground—he didn't even want to think about it, much less talk about it with Fehrenkamp. ''Ask your accident board if having a pilot in the backseat would have made any difference. All I know is that Joe wasn't too free with the controls. He could have had Chuck Yeager in the backseat and Joe would still have had the stick.''

Fehrenkamp stopped at the door, framed against the parking lot and trees beyond with the bag of takeout in his arms. ''You know, Scottie . . . we don't *have* an upper age limit.''

Then he was gone. Scott McDowell sat back and stared at his empty beer glass. He knew Les Fehrenkamp well enough to realize he'd just been offered another chance.

CHAPTER 23

On Thursday morning, after four straight twelve-hour days at Ellington and more hours at home, brooding, Mark got up early and jumped on his bike.

His first stop was a quick flyby at the astronaut office. His stated purpose—if asked—was that he wanted to pick up his schedule for next week. (Would he be scheduled for another flight in a T-38, for example? He was obviously going to miss this week, putting him an hour behind for the quarter.) His real goal was to make sure everybody knew he was still alive and active.

He got a partial answer to his quest when he picked up his schedule. The entire week, top to bottom, had him assigned to the Air Patch and the board. The only relief was that on Wednesday they had him scheduled to fly backseat in a T-38 again. If not for that, he might have just torn up the schedule.

He was lucky enough to find Jinx Seamans watching an early-morning broadcast from the current mission on NASA select. Seamans was the deputy chief astronaut, a former F-14 radar-intercept officer whose work as a mission specialist on three Shuttle flights had been described to Mark as adequate without being particularly good. With Seamans were three of Mark's fellow Worms, plus Sarah Wall, one of the few women Shuttle pilots in the office.

On the screen floated Dolores McCoy, a mission specialist on the current STS-95 flight. She was telling some reporter on *Good Morning America* what this particular mission was supposed to accomplish. "She sounds good," Wall said.

"She made a good recovery, then," Seamans said. "Yesterday she didn't want to get out of bed. Kubiak told the doctors she was practically green."

"How could they tell?" Wall snapped. McCoy was an African American; she wouldn't have been selected if she'd been a white male.

The mildly racist remark was something Mark had rarely heard around the office. Which isn't to say that all the astronauts were politically correct—in fact, they were quite open in their disdain for those who didn't fit. Usually, however, the targets were payload specialists, or foreign astronauts, especially the ones from the European Space Agency. Or people from headquarters who dared to make decisions that affected CB without having qualified for it.

The real irony here was that Sarah Wall was a pretty clear case of affirmative action herself. She met the qualifications on paper, of course, but her selection as a Shuttle pilot had still been political. It was obvious that America's female operational military pilots were overrepresented in CB. As Jason Borders had once told Mark, "There are maybe two hundred chicks with sticks in the four services and we've got five of them here. So two and a half percent of all the women who are military pilots are good enough to be astronauts. If they selected the same percentage of men we'd have about a *thousand* astronauts."

Wall wasn't finished with McCoy, either. "Her hair makes her look like the Bride of Frankenstein." In microgravity hair, like everything, tended to float up. Dolores McCoy's bouffant do gave her a dark brown halo.

"I told her to cut it," Seamans said.

Both of them talked as if the Worms weren't in the room. Mark took this as a sign of acceptance. Suddenly Seamans turned to Mark: "What's going on with the board?"

Not knowing what Seamans might have heard, Mark said, "The plane's been torn apart. Engines are being worked on at the shop here. Avionics went back to Collins. I'm on my way back over there right now. We're supposed to be down until we get results Monday."

Seamans nodded. "Try to get this thing wrapped up as quickly as possible." Then he drifted off. So, Mark realized, had everyone else.

He was still untouchable.

Mark was just about out the door when the picture on the TV cut to a scene of Mission Control. His eye automatically went to the capcom station, where Arnaldo Rivera was chatting happily with Dolores McCoy. Sitting right next to Arnaldo, looking smug—or was that Mark's imagination?—was Viktor Kondratko.

It wasn't the sight of Kondratko that did it. Not entirely. It wasn't the schedule. It wasn't Sarah Wall's remark. Or the disappearance of his three fellow Worms.

But all of them combined to send Mark down the stairs to the bike rack.

A few moments later he was pulling into the parking lot at the Kings Inn Ramada, just a few hundred yards east of the JSC main gate.

He stashed the bike behind a Dumpster near the office, then ran for Drury's room. He knocked . . . heard nothing . . . and feared that he was too late.

He knocked again. Finally the door opened. "Mark?"

"Sorry I didn't call. . . ."

Drury waved that aside. "As I get older I spend more time in the goddamn bathroom. Come in."

Drury's bag was closed and resting on the bed. His briefcase lay open. Plane tickets and reports all arranged with the precision Mark had come to expect. "You're lucky you caught me. I'm heading for the airport."

"Back to New Mexico?"

"Yep. Fly to El Paso, then drive to White Sands." He smiled. "We're going to take the X-39 out for a little air, I think." Drury closed up the briefcase. "What can I do for you?"

Mark thought back over the past few days. The medical report. The freeze-out. The hints from Kelly Gessner. "I really need to talk to you about the board's report."

"Aren't we moving it along all right?"

"There's something you need to know."

Drury weighed this for a moment, then opened his briefcase and drew out a business card. "I tell you what . . . give me a call at home tonight."

"I'll drive you to the airport."

"I have a rental car—"

"That's all right. I'm on my bike."

For a moment Mark could see the cold-eyed bureaucrat that Drury used to be. He had seen enough of Drury in action to recognize the signs. But it passed; he softened. Drury actually clapped him on the shoulder. "Let's go, then."

He allowed Mark to carry his bag.

By the time they reached the Airport Boulevard exit Mark had replayed all of Thompson's concerns. "Let me get this straight . . . Joe Buerhle was drunk or stoned when he flew that plane into the water?"

"Yes. There were significant traces of cocaine in his blood. More than enough to cause disorientation."

"Where did the tissue come from?"

Mark told him about the discovery without mentioning his own role in it.

Drury fumed. "So this Thompson fellow just happened to be there when they found it? That bothers me."

"I don't know."

"Well, that is a bit of a problem." He looked over at Mark. "What are you going to do about it?"

"I don't know that, either."

"This doesn't look good, you know. If it gets out." Mark was too busy making the turn into Hobby Airport to answer. "The agency is never good about acknowledging errors in the best of times. There's a hell of an institutional memory . . . we all remember what it's like to be raked over the coals on technical matters by some goddamn congressman who thinks pi is equal to three.

"Besides, Mark. It's all about belief. You can't *sell* people on the idea that going into space is necessary any more than you can *manage* a soldier into charging a hill." Mark had pulled the car to a stop in front of the Southwest terminal. "You're one of the believers, too, you know."

"Who gets hurt if this comes out?"

"The agency. Its practices, its management, its funding. If this is negligence, that's bad enough. You remember that first Simpson trial out in California? How they worked over the police forensics people? That's what you'd be facing. How can you allow some guy to get in a thirty-million-dollar plane with a load of drugs in his system? What kind of people are you hiring down there in Houston? Who's keeping an eye on the taxpayers' investment?

"Then you ask yourself, What if it wasn't negligence? Buerhle was a solid pilot, not some weekend warrior in a silk scarf. There is no way he would have gotten in that cockpit unless he thought he was able to handle the plane.

"So then you're talking . . . murder, I guess. Shit." Drury shook his head. "Well, I can see why you wanted to talk to me. What do you think we should do?"

"I suppose we should find out who did it."

"I'm too old to be a TV detective, Mark. I'm an adviser."

"And I'm even further down the food chain."

They unloaded his bag and checked it. "Here's my first piece of advice," Drury said. "Before you start turning over any rocks, ask yourself what good it's going to do the agency, Mark. And if you really want to have some fun, ask yourself what good this is going to do you, if this winds up in a newspaper."

"I'm wondering what will happen if it winds up in the newspaper and doesn't come from us."

"Good point. All right, since we're already skating on some thin stuff here, let's take a breath and see what happens. Nothing's going to happen with the board for three or four days, until the technical reports come in from Northrop and the others. Why don't you dig into this a little bit? See who was out at Ellington that morning and could have spiked Buerhle's coffee or whatever. Be discreet. And let's you and me talk Monday."

"Okay." On impulse, he put out his hand to Drury. They shook.

"Just don't get too clever, Mark. You're a smart guy, but this business is full of smart guys."

Mark caught a cab back to the Kings Inn, which took all his remaining cash.

His bike was gone.

PART III
CB

U.S. GOV'T
FCOD STS-96 MISSION SUPPORT ACTIVITIES
AS OF: 10/25/98
8:23 A.M.

FCOD Management Support

Launch:	KSC/OSR	Fehrenkamp
	JSC	Wescott
Orbit:	JSC	Fehrenkamp
Landing:	KSC	Fehrenkamp
	JSC	Wescott

Flight Crew

CDR	Joseph
PLT	Mecom
MS1	Teague
MS2	Holly
MS3	Whitefield
PS1	none

CAPCOMS

Ascent	Rivera
Entry	Rivera
Orbit 1	Smalley
Orbit 2	Kondratko

KSC Launch Support

ASP	Goode
Backup	~~Koskinen~~ Leslie
Comm Checks	Tappert
Switch List	Goode/Leslie

TAL Support

Ben Guerir	Borders
Moron	Scull
Zaragoza	Lemay

Mishap Representative

| JSC/MIT | Gessner |

Exchange Crew

| DW | Leslie |
| SC | Tappert |

SPAN		Contingency Action Centers	
0800–0800 Daily		KSC	Goode
11/19	Keimer	JSC	Vaughan
11/20	Takiguchi	DFRF	Thurgood
11/21	Decastro		
11/22	Wollaston	**Crew Recovery Team**	
11/23	Keimer	FCOD Mgmt.	Fehrenkamp
11/24	Takiguchi	Flt Surgeon	Lewis
11/25	Decastro	PAO Rep.	White

CHAPTER 24

Putting together Shuttle crews was the part of Les Fehrenkamp's job he liked most. He didn't even bother to hide it. The chief and deputy chief of CB had input, of course. He made sure to listen to mission operations, though given the institutional animosity between flight controllers and astronauts he was just as likely to do the opposite of what they wanted. But at some point he would sit down at his office computer on, say, a Thursday morning knowing it was his decision—his alone—that would be announced to the world the next week. In this case, the names of the astronauts who would fly STS-100 sometime next year.

At the moment there were 115 active astronauts—with another nineteen candidates, who could be discounted for the moment. Of the actives there were six who were on details—working in Life Sciences or the director's office at JSC, or detached to HQ. That left 109.

Of the 109 true eligibles forty-five were already assigned to upcoming missions, including the six who were on orbit this morning. That left fifty-four, still far more than were needed for a single crew. In fact, there was constant grumbling from other divisions that there were too goddamn many astronauts. The Shuttle manifest wouldn't support more than seven missions a year—with all the training these people got, they could easily fly one per year. In fact, some people had flown twice in a few months without doing a bad job at all. Seven missions a year times five and a half astronauts a mission equaled thirty-nine and a half astronauts.

Fehrenkamp didn't see it that way. For one thing, flying in space had never become as routine as flying an airliner . . . or even a military tanker or bomber. The training was much more intense; the stakes were pretty goddamn high. The odds of getting killed were ridiculous, still something like one in seventy! Those figures alone drove people out of the office after three or four flights. Sure, there were some guys who would stick around and fly forever—like Cal Stipe—but they were the exceptions. Danger junkies. True believers.

Fehrenkamp had enough astronauts for two years of Shuttle missions and figured that was bare minimum. At any given time only half of the astronauts were in mission-specific training while the other half waited, but while they waited they handled important technical assignments. CB was divided into seven branches: flight support, operations and vehicle systems, operations planning, EVA, robotics, computer support, and payload/habitation. A veteran astronaut headed each of those branches, and anywhere from six to ten veterans and rookies worked there, improving EVA techniques, for example, or debugging software at SAIL. There was work for them, all right.

Besides, after Russian money problems and Boeing screwups, the crews for International Space Station (ISS) missions would be getting named soon. The ISS missions would eat up a minimum of three years of an astronaut's career. No, as far as Les Fehrenkamp was concerned, he had too few astronauts, not too many.

There were some fixed data points that controlled the decision. STS mission 100 was manifested for launch nine months from now aboard the orbiter *Atlantis*. It would carry a crew of five on the tenth visit to the Mir space station and was known in the planning documents as SMM-10.

Each crew was commanded by a veteran, a pilot who had already commanded a mission, or a guy who had flown as pilot twice and done a good job. The pilot might be a rookie, might not. Given the nature of the mission, heavy on rendezvous and prox ops, it might be better to have a pilot who had already been through training and flown a mission. On the other hand, some rookies were quick studies, and if the commander was good . . . Well, that was what made this an art instead of a science.

Of the three mission specialists, one should be a veteran. Again, given that this was an important visit to Mir, it might be good to have a couple of veterans. In any case, training would go more smoothly if one of the mission specialists had worked with the commander in the past.

The commander was generally the first and easiest choice, because the pool of candidates for a given mission rarely exceeded four or five. The commander pool for STS-100 included a couple of senior types who had been around since the mid-1980s, each with three missions behind him. There was one pilot who had done a good job in his first command six months back. And there was another pilot who had flown a pair of missions from the right seat who deserved a shot at command. This pilot had already flown a mission to Mir, too, which didn't hurt.

The only mark against this particular astronaut—Steve Goslin—was that Joe Buerhle hadn't liked him. In their last meeting, the morning of Joe's accident, they had discussed this list of potential commanders, and Buerhle had put Goslin at the bottom. "In fact, I'd like to send him to Russia when we change directors there."

"That sounds harsh. Why?"

"I've flown with Steve. He's a pretty good stick, but he's wired way too tight."

"He is, or his wife is?" Fehrenkamp knew that Goslin's wife was an active evangelical Christian—pretty, but absolutely humorless, an unfortunate combination.

"This has nothing to do with his wife. But I got to know both of them pretty well during 90, and in my opinion there's no way Goslin should be in charge of a crew."

"He's inflexible?"

"That's a good word."

"I can't pass him over."

"Send him back to the fucking Marines, then."

Fehrenkamp always gave his chief astronaut a veto. If Buerhle didn't want Goslin, he certainly wasn't going to assign him anyway. But now Buerhle was dead. And Fehrenkamp believed in Goslin.

And even if the Marine needed to loosen up a bit, having watched several of his contemporaries go on to commands while he languished in a technical assignment should have encouraged the process.

Fehrenkamp consulted his matrix and checked off Goslin's name. The computer immediately listed the next available pilot, a Navy commander named Jeff Dieckhaus who had flown a single mission and could be counted on to provide support to a new commander. There were two of the five right there.

The matrix also listed three mission specialists Goslin had flown with, and their current assignments. One had just come back from another mission; there was no rush to recycle him this quickly. One was four months into an assignment as chief of the flight support branch. Too early to pull him out of there. Which left the third candidate, a good choice for the veteran in the mix.

Now he had a potential commander, a potential pilot, and one of the mission specialists. He looked over the matrix on the mission specialist, noting experience both in EVA and RMS, which meant Fehrenkamp could assign just about anyone in the pool to the other two jobs. Since there were still four or five members of the previous astronaut class who had yet to fly missions, Fehrenkamp added two rookies to the matrix.

And looked it over. A Marine commander, a Navy pilot, a veteran civilian mission specialist, a rookie Air Force mission specialist, and a rookie mission specialist from the European Space Agency. Four men and a woman. Another regular World War II bomber crew.

The only slight problem was the European mission specialist, an Irish astronomer Fehrenkamp simply didn't know well. But his trainers spoke highly of him, and he had done a good job in support down at the Cape.

Well . . . this would be a question for Goslin. He always let a commander have one veto.

It was too early for Valerie to be in, so he picked up the phone himself and dialed a home number. "Steve, it's Les Fehrenkamp. Stop by and see me on your way in today."

Goslin would know that STS-100 was about to be named. He would be aware that he was in the small pool of potential commanders. He would have to suspect that the assignment was why Fehrenkamp wanted to see him first thing.

It was only a few minutes after seven on a Thursday, and Les Fehrenkamp had already made a Marine pilot one happy man.

This is great. This is outstanding," Steve Goslin said an hour later. He had come into Fehrenkamp's office suspecting it was good news, but still a little unsure. Once Fehrenkamp had told him that, yes, he was the commander of STS-100, Goslin had actually slumped in his chair. "You're going to have to stay loose with your training," Fehrenkamp warned him. "This mission wasn't even on the manifest until last year." STS-100 was intended to rendezvous and dock with the Mir space station, to pick up and return to Earth the last of half a dozen NASA long-duration visitors to the station. At this point in time that last visitor was scheduled to be Cal Stipe. There was already talk of letting Stipe stay on past SMM-10 to a new mission, yet to be scheduled. This was all related to the continuing delays in launching the first elements of the ISS. And the survival of Mir itself.

"I'll hang loose. I mean, it's still a rendezvous and docking. The business of whether we come back with the same number of bodies we go up with isn't going to keep me up nights."

"I didn't think it would." Fehrenkamp could see Goslin unwinding . . . his confidence growing. "Anything else?"

"Yeah. I don't like that crew. Well, one of them. The ESA guy."

"He's qualified."

"That means he hasn't screwed up while we've been watching him, Les. It doesn't mean he was really competitive in the first place."

"Almost ten percent of CB has been selected elsewhere, Steve. That's a mandate from heaven."

"If I have to take him, I'd like another MS."

"Your mission is manifested for a crew of five up and six down."

"I've heard that changes sometimes occur."

Fehrenkamp smiled. He liked a commander who was willing to fight for his crew, to act like a leader. Within reason. "We're going to announce a crew of five. What happens down the line is anybody's guess. A lot of it is completely out of my hands."

Now Goslin smiled. "I don't believe that any of this is out of your hands, Les."

"Let's say I bump our ESA fellow to the next mission. Do you have anyone in mind to replace him?"

"How about Kelly Gessner? I haven't flown a mission with her, but we logged a lot of time together in the STA."

"She's just coming off another flight. I was hoping to use her in management for a year or so."

Goslin made a face. "Can't you use her in management *next* year?"

Fehrenkamp smiled, more to himself than to his guest, because he had wanted Kelly on Goslin's crew all along. But he needed *Goslin* to make the request. "All right, Steve: consider Kelly on your crew—with the ESA guy." Goslin wanted to protest but could clearly see that the deal was done. He'd won one and lost one. "Obviously I need you to keep this quiet until I'm ready to announce it."

"I've waited this long . . . a few more days won't kill me."

"Did you really think you weren't going to get a command?"

"Les, Joe Buerhle made it clear that as far as he was concerned, I was the invisible man. I figured I was on my way back to the Marines."

"Well . . . Speak no ill of the dead." He stood up and held out his hand. "Congratulations, Commander."

Once Goslin was gone, Fehrenkamp sat back in his chair to think about when and how and what he was going to tell Kelly Gessner.

NASA N E W S

National Aeronautics and
Space Administration
Lyndon B. Johnson Space Center
Houston TX 77058
281 481-5111

October 23, 1998
Shannon Crosby
Headquarters, Washington D.C.
(Phone: 202/358-1780)

Lou Wekkin
Johnson Space Center, Houston TX
(Phone: 218/483-1511)

RELEASE 98-111

RAGER NAMED DIRECTOR OF OPERATIONS, RUSSIA

Astronaut Jerome Rager (Lt. Col., US Army) has been named NASA director of operations, Russia, replacing Calvin Stipe at the Gagarin Cosmonaut Training Center near Moscow.

In this position Rager will support NASA astronauts currently visiting the Mir space station under Phase I of the Shuttle/Mir program, and the first visits to the International Space Station. He will serve as the primary link between NASA and Gagarin Center management, coordinating all operations involving NASA or contractor personnel.

Rager, 39, has flown two Shuttle missions and is currently assigned as backup commander for the first ISS increment, scheduled to commence with a manned Soyuz launch to the Russian-built control module in the spring of 1999.

Stipe, 51, is a five-time Shuttle flight veteran. He is currently assigned as the seventh Shuttle/Mir crew member and has been training on Soyuz-Mir systems and in the Russian language. He is to be launched to Mir aboard Soyuz *TM-30* next month and should break the all-time American space endurance record.

For complete biographical information, see the Internet home page at http://www.jsc.nasa.gov/bios/

CHAPTER 25

Mark arrived at ops two hours before his scheduled takeoff time because he knew that he had no helmet, no parachute. He only had a flight suit because he'd bought two of them before taking survival school. Worst of all, he had to drive the long way around because his bike had been stolen.

It was a good thing he'd allowed the extra time. When Mark reminded Harry, the equipment man, about his situation, it seemed that it would take an act of Congress to get those items replaced. That was just Harry, however. He was great at his job, as long as you didn't throw him any curves. He found Mark a new helmet, and even helped him pack a new parachute. They were out on the apron when Cal Stipe walked up to them with his helmet under one arm and his chute slung over his shoulder.

"Well," Stipe said, "this is *one* thing you obviously know how to do."

From most astronauts that would have been a dig, but Stipe was smiling. Mark stood up and shook hands with him. "It may be the only thing, if you ask around."

"We'll talk about that. Ready to get back up on that old horse?"

"Yeah. I've got a flight in . . . God, fifteen minutes." He had been so preoccupied with getting ready to fly that he'd just about forgotten the flight itself.

"I know," Stipe said. "You're flying with me."

"I thought—" Mark said, then shut up. He hadn't thought anything about who his pilot would be, but flying with Stipe was as good, if not better, than being with one of the pilot astronauts. For one thing, with almost twenty years as an astronaut behind him, Stipe had more hours in the T-38 than any other pilot, something like three thousand, which was more than some of the pilots in Mark's Worm group had in all aircraft put together. There wasn't much about the T-38 that Stipe didn't know.

Best of all, even though he had all of the traditional pilot's skills, he had none of the traditional attitude. He was the one senior astronaut who had gone out of his way to be friendly to the Worms. The only time Mark had gotten tipsy during his time in Houston had been with Stipe and Kondratko. Well, maybe a little more than tipsy. All Mark really remembered from the evening was Stipe and Kondratko exchanging dirty jokes in Russian.

Mark quickly ran upstairs to the duty office to sign out, then back down to the apron. Stipe was in the middle of his walkaround on bird number 916. "I always start at the left nose, pilot's side," Stipe told him. Mark had been trained to do his own walkarounds while staying out of the pilot's way. This was the first time anyone from the astronaut office had bothered to let him take part in the process. "Examine the intakes, the Pitot tube, landing gear pins, then work your way all around under the wing to the other side, looking for leaks of hydraulic fuel. Nothing. A good, clean bird."

Stipe went up the ladder and down into the seat. Mark followed, pulling his straps on, oxygen connectors, helmet and mask. There was a whole other checklist to run through once you were in the cockpit. Batteries and radio switch. Rudder trim. Ejection handgrips. Stipe made him part of everything without ever being condescending.

Mark felt as though he were going through this for the very first time. He tried to slow his breathing . . . to relax. To forget about the ejection handgrips.

"NASA 916, you're cleared to start."

Stipe acknowledged the call, then looked over at the crew chief, twirling his finger in the air, then hitting the starter button on his console. The crew chief was hitting his own starter, a midget-sized turbojet known as the palouste, which would blast four hundred pounds of exhaust into the T-38's twin engines to get them turning.

Within moments bird 916 was blowing exhaust out of its left tailpipe. Engine RPM and oil pressure were green. They repeated the procedure for the right engine, then the crew chief unhooked the starter and Stipe called Ellington Ground for permission to taxi.

They reached the departure pad, then waited again, this time for Ellington Tower to clear them for the runway.

Mark tried not to think about what had happened last time. Then gave up and wallowed in it: what were the chances of an accident happening again?

Their turn, now. Throttles forward, and just like that you were up. The T-38 had twin engines and a wonderful little lift over drag . . . that is, a hell of a lot of lift compared to drag. It would rotate in a few hundred feet and take you straight up. Today it was straight up and to the southwest, the Gulf Freeway passing behind. Always had to avoid the Hobby control zone farther west; turn east, right over JSC.

So far so good.

"I'm not big on acrobatics," Stipe said. "Hope you won't be too disappointed with a little stroll out and back."

"Just bring me back alive," Mark said. Stipe laughed.

"I have a confession to make," Stipe said as they continued streaking south toward the Gulf. "I asked to have you assigned to me."

"Thanks."

"You're going to have to, uh, reestablish yourself, you know."

"Am I?" Mark said, realizing that Stipe was undoubtedly telling him the truth.

"Pilots are very rational individuals about most things, but flying brings out their superstitions. And astronauts, because they are sort of superpilots, are supersuperstitious, if that's a word."

"Nobody wants to fly with me."

"Let's just say there was a distinct shortage of volunteers to take you out for your first flight after the accident."

"Well, then, thanks again."

"Buerhle was very popular in certain circles, you know."

Mark saw an opening. Since dropping Drury at the airport he had done damned little in the way of investigating. Other than try to figure out where his bike had gone. He was hampered by the lack of any real contacts inside the power structure of the astronaut office. The people he knew best were just the Worms, the last to know. "Sounds as though there were some people who didn't like him."

"Any boss makes enemies."

Stipe aimed the T-38 well out into the Gulf. Mark wondered if they would be flying over the spot where he had ejected into the water. "I thought Buerhle was universally loved."

"He could be a cold son of a bitch, even to his friends. Do you know Scott McDowell?"

"Vaguely." All Mark really knew was that McDowell was one of the dozen lead flight directors. Sometimes he showed up around the Air Patch because he was also a former Air Force pilot.

"Joe Buerhle's best buddy. I mean, they own a plane together. But Scott McDowell was never going to be selected as an astronaut as long as Joe had anything to say about it."

"Why not?"

"Joe had very high standards. I mean, you should be damned honored you made it into one of his selections. He just never thought Scott was a good enough stick."

"Even for MS?" You didn't need to be a pilot to be a mission specialist. Mark was proof of that.

"It all has to do with your attitude toward your job. Scott lets things get to him . . . he's got a mean temper. That may be perfect for a flight controller. Those guys are beating the shit out of everybody all the time, anyway. But Joe thought he'd be a disaster—well, not a disaster. Just not as good as some of the other candidates. I know, because I was on one of the boards that didn't select McDowell. He'd given Joe Buerhle as one of his references, and Joe just sank him."

Mark found this fascinating. He wished that he and Stipe weren't just sharing a T-38 cockpit for forty minutes but were sitting side by side on some long transcontinental airline flight, preferably knocking back a few cocktails. "You're sure it wasn't something else? Some woman problem?"

"Well, it's *always* something else. But that's the heart of it."

"Wow."

"I'm not saying I think it's true, about Scott being a bad choice for astronaut. He just has a perception problem. And so, my friend, do you."

Mark was just as happy to accept Stipe's advice on this. "What should I do?"

"Fight it. Be aggressive. I know ASCANs are supposed to be seen and not heard, but you're going to find yourself slid out the door if you don't start acting like you belong in CB. As if we're lucky to have you. Attitude alone won't do it, of course. But start from there."

"Okay."

"Don't let Fehrenkamp push you around, either. He loves to play games with people, but he has a lot more respect for people who come right back at him. Like Gessner."

"Kelly Gessner?" Mark was desperate to hear more.

"Oh, shit," Stipe said. For an instant Mark thought, Oh no, here we go again. "We're out of time."

The T-38 banked to the left. And with Stipe concentrating on setting up for his approach and landing, Mark kept quiet.

After Mark had showered and changed he went out to the parking lot. He was just about to get into his Explorer when Steve Goslin drove up in his car. As the Marine got out, he nodded hello at Mark. With Stipe's advice still fresh, and remembering that Goslin had, with Stipe, been one of those gathered around the secretary's desk in CB the night Buerhle died, Mark wasn't just going to let this opportunity pass.

"How's your daughter doing?"

Goslin seemed at a loss for a moment. "She's fine. One of those strep throat things. Woke up with a fever of a hundred and four."

"I wish she'd picked a different morning."

Goslin just blinked at him. "Well, I don't think she had much choice."

So much for Mark's attempt at humor. He realized that he didn't much like Steve Goslin—he had mean little eyes. Piss holes. That's what they called them back in Iowa. "I'm glad she's better now."

He opened his car door. "Were you out?" Goslin asked, as if the concept of Mark in a cockpit again was unimaginable.

"Yeah," Mark said, grinning. "And this time I couldn't figure out how to fuck things up."

Goslin blinked again. "You know, I'm sorry." He just stood there, a martyr.

"For what? Your daughter was sick. I don't know what happened to Buerhle, but it sure wasn't your fault."

"Well," Goslin said, "I guess I'll see you around." Clearly uncomfortable, he headed toward Hangar 276, leaving Mark to wonder if, somehow, Goslin were actually apologizing for some *other* action.

But what?

CHAPTER 26

Drury hated to travel on Sunday, especially Sunday evening, especially going east on Sunday evening. Here it was, early evening by his internal clock, yet the airport seemed practically deserted, as if it had just received the last flight of the day. He knew from experience that nothing would be open. As an added bonus it was drizzling.

In the Apollo days he would have hit town and been heading for a bar or nightclub before bothering to unpack. Of course, in the Apollo days he would not have been traveling alone. They hunted in packs in those days. Even the relatively small towns like Cocoa Beach or Huntsville roared whenever the NASA team came to town.

Now all his contemporaries from the Apollo days were dead or retired. Scattered to Florida or Arizona. A few remained hereabouts, in the JSC community, but they were rarely home, he had discovered.

Maybe he had just hung on too long.

He had long since learned to keep his luggage to a single carry-on, though carrying it had gotten more difficult lately. He was waiting for a cab when he saw a gray Ford Explorer, wipers slapping, pull up to the curb.

"Don?" It was Mark Koskinen. "Need a ride?"

What was he doing at Hobby Airport on a rainy Sunday night? Don Drury was afraid he knew the answer. "Sure do," he answered.

There wasn't much traffic, but what there was refused to move. Drury felt blinded by the sheen of water on the windows, the way it distorted the lights. He never rented cars anymore. He didn't like driving in strange cities at night, and had been absent from Houston long enough for it to qualify as a strange city.

Mark asked the obligatory question about Drury's flight. They chatted about the current mission, which was still docked with Mir. Drury was grateful that Mark had his radio tuned to some all-news channel, keeping the volume low enough so that it couldn't actually be listened to.

Drury waited for Mark to bring up Joe Buerhle and the T-38. He wondered if Mark realized just how easy it was to crash a plane like that. They finally got on the 45 freeway headed south. And Drury was tired of waiting. "What did you find?"

"At least one guy who hated Buerhle enough to want him dead. And who has already benefited."

"Okay."

"His buddy, Scott McDowell. Apparently Buerhle had kept him out of the astronaut office, and he knew about it."

"You know this for sure."

Mark turned and looked at him. He was practically blushing. "I don't know *anything* for sure."

"I was going to say that, even if you did, there's a couple of long steps from a possible motive to commission of this kind of crime."

"He was at Ellington the morning of the accident."

"And, yes, he could have spiked Buerhle's coffee. Can you imagine what a defense attorney would do to that?"

"Very easily."

"What else?"

"Nothing concrete. There's another astronaut, Goslin, who had a grudge against Buerhle. He was the guy I was supposed to fly with that morning, but he was a late scratch."

"So he wasn't even at Ellington."

"Well, that's the funny thing: turned out he *was* there, after all."

Drury didn't like the sound of this. Not the facts—those were practically irrelevant. Joe Buerhle was dead; nothing was going to bring him back. But here he had young Koskinen—a very bright young man, supposedly very levelheaded—convincing himself that a member of the JSC family had killed another one. What would happen if he let this thing get out of control?

He had been in a situation like this before, starting in Washington, January 1986. He had watched the Mission 51-L launch on a cold day in late January the way everyone else did, on television. He had just described to Dorothy, his new secretary, how Christa McAuliffe—the schoolteacher who was going to make a Shuttle flight—would be feeling right then. "She's been sitting on her back for a couple of hours now wearing gloves and a big helmet. She's probably very uncomfortable." There was main engine start, solid rocket motor ignition. "Now she's hearing thunder from the SRBs and feeling a little shook up." Drury didn't think he could adequately describe the violence of a Shuttle liftoff. He himself only had reports, though he had seen some handheld videotapes taken by crews and talked to enough of them to realize what a terrifying experience it could be.

"She'll start to feel as though her seat is tilting back. The Shuttle goes into orbit with the tank up and the orbiter hanging below it." Things seemed to be going well, routine calls from the capcom to Dick Scobee, the commander. Drury thought the ascent seemed a trifle sluggish, almost as if *Challenger* was fighting a strong wind.

Then he saw the picture erupt in a silent geyser of orange. "Oh, Christ."

Dorothy had never seen a Shuttle launch before. "What's happening now?" she said.

"They're dead."

Dorothy, a black woman in her late twenties, looked at him and frowned. "I'm sorry, Mr. Drury, but that isn't very funny. . . ."

"I'm sorry, too, Dorothy." He went on, as gently as he could, to explain how that flash on the screen meant that something had gone terribly wrong during the one phase of ascent from which there could be no recovery. All of this was being confirmed by the words from Houston. "Flight dynamics officer reports the vehicle has exploded." "Radar is reporting discreting sources." And the pitiless eye of the camera was showing a shower of pieces falling into the ocean.

The ocean.

Drury was assigned a role in the recovery team. Although there were something like thirty cameras covering the *Challenger* during its ascent to go with miles of data recorded right up to—and, as it turned out, milliseconds past—the moment of the explosion, the true search for the accident's cause would focus on the hardware itself. Hardware which was scattered over several miles of water.

So it was that Drury happened to be in the wrong place at the wrong time when, six weeks after the disaster, one of the salvage ships reported that it had located the wreckage of the crew cabin.

Drury assumed at first that the crew had been vaporized instantly. He had learned over days and weeks that the orange-and-white cloud was caused by the sudden mixing of volatile fuels . . . that the orbiter had actually suffered an aerodynamic breakup, that several pieces, including the rugged, self-contained crew cabin, had flown free of the initial "explosion" and arced even higher into the sky before falling sixty thousand feet to the water.

It was accepted—though rarely discussed—that the crew had probably lived through the breakup only to die on impact. In early March one of the recovery vessels, the USS *Preserver*, found proof . . . the cabin itself, lying half crushed in a hundred feet of water. It shouldn't have taken that long: a battered astronaut helmet along with other materials from the crew cabin had been recovered floating on the water three days after the accident, and it was fairly simple to backtrack to a projected impact circle less than a mile across. One of the recovery ships even got a sonar contact within that circle, Target 67. But to Drury there was no real desire to find the crew cabin. What were they going to learn? The crew was dead. The important pieces of *Challenger* that needed to be recovered during that horrible winter weather were the solid rocket motors, the main engines, the equipment that might have caused the accident.

Target 67 was ultimately reached on Friday, March 7, by the *Lucy*, an Air Force vessel, an old utility landing craft equipped with a crane and winches. Alerted to the discovery, the *Lucy* was replaced on station by the *Preserver*. The next morning its Navy divers and one of the astronauts aboard were able to confirm that, yes, this was the *Challenger* crew cabin, and swim inside. They found that all seven seats had been torn from their mountings and flattened into a cake of metal, wire and human remains.

Having received the coded message that "Tom O'Malley" had been found, Drury was waiting at the pier at Port Canaveral that night as the *Preserver* put in. The astronaut remains had been placed in black body bags and the bags inside three plastic garbage cans. There had been some discussion about taking the remains, if recovered, to Hangar L at the Kennedy Space Center. Hangar L was the Life Sciences building.

But nothing had been decided. Hangar L wasn't ready. Worse yet, it was a civilian facility, meaning that the local Brevard County medical examiners would have the right to examine the remains. Preferring to have the astronauts examined by military pathologists, Drury decided to send them to the morgue at nearby Patrick Air Force Base. He got into a pickup truck with an Air Force sergeant, and drove the five miles down Highway A1A to Patrick. He never looked back.

There was a dispute later between the local medical examiners and NASA, but a few phone calls smoothed that out. Drury just wanted to put the whole matter behind him. He was horrified enough by what he had seen over the past few years and what he was hearing from the commission investigating the disaster.

Years later he wondered if he had done the right thing. He saw public officials destroyed for improprieties that were relatively small compared to his evasion of justice. Yet . . . it had felt right at the time. He had not wanted autopsy pictures to wind up in the *National Enquirer*—or *Life* magazine. The families had suffered enough. The agency had suffered enough. He felt he could still defend that decision.

And now he was faced with another one. "You're a smart young man, Mark. Everyone says so and I can see it myself. You can certainly imagine what would happen to you if you took that specific information into a court of law."

"I'd be chewed up and spit out."

"Very likely. But just put that aside for the moment. Let's say no one challenges you on the whereabouts and actions of McDowell and Goslin that morning.

"Your whole case is still built on this piece of information: some tissue *allegedly* recovered from the wreckage of the plane flown by Colonel Buerhle was *suspected* of having *traces* of a narcotic in it. Note the emphasis?"

"Noted. I'd have to be able to create a regular chain of evidence."

"You got it." He paused to let that sink in. "Did you know my background was in chemical engineering?" This was true: his first job in the space business had been in propellants.

"No."

"Let's just say I know enough about that field to ask the right questions, and I'm telling you the amount of this stuff—"

"Cocaine."

"Whatever, is going to be another problem. Maybe a . . . a cold medication would give the same tox result."

"I know where you're going with this, Mr. Drury, and I appreciate it. But you have to remember one thing: I was there. I *heard* Joe Buerhle . . . freak out."

That was both Mark's best and weakest point. "I'm not going to diminish what happened to you in any way, Mark. I'm not suggesting you're wrong. What I am suggesting is that there's no . . . fucking . . . way you're ever going to prove it. All you're going to do is hurt the agency and ruin your chances of flying in space."

They had long since turned off I-45 onto NASA One, a dreary sight on this rainy night. Now they were pulling into the Kings Inn. The car stopped.

"What would you do if you were me?"

"I'd wrap it in a white light, son. I'd place it in a mental footlocker with Jesus and Bigfoot and the national debt . . . all the sacred mysteries."

Drury opened the door, got out, and reached for his bag. "I've got it," he snapped as Mark moved to help him.

He leaned in to deliver the final punch. "Tomorrow morning we're going to examine the evidence on that plane. If something mechanical turns up, we will deal with that. I'm afraid I'm not going to be very tolerant of any wild speculation in this other venue."

"I hear you."

"Nor do I want any clever little blind items in newspapers. I don't even want to think this is going to wind up in your memoirs when you become the first man on Mars. I swear I'll come back and haunt you."

It was an old technique—jolly them a little while you smoke 'em with the bad news. Mark couldn't help smiling. "I understand perfectly."

Drury rapped on the door. "Good boy. See you tomorrow." He went into the lobby without looking back, hoping that young Mark Koskinen was as smart as everybody said he was.

CHAPTER 27

Well, then," Don Drury said to the assembled board, "you've heard the
evidence from the contractors. There are no anomalies in the engines,
the control systems or the airframe. . . ."

He shuffled his papers and adjusted his reading glasses. Kelly looked at
the others around the table. They had moved out of the cramped little maintenance office, where there was no room, into the hangar itself, where there
was too much. Every movement of a chair or dropped pencil echoed like a
rifle shot.

In a way Kelly was glad; the noise forced her to return her attention to
the meeting, instead of thinking about Les Fehrenkamp's call that morning.

He wanted her to think about going into space for a third time, as a
mission specialist in STS-100, Steve Goslin's crew. "Is this an assignment
or an offer of an assignment?" she had asked.

"At the moment, an offer. You just got back; you're under no obliga-
tion. I want you to take at least a day to think this over."

Kelly planned to do just that. When astronauts returned from a Shuttle
flight they were on call for debriefs, first of all. But once those wound down
they were usually given some free time. In fact, the attitude was, Let us
know when you want to go back to work. You couldn't screw off for the
next six months, but you could lie low for several weeks, if that's what you
needed. Almost nobody wanted to go back through the training grind right
away.

"The board's going to start on a report today," Kelly had told Fehrenkamp.

"Don't keep me in suspense. Am I going to be called to Washington
to testify?" That was a typical Fehrenkamp attempt at humor.

"I think you can sleep well, Les. No one is going to hang maintenance problems or poor training on you. It's just going to come down to probable pilot error." Fehrenkamp had seemed pleased, and made her promise that they would talk again as soon as possible.

She'd based that statement on nothing more than her sense of the board. Yet, here she was, hearing Don Drury saying that very thing.

"I propose that we start drafting a preliminary report concluding that NASA 911 could only have crashed because of pilot error. Do I hear any dissent?"

There was silence around the table, from Thompson, from the Northrop, Collins, and Pratt and Whitney people. Mark Koskinen seemed to be examining the table in front of him for manufacturing defects.

Kelly raised her hand. "What are the ramifications for a finding of pilot error?"

"We're only talking about probable pilot error, not a definitive finding thereof. If we did that, it might impact insurance settlements and whatnot. But we're only saying, Look, we can rule out mechanical and weather problems. We have a survivor who was in the cockpit until just before the crash, and his testimony is consistent with those conclusions. The only cause we can't *rule out* is pilot error."

Kelly would have to be satisfied with that. Drury started passing around sections of a Form 6120, the standard accident document of the National Transportation Safety Board. "I've got this whole thing on diskette, so we can break it into sections and then swap them around. . . ."

There would be a summary of the accident, including weather conditions, communications between Ellington and Houston traffic control centers, the flight plan. Then a history of the aircraft itself. Description of the damage to aircraft and victim. Personnel information.

"All right, then, let's get to this."

They broke for lunch early, right around eleven, with a good chunk of the work already done. The writing of an aircraft accident report, Kelly discovered, was fairly cut and dried, almost like filling out a Form 1040. Much of it was existing boilerplate text; you only had to fill in names and dates. The work had proceeded smoothly, with Kelly working on the section detailing the history of NASA 911.

Mark Koskinen had asked to work on the personnel section with Drury, and she could not help overhearing him questioning several statements over and over again. Always with great deference but still persistent. When she caught up with Mark at the vending machine, she asked him why he was torturing Drury so much.

"I just wanted to make sure we were being fair."

"You and Mr. Drury are getting along?"

"He's a space pioneer. A legend. Why wouldn't we get along?" There was a slight edge to the statement, but before Kelly could explore it, Mark said, "You seem distracted."

She laughed. "I think you're right. I'm being offered another flight." Mark's eyes went wide. "So what do you think I should do? Should I take it?"

She expected an automatic "Yes!" but Mark surprised her by asking, "Who's the commander?"

"Goslin."

"Do you trust him?"

That was another surprise, and on target, because she *wasn't* sure that she trusted Steve Goslin. Yes, he was technically competent. Almost all of the Navy and Marine aviators who came to the astronaut office were better than their Air Force counterparts, though the blue suiters wouldn't agree. Joe had told Kelly—the one time he had come close to admitting it—that it was because of career choices. The Air Force had more command opportunities for pilots, so a lot of the good sticks weren't interested in NASA. Kelly also suspected it had something to do with being able to handle carrier landings. "I'm not sure."

"He strikes me as pretty stiff."

"You don't have to be Robin Williams to command a Shuttle crew."

"True. But it might be a sign that he lets things bother him."

"Sounds to me as though you've been thinking about Steve Goslin a lot."

"I've been thinking about everything a lot."

"I suppose I would, too, given what's happened."

"And I don't think I'd fly with Steve Goslin."

"Really? If Les Fehrenkamp called you on that phone over there and told you he wanted you on STS-100, you'd say no."

"Yep."

This boy was just full of surprises. "*You* haven't been paying a lot of attention to your Commandments."

"What can I say? As a Worm I'm a failure."

"Why don't you tell me what's going on?"

"Nothing's going on."

"Bullshit. And you're dying to tell someone. It might as well be me." Mark still looked at the floor. Kelly sighed and lowered her voice even further. "It probably doesn't look like it to a Worm, but we do look out for each other. CB's a family."

He was shaking his head before she even finished. "It's the family that's got me worried."

She spread her hands, wondering why she was going to all this effort. Koskinen wasn't that cute. Finally he smiled. "All right. It might as well be you."

And he told her everything. At least, she hoped it was everything. The tissue found in the wreckage of the plane. The test results. The possibility that Joe had been drugged. The suspicious rumors about Scott McDowell and Steve Goslin. The complete and utter stall Mark had gotten from the great Don Drury.

"Wow," was all she could say.

"Maybe you should take some time to think this over. I have a pretty good idea what it sounds like. . . ." He started walking away, but Kelly grabbed his arm.

"Oh, no. We're going to look into this, you and me."

"That'd be great," he said, with genuine relief. "Because I'm in way over my head."

"I owe it to Joe, if nothing else. I liked him." She would probably have to tell Mark about her and Joe, but there had been enough personal revelations for one lunchtime. However, she was telling the truth. If Joe had been doped, she sure didn't want some accident report claiming "probable" pilot error.

"So . . . what are you going to do about that crew assignment?"

"I guess I have to take it, don't I?" Kelly said. "How else am I going to keep an eye on one of our suspects?"

HARRIMAN ASTRO
"Where the Future Begins!"

October 21, 1998
193 Porcaro Road
Suite 100
Las Cruces NM 88010

SPACELIFTER SCHEDULED FOR FLIGHT TEST

The X-39 Spacelifter, the prototype single-stage launch vehicle developed by Harriman Astro for NASA and the Department of Defense, will be rolled out to Launch Complex 35 at the White Sands Missile Range, the first step toward qualification flights scheduled to start next spring.

The fifty-foot-tall Spacelifter, built of composite materials and using off-the-shelf electronics and propulsion systems, will undergo a series of fitting checks which will also help train its ten-person ground crew.

Program director for Harriman Astro is Andrew Delos. Donald Drury is launch director.

Interested media should contact James Hardesty at (505) 788-8300.

CHAPTER 28

Jesus, Scotty, when did you start running?''

Scott McDowell had his hands on his knees and his eyes closed and was trying to force more oxygen into his lungs by willpower when he heard a voice behind him. He raised his head and saw Carl Strahan, one of the other flight directors. ''About half an hour ago,'' McDowell admitted. He knew that he looked like hell, but, then, so did Strahan, who was twenty pounds overweight and whose ''JSC Chili Cook-Off 1997'' T-shirt was soaking wet.

Strahan seemed to welcome a chance to take a break. ''I wish I had a cigarette.''

''Nobody's stopping you,'' McDowell said, though he knew he would throw up if he got a whiff of tobacco right now.

''Oh, check this out . . . our flight crew.''

McDowell followed Strahan's nod and saw five really healthy individuals jogging the other way. It was the astronaut crew for STS-98, one of the upcoming STS missions. McDowell's next mission. ''Delahunt and I still have a couple of issues to work. Maybe I should just tackle him.''

Delahunt was the STS-98 commander, a Navy pilot from the old school. He practically had his crew saluting, and McDowell could have sworn that during one of the sims he'd heard him call somebody ''Mister.'' Strahan laughed. ''You'd be better off trying to run him down with a car.''

Astronauts and flight directors went through a complex bonding ritual that started with mutual respect, degenerated into open hatred, and only returned to respect and possible affection toward the end of a mission. Right now McDowell and Delahunt were in the phase of open hatred. ''I'll let him go for now,'' he said.

"That doesn't sound like Scott McDowell," Strahan said. McDowell knew he had a reputation as the most aggressive flight director in the office. Aggressive when it came to putting astronauts in their place, that is. There were no flight directors who were not aggressive when it came to mission rules. "Are you feeling all right? Wait a minute . . . you're jogging . . . you're going easy on your crew . . . is that a new haircut? Are you in love or something?"

"Fuck you," McDowell said. And though it was the last thing he wanted to do, he started running again. He kept himself in reasonably good shape. His weight was maybe ten pounds greater than it had been when he was on active duty, and that was ten years back. Aside from an occasional cigar on the golf course, he didn't smoke, was a social drinker, and preferred salads over the machine food that fueled endomorphs like Strahan, who was still huffing and puffing along the road far behind him.

But this morning was the first time he'd gone running in . . . well, since the last time he'd applied for the ASCAN group. He didn't know how much good it was doing him—his knees were killing him and he'd spent as much time walking as running—but he felt he was changing his life. He had already started looking around his office at the MOD and thinking about how much he would miss it when he moved across the lawn to 4-South.

He reached the west gate and turned around. Thinking about his failed applications got him angry at Joe Buerhle all over again. He was just now starting to realize how often he'd been angry with him.

Like that first year they'd owned the Pitts. They had picked a long weekend to fly it up to Oshkosh, Wisconsin, for the big air show. The trip up was uneventful—they had quite a good time catching up with a couple of old buddies from Cannon, and McDowell had nailed this blonde named Jennifer in an RV.

It wasn't until Sunday morning, when they were getting ready to fly back, that Joe had told McDowell his news: he had been assigned as a pilot on his first Shuttle mission, STS-64, scheduled for launch in eleven months. That was great news for Joe, and McDowell had been happy for him.

But it also presented a problem. "Joe," McDowell had asked, "did you clear this trip?"

"No."

"What about the restrictions?" Two astronauts had died in off-duty air crashes in the past few years. The first one had killed an ASCAN named Steve Thorne. That was a tragedy, but it was over and done with.

A couple of years later, Dave Griggs, a former aircraft ops guy who joined CB, had been up in Arkansas doing acrobatics with an old AT-6 when it flew into the ground. That was a bigger problem, since Griggs was training for a mission and had to be replaced. So Les Fehrenkamp created a reg forbidding astronauts who are assigned to missions from flying anything other than NASA birds without permission. When Hoot Gibson collided with another plane during a Formula One race in Texas a year later, a race that had not been cleared, he lost a mission and went on some bizarre NASA-style punishment routine for a year.

"Don't you think that's a little risky?"

"Who's going to tell? Nobody knows we're up here but you and me."

"And a half dozen people we talked to."

"Most of them don't know I'm an astronaut. I'm just another flyboy."

"All it takes is one, Joe."

"Look—I'm a pilot. I like to fly. And that's what I'm going to do. If Fehrenkamp and the others want a bunch of Boy Scouts, I'd rather know now."

"They've got a whole bunch of Boy Scouts, Joe. And any one of them will be happy to take your mission."

"They're not gonna find out, Scottie. They're not gonna take my mission. Besides—" Buerhle had smiled. He looked like a guy who was ready for a fight. "Hoot Gibson got a new mission, and where is he now? That naughty boy?" McDowell knew very well that, in spite of his sins, Hoot Gibson had wound up being named chief of CB.

That might have been the end of it, except Joe, who often went one word too far when he got worked up, had added, "Don't be such a goddamn pussy."

Well, maybe that was his whole problem. He was too conservative, not a real silk scarf guy like Joe. But he was alive, and he was going to do what Joe had kept him from doing.

He stopped at the gym to shower and change before going up to the MOD. When he got there, his secretary was frowning at a message. "Am I late for something?" he asked.

"I just got a call from Life Sciences. They want to see you over at the clinic," she said.

Carl Strahan came in at this point. Even though he'd showered and changed from a T-shirt and shorts to gray slacks and a white shirt, he still looked damp. He overheard the business about McDowell's appointment. "Why do you need a physical?"

"That's my secret, Carl."

"You're applying again."

All McDowell could do was smile.

"You bastard."

He couldn't wait until they were on opposing teams.

CHAPTER 29

Here we are," Kelly said, pulling into the parking space behind her condo. "I could have walked," Mark told her. It was true. His own place was literally about six blocks north of Kelly's.

"Look, half of CB lives in these few square miles. The only exceptions are some of the lifers who want the whole ranch experience. They're out in Friendswood getting nervous every time it rains."

Two days had passed since the last meeting of the accident board. On Friday Mark had spent the morning at Ellington writing and rewriting his part of the report with Northrop One. Drury wasn't around; Kelly had popped in and out. Her manner had been cool and completely professional; Mark wondered if he had imagined their conversation.

Then it was back to JSC for a briefing on changes in the International Space Station assembly sequence. There were continuing problems with the actual construction of both American and Russian elements. Most of the other Worms were there, including Kondratko, who had his own unique perspective on the problems. ("My people are thieves and yours are liars. Or the other way around.") Everyone hung around later to speculate about how this would affect them, since the Worms had essentially been selected for ISS missions. For a moment it was just as if the Buerhle accident had never happened.

Allyson had flown in that evening, and they had gone out to dinner way over on the west side of Houston, where the real Texas money people lived. And somehow Mark had not managed to find any time to do any detective work.

But Kelly had called him first thing Saturday. "I'm going to pick you up and we're going to talk about this."

Allyson had been intrigued. "Oh, hanging out with one of the women astronauts, are we?"

"It's strictly business." Mark had not told Allyson about the drugs and his suspicions. He was still afraid of how it sounded.

"This is the pretty one from that last flight?" Allyson followed Shuttle missions.

"She was on it, yeah." Of the many minutes Mark had devoted to thinking about Kelly Gessner in the last forty-eight hours, only a fraction related to her beauty, or lack thereof. He was more interested in whether she was on his side or not.

Kelly's condo surprised Mark. It was a typical living room and kitchen downstairs, two-bedroom upstairs layout, much like his own, but it had been decorated. "You've got real furniture," he told her.

"Well, I've been living here for seven years. NASA does pay me, and if you look around you'll see some stores. You can't work all the time."

Mark couldn't help seeing that on Kelly's wall were two gag crew photos from her Shuttle missions. One showed Kelly's STS-76 crew—including Joe Buerhle—in costumes from *Star Trek:Voyager*. The other had the STS-95 group, which included crew members from three different countries, in a collection of awful "native" garb. Kelly was dressed like a sexpot Pippi Longstocking, complete with enormous fake breasts. "I didn't think NASA did those anymore."

"They never admit it. I'm sure you can see why."

"You make a great Romulan."

She gave him a look.

"That's really not very impressive," Mark told her as they headed for the kitchen. "Not even a Tinkertoy orbiter or STA."

"I send all that stuff to my brother, Clark," she said casually, opening the refrigerator door and, without asking, handing Mark a beer.

"How old is he?"

"Thirty-eight. Older than me, if you're keeping track."

"And he collects model airplanes?"

Kelly forced a smile and changed the subject by moving into the living room. She stood there glancing at her telephone answering machine, which showed half a dozen messages. "You don't call people back much," Mark said.

"Not for the last day or so." She flopped on the couch and looked tired. "Man."

"What did you find out?"

Kelly rubbed her eyes. "I talked to some of my old friends at the Patch yesterday. As near as anyone can recall, Steve Goslin was present prior to the time Joe took off. His daughter had started feeling better, and he had come in hoping to catch a later flight."

"Okay. That fits."

"Did you know Scott McDowell was hanging around until you guys took off? Turns out he was the guy who was supposed to ride backseat with Joe."

Mark vaguely remembered seeing McDowell in the locker room, but that had been a good ninety minutes before takeoff. "Why was he sticking around?"

"He told me it was because of some Fehrenkamp meeting . . . but get this: there was no Fehrenkamp meeting that anybody remembers from Wednesday morning. And ask yourself this . . . why would Fehrenkamp have a meeting at Ellington that would concern Scott McDowell? Joe Buerhle, yeah. Boyd Akin. It would be about the fleet, not about some MOD crap."

"All right . . . so the two people with the biggest grudges were present. I have to ask this: how many other people were there?"

Kelly got a strange smile on her face and said, "Check this out."

She led him over to her computer, which was showing a Grand Canyon screen saver. She hit the escape key, revealing a list of names on a small spreadsheet. "Over forty people?" Forty-one, to be exact. Mark suddenly felt that this was useless . . . he was in over his head.

"It's not quite that bad." Kelly sat down and began clicking across the screen. "Seventeen of those names belong to aircraft ops people. Other pilots, secretaries, DynCor." She clicked on one of the vertical lines of the spreadsheet, reducing the number of names to twenty-four. "Another thirteen were in the air at the time, or from launch minus one hour. I don't think they could have dumped anything in Joe's coffee." Another click; down to twelve. "Five of the others happened to be the crew of STS-96, which was getting ready to fly to the Cape later that morning. No one's exactly sure that they were present when you and Joe took off." *Click.* Six names left.

"Fehrenkamp was. I saw him."

"He's one of the finalists. Goslin, McDowell, Joe. Cal Stipe was still waiting to take off. And Fehrenkamp."

Mark saw that his own name was on the list. "And me."

"It's a motley crew."

"Is there a murderer in there? Someone who hated Joe Buerhle enough to just . . . take a chance and kill him? Who the hell would be carrying some of that stuff around, anyway?"

"Gee whiz, Mark, if you're going to ask tough questions, remember that we just arbitrarily ruled out the aircraft ops people."

"If they did it we'll never find out."

"That's why I eliminated them." She tapped the screen. "We've got two people in here with giant grudges against Joe, Scott McDowell and Steve Goslin. And two others we just don't know about, Fehrenkamp and Stipe." She turned her head and smiled at Mark. "And you, of course."

"Don't look at me. I barely knew the man." He had found that look unsettling, mostly because he could see quite clearly that, yes, Kelly Gessner was the cute one.

"Fehrenkamp is a long shot. If he had a problem with Joe, there were lots of ways he could have punished him. Stipe . . . he seems above this all, somehow. He's got a long mission coming up, and whenever he's in mission training he's not thinking about anything else."

"So it's back to our two star suspects."

"Goslin's career was dead as long as Joe was chief of CB," Kelly said. "And we've learned that Scott McDowell's selection was also stalled by Joe. And that Scott knew it."

"Would McDowell have access to coke?"

"He's wound pretty tight. Why not?"

"What about straight-arrow Steve?"

"That's tougher. But he told me once his brother was a vice cop. . . ." She drummed her fingers on her desktop. "So, Koskinen. You're supposed to have the highest I.Q. in your group." Mark had never heard that and didn't believe it. "What do you think we should do next?"

"All I know is that I don't want to call the cops."

"Not only cute, but smart. Let's let the Harris County sheriff's department stick to its business. I'm not sure they would even have jurisdiction, and can you imagine what they would do if NASA HQ started leaning on them?"

Mark was about half a beat behind Kelly, still wondering if he'd heard correctly. Had she called him cute? "Time for one last reality check," he said. "Would somebody really spike Joe Buerhle's coffee so he'd fly into the Gulf?"

"Someone might just have wanted him to screw up and look bad. Wrack up his plane. Lose credibility." She stood up and stretched. "Look, Joe was the boss. People hate bosses, and the people in CB are no exception. They might even be worse. You know what they say."

"What do they say?"

"As individuals astronauts are great; as a group they're assholes. There's a lot of truth to it. I mean, we have to pass a million tests to get these jobs—it never happens by accident or because you're somebody's son-in-law. We're just superior human beings, and we've got proof."

"Just don't get in our way."

She smiled again. "We aren't calling the cops. What are we doing? What do we want to have happen?"

Mark thought for a moment. "I don't know either Goslin or McDowell well enough to start hanging around with them. Assume one of them is a murderer—he'd be on guard. You know both of them. . . ."

"Only slightly better than you do, frankly. Let me put it this way: Scott McDowell isn't going to tell me much of anything. Goslin is strictly business, because as far as he's concerned I'm a slut."

"Anyway, what I said applies to you: the killer is going to be on guard." Then it struck him. "We've got to smoke him out. We've got to get both of these guys thinking that the board is coming out with some weird report . . . get them worried somehow. Make them think there's going to be a real investigation and that they're going to wind up having to testify." He was convincing himself only slightly faster than he was convincing Kelly. "It should just be a rumor . . . the astronaut equivalent of pillow talk. Something that will force our guy to make some kind of move."

Kelly thought this over for at least ten seconds, then put her arm around him and gave him a brotherly squeeze. "Okay. And I know who's got the biggest mouth in the whole office."

"Who?"

"Me." She held up a hand, preventing any protest. "Trust me."

"We've gotten beyond that point, I hope."

The expression on her face changed. She seemed younger, more relaxed. Happier. "Oh, I think we have."

A few moments later she was dropping him off at his apartment. He almost ran inside, feeling exhilarated at having a plan to somehow solve this problem, and for having spent this time with Kelly Gessner.

CHAPTER 30

Kelly walked into the sixth-floor auditorium just before eight o'clock on Monday morning and almost collided with Les Fehrenkamp. "Back to work already?" he said with a smile. She had called him at home on Saturday and told him she would be happy to fly with Goslin.

"I'm just a space machine," she said, only half kidding. Les squeezed her shoulder, then took his place up on the stage with Jinx Seamans. Kelly looked for Mark Koskinen and saw him lurking in the back with his Russian buddy, Kondratko, and some of the other Worms. She made as casual a wave as she dared, then took a seat about halfway back, leaving one on the aisle.

The Monday morning pilots' meeting was one of the astronaut office's few lasting traditions, dating back to the early 1960s, when the first seven Mercury astronauts had moved with the old Space Task Group from Langley, Virginia, to Houston. At Langley the seven men fit into one office: their schedules were largely their own business, though they tried to touch base with each other every Monday and Friday.

Shortly after the move to Houston, however, NASA added nine more astronauts to the team. Sixteen pilots didn't fit into one office. So one of the original seven, Deke Slayton, became the coordinator of astronaut activities, aka the chief of the astronaut office, and he started getting all the astronauts together every Monday morning at eight, at which time announcements would be made, schedules would be announced and problems would be worked out.

A few years later, at the height of the Apollo program, there were over sixty astronauts, Al Shepard was the chief and the pilots' meeting often resembled a raucous hoot in some naval air squadron—or so Kelly had heard. Now, of course, in keeping with the more mature NASA, pilots' meetings were much more sedate. There were guest speakers. There was an agenda. And the meetings were much larger. There were over 115 active astronauts, plus nineteen ASCANs—most of them would crowd into the auditorium. There were also at least forty support staff for CB alone, plus various hangers-on and friends of the family. Less than a third of the people at the pilots' meeting were pilots, but that didn't seem to matter.

The first order of business was Seamans's announcement of the STS-100 crew. "As they say on the Oscar show, please hold your applause until all the nominees are read. Steve Goslin will be CDR, Jeff Dieckhaus will be PLT. Mission specialists are Dave Freeh, Don O'Riordan and little Kelly Gessner." There was a smattering of applause and some laughter. Seamans thought of himself as a great wit.

As Seamans started running through some houskeeping matters, Mark slipped into the seat next to Kelly's. "Congratulations," he said. They actually shook hands. He was playing the earnest boy astronaut role as if born to it. Well, maybe it wasn't much of a stretch. For her part, it was like having public contact with a man with whom she was having a very secret love affair.

And how much of a stretch was that? Had she really told Mark he was cute? While they were discussing Joe's possible murderer? Had she become sexually desperate? Was this what happened to a woman in her thirties?

Seamans turned his meeting over to Cal Stipe. "I'm sure all of you know that Cal will be aboard Mir into next summer. He will be leaving for Moscow next weekend—is that right?" Stipe nodded, somewhat impatiently, Kelly thought. "He'll also be turning over the DO job to Jerry Rager. Until then, if you have any questions, go see Cal."

As Stipe took the stage, Kelly saw Steve Goslin kneeling next to Mark. "Can we get together right after this?" he whispered to her.

"Your office?" Kelly said. Goslin nodded. Of course, now it would be her office, too. Shuttle crews all got moved into a single office for the duration of their training.

"How's it going, Mark?" Goslin said just before he took off.

"Is it my imagination, or is he loosening up?" Mark said to Kelly.

"Amazing what getting command of your own mission will do for you." She nudged Mark with her elbow. "Let's get out of here."

"Don't you want to learn all about the Russians?"

"Please." She liked the Russians fine and looked forward to flying with any of them. She wasn't like Joe in that regard.

She and Mark headed toward Kelly's office. "Going for number three, huh, Kel?" One of the secretaries cheered her on.

"I didn't realize how popular you were," Mark said as they reached her door. No one else was inside; the rest of Kelly's STS-93 crewmates were still on leave or at the pilots' meeting.

"To know me is to like me, at the very least," she said. "Now . . . you may have noticed that there's very little privacy around here. We can use that to our advantage. Be having a phone call when Goslin gets finished with his crew meeting. It shouldn't take long and I'll give you a heads-up when it's going to start."

"Okay. What do you want him to overhear?"

"You're concerned. The board is dragging its feet. There are medical issues to be resolved. As if you're talking to a reporter."

He smiled and nodded. "What about McDowell?"

"I'll handle McDowell."

Goslin's speech to his four crew members had been mercifully brief. Something about the virtues of teamwork and still having fun while being aware that every time you lit off a solid rocket booster you were risking death. . . . It was about average, in Kelly's judgment. Not nearly as good as Jackson Willet's, but much better than her last commander's.

As the meeting ended and the office door opened, Kelly got Goslin's attention. "Steve? Have you been over to the MOD yet?" She saw Mark on the phone right outside the office, using one of the assistant's desks. Good thinking!

"No. Why?"

"They've certainly got a lead assigned to us."

"They do. Les told me that Friday."

"Why don't you go over and introduce yourself to whoever it is?"

Goslin frowned. "Right now?" He seemed to be trying to both overhear what Mark was saying and to justify his own reluctance to enter the sacred halls of the MOD.

Kelly realized she had to keep playing the role of Kelly Gessner, Shuttle veteran and ex-girlfriend of the late chief astronaut. She kept her voice low, and said, "They're probably wondering about you over there, Steve. Your turn to command should have come up a year ago. I would march right over there and show them that I was in charge."

"You're right." He shook his head. "I'm glad I got you on this crew."

"I've just had the benefit of a different perspective, that's all." Be humble. Goslin would only allow her so much independence, anyway.

"You've got to come with me, though."

"No, really, Steve—"

"That's an order from your commander."

"All right, if you put it like that." Sometimes men were easy to manipulate. "Who is our lead, anyway?"

"Scott McDowell."

"Oh, good," Kelly said.

Goslin's conversation with McDowell started off with ritual congratulations, promises to work together, then took a surprising turn. "Now," McDowell said, "before we go anywhere else, what was your problem with Joe Buerhle?"

"Gee, look at the time," Kelly said. "I think I'm going to get some lunch—"

"Don't go away, Kelly." Goslin looked determined and somehow holy, like a martyr. "I'll be honest: Joe thought I screwed up the landing."

"Did you?"

"I've gone over it about a million times in my head. I don't think so."

"Then Joe did."

"I'm not going to speak ill—"

"That's just it, Steve." McDowell gave Kelly a sidelong glance. "If we're gonna work together, you have to tell me the truth. I don't give a shit about Joe Buerhle's reputation. I want to know the facts."

Goslin looked at the floor for a moment, then raised his head. "Well, then, yeah . . . Joe screwed up." He waited for McDowell to challenge him.

"You're right," McDowell said quietly. "I looked at the tapes and reports last week. It was a CDR fault." He stood up and held out his hand to Goslin. "Look forward to working with you."

Goslin seemed relieved to get out of there. Kelly lingered. "I'll see you back in the office," she told Goslin.

As soon as the door closed, she turned to McDowell. "I'm glad to see the rumor isn't true."

"What rumor?"

"That you've gotten mellow now that you're applying again."

McDowell laughed. "Actually, I am. I really had to force myself to treat Goslin like shit. Now, if he'd been one of the astronauts I *liked*, I probably couldn't have done it." He got serious again. "He'll do a good job. He's a good stick."

"And the system will protect him."

"Speaking of rumors—"

"Me?"

"Gessner's so fed up she doesn't care if she flies again. Alternately, Gessner's tied up with that accident board. But here you are, on the crew."

"I guess Les just likes the cut of my jib," she said. "My prediction is that board will never reach a verdict. I'm moving on."

Now she had his interest. "Really?"

Correction. Men were *always* easy to manipulate.

NASA N E W S

National Aeronautics and
Space Administration
Lyndon B. Johnson Space Center
Houston TX 77058
281 481-5111

November 3, 1998
Shannon Crosby
Headquarters, Washington D.C.
(Phone: 202/358-1780)

Lou Wekkin
Johnson Space Center, Houston TX
(Phone: 281/483-1511)

RELEASE NO. 98-114

CREW SELECTED FOR STS-100, LAST SHUTTLE-MIR DOCKING

Two-time Shuttle veteran Steven Goslin has been named to command STS-100, scheduled for launch in June 1999. This planned ten-day-long mission of the orbiter *Atlantis* will perform the last rendezvous and docking with the Russian Mir space station prior to construction of the International Space Station.

STS-100 will also return astronaut Calvin Stipe to earth, concluding NASA visits to Mir.

Joining Goslin on the STS-100 crew will be Jeffrey Dieckhaus (Cmdr., USN), pilot; and mission specialists David Freeh (Maj., USAF); Kelly Gessner (civilian); and Donal O'Riordan (civilian, European Space Agency).

Goslin, 42, is a lieutenant colonel in the U.S. Marine Corps. He is a native of Norcross, Georgia, and a graduate of Georgia Tech. He was selected as an astronaut in 1989 and flew as pilot on STS-79 and STS-90, logging over 420 hours in space.

Dieckhaus, 37, considers Wausau, Wisconsin, to be his hometown. He graduated from the U.S. Naval Academy in 1981 and was selected as an astronaut in 1991. He has made one previous Shuttle flight, STS-92.

Freeh, 38, was born in Everett, Washington, and received a Ph.D. in physics from Stanford University. He was selected as an astronaut in 1995 and will be making his first Shuttle flight.

Gessner, 34, is a native of Orlando, Florida, and received an M.S.

from Rice University. She was selected as an astronaut in 1988 and has made two Shuttle flights.

O'Riordan, 40, is a graduate of Trinity College, Dublin, and a former engineer with the European Space Agency.

Stipe, 51, is a veteran of five previous Shuttle missions, and is scheduled to launch to Mir aboard *Soyuz TM-28* on November 16, 1998.

CHAPTER 31

Viktor Kondratko had lived in America for half a year and was continually delighted and appalled by it. Delighted by the variety of clothing and food and cars and houses—and by their quantity! And prices! And appalled by the paucity of ceremony or fellowship or camaraderie.

His first lesson had come the day he had arrived in Houston. There was no one to meet him at the airport. He was traveling light, of course: two suitcases. He spoke English. He had even made one trip to Houston prior to this, to be interviewed by Mr. Lester Fehrenkamp himself about his suitability for the Shuttle program. But on that trip he had been accompanied by two other Russian cosmonauts and one of their training managers, all of them veterans of the Moscow-Houston routine. He had clearly not paid sufficient attention to the mechanics of getting one's luggage . . . of arranging for a rental car . . . of finding one's way from the north side of Houston some sixty or a hundred kilometers south to the Johnson Space Center area. He faced all of this alone when he arrived for ASCAN training . . . and all of it took three times as long as it should have.

He barely made it to his hotel. And then, the next morning, had been forced to wait at the badging center for two hours while someone could be found to vouch for him!

Kondratko was a lieutenant colonel in the Russian air force. He had been a Party member, back when that had been a requirement for career advancement. He had attended a higher air force school and the Moscow Aviation Institute. He had been selected for test pilot school at Akhtubinsk—there was a desolate hellhole for you—and fought his way into the Buran shuttle program. When that had finally been canceled, he had somehow managed to convince not only his bosses at the Chkalov Flight

Test Center, but also the Gagarin Cosmonaut Training Center, to transfer him there.

He knew how to deal with a bureaucracy. But NASA still baffled him.

Then there were the ASCANs or astronauts themselves. Even back in Russia, where there was no single NASA-style group, but an air force team and a civilian team, a team of doctor cosmonauts and probably one or two others . . . there was still a sense of working together for a common goal. They ate together. They took classes together and shared notes. They discussed everything. Yes, they drank together, too.

Maybe the Russians had developed their own bonding rituals because almost every crew was made up of people from different teams and would have to work, essentially alone, in orbit for months at a time. Shuttle flights were short. Crews were large, training was compartmentalized, with pilots doing one thing and mission specialists another, and spread all over the country. And there were just so many astronauts in the office—over a hundred!

Kondratko felt he had gotten to know only two or three of his fellow ASCANs, the Worms. (What did it mean, that every ASCAN group gave itself a derogatory name? Maggots. Gaffers. Slugs.) It was one of the reasons he was so pleased when he happened to run into Cal Stipe, who suggested that they go out and have a drink. Not at some future date—tonight. Right now.

"Right now" was at least four hours in the past. Stipe and Kondratko had driven in Stipe's car all the way up the 45 to downtown Houston. At first Kondratko thought—hoped—Stipe was heading for one of the expensive gentlemen's clubs, an upscale strip joint. "Too much hustle," Stipe had said when Kondratko raised the question. "Besides, they're a little too public, if you know what I mean. I generally don't give a shit about what management thinks, but getting your picture in the newspapers at a strip club is just bad for your career."

Stipe had gone on to regale Kondratko with the story of one unlucky astronaut—a space veteran—who had been seen in one of these gentlemen's clubs. The gentlemen who had taken him there turned out to be government agents involved in a sting operation. The astronaut was innocent on both counts, but it hadn't helped his career at all.

Kondratko found this hard to believe. Not that you could ruin your career by being a little too wild, but that you could do that as a flown astronaut. "One of my friends, a test pilot, got kicked out of the cosmonaut detachment because he got divorced," he told Stipe. "It was a friendly divorce: his wife left him! And still they fired him.

"But there was another guy who had made a flight years ago, back when you got an automatic Hero of the Soviet Union medal." Awards like that didn't mean much in the USA, Kondratko knew, but they were like cash bonuses in the former USSR. Free travel for life. Go to the head of any line. Your children guaranteed admittance to any state university. The Hero medal was one thing—maybe the only thing—about the former USSR that Kondratko missed.

"This guy was a complete drunk. He kept getting assigned to new programs, then showing up late for training sessions, until finally they quit assigning him. He dumped his first wife, then dumped the girl he dumped her for.

"One day he ran off with someone else's wife in a car, drunk. Ran off the road and left her hurt! She didn't die, thank God. But he just ran away from the accident!"

"What happened?"

"They let him retire when he got to twenty years in the cosmonaut team. And got him a nice easy job at some ministry in Moscow. All because he was a Hero."

Stipe had laughed and laughed at this. "Maybe that's why no one ever says anything to me. I don't have a medal, but five flights count for something."

Five flights, with a sixth coming up. It counted for a lot with Kondratko.

Stipe patted him on the shoulder. "Don't worry, Viktor . . . if I run this puppy off the road, I'm taking you with me."

They wound up at a bar or tavern or saloon—Kondratko was never exactly sure of the difference—across from one of the big downtown hotels and worked their way through a wonderful meal of blackened fish and several drinks each. The ostensible purpose for the dinner was easily accomplished—Stipe wanted to pick Kondratko's brain for Russian gossip, what was being said at the Gagarin Center.

"Is NASA going to train station crews in Russia?" Kondratko asked. "I heard there was a big movement to stop that."

"I think that particular train has slid off the tracks," Stipe said with satisfaction. "This is all politics of the worst sort. There are a lot of people inside NASA and the contractor community who can't forget about the Cold War . . . none of them were old enough to *fight* it, but that doesn't seem to matter. They want Russia out of the space business. They want all of the International Space Station money spent here.

"They don't realize that without Russia, and the Europeans, and the Japanese and the Canadians, all pitching in, there wouldn't be a space station *at all*. Jesus, I've been part of review teams on two different designs for U.S. space stations going back to the early 1980s . . . there's no way for the U.S. to build a space station for less than about thirty billion dollars going in. That's the price to drive it off the lot. Then you talk about another couple of billion every year to operate it.

"The taxpayers wouldn't bite, and I can't blame them. Fifty billion dollars for an astronaut hotel? No fucking way, especially when they see old Mir rolling along up there. What do you suppose that cost to build and maintain?"

"I don't know how maintained it is," Kondratko said, half joking. He also felt inadequate in the face of Stipe's passion. Nor did he have any idea how much Mir cost. Well, he might have been able to get that figure if he hadn't had four—or was it six?—drinks.

"It costs about *one tenth* as much. Christ," Stipe said suddenly, "let's get over to the bar."

Kondratko stumbled once getting out of his chair. He was at Stipe's mercy. Oh, well; there was no astronaut he trusted more.

They were well into a second round of drinks at the bar when Kondratko, who had been watching hockey on the overhead TV, noticed that Stipe was laughing with a girl on the stool next to him. Not a girl, he corrected himself: a grown woman, in her late twenties. She had blond hair and a round face and wore some kind of tank top leotard which showed that she had nice breasts. Her name was Tamara, she said, when Stipe introduced them. She worked in the audio business, selling speakers for CD players and stereos.

Tamara was a lovely name . . . a Russian name. It was *his wife's name*, his wife, who was probably off at her job in the Gagarin Center at this moment. He had rescued Tamara from a dreary life in Akhtubinsk and taken her to Moscow. She forgot that from time to time, but Kondratko didn't. She couldn't come to Houston—not while Kondratko was just a Worm—so what was he to do? Kondratko decided that he was in love with this Tamara.

It turned out that Tamara was at the bar with her friend, Molly, who was tall and dark and not nearly as attractive to Kondratko as Tamara. It didn't seem to matter: Molly parked herself right next to Stipe, who some-how, strangely, wound up examining an injury of some kind to Molly's knee.

Molly worked in the same office as Tamara and the two of them were out this Monday night celebrating a big sale to Home Depot. The women had had a few drinks themselves, because they got a bit too excited when Stipe actually told them what he and Kondratko did . . . that they were as-tronauts. "Well," Stipe said, "I think Viktor is actually an unemployed Russian spy. So be careful what you say around him."

He and Tamara had their arms around each other's waists by now. She leaned close to him and said, "Do Russian spies know how to make love like James Bond?"

"Who do you think taught that guy?" And then they were kissing.

Somehow it developed that Tamara was going to drive Kondratko while Molly was going to ride with Stipe. They were all going to Molly's place, which wasn't far. The women ran off to make one last trip to the ladies' room, and Stipe turned to Kondratko. "I hope that Russian spy stuff didn't bother you," he said. "It just slipped out."

At this moment Kondratko loved Stipe like a brother. "How can I be offended? I *am* a spy." He watched happily for the reaction on Stipe's face. "Not for the KGB, which doesn't exist anymore. Or any of those guys. For myself. I collect information."

Now Stipe was losing interest. "Oh, really."

Kondratko wanted to prove he knew something. "You know Mark, my friend?"

"Our bailout expert? Sure."

"He was on the phone in the office for one hour today about the Joe Buerhle crash."

"What about it?"

"He was telling someone there's something funny about what happened, that the board can't agree on a verdict until some medical results come in."

"Why would he be saying that? Any idea who he was talking to?"

"No." That was as far as Kondratko got, because Tamara and Molly were back, and the four of them staggered out into the cool, damp night air. Nothing like Moscow or even Akhtubinsk. More like one of the resorts in the Crimea.

Molly and Stipe headed for his car while Kondratko and Tamara stopped at hers. "You are so beautiful," Kondratko blurted in Russian.

She formed the beginning of a smile . . . unsure what to say. "I'm sorry."

He told her in English this time. Then he recited two lines from a Pushkin poem. Then they were kissing again. "Oh, God," she said, and Kondratko wondered if she was upset.

Then she opened the back door to her car and slid inside. She held out her hand for him, and he joined her. In a moment they were on their sides, and lovely Tamara was pressed back against the seat. "I can't believe I'm doing this," she said. "I hope a cop doesn't find us."

"I'm a hero," he told her. "Trust me." His hands had pushed up her skirt, finding her panties, wriggling inside them. "Do you want these off?" he asked.

"I don't care!" she said, fumbling with his belt.

For one moment Kondratko wondered about Stipe and Molly. Were they in the backseat of his car? Or on their way to Molly's place . . . would they wait, and wonder?

Stipe was his brother now. He would want this for him.

But there was something else he'd wanted to tell him about Mark's conversation today. Someone else had been listening to him . . . who?

Goslin. He remembered it because Goslin had quickly walked off, as if he hadn't liked what he'd heard.

Then he felt Tamara's hand on his cock, peeling back the foreskin. "This will be something new," she said.

"Yes," he said, crushing her panties and pressing himself into her.

CHAPTER 32

Mark survived his second postaccident flight in a T-38 on Tuesday morning. This time his pilot was Jason Borders, a fellow Worm, who bitched all the way to the operating area about his technical assignment to the Shuttle Avionics Integration Laboratory (SAIL).

SAIL was the place where the specific computer programs for each Shuttle mission were developed and debugged around the clock. It was widely considered to be both the best and the worst technical assignment an astronaut or ASCAN could have.

"They treat you like God over there," Borders said, "which is a nice change from CB. But to be sitting there in their little cockpit playing commander eight hours a day . . . going over the same ascent profile again and again. I don't know how much of it I can take."

The orbiter's computer systems had been upgraded at least twice since missions started flying, but they were still several generations behind a home computer when it came to memory and speed. For the last few years crews had often carried laptops into orbit to do most of their work.

"Come on, Jase, SAIL is where you really wind up knowing orbiter systems. All the best Shuttle commanders, like Crippen, were computer *masters*." This seemed to soothe Borders.

"When are you going down to the Cape?" he asked.

"Soon," Mark said. If Borders hadn't noticed that Mark's name had been crossed off the STS-95 support list, why tell him?

Thinking about his shaky status only made Mark want to thump Borders on the helmet and tell him to fly fast. He was absolutely certain things were simmering back at JSC, and didn't want to be over the Gulf when they boiled over.

" 'Thou shalt not complain,' " Mark said, quoting from the Commandments. " 'Maketh survival look easy.' "

"I hear you."

As soon as he'd changed and thanked Borders for the flight, Mark went over to the hangar, where he found Don Drury all alone at his desk, reviewing an inch-thick document with a red pencil in his hand, much like a high school teacher correcting a theme. "Sit down," he said.

"Where's everybody else?" Mark asked.

"Scattered like the wind."

"Are we finished?"

"That's what I wanted to talk to you about." He spread his hands. "What has your investigation produced?"

Mark debated the wisdom of telling Drury what he and Kelly were up to, and instantly rejected it. He chose instead to be aggressive. "You mean, the informal investigation that nobody wants me to undertake?"

Drury smiled. "That's all we have going."

"Why do you care?" Mark tapped the report. "You're all ready to send this thing out."

"Tell me I shouldn't. Give me a reason to revise it."

"You know I can't do that."

"Then what do you expect me to do, Mark?" Drury sighed. "I was asked to head up this board and to produce a result *quickly*. That was my mission and I accepted it. I take promises like that very seriously. That's one big difference between my generation and yours, I'm afraid. When we said we'd do something, whether it was going to war or flying to the Moon, by God we did it. Your generation, from your elected leaders on down, seems to think commitments are just . . . conversation."

At that moment Mark felt a mixture of pity and admiration for Drury. He realized that much of what he was saying was right; he had seen it in himself, that willingness to quit, move on, start over, change direction.

But people like Don Drury went to the Moon by the end of the 1960s because President Kennedy stood up before Congress one day and said they should. "Look," he finally said, "I understand that you need to make some sort of judgment. Go ahead! I'm not officially part of the board anyway."

Drury extracted a piece of paper from near the top of the stack and passed it over to Mark. It was a signature sheet with all their names and affiliations neatly typed in. Everyone else had signed it except Thompson and Kelly. "For some reason, I can't seem to get in touch with either of these kids right now. The only thing they have in common, to my old eyes, is an association with you."

Mark understood why Kelly wouldn't have signed the report. He was pleased that Thompson hadn't, either. "I'm just the guy who punched out of an airplane, Mr. Drury. I may have screwed my astronaut career. Why would either of these people listen to me?"

"Maybe you've told them something you aren't telling me."

"You weren't interested."

"I'm asking now."

Mark saw barely restrained anger in Drury's eyes. He had pity for anyone who had crossed this man during the Apollo years. "I don't have any hard information to give you."

"No . . . just more rumors."

Mark stood up. He realized he was shaking with barely restrained anger of his own. "If you don't need me for anything else, I think I'll be leaving."

Drury suddenly slammed his hands down on his desk, struggling to get to his feet. For a moment Mark thought he was going to launch himself at him. "I'm going to give you and your friends forty-eight hours from right now. Friday noon I send this paper over to Fehrenkamp *with* their signatures or *without* them."

"I think that's fair," Mark said.

"I don't give a shit what you think," Drury said. "I'm just trying to do a job."

Barefoot, wearing shorts and a T-shirt, Allyson cooked dinner that night, a process she found especially amusing. "You've got appliances and utensils, honey, I'll give you that much. But they all look new."

"Hey, I can open a box of cereal and make a salad. I can do hamburgers and hot dogs."

"Those aren't meals, those are snacks."

"You know what my hours are like."

"Are mine any better?"

"I've seen your kitchen, young lady, and *your* appliances don't get any more use than *mine*." She laughed. It was all play, anyway; Mark made a point of actually cooking at least one dinner for himself every week, usually on Sunday night. "You know . . . I like having you here," he told her with no prompting at all.

She put her arms around him. "I was hoping it would help if you had someone to come home to for a few days."

"Maybe more than a few days." Oh my God, what was he saying? "At least you're getting to know the area a little. . . ." That was just as bad!

She smiled. "It's a nice little area. And I'm really enjoying your car. Sure you don't want to sell it?"

"Only if you get my bike back."

They kissed, then Allyson suddenly pulled away. "I'm not ready for another one of *those* conversations, not on an empty stomach, at least. And I don't think you'll be ready for that conversation until you've gotten your big space flight, so let's not kid ourselves." She turned back to the stove. "What excitement do you have planned for me after dinner?"

"Well, precoital, I thought we'd watch some TV. There's supposedly this new soap about NASA—"

"You're kidding. TV shows are all about sex and murder, aren't they? How much of that goes on around here?"

"Hey, it's TV. Besides . . ." He slid his arm around her as she passed and pulled her close. As they kissed he ran the back of his hand up Allyson's bare thigh.

"All right," she said. "You're convincing me about the sex part." She turned away, and he wondered when and how he was going to explain to her about the murder part. "Tomorrow night, though, we're getting take-out," she said.

"Yeah . . . we don't want to make too many radical changes at once."

Their lovemaking, later that night, was surprisingly intense. For a not-so-brief moment he forgot about NASA and flying the Shuttle and Joe Buerhle . . . none of it mattered.

About ten-forty, unable to sleep, he went downstairs and dialed Kelly Gessner's number. He told himself it was all about Goslin and McDowell— what had she told them? How had they reacted? Was she really hiding from Drury? And didn't he need to tell her about Drury's deadline? He told himself it had nothing to do with him and Allyson . . . it wasn't just because he wanted to hear her voice.

"Hi, this is 555-1932. Leave a message." *Beep.*

He glanced at the clock. Ten-forty-five. Where was she? And why did he care?

CHAPTER 33

Kelly was rebounding from her STS-93 mission when Mark called. Several of the experimenters plus the mission scientist from Marshall were in town for their debriefs and they had begged her to join them at Le-Roy's for dinner. She felt she owed them that much; anyone who could bore through the combined bureaucracies of the scientific community and NASA to get an experiment into space had an unusual amount of patience.

Besides, they were a fun bunch, if you liked pale, obsessive men with scraggly beards. That was unfair; only six or seven of the dozen had scraggly beards. A couple of them were athletic, even good-looking. And another two were even women.

And Kelly was the only crew member available. Everyone else was on vacation or conveniently out of town, even the two payload specialists, who had come from the experimenter community. Payload specialists had to relocate to Houston for the year prior to the mission, and therefore tended to go back home at any opportunity.

So Kelly had done her best to provide the NASA equivalent of star power. She told stories about the astronaut office and the mission operations people. She managed to dish—in a friendly way—the boneheaded crew member who had gummed up as many experiments in orbit as he had done right. The experimenters were in a better mood now than they had been during the mission. Watching astronauts and flight controllers ruthlessly altering or simply eliminating their experiments while they could only sit there, powerless, was painful. But the pain diminished with time— like that of childbirth, Kelly figured—and with a lot of beer and Cajun cooking.

Now she was home for what seemed like the first time in a year. It was too late to start the postmission cleaning; that was a job for a Saturday morning. And given that she had just allowed herself to be talked into another mission, it might be another year before the condo returned to normal.

Eventually she was going to have to admit that its current state *was* normal.

She heard Mark's message—the only one on the machine—then sat down with the TV remote. She flipped through about sixty channels on TV and was about to give up when she landed on the Discovery Channel. She had watched this show a couple of times before. A former astronaut she knew worked there as a host sometimes, the kind of thing Kelly thought she might try if—make that when—she left NASA. Tonight's program just happened to be about the uses of military aircraft in the Gulf War.

It made her think about Joe. The war had preceded their time together—it was before she was even in the astronaut office. But they had talked about it from time to time. "I've spent a lot of time learning how to fly the orbiter," he had said once. "Now if you take that and multiply it by about five, you'll have the amount of time I've spent learning how to drop bombs and wax bad guys in an airplane."

He had seriously considered leaving the office to go back to operational flying. But at the time he was in training for his first flight. Walking out of NASA at such a delicate moment would have effectively screwed him at the space agency for all time to come.

Also . . . in the fall of 1990, who knew it would ever come to real shooting? And when it did, in January 1991, it was already too late. Joe admitted that he had called a buddy at the Pentagon and had been told, "We don't need you. It's not as though we don't have a bunch of pilots who are dying to do this. You haven't been in an Air Force cockpit for four years. You would need to be requalified for the 111, for night flying, for combat, for ops. Let's not even discuss the fact that you're a middle 0–5 and should be running your own squadron, not flying wing for some thirty-year-old captain, which is what you'd wind up doing."

The conclusion was, Joe Buerhle was not going to get into the Gulf War with the USAF. So he, like all of the other highly trained military pilots in the astronaut office, had watched the Gulf War on television. The total domination of Iraqi air by the American forces, and the relative ease of victory, had only made it more painful.

Thinking of Joe got Kelly thinking of her silly suspect matrix. She clicked off the TV and booted up her computer, brooding that a whole day had passed since Goslin and McDowell had been made aware that they had not gotten away cleanly. And nothing had happened.

She wasn't exactly sure what she had expected—something along the lines of Steve Goslin breaking into a visible sweat and confessing his evil deed. Or Scott McDowell taking up the Pitts and deliberately flying it into the ground, leaving behind a revealing note. Neither action was likely. The business about McDowell wasn't even nice.

The killer might contact Don Drury, of course. Or one of the people on the board. (Did either Goslin or McDowell know the other members of the board? She suddenly wished she knew.)

Of course, there was still a little time. Maybe a whole day.

She closed the file and ejected the disk. As she placed it on her desk, she noticed a pair of disks sitting to one side. The two she had gotten from Joe's house. She wondered what was on them.

The first—labeled "NOFORN," a Joe Buerhle joke, since "No Foreign" was a security label for some kinds of confidential documents—had a bunch of dated memos in its file directory. Kelly opened up a few and saw that they were routine CB material . . . Joe to the schedulers, Joe to branch chiefs, Joe as official rater for the military guys.

Now, here was something interesting. A file called "Defcon3." That was old Cold War jargon for a level of defense readiness. Kelly opened it and saw that it was notes for a memo to not only Les Fehrenkamp but to Dr. Hutchins, the director of JSC, and several people at headquarters. The distribution list alone was a good third of a page.

> *As the veteran of four Space Shuttle missions and chief of the astronaut office I have seen the best and the worst the American manned space program has to offer. . . .*

It was Joe in one of his rare speechifying moods, where he managed to sound like any one of a hundred astronauts. Clearly he had labored over this memo, and it still didn't seem to be finished. One paragraph stood out. In fact, it was still separate from the rest of the memo, as if waiting for surrounding support:

> *The decision to accept ESA, Canada and Japan as partners on the space station was questionable, though understandable. The decision to give Russia an even greater role was indefensible. Our entire*

*program is now hostage to the steadily deteriorating capabilities of
a nation that until quite recently was our sworn enemy. I can no
longer remain silent. I intend to use whatever power and influence
I have to change this situation now. For the space station to succeed—for it to be a safe place to conduct earth orbit operations—it
must be built and launched by our people only.*

There were several versions of the same thought. What struck Kelly was
Joe's vehemence—and his intention to make this some kind of holy war.

Would it have worked? He was chief astronaut, merely the first among
a lot of equals. Of course, most of his equals would have supported him.

Suppose the astronaut office had gone on strike over the matter?

Better yet . . . what would have happened if CB had merely *threatened*
to go on strike?

Kelly wondered who else knew about Joe's plans.

She found nothing else on the "NOFORN" disk. She turned to the
second one, labeled "TK." Oh, yes, Talent Keyhole, another classification
from the intelligence world.

There was only one file on this disk, named "paranoia."

*I'm noting these events for my records, because I don't know how
much I can trust my memory. Simply put, I think someone is trying
to kill me.*

Kelly found herself sitting straight up in her chair.

The document wasn't long—more of a chronology going back a few
months, to July, shortly after Joe was named chief astronaut—with three
entries.

One dealt with the Pitts belonging to Joe and Scott McDowell. "Sheered
control line." That sounded dangerous.

The second was about Joe's car. "Both front brakes" had been tampered with out at Ellington one morning when Joe was flying. He had noted
it was during "bad weather."

Kelly remembered some of this. She had been deep in mission training
by then, but during one of her weekends home had wound up driving Joe
or letting him use her Volvo.

That had also been the last weekend they spent together.

The third was merely one word . . . "Kelly?" Kelly what? Kelly a suspect? Kelly a target?

All right, she thought. Let's assume Joe's notes are correct . . . that someone tampered with both his plane and his car in hopes of killing him, that both attempts failed. It would mean that someone had been after him for months, not just the last week.

Did this help or hurt the case against Goslin? He certainly knew his career was in trouble the moment Joe became chief astronaut. He would be around the Air Patch.

McDowell? His last failed application for the astronaut office took place prior to both attempts. He wouldn't have been around Ellington as much as Goslin . . . but obviously had a better chance to screw with the Pitts.

She knew no more about Goslin and McDowell than when she opened the files.

It was clear that there was a lot she had missed during her training and mission. Joe's crusade. He might have made enemies other than Goslin and McDowell. And these enemies were clearly willing to keep trying until they succeeded.

She suddenly felt frightened. Ridiculous: she was tired and it was late. Yet . . . Joe was dead. The accident was mysterious. And from these files, he had had other close calls.

She looked at her clock—11:45. It was really too late to call Mark. Yes, like hers, his life might be in danger . . . but evidence on the message machine suggested that he was home. She couldn't imagine Goslin or McDowell or the Mysterious Enemy moving against him there.

He should be safe until morning.

CHAPTER 34

On Wednesday evening Mark called and said he'd be a little late, something about working on the Regency trainer. He had managed to call in an order at Le-Roy's, and it would be ready at eight, if Allyson could pick it up.

She was happy to do so. She had spent the afternoon with her laptop plugged into Mark's modem—an intimate, even sexual, gesture—checking with her office in L.A. She was on vacation, but it never hurt to show those above and below her that she was still part of the team.

It was also a bit of a test, to see how much she missed being at Hughes. So far the answer was, not a hell of a lot. Besides, even if she and Mark got married, a move to Houston wouldn't necessarily mean leaving Hughes. The company had several support contracts with JSC, and a program monitor like Allyson could easily get a transfer.

As for the reality of living in Houston, specifically in the Clear Lake area, that was a different matter. Her community of Westchester was one of a dozen suburbs in the South Bay area of Los Angeles, but it also had Los Angeles and Westwood and Santa Monica and Long Beach close at hand. As far as Allyson was concerned, greater Houston, with its urban amenities, was just a rumor. Living in Clear Lake would be a lot like living in, say, Palmdale. Or Provo, Utah.

It wasn't that the people all fit in the same class, far from it. She had seen quite a blend of white-collar engineer types and Texan ranchers or oil rig workers. There were even engineers who affected the big hat, rancher style. But Allyson wasn't sure that she wanted to make a life among either. She suspected she would miss the beach crowd, the showbiz fringe.

Then there was the Gulf Coast weather. Thick, humid, buggy, prone to sudden rain. And this wasn't the worst time of year!

Oh, well, why worry now? She had deftly postponed the whole marriage discussion for at least a year. Or, as her sister put it, she had moved it thirteen eggs into the future.

It was pouring down rain as she splashed through the parking lot to Le-Roy's. The refrigerated air immediately chilled her. She should have worn a jacket.

The place was busy for a Wednesday night . . . mostly couples without children, she saw, in addition to half a dozen singles waiting for takeout. She edged up to the window. "Order for Koskinen?"

The girl behind the counter frowned. "I thought it was ready. Let me check. . . ." Fine. It would give her time to get thoroughly chilled.

Through the front window, cloudy from condensation, she could see the lights of cars racing up and down Galveston Road. Beyond it were the lights of Ellington Field. At this time of night, in this weather, it looked forlorn.

"I don't believe I've seen you around here before."

Allyson turned, smiling to herself. Oh my God, she thought instantly, someone is trying to pick me up. "I haven't been here before," she said, adding, "And depending on the clientele, I might not come back."

The man laughed. He looked fit and seemed confident, just like Mark, adding a few years. He was drinking a beer. "That would be a shame. I don't see women as pretty as you in here very often."

"You should have said 'never,' " she told him.

He had the grace to laugh. "Next time I'll do better." And he plunged out into the rain.

"Koskinen order?" Allyson turned and saw the counter girl holding up a paper bag and gesturing to her. "I thought I put this out here. Maybe somebody moved it." Well, it was here now, the name "Koskinen" written on it in black felt-tip.

Allyson paid, then went out into the rain herself.

Inside the car the rich aroma of Cajun food was too much to resist. She barely had her seat belt buckled before she started digging into the bag. Mark might be annoyed, but it was already after eight and she had not had much in the way of lunch.

Not the shrimp. That would be too messy inside Mark's Explorer. Oh, here were some fritterlike things . . . a couple of quick bites would do her a lot of good.

Now all she had to do was navigate through the rain back to the condo. Right on Galveston Road, then it was just a mile to the left turn at Clear Lake Boulevard.

She wondered where Mark was right now . . . it was probably a blessing that he didn't have the bike, because he would feel obligated to ride it home in the rain.

The traffic was slow; drivers were taking it easy because of the poor visibility. There also seemed to be some police activity up ahead on the northbound side . . . a cop had pulled over some speeder, apparently.

Whoops! Allyson slammed on the brakes and caused the Explorer to skid. Her heart beat wildly as she realized how close she had come to ramming the car in front of her. What the hell was the matter with her? She'd driven in Los Angeles most of her life. This was *nothing*.

The traffic started moving again, slowly. The left turn onto Clear Lake was nerve-wracking, since there were so many cars stacked up doing the same thing that Allyson was left in the traffic lane. Horns screamed behind her, doing that annoying Doppler shift down the scale as they passed.

She was across—

—and not feeling good at all. There must have been a ton of sodium in those fritters, because she had an instant headache. Christ, it was even making her eyes water. So much for dinner—

She realized she was breathing hard, as if she'd just sprinted a hundred yards. The wheel of the car felt doughy in her hands, as if she were losing feeling.

Only one more light to Space Center Boulevard, then it wouldn't be far. . . .

Was that a red light? She hit the brakes—

—just as she saw the truck.

CHAPTER 35

I think you've got the makings of a problem," Drury told Fehrenkamp.
They had just returned to Fehrenkamp's house in River Oaks from dinner
at the country club. It was an impressive home . . . three bedrooms, tile
floors, a kitchen large enough for a game of handball. Drury noted that all
of the homes in this development seemed impressive and expensive. Who
owned them? With his experience in government, he could have guessed to
within five hundred dollars what a civil servant like Les Fehrenkamp made
in a year, and it would take a lot of stretching to cover a down payment on
something like this.

But small talk about mortgages, even small talk that masked questions
about the source of outside money, wasn't on Drury's agenda. "Your accident board."

Fehrenkamp floated around the kitchen—the man was practically
weightless—making coffee. "I like to think of it as *your* accident board,
Don." He called to Drury in the living room. "That's why I made you
president."

"Remind me to thank you again." He noted the pictures on the wall.
A woman—Fehrenkamp's ex—or was it late—wife. A son. Well, a young
man of some kind.

"You're supposed to deliver a report Friday. Is that going to be a problem?"

"It might be."

"Well, assume I'm listening with full attention."

Drury always assumed that with Fehrenkamp. In fact, he would have
preferred to have him a little distracted. "I can't discuss the facts with you,
Les. You don't want me to."

"Understood. I have no desire to wind up before a congressional com-mittee. But there must be something you can tell me . . . you raised the issue."

Drury settled into a couch that was too soft. "It's your two astronauts. They're giving me the runaround."

Fehrenkamp entered the living room and set a cup of coffee in front of Drury, then took a chair across from him. "They're astronauts," he said. "We hire them because they're a mix of team player and bullheaded self-starter."

"These two are a little heavy on the bullheaded side."

Fehrenkamp thought that over. "I think you have to expect them to, ah, aim higher than the other members of the board. It's their ass in those planes. And Joe Buerhle *was* their boss."

"I expect that. I guess I just want to know if there's anything else I should know about them. . . ."

"I think," Fehrenkamp said after another pause, "that you'll find the, ah, team player side of them will win out, once you make the decision. Once you tell them, This is it, you're outvoted.

"At that point, feel free to remind them that the ultimate judge of their behavior is their old friend Fehrenkamp. Kelly Gessner was just assigned to a crew, and that could disappear with a phone call, as well she knows. Mr. Koskinen is even more vulnerable. *He* could disappear from the office with a phone call, and never get a flight at all.

"They might grumble and bitch, but they'll sign. And I don't think you have to worry about them going public later."

At least Fehrenkamp was willing to give him a stick to beat the astro-nauts with. Drury realized that this was the best he was going to get without telling Fehrenkamp everything Koskinen had told him. He hadn't wanted to do that because he didn't want to be used. And, let's face it, he had promised the young man that he wouldn't spill the beans.

There was also the nagging thought in his mind that the young astronaut *might just be right.* Don Drury had lied in the past to protect the mission—knowing that he would take the fall if he got caught. He would lie again, if the circumstances justified the action. But covering up negligence or an honest mistake or a great big mistake was one thing. Covering up a murder was a whole different deal.

He had offered Fehrenkamp his own opportunity to wave him off, to send him a message. Yes, there's something dicey here. If it were up to me, I'd simply—

But he'd received no signals, nothing to indicate that he shouldn't just follow his instincts. And solve the problem the best way he knew.

Drury believed that problems should be solved inside the family. Behind closed doors, away from the windows, out of the neighbors' hearing.

Speaking of the neighbors . . . "Tell me, Les, where the hell do people around here find the money to pay for these houses?"

CHAPTER 36

Mark was in a good mood, all things considered, when Greg Yakubik dropped him at the corner. True, there had been no progress on the Goslin or McDowell fronts. But Mark had begun to feel like a real Worm again. Even the moderate soaking he got scooting to his door didn't change that.

Allyson wasn't home and the house was dark. He looked at his watch—8:20. And he was hungry.

Well, she might have gotten lost on the way to or from Le-Roy's. Or there might have been a crowd.

He switched on the lights, then went upstairs to the bedroom. To warm up he stripped out of his clothes and stepped into the shower. When he came back downstairs in a T-shirt and shorts it was 8:45. And still no sign of Allyson. No messages on the machine, either.

He wasn't used to having unscheduled time. He could have read a book—when was the last time he'd done that? He could have watched *Sports Center* on ESPN. But, wait, what season was it? Wasn't the World Series about to start?

He picked up the workbooks from his session on the Regency trainer today. After three weeks of concentrating on the T-38 and not being allowed to think about his job at the Cape, it had been fun. And possibly productive. He knew that once he got that material into his head, it was there for good—

The door buzzed.

Allyson, finally. He would tease her about misplacing her keys. But when Mark opened the door he saw a Clear Lake police officer who looked vaguely familiar. Wait—this was the same guy who had taken the report of

Mark's stolen bicycle. Officer Laatsch. "Don't tell me," Mark said. "You found my bike."

Laatsch looked nervous. "Mr. Koskinen . . . do you know an Allyson Morin?"

Mark suddenly felt very worried. "Yes."

"I'm very sorry to tell you this, Mr. Caulkins"—he was so shaken he couldn't even get the name right—"but there's been an accident—"

"Is Allyson hurt?"

"She's passed away."

Take a breath. Take another one. "Okay," he said, feeling strangely calm. "What happened?"

Laatsch consulted a notebook. As far as they'd been able to determine, Allyson's Explorer had run a red light at the intersection of Clear Lake and El Camino, and collided with a Federal Express truck. That had been bad enough, but the initial impact spun the Explorer around on the wet pavement. A pickup truck coming the other way had smashed into the driver's side. "They took her to Memorial Southeast," Laatsch said, naming a hospital on the other side of I-45, "but as I understand it she was probably dead at the scene." Mark nodded. They were still standing in the doorway. "You probably heard the sirens."

"I was in the shower."

Laatsch nodded and consulted his notebook again. "I just want to confirm this—Miss Morin was using your vehicle with your permission."

"Yes." It suddenly occurred to Mark that he might be in some kind of legal or insurance trouble. But, really, how important was that right now? How important was anything—being an astronaut? He should have skipped the trainer and come home!

No, don't start that. Concentrate on what needs to be done. "You probably need me to identify her."

"Yes, sir. And if there's anyone else who should be notified . . ."

Mark realized he'd been holding his breath. He let it out, and felt weak and tired. "I'll handle it."

It was after midnight before Mark ran out of people to call and decisions to be made. He had identified Allyson's body—badly bruised and swollen. She had died of a broken neck in the second impact, they were saying. Mark had no strong opinions about whether death should be instant or with some kind of warning. He preferred to avoid the whole business, though with Joe Buerhle and now Allyson, death seemed to be closing in on him.

Before leaving his condo he had grabbed the Rolodex card with Allyson's parents' address and phone number. That had been a difficult call—they were a fairly close family, since parents and Allyson and sister Colleen all still lived in the L.A. area. About all he could do was give them the awful news, assure them that he was with Allyson—with her remains—and that he would call them in the morning about arrangements, although parents and sister naturally wanted her buried at home.

Then, my God, the arrangements. First there would be the routine Harris County autopsy, then the body would be released to a funeral home. (Which one? Which one had handled Joe Buerhle?) The funeral home would manage the business of shipping the remains back to Los Angeles, where another funeral home needed to be waiting . . . that decision could wait until morning. Mark simply said yes to most questions and offered to pay whatever it would take.

There were also other matters. The drivers of the two trucks involved in the collision, and another driver who had tail-ended the FedEx vehicle, had all been injured, though none seriously. Two of them had been brought to the emergency room, and Mark thought he should at least see how they were doing. The phone calls to L.A. had been difficult; meeting the other victims had merely been awkward.

Ultimately there were no more decisions to make, no more bits of information to absorb. One of the E.R. nurses told Mark he should go home and rest.

Mark knew that there were local people he should call. Kondratko, certainly. The Russian pilot had known Allyson. But it was after midnight. Why ruin Kondratko's evening? He would have to call Fehrenkamp, because he would be out of the office for several days. Drury. Christ, it was Thursday now, and tomorrow was the deadline for the board!

He also needed a ride home: Laatsch had driven Mark to the hospital.

The number he called was Kelly Gessner's.

NASA NEWS

National Aeronautics and
Space Administration
Lyndon B. Johnson Space Center
Houston TX 77058
281 481-5111

November 6, 1998
Lou Wekkin
Johnson Space Center, Houston TX
(Phone: 281/483-1511)

RELEASE NO. 98-113

PRELIMINARY CAUSE OF T-38 CRASH

An Accident Investigation Board studying the crash of a NASA T-38A on October 14, 1998, has ruled out mechanical and maintenance errors, weather or other aircraft as possible causes, Board President Donald Drury announced today. Drury went on to note that the Board's final report is still in preparation and that this determination is only a preliminary one.

The preliminary judgment allows the Aircraft Operations Directorate of the NASA Johnson Space Center to resume a full flight schedule.

Pilot error remains among the possible causes for the crash, which killed astronaut Joseph Buerhle.

The Board is composed of representatives from Northrop-Grumman Aviation, Collins Avionics, Pratt and Whitney, and NASA.

-end-

EDITOR'S NOTE: Images of the NASA T-38A aircraft are available via the Internet at the Johnson Space Center's on-line photo archive. The World Wide Web URL is: http://www.jsc.nasa.gov/PhotoServer/photoserver.html

CHAPTER 37

Between the evenings at Joe Buerhle's and travel for STS-93, Kelly hadn't spent a lot of time at home in the past year. She made a date with herself to spend Saturday night home, alone, just catching up on chores. There were bills to pay. Books to rearrange on the shelves. Obsolete food to be purged from her refrigerator. A Rolodex to be updated.

And recycling to be sorted and taken out. Lots of recycling.

She was in that phase of her Saturday night mission, returning from the bin at the corner of her building, when she spotted Steve Goslin on the sidewalk. The mere sight of him raised a shiver in her recently discovered paranoia gland, until she remembered that they were, in fact, neighbors. And that Goslin had his two daughters with him, one wobbly on a pink bicycle with training wheels, the other walking.

Goslin seemed unusually subdued for what should have been a happy family outing. "Are you feeling all right?" she asked him. "How about a beverage?"

"Thanks, but . . ." He nodded toward the girls, who had ceased their progress and were now conferring over some crack in the sidewalk.

"They're getting big."

"I don't think she's quite big enough for that bike, yet."

"Fathers always try to hold their daughters back, Steve. Get with it; next thing you know, it'll be lipstick and a date."

"Even Shuttle commanders have to take orders."

At least he laughed. And his two daughters looked adorable. "You heard about Mark Koskinen's girlfriend," Kelly said casually.

"That was terrible," he said. "He's having a very bad streak." Just then one of the girls tugged at his jacket. "I'd better get going. Thanks!" He waved as he followed the girls down the walk.

Kelly had heard all about the accident from Mark, of course, though by the time she picked him up he was so exhausted that there hadn't been many details. One thing she had insisted on was this: she and Mark were going to sign the preliminary board report Friday morning. Right or wrong, Mark had other things on his mind right now. They deserved his attention, not Joe's accident.

She hadn't been entirely certain that he had agreed to that, but when she dropped by Ellington Friday morning she saw that he had beaten her to it: she signed below his name. There was only one signature missing, in fact, that of Walter Thompson of the NTSB. Well, that was Don Drury's problem.

Unsurprisingly, Mark had not come in to the astronaut office, either. Kelly found when she arrived that the word about Allyson's death was already out, which saved her from having to tell the story over and over again.

In keeping with her futile attempt to get current, she had spent the rest of the day catching up on correspondence. A Shuttle flight generated hundreds of requests for autographs, photos. Some of the people in CB were pretty casual about responding—if not downright hostile—but Kelly religiously worked her way through most of the pile. It kept her from thinking what a bad detective she was. Two whole days had passed since she had let slip that there was something odd about Joe Buerhle's death, and neither of the two leading candidates had done anything to indicate that he was feeling guilty or nervous. Maybe the killer was just cold-blooded enough to ride this out.

Or, maybe, Joe Buerhle's killer was not Steve Goslin or Scott McDowell. Kelly suspected this was a lot like real police work, that she just needed more patience and more evidence. But where was she going to get more evidence? While trying to train for a space flight, that is.

This evening Steve Goslin certainly hadn't struck her as a cold-blooded killer, but rather as a suburban dad indulging his little girls. She was ready to scratch him off her list, anyway, cop brother or not.

Which would leave Mark and Kelly with McDowell as their major suspect. How was she going to justify an interest in his activities? McDowell was the kind of man who took the slightest sign of female interest as proof that a relationship was inevitable.

Yes, he was a good-looking guy; Kelly could see how a woman would be interested in him. Had she never received Joe's perspective on the real Scott McDowell, she might have given him a try herself.

She was putting leftover Halloween candy back in its bag when the doorbell rang. She was careful enough to look out the window before opening the door—

It was Mark Koskinen, looking terrible.

"Trick or treat."

Kelly handed him a Nestlé Crunch bar. "You're such a tall fella that I should probably give you two."

"I could use them. They'd be dinner."

She invited him in. He not only ate a pair of Crunch bars but managed to down three Milky Ways. "Mark," she said, "I'm going to make you a sandwich." Which she did.

She had barely gotten the peanut butter out of the cupboard when he came into the kitchen. "I got the autopsy report on Allyson a little while ago."

"Anything unusual?"

"Check this: there were traces in her blood of the same controlled substance that was found in Joe Buerhle. Coke."

Kelly actually dropped the peanut butter jar. "Good thing it's plastic," she said as she picked it up. "How did she get it?"

"My friend at the coroner's office says it could have been in something she ate just prior to the accident."

"Are you thinking—"

"That our killer has struck again? You tell me. My judgment isn't too reliable now."

"Well, it depends. Why would our Joe Buerhle killer go after Allyson?"

"Maybe he was aiming at me," he said quietly, like a man laying out a trump card in a game of euchre.

Apparently Mark had received the call from someone named Todd at the coroner's office around noon and had immediately started retracing Allyson's steps that evening. "Here's what I've come up with. I called in an order to Le-Roy's from CB at, like, six-thirty. There were all kinds of people around who could have heard me say I wouldn't be picking it up until eight. That I would be picking it up."

"Then Allyson shows up instead—"

"And gets the bullet that was meant for me."

Kelly was trying to visualize the terrain. The astronaut office. The weather. Le-Roy's. "Well, there was certainly time for someone to get from the office to Le-Roy's."

"How hard would it be to add something to a paper bag when it's busy and nobody's looking? If it's somebody they know? An astronaut?"

"It's possible." It seemed all too possible, but—

"I'd love to know where Goslin and McDowell were between six and eight that night. I know Goslin was still in the office when I made the call."

Kelly put her hand on Mark's. "You're not going to like this. Goslin may have been on the sixth floor when you made the order, but from about six-thirty to eight-thirty he was over in Building 5. With McDowell—"

"And you?"

She nodded. "And the whole 100 crew and a dozen other people besides. We were just discussing the training schedules for the next couple of months. . . ."

The kitchen suddenly seemed too quiet. "Well, then," Mark said. "That's it." He took a careful bite out of the peanut butter sandwich.

"I'm sorry."

"We were making a circumstantial case for murder. Unless we want to assume that whoever killed Allyson didn't kill Joe Buerhle, which means there are *two* murderers running loose, and I don't have the faintest fucking idea what to do in that case."

Kelly took him by the hand and led him out of the kitchen. "I tell you what you're going to do," Kelly said. "You're going to put this out of your mind. You're going to get on a plane tomorrow and fly to Los Angeles, and be with Allyson's family. They need you now."

"What about you? If someone tried to kill me, they might try to go after you, too."

She smiled. "I'll be very careful about what I eat. Maybe I'll hire Les Fehrenkamp as my food taster." Mark managed a laugh. "I think I can manage until you get back."

"And then what?"

"We go to Plan B. That's what astronauts always do. You have a Plan B, don't you?"

"By Monday."

She rubbed his shoulder. "Monday." And without ever deciding to do so, Kelly put her other arm around Mark's neck. They kissed . . . hesitantly at first, then with much more vigor. Oh my God, Kelly thought.

Just as suddenly, and with as little warning, it was over. "I'd better go," Mark said.

"I think so. But we're not done with this."

He looked at her. "No, I don't think we are."

CHAPTER 38

Les Fehrenkamp had many operating rules for the astronaut office. The LASCANs had their Commandments, of course, which were certainly in the spirit of Les's rules but were narrower in scope, designed to reach the goal of that all-important first, and possibly only, flight in space.

Fehrenkamp's rules were not written down and never would be, but were implicit in his actions. This allowed him to break his own rules when needed. Besides, the more astute astronauts discovered them on their own, thus justifying their continued assignments to missions. Those who never figured them out just faded away.

Seniority counted, was one of them. Astronauts who had been in CB longest got first crack at missions. If they were unavailable, then the new folks would step up.

You get one chance at redemption, was another. With the travel, the notoriety, the risk, the competition, being an astronaut was a complicated job. Even the best of them made mistakes. Fehrenkamp felt that anyone who made an honest mistake would get one chance to prove that he or she had learned. Usually by having to work for a year at the worst possible job Fehrenkamp could find or create.

Astronauts don't make policy. If there had been a scale showing the importance of the rules, this would have been number two, right behind *The director's word is law.* The hundred-plus astronauts in the office were a fairly diverse lot, given the obvious common interests in aviation, technology and spaceflight. There were Republicans and Democrats, career military officers and civilians who had marched in protests, pilots and nonpilots, genuine scientists and probably some outright thrill-seekers. And now Americans and foreigners. Take any budgetary matter, any NASA decision, whether to fund the Spacelifter or build another orbiter, and you could have forty different opinions.

When the American public thought of NASA, it thought of astronauts. It was bad enough for the space program that you still had venerable planetary scientists—space probe people like James Van Allen and Bruce Murray—who would trash the Shuttle program. Suppose the dissenting views came from people who had flown in space? It would mean chaos. It would politicize the office. It would destroy the sense of teamwork that made everything possible.

It was why Fehrenkamp went to see Cal Stipe on a Sunday morning, just hours before he was to catch an American Airlines flight to Moscow.

Doing a flyby, as Fehrenkamp called it, required a little planning. You had to make the preflyby call, one of those "I'm going to be out your way tomorrow morning" things, and then have a quasi-legitimate purpose. In this case, some official NASA photos of Stipe with his two Russian crewmates needed to be inscribed for some headquarters personalities and some on Capitol Hill. It was just the kind of detail that Fehrenkamp often handled personally.

Stipe lived west of JSC in Pearland, in a woody area that backed up on a creek. Some years back the creek had flooded Stipe out; with typical Stipe bullheadedness he had remodeled his place so that a future flood would just be an inconvenience, essentially moving his living room, bedroom and valuables upstairs and turning the ground floor into a cement-floored playroom and gym. Another Stipe trait was that he usually got sidetracked before finishing a job, and so nothing was quite finished. There was still lumber piled next to the driveway, for example. Fehrenkamp wondered what the neighbors thought, then remembered that this was Houston, where urban zoning was a sign of twentieth-century decadence. The neighbors' places, in fact, looked just as unfinished and cockeyed as Stipe's did.

There were only three bags waiting in the downstairs when Fehrenkamp entered. "You travel light," he told Stipe.

"Shit, Les, I've been living over there, off and on, for a year. Most of my stuff is at Star Town." This was true: there were half a dozen NASA apartments in the formerly closed city that housed the Gagarin Training Center. Les hadn't noticed many Americans making a home there, however; rather, they treated it like a hotel.

"What time is your flight?" Fehrenkamp said, knowing full well when it was leaving.

"Two-thirty. I'll be heading out at noon."

"Let's get these signed, then." Fehrenkamp produced the stack of photos—each one tagged with a yellow Post-it giving the recipient's name. All of them had already been signed by the cosmonauts, then pouched back to JSC. Stipe collapsed on the floor in a lotus position and went to work. "How are you getting along with your crewmates?" Fehrenkamp asked.

"Sasha and Sasha?" Both Russians were named Alexander. "Really good. They're young, but they don't mind having the guy in the third seat point some things out to them."

"Giving them pointers on the Soyuz systems, I bet." Fehrenkamp was joking, but he could easily picture Stipe correcting his Russian commander and flight engineer on some business.

"Very gently." Stipe continued to sign, methodically, like some best-selling New Age author, his name almost microscopic.

"Oh, by the way," Fehrenkamp said, segueing into the real purpose for his visit. "I'd really appreciate it if you'd lie low on this whole NASA-Russia relationship business."

"What do you mean, Les?" Stipe glanced up. "From what I can see, the relationship is all worked out. Everybody's happy."

"Right now. But things can change. And given that you're going to be up in Mir for eight months, you're not going to be in the loop on the latest guidance."

Stipe finished signing and stacked the photos. "Well, you know, Les, that might be a bit of a problem for me."

"You know the limits of communication with Mir as well as anyone." They were horrendous: the crew had full communications capability with the ground for only a third of every workday, so naturally those comm sessions were jammed with housekeeping matters. There was no way for an American astronaut to, say, chat on the phone. It had proved to be a major psychological problem for Americans on Mir so far.

"That's not what I'm talking about," Stipe said. "You want something to drink?"

"No, thank you." He watched Stipe get to his feet, then head to the kitchen. He was awfully limber for his age—any age. "What are you talking about?"

What Fehrenkamp heard was the buzz of a blender. Stipe reappeared a moment later, drinking some sort of yellowish goo right out of the mixer. "I'm NASA's representative to the Russian manned space program, Les.

I'm not going to just keep my mouth shut and I'm not going to, you know, leave my opinions back on Earth. If I start seeing big bad changes in policy, I'm going to say something."

Fehrenkamp weighed this. He wasn't used to having astronauts argue with him—well, astronauts other than Stipe. "How'd the Buerhle thing turn out?" Stipe said casually.

"The only cause the board couldn't rule out was pilot error." This was something new: Stipe was *fighting back*. Did he know there were rumors about the board's verdict? Fehrenkamp suddenly wished he had not chosen to come by.

Stipe shrugged. "Well, that was my guess from day one."

"I'm going to be honest with you, Cal. We've always been open with each other—"

"Have we, Les? We've known each other almost twenty years . . . how open have we been?"

Before Fehrenkamp could formulate a reply—a defense—Stipe reached out and put his hand on Fehrenkamp's face. "I remember an evening at the Cape some years ago. Do you?"

Fehrenkamp remembered all too well, a conversation in a hotel room. He remembered the preliminary and aftermath, that is. He wasn't entirely sure there had been any . . . contact. In those days, before the Shuttle even flew, he had often drunk more than he should have. It was one of the reasons his marriage failed.

It was not how he lived now. He was not gay.

"Why don't you take your hand off my face," he said quietly. Stipe did so. "I've made my point. Obviously you've made yours," Fehrenkamp said. "I think I'll be going." He tried to keep the sarcasm out of his voice. "Have a nice flight."

As he drove away, Les Fehrenkamp decided he had had enough of Cal Stipe. Had it been a Shuttle mission, a way would have been found to bounce him off it. Since this was a Russian launch—well, there was no way he was going to share his annoyance with them.

But Stipe was through in CB as long as Les Fehrenkamp was director.

CHAPTER 39

On Tuesday Mark returned to the astronaut office. Had he wanted, he could have caught a late flight on Sunday and returned in time for the Monday pilots' meeting, but realized he didn't particularly care.

In the last month, now, he'd missed two of the meetings. Clearly he was breaking Commandments all over the place. He did manage to get into the office even earlier than usual, before seven.

He found his most recent schedule sitting on his desk, opened it and saw that he was still technically assigned to Don Drury's board, with the exception of a T-38 flight on Thursday. In a way he was glad, because he had a mental shopping list of errands to do, number two being "Buy a new car." He was driving a rental he had picked up at Hobby Airport late Monday.

Number one on the list wasn't a housekeeping matter; it was "Talk to Fehrenkamp" and find out when or if he was ever going to be allowed to move down to the Cape. He quickly learned that talking to Fehrenkamp this morning was going to be impossible: the director was on his way to the Cape to greet the crew of STS-95, which would be landing this morning.

Mark glanced at his watch, saw that the landing, in fact, was imminent, and went looking for a TV.

NASA Select was playing in the conference room. There was a shot of Mission Control, with Arnaldo Rivera serving as entry capcom and Viktor Kondratko sitting next to him.

The orbiter *Atlantis* had already fired its maneuvering engines out over the Pacific, beginning its long fall across the United States. Its reentry path ran from southern Canada across the middle of the United States, too far north to be seen from Houston.

This mission also had some cockpit views from the helmet of the pilot, Sandra Rhodes, uplinked through a Tracking and Data Relay Satellite. Things seemed to be going well. The cockpit windows glowed, as if the orbiter were flying through an oven, and there was an occasional bump, which might have been Rhodes shifting in her seat.

Now that it was well after seven, the astronaut office was coming alive, and Mark realized that others had joined in to watch the landing.

"Come on, Ron, bring her home." Jason Borders addressed the TV screen as it showed the orbiter from the ground. Even through the TV speakers you could hear the double *crack!* of a twin sonic boom.

"Orbiter *Atlantis*, going around the alignment circle, setting up for final approach," the public affairs officer said. "Sonic booms rolled over the Cape as the orbiter goes subsonic. . . ."

Mark received pats on the back—even a squeeze on the arm—from people he'd never spoken to. He decided he was glad to be here this morning, especially when the view on the screen showed what Sandy Rhodes was seeing out her window . . . the runway at the Cape, seemingly impossibly far below, yet growing larger every second.

Back to the external view . . . the winged orbiter flaring for landing . . . condensation trails swirling off the wingtips . . . gliding onto the runway . . . the *whoosh!* as it passed the camera position and kept rolling. Eventually it stopped. "Welcome home, *Atlantis*," Arnaldo radioed.

"Looks easy, doesn't it?" one of the pilots said. The impromptu gathering broke up. Mark found himself alone in the conference room, watching the orbiter as it sat on the runway with its convoy of sniffer trucks approaching it.

He had covered a lot of territory, geographical and otherwise, in the past four days.

The family delayed the funeral to Monday on the grounds that Sunday was the wrong day for such an event, leaving Mark with more free time than he really wanted. He wished, briefly, that Kelly were in town, then hated himself for even considering the thought. A week ago he had been thinking about marrying Allyson!

Arriving in L.A., Sunday he took his rental car—he didn't even want to think about his credit card bill for the month—and drove north from the San Fernando Valley toward Lancaster and Palmdale. He turned off on Pearblossom Highway, right near a spot where, according to space lore, Neil Armstrong had lived during the time he was a test pilot at Edwards, a few miles to the north. Supposedly Armstrong had a car that often had trouble starting, so he would simply let it coast down the steep slope of the highway until it caught. Then he would roar off to fly the X-15 or something.

Fifteen miles due east along the foothills of the San Gabriel Mountains was the dusty hamlet of Pearblossom, home of the Juniper Hills Glider School. Mark had come out here at least once a month all during his time in Los Angeles—especially after his first application to NASA had failed—in order to build up time in sailplanes. Judy, the dispatcher, still had his name and records on one of her index cards. She gave no sign at all that she knew of Mark's current job, but she was able to set him up with a plane and a tow.

Mark took off around ten, when the autumn thermals were beginning to pound the San Gabriels. It felt strange to be in such a stripped-down cockpit—the sailplane needed few instruments beyond an altimeter, and the rudder and stick dated back to the Korean War, at least. Even stranger to be the pilot in charge, especially when the tow plane cut him free at ten thousand feet.

It was quiet, except for the rush of the air over the canopy. Mark let the thermals carry him up for a while, then banked north to make a big loop out toward the dry lakes of Edwards Air Force Base.

As he came around, bearing west, he could see all the way to the big aircraft plant in Palmdale, which got him thinking about Don Drury's Space-lifter, currently a-building in a similar place. Mark wondered what it would be like to work out here, in what was essentially a dusty, windy gateway to nowhere. There was a theory in aerospace circles that projects got built faster and better in miserable places like Palmdale, White Sands, or China Lake because no one wanted to stay there for long. "Finish this thing so we can go home!"

What a change from JSC, where everyone seemed to be rigging for a long haul, to fly the Shuttle into the middle part of the next decade, and to operate the ISS even longer.

If you wanted, you could see your entire career unfolding in front of you.

Mark wondered if that's where he was headed—even if the events of the last few weeks had ruined his chances of flying in space, NASA was committed to finding Mark a job. He was a civil servant, after all.

What a joke. NASA was a joke. Did he want to go back? Suppose he just walked out on the whole thing. What would Allyson have thought about that?

Suddenly there were tears in his eyes, not just tears of grief, but also tears of guilt. Allyson had died because of something he did. That's why he had to go back to NASA . . . he had to find out what had killed her.

Eventually he left the conference room and returned to his office. He studied for a while. He dropped by Kelly's office and learned that she was out at Ellington until early afternoon, flying.

Nobody he knew was around the office, so at noon he walked down six flights and headed for the commissary, blinking in the bright sunlight after what must have been a couple of hours of soothing darkness.

At a table not far from his he saw a bunch of guys from the MOD, including Scott McDowell. They were a bit raucous, celebrating the successful completion of another mission. Even though Kelly had essentially cleared McDowell, Mark watched him, waiting for some kind of slip.

It was all he could do, right now. He needed to talk to Kelly. They needed to have a plan. There had been other people besides Goslin and McDowell at the Air Patch the morning of Joe Buerhle's accident, Kelly had said so. All they needed was to place one of those people at Le-Roy's on Wednesday night. Get the name, then you can find the motive.

When Kelly didn't show right after lunch, Mark went over to Building 5 and spent several more hours on the Regency trainer. He was barely able to concentrate; good thing this was a self-grading system. A training supervisor would have called the whole thing off and told Mark to go home and get it together.

He happened to be heading back to Building 4-South when he ran into Viktor Kondratko walking along the duck pond on his way out of the Mission Operations Building.

"Mark!" They had not seen each other since before Allyson's accident. Kondratko embraced him. "You got my message?" The Russian had left a wonderfully pained and sympathetic message on Mark's machine.

"Thank you."

"Come with me."

"Where are we going?"

"To Ellington. To greet the crew."

The last thing Mark wanted to do right now was go to Ellington and greet a tired group of Shuttle astronauts. But Kondratko, who was now connected to the mission, insisted.

In the car he said, "The funeral, it was horrible as these things are?"

"Even worse." Her parents had been devastated, yet they had somehow found the strength to console Mark. This showed special courage, because they had never really liked him.

"You will work. The pain will never leave, but you will learn to stand it."

"I hope so."

There was a line of cars waiting to get into the Ellington parking lot. Kondratko and Mark wound up sitting. "I heard she was coming from Le-Roy's," Kondratko said, nodding in the general direction of the restaurant.

"Yeah. She was just picking up some dinner."

"This was Wednesday night." Mark nodded. "I was in Le-Roy's Wednesday night."

Mark suddenly sat up a little straighter. At the same time, traffic began to move. "What time?"

"I got there a little after eight." He gave half a smile. "Don't think I'm a bad man, but I was meeting a girlfriend."

"I don't think you're a bad man, Viktor," Mark said, though he was getting less hopeful that he would learn something valuable. "You're sure it was after eight?"

Kondratko thought. "Yes." He aimed a finger at the dashboard radio. "I had just listened to the news at the top of the hour."

"Oh, well. So you certainly didn't see her."

"No. I wish . . . I wish." He shrugged. "I don't know what I wish. Forgive me."

"It's okay." Mark figured it was worth one more question. "Did you happen to see anybody else we know? Anybody from JSC?"

"Of course!" Kondratko said. "He was waiting there for me. I was actually a little late."

"Who?" *Who*, goddamn it!

"Calvin Stipe."

PART IV
THE MOD

NASA N E W S

National Aeronautics and
Space Administration
Lyndon B. Johnson Space Center
Houston TX 77058
281 481-5111

November 11, 1998
Lou Wekkin
Johnson Space Center, Houston TX
(Phone: 281/483-1511)

RELEASE NO. 98-119

COUNTDOWN COMMENCES FOR MIR-30

The final chapter in Phase 1 of NASA's Shuttle-Mir program begins this week, as astronaut Calvin Stipe prepares for launch to the Mir space station with a pair of Russian cosmonauts.

Tomorrow Stipe is scheduled to leave the Yuri Gagarin Cosmonaut Training Center, near Moscow, and fly to the Russian launch center Baikonur in central Kazakstan. With Stipe will be Lieutenant Colonel Alexander A. Shabarov of the Russian air force, the mission commander, and Alexander V. Dergunov of the Energiya Space Production Company. Shabarov, Dergunov and Stipe will fly the 30th expedition to Mir.

Stipe is scheduled to return to earth aboard STS-100 in June 1999, though NASA HQ is weighing an option to extend the mission through the end of 1999 in order to gather unique biomedical data.

The Mir-30 crew will be launched by a Soyuz U2 rocket on November 16th.

CHAPTER 40

How are we going to prove this?'' Mark said. They were walking from Kelly's car into Le-Roy's.

"We're simply going to ask if Cal Stipe was here last Wednesday night around eight o'clock. I bet we can get a yes or no.''

"Suppose they say yes.''

"Then we try to figure how he might have doped Allyson's order.'' Kelly stopped short of the door and turned toward Mark. "If nothing else, it's something the police will eventually want to know.''

"If they ever dig into this. Right now they just think Allyson was some cokehead from L.A.''

"I think we'd like to change their minds about that,'' she said quietly, linking her arm in his.

He managed a smile. "I'll follow your lead.''

Kelly knew Mark was right in raising the issue of an eventual criminal investigation. Too many questions would trigger one, taking the matter out of their hands. The owners of Le-Roy's, for example, would certainly know that last Wednesday a young woman had gone directly from their restaurant to her death. If they had served her several beers, for example, they could be liable, so they were likely to be sensitive to queries. And the last thing Kelly and Mark wanted was a big discussion.

They ordered, and since the counter was too jammed to make a supposedly casual query, took a table in the front room. While they waited for the food, they had a beer. Mark seemed lost in thought. Kelly said, "Tell me what's on your mind.''

He laughed. When he spoke, he kept his voice low. "Stipe was at

Ellington, Stipe was here. Stipe seems to be the kind of guy who could get his hands on this drug.

"All we don't know is *why*. What could be so important that a guy like Stipe would kill two people?"

"It's all about Joe. You said it yourself: whoever killed Allyson was aiming at you. We put out the word that you were worried about some anomaly on the board. The killer decided to shut your mouth." Kelly had spent far too much time thinking about Allyson's bad luck. Stipe—assuming the killer was Stipe—might have hoped Mark, under the influence, would just injure himself. But Allyson was smaller, lighter. The dosage had hit her hard and fast. Harder and faster than Joe Buerhle.

"And could have been aiming at you, too."

"I suppose. Anyway, if it was Stipe, we're safe for the moment. He's in Russia now, and in a couple of days he'll be at Baikonur."

"When is he supposed to launch?"

"The date is November sixteenth. There's not much chance of that date slipping." She sipped at her beer.

Mark stared at what was, by now, an empty beer glass. "This is all so weird."

"Look at it this way: if astronauts are superhuman, they'll have super-human tempers. And, believe me, Calvin Stipe has superhuman arrogance."

"Come on. Everybody likes him."

"I don't know that anybody *likes* Stipe. We're all fascinated by him. I mean, he's the one total free agent in CB. We're all little marching drones compared to him."

At that moment a middle-aged woman with frizzy black hair came up to Kelly's and Mark's table. "Gessner, is that you?"

Kelly was genuinely glad to see the woman, who was Carla Spano, and introduced her to Mark. "Carla worked for Rockwell in CB up until a couple of years ago." Rockwell once had the support contract for the astronaut office. It turned out that Carla and another female friend had just come out for dinner. "We miss you up there."

"Honey, you astronauts barely knew I was there at all, you were always so darned busy!"

The little cluster at the table brought over one of Le-Roy's waitresses, however, to deliver plates of seafood for what she know knew were a couple of astronauts. As Carla and friend moved off, Kelly said to Mark, "Our moment is now."

She asked the waitress if she usually worked weeknights. She did. Last week? Yes. Was she working Wednesday night when Cal Stipe was in here?

The girl actually blushed. "He was so funny! He just kept ordering beers and making comments about people."

Kelly turned to Mark and announced. "You owe me dinner," she said pointedly. "I told you I saw Cal crawling out of here last Wednesday right about eight."

The waitress got a little frown on her face. "He's not in trouble, is he?"

"Just a little wager," Mark said, stepping into his role. He pulled some money out of his pocket as Kelly picked up a takeout bag and walked off with it. She opened it, looked inside, closed it. She imagined good old Cal Stipe walking off with a similar bag. Christ, he could have gotten all the way outside! Opening the bag, dumping white powder on the fritters, whatever. It would melt quickly; even if it didn't, who knew what Cajun spices looked like?

A whole minute had passed. Mark was still charming the waitress. Kelly walked back over, and only then did the waitress notice. "Did you order takeout?"

"No." She summoned up her friendliest smile. "My mistake."

The waitress moved off. "Now what do we do?" he asked.

"First," Kelly said, feeling pleased with herself, "we eat dinner."

An hour later they were back at Mark's apartment. "You must be a little relieved," Mark was saying.

"Why?"

"Your crew commander isn't a murderer."

She hadn't thought about that, but, yes, it was nice to have Goslin cleared. "Neither is my lead flight director."

"Would you like something to drink?"

"Anything." He went into the kitchen and Kelly looked around. Mark's place was so bare you'd never know an ASCAN lived there. Well, be fair. She remembered how busy that time had been for her . . . she had had the advantage of being a Clear Lake resident when selected. Starting a household while trying to keep to that schedule . . . Mark was lucky to have a roof over his head.

He was back from the kitchen holding a cup of water. "Would you believe it? This is all I have, except for a pint of milk that scared me."

Kelly laughed and accepted the water. "This is all I really wanted, anyway." God, that sounded like a high school girl out with a cute guy. *Don't make him feel bad!*

Of course, Mark was a cute guy. And they were out, in a way.

He flopped on the main chair and invited her to sit on the couch. "Well, we've got circumstantial evidence tying Stipe to these crimes. What do we do?"

"Go to Fehrenkamp."

Mark looked genuinely surprised. "I'm sorry, I thought you just said 'Go to Fehrenkamp.' "

"That's what I said." It had just popped out, but she had learned one thing in this business—to trust those first ideas. They were the result of her highly trained subconscious at work. "I mean, there's always the police. But as you said, the evidence is really circumstantial at this point. And for all the reasons we discussed earlier, up to and including the fact that Joe died in international waters, I don't think the police are the answer. Yet. Maybe never. We could try to deal with this all by ourselves. . . ." She trailed off.

"And haven't we done a fabulous job so far."

"Look, even if we had an ironclad case against Stipe right now—which we do not—we would have to somehow get him out of Russia! Without screwing up some hundred-million-dollar space mission! The only person I know who would tackle that is Fehrenkamp."

"I suppose you're right." He didn't look convinced. "I can just picture the look on his face when we tell him."

"Oh, it'll be priceless."

"You did say you'd be part of this, didn't you? Because he'll laugh me right out of NASA if I go in there alone."

Kelly set the empty glass on the couch and slid over to Mark. She put her hands on his arm. "I'm in this with you, okay?"

Here was another one of those potentially intimate moments. Mark sensed it too, and took her hands just as she was about to remove them. "Kelly—"

"You're going to tell me this is too soon."

"Yeah."

"You're right." It was a little early for her, post-Joe, to be starting a new relationship, too. "I'm going home right now."

"I think you have to."

They both elevated themselves to a standing position. Mark took her hand and walked her to the door. She found it charming.

It wasn't until she was unlocking her car that she remembered Joe's files! And the other alleged attempts on his life!

For a good ten seconds she thought she would march back up to Mark's and tell him.

No. No way. This information would keep. If she went back there, she was going to spend the night, and neither of them seemed ready for that right now, if ever.

CHAPTER 41

"That is one amazing story," Les Fehrenkamp said to Kelly and Mark. *Amazing* was the mildest word he could summon at the moment.

Mark sat across from him, on the couch. Kelly stood at the window, looking across at the astronaut office.

"Let me see if I've got this straight: Joe Buerhle was drugged, which is why he crashed, and then your girlfriend, Mark, was killed to keep you from talking." He found himself smiling, without any enjoyment. "Your purported killer makes a lot of mistakes."

"I think you were right, Mark. Les is too busy to think about this," Kelly announced, turning away from the window. Fehrenkamp caught her eye as she turned, and it was almost frightening. He had known her for the better part of ten years, had seen her tired, weary, frustrated in sims and briefings. But he had never seen pure, cold fury.

"Kelly, please. I think we all need to think about this calmly."

Kelly frowned, but joined Koskinen on the couch. "We've laid it out for you as calmly as we can, Les. I guess we were hoping that if you would trust us with a billion-dollar spacecraft, you would know that we wouldn't come to you with some half-baked story. This is fully baked."

"If I gave you the impression that I didn't believe you, or that I didn't want to listen, I'm sorry." He meant it. Still. "Who else have you told?"

"Don Drury knows part of the story," Mark said.

Fehrenkamp remembered Drury's hints to him that something was wrong. He wished now that he had pressed him for more information, not that the old bastard would have given it to him. "Which part?"

"That there was evidence that Joe had been doped, and that there might be people who wanted him dead."

"So it's the three of us and Drury," Fehrenkamp said.

Kelly said, "And, of course, the murderer himself."

"Yes," Fehrenkamp said. "Do you know who it is?"

"All the indications are that it's Calvin Stipe."

Whatever doubts Fehrenkamp had about Kelly's and Mark's story vanished at that point. Well, he still had questions about facts; he still didn't know what could be done. But emotionally he was now prepared to accept the ridiculous premise—that an astronaut had murdered another astronaut, and a second person besides. If there was ever an astronaut capable of cold-bloodedly killing a person, it was Stipe. "If true, it presents us with a number of challenges, doesn't it?"

"I don't suppose you can just yank him off his Mir flight?" Kelly said.

"Five days before launch? He doesn't even have a backup." Yes, there was an official NASA member of what the Russians called the second crew, but it was Jerry Rager, who was actually training for an International Space Station mission. He was only standing by in case of a catastrophe, such as Cal Stipe's slipping on the ice at Star Town and breaking his neck.

Of course, if *this* wasn't a catastrophe, it was damned close. "Are we agreed that this isn't something that can be made public?"

"You don't have to convince us," Mark said. He ran quickly through the various legal ambiguities—the accident in international waters, the fact of a preliminary board verdict of pilot error on Joe Buerhle's part, the lack of control over key evidence.

"We came to you for help, Les. The program can't stand a huge scandal right now. Or ever. But we can't just sit back and do *nothing*."

"I won't do nothing," Fehrenkamp said. "But I'm going to need some time." This was just another problem, and the way they got solved was with time and hard work. "From now on, I will handle this matter. You are to discuss it with no one, is that understood?"

They both nodded. He stood up. "Obviously I'll have questions for you in the next few days. It would be helpful if you both just wrote down what you've learned and where."

"Thanks, Les," Kelly said, looking relieved.

"I'm glad you trusted me enough to come to me." He clapped Koskinen on the shoulder. "We'll do something."

The moment they were gone he buzzed Valerie. "Tell Lisa Goode down at the Cape that I want her to plug Koskinen into the Cape Crusaders effective Monday. Call the MOD—McDowell—and see if we can't get the

STS-100 crew into sims." He wanted both of the astronaut crime stoppers to get busy.

"Then find me Don Drury."

While he waited for that call to come through, he dialed a number himself. Melinda Pruett at headquarters. If there was ever a time to use that channel, it was now.

CHAPTER 42

Each of the five times Cal Stipe had been launched into space was a little different. His first Shuttle mission, back in 1984, had gone very smoothly—the crew had launched the first time they had boarded the orbiter. The ride uphill, with Stipe on the flight deck in the rear left-hand seat, had been totally exhilarating.

The second one, in late 1985, had been anything but. For starters they had suffered through an RSLS—a redundant set launch sequence—abort, in which one of the Shuttle's main engines failed to come up to speed and the onboard computer had shut down the other two just a fraction of a second before the giant solid rocket motors had ignited. That hadn't been exhilarating; it had been downright frightening to wait, as Stipe had, on the mid-deck, feeling blind and helpless, with the orbiter swaying back and forth for something like fifteen minutes.

The third mission, early 1989, had been one of the first Shuttle launches to follow the hiatus caused by the *Challenger* disaster. For the first time Stipe had ridden into orbit wearing a launch escape suit, complete with parachute, instead of the relatively comfortable flight overalls. He had also been assigned as the jump master for emergency egress, the astronaut sitting right by the hatch on the mid-deck, responsible for blowing it and getting the crew hooked up to the slide pole and out the door.

On his fourth he had been back on the flight deck for ascent, with a clear view of the smoke and flame of launch, the launch tower and the entire coast of Florida rolling away, wondering just how easy it would be to force himself down through the interdeck access to the jump station if they happened to have an emergency that required bailout.

On his fifth he had been the flight engineer—the mission specialist 2, looking right over the shoulders of the commander and pilot, and he had been so busy making sure they were on the right cards that he hadn't actually thought about emergency egress.

Here was his sixth, and it was completely different.

For one thing, he was wearing a Russian Sokol pressure suit, a lightweight rig that had a soft helmet. For another, he was squeezed into a Soyuz command module, literally perched on the shoulder of the commander, his young friend Alexander Alexeyevich Shabarov, a thirty-three-year-old Russian air force pilot making his first space flight. Not that the position was uncomfortable; far from it. Like the early Mercury and Gemini spacecraft, Soyuz had seats that were molded to the shape of the occupant.

This made life difficult in many ways. The crew launching in this Soyuz would be returning in an entirely different vehicle some months down the line. These seats, then, would have to be removed and replaced with those made for the current Mir crew. That would be one of Stipe's jobs, in fact, once he reached the Russian station.

On the other side of Sasha-1 was Sasha-2, Alexander Vladimirovich Dergunov, who was forty-two, a chain-smoking civilian engineer from the Energiya Space Production Company, and the veteran of two visits to Mir already. The Russian system of having a rookie commanding a crew of two veterans struck Stipe as strange, but they had done things this way for years.

There had been a whole different set of prelaunch traditions, too. There was no breakfast for the crew with a cake, for example. There was, instead, a march out of the bus bringing the crew to the launch complex, and an address to the members of the State Commission, led by some Russian three-star general. Sasha-1 had handled this very well, saying something about "fulfilling the goals of the Russian Federation."

When the bus headed to the pad, Stipe learned about an even more curious Russian tradition: they stopped the bus halfway so the crew could clamber out, unzip their suits, and urinate against the wheels!

It had been explained to Stipe that Yuri Gagarin did this on his way to the very first Vostok launch back in 1961, and apparently it had been done— for luck—ever since.

Forget that it brought no good luck to Vladimir Komarov, whose Soyuz 1 crashed in 1967, or to Dobrovolsky, Volkov and Patsayev, who were found dead in Soyuz 11 in 1971. Maybe they hadn't urinated on the way to the pad! Stipe wished he had asked.

There was no countdown, per se. Yes, Soyuz TM-28 had a target launch time, and there were certain prelaunch events that had to happen at certain times, in the proper sequence. But the voice in Stipe's headphones merely announced certain milestones, the most recent being "Fifteen minutes."

The whole process seemed less cluttered—quieter, more routine than preparations for Shuttle launches. There were fewer people in the crew. And since most Russians assumed Stipe, as a foreigner, was not fluent in the language—a mistake—he was largely left alone.

As he probably would be on Mir for the next six months or more.

That was fine. That was exactly what Cal Stipe wanted. He had spent most of the past year in Russia, through a cold, endless winter and an all-too-brief, though beautiful, summer.

It had only been on his trips back to Houston that he had felt unhappy. More than unhappy. Furious at things and people. Especially this last trip—

"For Granite-3. Are you listening, Granite-3?"

That was the voice of the Russian communications operator in far-off Korolev, outside Moscow, at the flight control center. Granite-3 was Stipe's call sign.

"Granite-3 is listening," he acknowledged in Russian.

"We are connecting to Houston . . . ," the operator said.

Houston! There was no scheduled comm session between Stipe and Houston at this stage! He could feel his heart rate quicken. . . .

"Cal, this is Les Fehrenkamp." Fehrenkamp? He never called a flight crew. *Never.*

Was he going to stop the launch? Could he do that?

"Nice to hear from you, Les." He kept his voice calm.

"We know you're going to be on orbit for a record amount of time, and just wanted to take this last opportunity to wish you a safe trip. And to ask you to stay loose. Plans could change."

What did that mean, plans could change? Of course they could change! Shannon Lucid had wound up spending six more weeks on orbit than originally scheduled. Foale had almost been brought home early. Why was Fehrenkamp telling him this?

"You know me, Les. Mr. Flexible."

"I'm counting on that, Cal. See you when you get back."

And that was the end of it. "Phone call from the president?" Sasha-2 said. Unlike Sasha-1, Sasha-2 spoke fairly fluent English.

"Just my boss," Stipe told him. What did Fehrenkamp know? What did he think he knew?

"Five minutes," the operator told them. They lowered their helmet face-plates. Sasha-1 flicked the rubber ball hung on a string from the control panel in front of him. They would know they were reaching microgravity when it floated.

Stipe could hear the wind brushing against the side of the spacecraft, even through the launch shroud. It had not only been windy but cold at Baikonur this morning. A Shuttle would not be launching in these conditions.

"Here we go," Sasha-2 said. It was a single Russian word, *poyekhali*, the same thing Gagarin had said at ignition on the first Vostok.

From far below them came a rumbling as twenty engines ignited and began to build up thrust. Another few seconds, and with the feel of an elevator rising, the Soyuz and its carrier rocket began to lift off.

Stipe wished he had Fehrenkamp on the line right now. Because whatever he'd had in mind . . . it was too late now.

CHAPTER 43

"All right, that sure as shit didn't work," Rick Delahunt said over the radio. The tension in his voice was apparent; it was that throat-strangling dryness you never heard from Shuttle commanders in flights, and a good thing, too.

"Concur," Scott McDowell said. "We'll do a data dump and move on."

Delahunt was the commander of STS-97, a Shuttle mission scheduled to carry one of the first pieces of the International Space Station into orbit ninety days from now. He and his crew of five had just killed themselves. Fortunately for them, they were lying on their backs in the motion-base simulator in Building 5, not an orbiter ascending from the Cape.

A crew was usually put together nine months to a year before a scheduled launch. By that time even a real Worm—a recently graduated ASCAN—had a basic understanding of Shuttle systems and operations. The goal over the next year was to train that person to perform a specific mission . . . to deploy a satellite, to operate a specific suite of experiments, to do an EVA . . . or some combination of all three.

Most of this training took the form of simulations. In the first weeks the crew did single-system training, working with instructors on various phases of Shuttle and payload systems. Then came mission sims, where the whole crew would be brought together in a mockup of the cockpit, at the mercy of the simulation team.

Four months before launch the joint integrated sims started, and instead of merely dealing with a sim team of four to eight people, a crew had to perform for a flight director and his whole team, which could number up to seventy-five. A JIS was not the time a crew wanted to be seen making mistakes. And it was just the time when McDowell and every other flight director wanted nothing more than to have them die by their own mistakes.

The sad truth was that Scott McDowell, like other flight directors, *loved* to kill astronauts. It was not now, and never had been, personal. Flight directors treated astronauts like shit for professional reasons. The tougher they were on the ground, the easier things would go on orbit. That was the theory, at least.

According to the unwritten and unspoken rules of this game, they weren't to be killed by a big, unsolvable problem. No *Challenger*-style O-ring failures, no tiles unzipping from the underside of the orbiter during reentry. There were no contingency cards for disasters.

What you wanted were *problems*, like a propellant leak in the orbital maneuvering system that occurs just prior to the final de-orbit burn. The crew takes a minute too long to restring the computer controlling the fuel feeds, so they miss the burn opportunity. Just then the weather at KSC turns bad, and there's a late-winter storm at Edwards. There's your crew . . . sitting there with egg on its face, asking that delicious question, "All right, Flight, any suggestions?"

The best, of course, was simply having them kill themselves. The Shuttle main engines were a dream for this kind of malfunction. There were three on every orbiter, and they were not only among the most powerful ever developed anywhere in the forty years of spaceflight but, unlike the others, they were nominally reusable. That is, they came back from a mission and with a million dollars of refurbishment, flew again.

They were tricky beasts, too. Machines that were designed to combine supercold liquid oxygen and hydrogen in a controlled explosion. Millions of pounds of the stuff in *seconds*. The turbine pumps alone were a regular triumph of engineering.

So it was entirely fair to throw a main engine malf into an ascent. Redline on one of turbines . . . shut down an engine. Oops, didn't get it shut down in time . . . something broke in another engine, too. With two engines out you couldn't even make a transatlantic abort; you had to come back to the Cape.

And if you were on that wonderful fifty-one-degree trajectory for a space station mission, there were even more opportunities to find yourself out of luck. McDowell had listened as Delahunt's pilot reported, calmly, two engines out at four minutes into the ascent, a point where the Shuttle would be well out over the Atlantic. Their only option was to go through pitch around and start burning the surviving engine to make sure they had the energy to get back to the Cape. And, of course, they didn't, because they had launched with tailwinds, which were now headwinds. McDowell had enjoyed the long minute, two minutes, three minutes, until Delahunt finally admitted that they weren't going to make it and it was time to think about bailing out. . . .

"Relax, Rick," McDowell told Delahunt. "This is just the first of many ascents in the first of many sims." Which was true. But everyone working the sim would be thinking, If this were a real flight, these guys would be *dead*. Or, if they were very lucky, floating in the middle of the goddamn Atlantic . . . but the orbiter would be gone! A two-billion-dollar vehicle, one fourth of the entire fleet! Why? Because they didn't see some approaching redline on one of the engines. Because they weren't fast enough at shutting it down.

The voices from inside the simulator were clipped, because Delahunt and his pilot were feeling the stares from the two mission specialists behind them, saying, *Our lives are in your hands, guys. Try not to kill us for real.*

"You didn't kill them already," Carl Strahan said. As the lead flight director, he had been quietly monitoring the sim. Now he stood next to McDowell at the console, hands idly playing with his unplugged headset.

"They killed themselves, Carl."

"You threw a main engine malf on their first sim? Jesus, Scott, don't you think that's a little harsh?"

"If they're going to get a main engine malf, it's going to be in the first five minutes of a flight," McDowell said, feeling defensive. "Besides, isn't this how we crystallize them?"

Crystallization was the point at which a Shuttle crew not only knew its procedures but also trusted itself to take the right steps automatically. You certainly wouldn't launch a crew that hadn't crystallized; you also didn't want them crystallized too early. It was a delicate process, like growing an orchid.

"It's also how we destroy them." Strahan was the lead director for STS-97; McDowell was merely the flight director for ascent and entry. "You're sure this application isn't affecting you?"

"A month ago you were afraid I was going to be too soft."

"Hey, it could have gone either way." Strahan smiled. "Maybe you don't want any of us to think you've turned to the dark side of the Force. The word is *overcompensation*."

McDowell shook his head, but wondered if he *was* trying a little too hard to prove he was still the toughest son of a bitch in the valley. The system made it hard not to want to whale on crews. Because of the rotation, McDowell had come off STS-94 just as STS-97 was going into the joint integrated sim phase. So he was, in effect, meeting this new crew just when his tolerance for astronaut arrogance—never notably high—was at its lowest.

Astronaut arrogance hit its peak about halfway through a mission, when the crew realized it had (*a*) survived the trip uphill to orbit, and (*b*) was no longer so sick and miserable that it could barely function, and most importantly, (*c*) was *up here* on orbit while Flight was *down there* in Houston. What was Flight going to do if the crew did things its way . . . call a cop?

If the crew had a good landing, the debriefings would be a nightmare. Every decision made on the ground that had not, for one reason or another, worked on orbit would be mercilessly dissected. McDowell had seen rookie astronauts who, prior to launch, had been so cooperative you'd think they were humble payload specialists, turn into raving maniacs. *I told you guys this equipment would be a fucking problem on orbit, and it was.*

"You may be right," he told Strahan

"I know I'm right. Frankly, I'm a little worried about you as the lead on 100."

"That's still a long way off." It was only November; the launch wasn't scheduled until June.

"I know. Just give me the Scott McDowell we knew and loved. 'He was a cruel man, but fair.' " Strahan was a fan of the old *Monty Python's Flying Circus* TV series.

The next ten ascents went well, and McDowell could hear Delahunt's team coming back to life. He could just imagine the Navy captain marching his team out into the beautiful autumn afternoon, perhaps for some midday jogging.

As he headed for the stairs he found Kelly Gessner waiting for him. "Buy you a salad, sailor?" she said.

"Sure. If you've got the time. . . ."

They headed south, past the old and new Buildings 4, and talked about the upcoming STS-100, which would not become McDowell's prime mission for several months, at least. Nevertheless, he was still interested in how the various timelines, the mission-specific software and the crew training schedules were shaping up. Everything seemed to be fine. "The only problem,'' Kelly said, ''is that this is probably going to be the last Shuttle-Mir docking, and already you can see people looking past you to the International Space Station.''

''Well, I wish I knew why we were going to Mir for the ninth or tenth time, when we should be concentrating on the ISS.''

They were in line at the cafeteria now. McDowell looked longingly at the Mexican food special. Not today, alas. ''Come on, Scott,'' Kelly said. ''How are the Russians going to stay in the space business if we don't help them out?''

''Who needs them?''

''They're building the station core, aren't they? It's going to be pretty hard to start hooking up our pieces if we don't have that.''

''We could have built our own in the same amount of time, and you know it.''

They sat down near the window. The cafeteria seemed crowded today, but perhaps it was every day; McDowell was rarely in the place. ''Well, then,'' Kelly said quietly, ''maybe we're just making a special trip to pick up Cal Stipe.''

''I've got a better idea: let's just leave him there.''

Kelly gave him one of those looks. ''Don't tell me *you* have a problem with Cal.''

''He's fine, if you like the arrogant, manipulative type. He cooked up this long-term mission all by himself and sold it to HQ.''

''Come on.''

''You and Joe must have talked about it. He and Stipe had a titanic fight about the whole thing.''

''I was probably busy training. He never mentioned it.''

''This was months ago. Joe was never a big fan of the Russian business, even before he became chief of CB. I think he saw what Stipe was doing and decided that it had to be stopped.'' He realized he wasn't as hungry anymore. Poor Joe. ''I guess it doesn't make any difference now.''

''No, I suppose not.''

''So,'' he said, ''what did you want to talk to me about?''

''You're the lead flight director on my next mission. Do I need any more reason to talk to you?''

''You took me out to lunch.'' He smiled, because he had a pretty good idea why Kelly had just happened to find him. ''In some cultures, that would be considered a date.''

"In that case, I've enjoyed myself and hope you have, too."

"We could go on a real date."

"Would this be before or after you break up with your Boeing honey?"

Sometimes it was easy to underestimate Kelly. He never knew what she knew. Still. "However you'd like it."

She just started laughing. "Scott, you are a genuinely bad man."

"I'm trying to be open and honest. Isn't that what women want?"

"I guess it all depends. Telling a woman that you'll, uh, overlap her with another one is open and honest, I suppose. But not, really, the kind of thing I want to hear. And your Boeing honey probably doesn't want to hear that, either."

"You and I have been circling each other for years. Nothing was going to happen as long as Joe was in the picture, but he's not. Don't tell me you haven't wondered. . . ."

She wadded up her napkin, dropped it onto her plate, and leaned close to him. "It was nice talking to you. Let's not have another conversation like this again." Then she got up and walked out.

McDowell leaned back. Had that gone badly? Or had it been perfect? He would know in the next few weeks; he was patient in these matters.

There was a long time to go before the launch of STS-100.

CHAPTER 44

"Look at all this stuff." Viktor Kondratko shook his head at the piles of books and loose papers that had grown on Mark's desk in the past week. It was all from the Shuttle flight data file, material on ascents, including the very key configuration of switches in the cockpit.

"Each Shuttle flight generates more paper than it carries in payload," Mark said.

"Is that true?"

"I have no idea, but it sure sounds plausible."

"I'm only surprised that you haven't taken over the twins' desks." The twins were their office mates, two veteran astronauts who happened to share a chance physical resemblance—both were slim, balding military men with mustaches—and nothing else. One was a laid-back Navy flight surgeon who was training as a payload commander for a Spacelab mission; the other was an edgy Army special ops helicopter pilot on a detached assignment as assistant to Dr. Hutchins, the center's director. Neither could be found in this office more than twice a month.

"The moment I did, of course, they'd move back in."

"Is that what you call Murphy's Law? 'Everything that can go wrong will go wrong'?"

"Koskinen's Corollary. 'The moment you try to pull a fast one it's already too late.' "

Kondratko hefted one of the books. "I should review some of this material, too." He was not remotely enthusiastic about it, and quickly dropped the book back on the pile. "When do you go to Florida?"

"Monday, after the pilots' meeting." His new schedule had finally put him back on track. Effective Monday he was assigned full-time to the flight support branch of the astronaut office, specifically with the astronaut support team—best known as the Cape Crusaders or C-squares—at the Kennedy Space Center. He was to spend all next week at the Cape with the four other Crusaders, one of whom he would ultimately replace. His new boss in flight support had told Mark he would probably be spending three days a week there for at least six months, possibly as much as a year. Only then would Mark be likely to be assigned to a flight crew, though it was just as likely that he would have to work a second tech job before that happened.

He didn't care. Starting the tech assignment was one small step out of ASCAN limbo, one giant leap out of ejectee hell.

There was a knock at the open door. It was Kelly Gessner, looking intent. "Mark, do you have a minute?"

"I am needed in Building 9," Kondratko said. He smiled at Kelly. "Door closed?"

"Yes."

With a wink at Mark, Kondratko was gone.

"What's up, stranger?" Mark said. He and Kelly had not exchanged more than half a dozen words since their meeting in Fehrenkamp's office, now almost two weeks in the past. It certainly hadn't been Mark's choice. Kelly had been sent out of town for several days on a speaking tour. And Mark had been concentrating on a new job and a new car. There had been communication, of a sort: Kelly had left several messages on Mark's phone machine, complaining of conditions in New Mexico or was it New Hampshire? Wherever she was speaking from at the time. Mark had left some E-mail in return.

"I've been bad."

For more than a couple of seconds Mark thought Kelly was kidding. "So you came here to be spanked . . . ?"

It was clear she wasn't kidding. She sat down on one of the twins' chairs, and realized there was dust on the arms. "God, this guy isn't around much." She brushed off the dust. "Fehrenkamp told us to let him handle our problem." She looked at Mark and raised one brow. "I got tired of waiting."

"What have you done?"

"I spoke to Scott McDowell. I didn't tell him why, so, naturally, he thinks it's because I want to sleep with him."

"Well, thank God for that." He said it lightly, but the idea disturbed him. Jealousy again. His primary emotion.

"He just . . . volunteered all this stuff about Joe and Cal Stipe. I mean, we were looking for a motive, and there it was."

"And what was the motive?"

"Joe was really against the whole Russian involvement in the program. The international stuff. He saw that Cal was in bed with those people and tried to do something about it. Stipe knew."

"And that was the reason he killed him?"

"Would you like it better if it was over a woman? Or a card game? Or a . . . a wallet? That's what most murders are about.

"Come on, Mark. This was a big deal. This was one of those future-of-the-human-race decisions. You must know that if we don't build a space station now, it's never going to be built. Not by this society, anyway. The U.S. and Europe are going to be too old."

He had not thought of it in those terms, but saw the truth. It was as if the United States had had the will to go to the Moon, and been so exhausted by the experience that the business of building a habitat or laboratory in Earth orbit—an easier task, in comparison—was too much.

That was too simplistic. The Apollo program had been driven by the Cold War. It had been run by people like Don Drury, who had learned their lessons about life in World War II. And even with a Cold War and a bunch of hard-driving vets, Apollo could just as easily have never happened. All that would have been necessary was for Nixon to have been elected in 1960 instead of Kennedy.

"So Joe Buerhle's death was more than just a murder . . . it was a po-litical act. An assassination."

"Yeah, I guess that's it." She drew her knees up and hugged them and, for a moment, seemed younger, more fragile. "What bothers me is that I could find this out fairly quickly. Les Fehrenkamp could have, too, with all his sources and contacts. But he didn't. Or, if he did, he didn't do anything."

"Except let Cal Stipe get launched to Mir."

"Yeah."

"Where, legally, he can't be touched." Mark was almost blushing. "Uh, I've been bad, too."

"What a couple of comedians." She shook her head. "What have *you* done?"

"I called up one of the legal affairs people at headquarters. I told her I had a letter from some high school kid in Marshalltown, Iowa, asking about crime in space."

"What were you supposed to tell your correspondent in Marshalltown?"

"Under the various treaties—United Nations things about return of astronauts, all that—a spacecraft is legally considered an extension of a sovereign nation, even if a chunk of it lands in your backyard. So even if Fehrenkamp had the evidence to get an indictment against Stipe, we'd still be nowhere, because he's legally resident in a foreign country, and—"

"And we don't have an extradition treaty with Russia." She smiled. "I may have asked a few questions myself."

"I think the problem could be solved, but only by dragging HQ into it, then the State Department, then the Russian Space Agency and their foreign affairs people. . . . I mean, you might as well call *Sixty Minutes*."

"And nobody wants this story to get out," she said, with a touch of what could only have been bitterness. It was enough to make Mark second-guess himself: why didn't he want this story out? Who was he protecting?

The answer was obvious, of course. Kelly had just mentioned it: the future of the space program. That was the end that justified these particular means.

Besides . . . there was the remote, but still real, possibility that he and Kelly had this *all wrong*. An unsupported charge that got to the public would do just as much damage to the space program as the real thing. More, perhaps, because then NASA would seem not only evil but incompetent.

"Still," Mark said, "I'm surprised Fehrenkamp didn't do *something*. Why didn't he cook up some reason to delay the launch? He could have had one of the doctors diagnose Stipe with a virus. . . ."

"There's something very odd about the whole Stipe-Fehrenkamp dynamic," Kelly said. "I've never been able to figure it out." She drummed her fingers on the desktop. "I'd better get going. Meeting with the High Commander."

"Who?"

"Goslin. This assignment has gone right to his head. Not in a bad way; it's mostly funny. But the whole crew is supposed to be in his office at three to discuss designs for the patch. I had a memo on my desk telling me about it."

"Is this typical?"

"Not entirely. Most pilots get to be commanders in the normal course of events. But Goslin was passed over for so long . . ." She abruptly changed the subject. "What about you? Down to the Cape?"

"Yes."

"Well, then, what about us?" Mark couldn't believe what he'd just heard. Before he could respond, Kelly went on: "What should we be *doing*?"

"Following Fehrenkamp's orders, in our fashion, I guess." Had she noticed the expression on his face? If she had, was that bad? Christ, this was like being in high school. "I was thinking I might talk to Thompson, that guy from the NTSB, when I get back. You should come along."

"I'd love to. Let's take him out and get him drunk. Maybe he'll know what to do."

"In the meantime, well, we know where Stipe is at any given moment. We wait for Fehrenkamp to do something."

"That's another thing that worries me," Kelly said, standing up. "Whatever it is he ultimately decides to do, we'll never see it coming. He's Fehrenkamp."

CHAPTER 45

Kelly had been looking forward to seeing Mark, to talking with him, for a week. And yet she was relieved to escape from his office. There was no sense fooling herself, either. *It was all because of Joe Buerhle.*

When was she going to tell Mark that she and Joe had been lovers? When they finally went on a date? Maybe midway through the first entree? Or should she wait until their wedding night? "Honey, I've got a little confession to make." God.

Had she actually thought "wedding night"? That was getting ahead of herself. Next thing she'd be writing "Kelly Koskinen" in her notebook. The name sounded as though it belonged to a woman doing Action Weather in Birmingham, Alabama, or maybe the Quad Cities.

She had grown too used to treating the relationship with Joe as if it were illicit, as if he'd been a married man. Skulking around had gotten to be a way of life.

She could have told Mark the moment they met. But, then, it would have sounded ridiculous. "Hi, yeah, we're on this board together even though I was sleeping with the victim. Shh. Nobody's supposed to know."

Well, how about when she picked him up at the hospital when Allyson was killed? "I'm really sorry, Mark, but I know just how you feel. You see, I lost Joe Buerhle—" It had already been too late then.

No, at some point in their early meetings at the Air Patch she should have taken him aside and said, "Mark, I'm afraid I haven't been entirely open with you." And, for that matter, with NASA in general and Les Fehrenkamp in particular. It would have been embarrassing, yes, but how embarrassing was this?

What she needed to do was march back into Mark's office, close the door, and tell him. To her surprise, she found herself doing that very thing.

Except that there was no answer to her knock. "If you're looking for Mark, he just took off," Shannon told her.

"Is he coming back this afternoon?"

"I don't think so. He mentioned something about test-driving a new bike."

"Kelly!" Steve Goslin was calling her from the door to his office. "We're starting."

She had tried. She had wanted to do the right thing.

The proposed mission patch for STS-100 was heavily symbolic. Well, all of them were. This one was symbolic in a way that made Kelly uncomfortable.

The patch showed the Mir space station against a black background with a sliver of blue Earth below and an orbiter above. It was ovoid, with five names bordering the image: "Goslin Dieckhaus" across the top, "Freeh Gessner O'Riordan" across the bottom. There was a little European Space Agency logo between "Gessner" and "O'Riordan." All very standard.

Except that the Mir looked like a cross. And the orbiter's lines had been softened so it looked like a damned angel. The artist had even airbrushed a plume from the reaction control system rockets, which suggested a halo. Ten points' deduction for inaccuracy: an RCS plume shot out a hundred feet, like a gassy stream from a hose.

Kelly looked at Jeff Dieckhaus, who seemed enthusiastic. "I'd be proud to wear that, Steve," he told Goslin. Well, pilots did have to find a way to get along with their commanders; either Dieckhaus didn't care about the patch or he was another Holy Roller like Goslin.

"Thanks. Any other thoughts?"

David Freeh raised an eyebrow, which made him look like *Star Trek*'s Mr. Spock. "Interesting symbolism," he said, choosing, as a space rookie, to stay noncommittal.

Goslin turned to Kelly. "What do you think?"

"Well, the Mir configuration is out of date. Remember what happened a couple of years ago?" One of the early Shuttle-Mir docking missions had designed a patch which had a rather fanciful version of the Mir station, which some Russian space officials took as insulting. (It happened to be released the very week another NASA official, in a communication with a pair of Russian cosmonauts, called them by the wrong names.) On the scale of international incidents, with the Cuban Missile Crisis rated a ten, this was a one-point-five. But NASA didn't like international incidents of any kind, and HQ had landed hard on the crew.

"I suppose you're right," Goslin said.

"And you don't have Cal Stipe's name in there." Kelly was enjoying this a bit too much. "He may not be an up crew member, but he's coming *down* with us."

Goslin picked up the sketch. "It's only preliminary." He sighed. "Besides, I showed it Fehrenkamp and he said we might not be able to use it looking quite like that."

"Did he give you a specific objection?" Kelly asked. Now she was starting to feel sorry for Goslin. The design was clearly his—probably executed by his wife. She didn't really look down on religion or God. She believed in some kind of God herself. Just . . . not Steve Goslin's. She also sympathized with anyone who received one of Les Fehrenkamp's "suggestions."

"No. He just told me to sit tight, get into generic training, that the only thing about this mission that was set in stone was the fact that we were going to Mir. Anything else might change."

"Including crew members?" That was Freeh again, suddenly insecure.

"I asked him the same thing. 'Especially crew members,' he said."

Kelly knew it was hopeless to second-guess a Fehrenkamp rumor. "Especially crew members." It could mean that one or more was being added. It could also mean that one or more was being removed.

Was this a message to Kelly? Keep quiet or you lose the mission? Or something else?

Maybe it was time she sent Les Fehrenkamp a message of her own—

From the *Houston Chronicle*, November 25, 1998

CHIEF ASTRONAUT CRITICIZED RUSSIAN
ROLE IN SPACE STATION
By Brad Whitsett, *Chronicle* Staff Reporter

Joseph Buerhle, the astronaut killed in last month's crash of a T-38 jet in the Gulf of Mexico, was a bitter opponent of Russian involvement in the International Space Station (ISS) Program.

Buerhle, the chief of the astronaut office at the time of his death, was apparently planning to do battle with high-ranking NASA officials over what he termed "a disaster in the making." The statement is contained in a preliminary draft memo obtained by the *Chronicle*.

The Russian Space Agency is managing the construction of the ISS Service Module (SM), a module that is to serve as a key component of the station. The SM has been subject to delays caused by the ongoing financial crisis in Russia, though it is still officially scheduled for launch this coming April.

"NASA and the current administration made a horrendous political decision on what should have been a straightforward engineering matter," said Ian Harvey of A-Team, a local ad hoc group that has been publicly critical of ISS management. "We're supporting Mir, which is not only falling apart, it has proven itself to be dangerous, and spending millions to 'internationalize' the ISS, when that money could have been used to build it ourselves, and build it better."

Buerhle's documents are also critical of agreements to augment NASA's astronaut corps with international crew members.

A NASA spokesman had no comment.

CHAPTER 46

Don Drury read about Joe Buerhle's memo when he picked up *USA Today* in the El Paso airport. The story was on page 2, thank God, though just the fact that it got picked up by the McPaper was bad enough.

Les Fehrenkamp must be throwing a fit.

Drury picked up his car and headed north toward Las Cruces. This was a drive he made twice a month of late, and it never bored him the way going home to Houston had. Of course, he had only lived in this barren corner of New Mexico and Texas for a couple of years. There were fewer bad memories here—just big skies and open spaces.

It had been the open spaces that brought the Army out here in the first place, over fifty years ago, to fire off its captured V-2 rockets. They had taken a corner of the Fort Bliss artillery range and expanded it north, including the Trinity site, where the first atom bomb had been set off. Drury would have enjoyed being at White Sands in those days, when his work at Langley was all serious aeronautical engineering, and rockets were comic book stuff.

Eventually, of course, bigger rockets had required a bigger test range, and the military had gone to the Florida coast. But White Sands had survived all these years as a home to antimissile systems tests, small sounding rockets, death rays, and now the X-39 Spacelifter, a prototype for a comic book spaceship, intended to blast itself into orbit without dropping pieces of itself along the way, then to come down the way it went up . . . tail-first to a concrete pad, much as the Apollo lunar module had settled to the surface of the Moon.

Drury still wasn't sure the Spacelifter was going to lead to a real spaceship any time soon. For one thing, it was horribly underfunded, drawing money from NASA, from several offices in the Air Force and Navy, and even from a couple of corporations. For another, the forty-foot-tall Space-lifter was still little more than a scale model. Its engines were capable of lifting it several thousand feet in the air and maybe up to several hundred miles an hour. That was a far cry from the 17,500 miles an hour needed to reach orbit.

But it was worth a try. And working on it out here at lonely White Sands took Drury back to the days when there was no NASA, no big centers.

No scandals.

When he got in range of Las Cruces Drury used his cell phone to call home, reaching his wife and asking her if the *Albuquerque Journal* carried any more on the Buerhle situation. Yes, but it was all more of the same. Nothing about the crash. Nothing about the investigation. No mention of Don Drury, in fact. He offered Ginny his undying love and gratitude, then hung up.

He was essentially through with the board. Yes, a formal report was being written, and in several weeks that would have to be delivered, and there would undoubtedly be a press conference. But the preliminary report had gone out into the world. There had been no challenges, no dissent from anyone, including those two astronauts.

This business of a Joe Buerhle memo bothered Drury, though. It was just the kind of nasty story that would attract some investigative reporter, not one of the local yokels who was either in love with NASA or intimidated by it. Someone who could easily make a link between Joe's criticisms and his untimely death.

Investigative reporters had to know how things got done in the real world, that people often sat around discussing actions that were unrealistic, stupid, even illegal. Drury still remembered the investigation of the *Challenger* disaster, how pathetic those NASA guys from Marshall had sounded when their telephone conferences from the night before the fatal launch were played publicly.

What bothered Drury was knowing that an editorial meeting at the *Washington Post* wouldn't sound much different. Was that why reporters went crazy if you tried to tape their interviews with you? He also knew that his opinion meant nothing. Whether or not there was anything dicey about Joe Buerhle's death, just the *appearance* of scandal would be fatal to NASA, an organization that had to justify its existence all over again every year.

Had those astronauts leaked the memo? Not likely. Astronauts had a vested interest in the survival of NASA, in their chances of flying in space. That was the carrot that kept them in line.

Hell, it could have come from some secretary in the astronaut office. In any case, it was worth a call to the Johnson Space Center. "Les Fehrenkamp," he said.

It didn't take long. "You were next on my phone list," Fehrenkamp said. "Where are you, anyway?"

"Highway Twenty-five, about three miles south of Las Cruces."

"I take it you saw the story on Joe Buerhle."

"I did."

"Is this what you tried to warn me about?"

"No, it isn't." As briefly as he could, Drury told Fehrenkamp about the suspicions raised by Koskinen and Gessner, the fact that someone had, in fact, killed Joe Buerhle. It still sounded faintly unreal, but, then, so did many things these days. "I did nothing with that because they never took the next step. But I would hate for you to get any unpleasant surprises, given what's in the papers."

Fehrenkamp seemed to be weighing his answer. Or else Drury was losing the connection. "Les?"

"I'm here." Another pause. "Well, obviously it would have been better to have this information several weeks ago—though I can understand your reluctance to be specific. What would you do?"

"I wouldn't waste much time looking for the leaker; try to run this thing to ground, see if there is any connection. You won't know what the potential damage is until you get the facts."

"Suppose there is a connection? Suppose there's evidence that one of our people is a murderer?"

The thought actually chilled Drury. "No one can ever know that, Les. I can't emphasize that enough." There was nothing but static on the line. "Les?"

He'd lost him.

CHAPTER 47

Mark's week in Florida was a dream—and a nightmare. A dream because it was the first time since becoming a Worm that he felt he was making a contribution to the program. Working as a C-square certainly made him feel like a real astronaut. The orbiter *Columbia* was currently in the assembly building prior to being rolled out to Pad 39B, and Mark had been allowed inside the cockpit. He dressed in the whites of a pad crew member and crawled through the side hatch, to be confronted for the first time—he hoped not the last—by a world turned sideways. The orbiter's two cabins were oriented like an airliner's—the local vertical being perpendicular to the direction of flight. Since the direction of flight on ascent was up, the cabins were tilted on their backs. The seats for the three mid-deck crew members appeared to be mounted on the left wall and suspended from the floor. The lockers containing food and equipment were on the ceiling. The access hatch leading up to the flight deck was to Mark's right.

It took some getting used to. So did the smell, a combination of gym socks, machine oil and garlic from someone's lunch. Nevertheless, he managed—with Lisa Goode's expert guidance—to snake his way to the flight deck and pull himself up to the right-hand pilot's seat. Lying on his back, he could easily picture himself on Pad 39B. Instead of a covered window, he would be looking at blue sky and launch structure.

That was the dream.

The nightmare was the fact that it was Thanksgiving week, and the work was lonely as well as tedious. Since the actual flight crew was off in the simulators in Houston, the C-squares were required to be present for all vehicle testing and countdown demonstrations. This meant a lot of hours sitting around waiting. Then there was the matter of living in Cocoa Beach and environs, a wide area along the big beach highway dotted by fast-food places and motels. It made Clear Lake feel like Paris.

Nevertheless, when Mark flew back to Houston early Friday afternoon—backseat with Major Andrew Szurlie, USAF, one of the other C-squares, giving Mark his weekly flying quota—he knew he'd be able to handle the job. He even looked forward to returning.

He made the obligatory flyby of the astronaut office, even though it meant taking a major detour. Being absent for almost five days—something which would happen more and more—felt like returning to a grade school classroom after an illness. Things seemed to have changed in small ways.

He also hoped he might run into Kelly. They had exchanged brief E-mails, hers to Mark full of advice on the C-square job, Mark's to Kelly consisting of questions. When did she start sims with her crew? *First one this week.* Why was Goslin weirded out? *Still thinking Fehrenkamp or the Shuttle program managers were going to throw him a curve.* What were people saying about the Buerhle article? *The few people who made comments seemed to agree. The international astronauts pretended to ignore it.*

And what the hell was Fehrenkamp doing? *Your guess is as good as mine.*

Kondratko was in the office, looking uncharacteristically serious. "Just in time," he said by way of greeting.

"In time for what?"

"Our meeting with the big boss."

"Who? Fehrenkamp?"

Viktor nodded. "I was called out of my sim and told to meet you here. We are to go to Building 2, ninth floor immediately."

Mark could feel his self-confidence leaking away. He had just started his technical assignment. Surely he couldn't have screwed it up already. Kondratko wouldn't be involved in any discussions about the Buerhle matter.

There was no possible reason—no possible *good* reason—why Fehrenkamp should want to talk to Mark and Kondratko. "Do you have any idea what this is all about?"

"None."

"You look worried."

Viktor dismissed that by waving his hand. "I'm sad today for other reasons. It's my daughter's birthday. Lenochka is six. She's in Moscow and I'm here. Today I wonder why."

"When do you get to go home again?"

"At Christmas, provided the 91 mission doesn't slip anymore."

"It must be tough, spending a year away from your family."

Viktor shrugged. "Sometimes it's tougher than others."

Mark dropped his briefcase on his desk and glanced out the window, which looked toward Building 2. He was sure he saw Fehrenkamp standing there . . . watching them.

Go right in," Valerie, Fehrenkamp's secretary, told them. "He's expecting you."

Of course, Mark thought; he watched us walk over here!

Fehrenkamp was seated at his desk when they entered. He didn't get up, didn't shake hands, but merely nodded them to the couch. "Thanks for coming in on such short notice." Then he rocked back in his chair. "How do you two like your current assignments?"

Mark couldn't help glancing at Kondratko. "I just started mine this week," he said, trying to sound relaxed. "I like what I've seen of it so far."

"And I'm very happy as a capcom," Kondratko said.

Fehrenkamp raised his eyebrows. "So, if I told both of you that I needed you for something else, you'd be disappointed."

Mark looked at Kondratko again. What the hell was this all about? Which Commandment applied now? "I, ah, don't think we're saying that."

"We're part of the team," Kondratko said. He sounded just as craven as any American ASCAN.

Fehrenkamp smiled. "Good. Because I need you both to come fly a mission for me."

The room was so silent for a moment that you could hear Valerie the secretary shuffling papers in the outer office. "Great!" Mark heard himself saying, knowing there was something damned odd about this.

Kondratko said, "Which mission?"

"STS-100, our last Mir docking."

"I thought the crew had already been assigned," Mark said.

The beginnings of a smile, nothing more, appeared on Fehrenkamp's face. "Crews have been expanded in the past. There's plenty of time for you two to integrate with the other five and get ready."

Mark's heart was beginning to beat faster as the implications of Fehrenkamp's words struck him. He was getting a mission assignment! He was going to be sitting on Pad 39B, and within a few months!

"I'm going to hate myself for asking this," Mark said, "but we're still technically astronaut candidates. Isn't there some rule . . ." He didn't want to say, A rule that prevents us from flying. He also realized that he and Kondratko would be jumping over about half of the members of the previous ASCAN group, who had yet to be assigned a flight. That wasn't going to make people happy.

"Technically. But anyone can fly on a Shuttle if the appropriate officials decide they can do so. And in this case, I'm the appropriate official.

"Yes, there are some U.S. codes that limit certain activities in a spacecraft to those who have qualified as pilots or mission specialists. But you *will* be qualified before the launch, so even that doesn't apply.

"I'm doing this because HQ has absolutely, positively indicated that 100 will be the last Mir visit. Viktor, you've already trained on Mir for years, more than any of the other people in the pool. It seems natural to use your expertise."

Mark waited for Fehrenkamp to rationalize his assignment. Instead, Kondratko said, "What will we be doing?"

"Your actual roles in the mission are still in flux, as are experiment plans and schedules. One thing that will be necessary, I think, is for both of you to qualify as EVA crew members. We're discussing an extension of the EVA development test program to allow for four people to be outside Mir at the same time." A good half of mission specialists eventually went through the EVA syllabus, anyway, but Mark had thought it would be two or three years in the future.

"How public is this assignment?" Mark asked.

"Not very, for the moment. In fact, Steve Goslin will be the next to know, bringing the total, including you two, to exactly five." So Fehrenkamp had talked to them without getting the approval of the mission commander. No wonder Goslin was in a grumpy mood these days. "I anticipate an announcement at the pilots' meeting Monday. I won't say don't tell your friends and family. I would ask you to be discreet."

He stood up. Mark and Kondratko did so, too. "Good luck. I know you'll both do a good job." And that was it.

What an amazing six weeks you've had," Kondratko said the moment he and Mark were in the outer office. "What is it you say? From the shithouse to the penthouse?"

Mark started to correct him but wound up laughing instead.

The intercom on Valerie's desk made its trilling noise. "Mark," she said, "Les wanted one more word with you."

"Not both of us?"

"You."

Kondratko grinned and slapped Mark on the back. "Try not to make the big boss change his mind." He went out as Mark reentered Fehrenkamp's lair.

"You and I still have several items to discuss."

"I was wondering about that." Fehrenkamp had not addressed the reason for Mark's assignment, nor had he tested any rhetoric suitable for a cover story.

"This is all about Stipe, of course. I've been conducting a quiet investigation of my own, and—well, let's just say I wish he was where I could get my hands on him.

"That may, in fact, become your job."

"To put my hands on Cal Stipe aboard Mir?"

"In essence. I'm sending you there to bring him back. Frankly, there are better candidates." Mark agreed: his office mate, the special ops guy, for one. "But I'm determined to keep this whole matter as private as possible. You're already . . . contaminated."

"What about Kondratko?"

"We'll have to infect him, too, at some point. The sooner the better. And Goslin, though I would like to keep him concentrating on his flying without distractions for as long as possible." Fehrenkamp examined his desk calendar. To Mark's eyes, he suddenly seemed tired. Mark could only imagine the number of balls Fehrenkamp juggled on a regular basis, and the Buerhle matter was anything but regular. His voice was actually hoarse when he spoke. "The public justification—I should say, the message that will be delivered in CB—is that your military space operations background fits a classified Department of Defense experiment that will be conducted aboard Mir in conjunction with the Russian Military Space Units. Kondratko fits in here quite nicely, too." Mark got the impression that Fehrenkamp had only now made that connection. Fehrenkamp actually smiled as he warmed to his own sales pitch. "What you and I and Kelly will know is that the classified experiment involves the . . . the extraction of a dangerous element from a space station."

"I feel as though I'm being deputized."

"That's been discussed." He seemed finished. "Questions?"

"No."

"You have something you want to say."

Fehrenkamp was right. "I'm just a little worried that this is going to be hard for some people to accept."

Now Fehrenkamp got sarcastic. "And, what, you won't be Miss Congeniality anymore? This is not a popularity contest, Mark. No matter what you do, people are going to be unhappy. As my father used to say, that's the price of doing business."

As Mark headed out of Building 2, feeling more energetic than he had in weeks, he stopped at the duck pond, just to savor the moment. Obviously he had to call his parents and his sister. Just as obviously, he wanted to see Kelly.

The detour to the duck pond saved him from a collision with Steve Goslin, who was hurrying down the sidewalk on his way to Fehrenkamp's office. Poor Steve. He was going to find out that he had two additions to his crew, and still wasn't going to be told the reason why.

What was it they used to say? NASA means Never A Straight Answer? Mark tried to remember where he'd heard that.

When he got back to the astronaut office it was well after 5:00 P.M., and quiet. He asked one of the secretaries if she had seen Kelly Gessner. "I think she just left a couple of minutes ago. You can probably catch her—"

Mark was already running for the back stairs with his briefcase.

At the base of the stairs he turned right. Sure enough, there was Kelly up ahead, walking with some youngish-looking man about her height. Mark headed toward them, wondering if this was a JSC person or a tourist. He was about to call Kelly's name when he saw Kelly *take this person's hand.*

He closed his mouth. Now they were laughing about something, and she *was putting her arms around him!*

Mark cut directly across the lawn, running until he was out of sight behind a building. Kelly had some man in her life? How had he missed it? Why hadn't she told him?

He caught his breath and made sure Kelly and the man were gone. Then he headed for his new Explorer. To hell with her. He had calls to make. He was going into space.

CHAPTER 48

Steve Goslin didn't think of himself as an angry man, merely a tough one. It went with the job—not being an astronaut, but a military aviator. You took orders and you gave orders. You ran the risk of being killed and you often exposed others to the same risk. You did it because you believed in what you were doing. Defending the United States, and by extension your family. If questioned, Goslin would have been happy to tell anyone how protection of women and children was the true foundation for civilization. He could get quite emotional on the subject.

He knew that orders had to be followed, even if you disagreed with them. Nevertheless, a whole day and a half after getting his orders, he was still a little bit angry.

Fehrenkamp had warned him that he faced changes in his mission. You could not say the man had totally sandbagged him. But to arbitrarily add two crew members! And not just regular crew members—ASCANs! Goslin could think of a dozen people in the office who would be better choices for those two seats, if you had to have them.

The complications were immense. Now he had seven crew members going up and eight coming down. *Atlantis* was theoretically configured for a crew of eight: it had returned eight crew members for the first Shuttle-Mir docking back in 1995. STS-86, back in 1997, had been configured to bring back eight, though no one liked to talk about that. (There had been worries that Mir would fail and the UP crew member might not get to stay.)

But now there would be two additional voices on the comm links, two more bodies to be maneuvered around, two more mouths to feed. Jesus be praised, the mission called for the SpaceHab module to be installed in the

247

payload bay. It literally gave the orbiter a spare room. But things would still be crowded.

And this business of a four-person EVA. And talk of some military development test objectives. None of it seemed very well thought out to Steve Goslin so far. Yes, the launch was still six months off. But he felt he had wasted his first month as commander. And by simply informing him of these decisions, rather than inviting his input, Les Fehrenkamp had treated him badly.

"Just so we have one thing perfectly clear," he said to Mark Koskinen and Viktor Kondratko the moment they had ordered breakfast, "as far as I'm concerned, you guys are payload specialists. The manifest will call you MS4 and MS5, but you are passengers. You might not get out of the middeck the whole time."

They were at the Denny's a few hundred yards east of the main gate, a regular tourist trap that most astronauts or center people wouldn't have been caught dead in. It was a few minutes after seven on a Monday morning. Very shortly Jinx Seamans would be announcing the assignments at the pilots' meeting and all hell would break loose.

The Russian set down his coffee. "Colonel," he said, "we did not assign ourselves."

"We think it's weird, too," Koskinen said. "But what were we supposed to do? Say no?"

"I guess not." Goslin moved his own coffee aside so the waitress could deliver his breakfast. Had he really ordered the Grand Slam? "I just want you to know that I still don't see the justification. Weeks may go by before you feel as though you're really getting any productive work done."

"We understand," Kondratko said. "We still have classes to attend."

Goslin smiled. "You have a gauntlet to run, you mean." The group of ASCANs selected prior to the Koskinen-Kondratko group was very large. Only two or three had flown, with another handful assigned to missions. A good half, perhaps as many as a dozen, were going to look at these two ASCANs—ASCANs!—as if they had somehow jumped the line.

"I'm changing my phone number," Koskinen said. "I might even move." Well, he had a sense of humor about things. "At least Viktor has the perfect answer." He turned to the Russian. "You've been training for six years now."

"Viktor's place on a Shuttle-Mir crew makes a certain amount of sense," Goslin said to Mark. "Yours is going to be a lot tougher to sell."

He thought about Mark's background and what little Fehrenkamp had told him. "There isn't something classified going on here, is there?"

"If there were, I could hardly tell you."

"Even though I'm the commander."

"This is a civilian agency," Koskinen said. "Does NASA even do 'classified'?"

"No, it does something even worse, which is pretend nothing secret ever goes on." He waited. "You guys aren't telling me no."

Kondratko spoke up. "I could be with the KGB. Do you think I'd be entrusted with your secrets?"

Now Goslin was getting a tight smile. "There isn't any KGB these days, and even if there was and you were on its payroll, NASA is full of people who would tell you whatever you wanted to know. And you *still* aren't telling me no." He sighed. "I guess I'll just have to wait until someone tells me."

"Same here."

Goslin felt he had accomplished something. If nothing else, his anger was gone. Clearly Koskinen and Kondratko were also following orders. They would all have to trust that Fehrenkamp, and Hutchins, and the program people knew what they were doing, because spaceflight was no place for improvisation. He offered his hand to Koskinen, then Kondratko. "I've had my say. Welcome aboard."

Both of them thanked him.

He glanced at the check, counted out cash and an automatic 15 percent tip, then stood up. "We've got a sim right after the meeting. Come and meet your crewmates."

He walked out feeling quite good. He had a better idea of what lay ahead of him now. A period of trial, then the triumph. A good Christian would not only endure it but welcome it.

NASA N E W S
National Aeronautics and
Space Administration
Lyndon B. Johnson Space Center
Houston TX 77058
281 481-5111

December 1, 1998
Shannon Crosby
Headquarters, Washington D.C.
(Phone: 202/358-1780)

Lou Wekkin
Johnson Space Center, Houston TX
(Phone: 281/483-1511)

RELEASE 98-138
(EMBARGOED FOR RELEASE UNTIL 12:00 P.M. E.T.)

NEW CREW MEMBERS FOR STS-100

Astronauts Viktor Kondratko and Mark Koskinen have been added to the crew of STS-100, the tenth and last Shuttle-Mir docking mission, scheduled for launch in June 1999. They will take part in the seventh Space Station Development EVA Test, which has been added to the mission.

"We continue to learn more about workloads relating to long-duration missions," said flight crew operations director Les Fehrenkamp. "The 100 crew already has its hands full with materials transfers. We realized that we needed more hands."

Fehrenkamp noted that one of the new crew members, Viktor Kondratko, is an astronaut from the Russian Space Agency who has trained extensively on Mir for several years.

The STS-100 crew, previously announced, is commanded by Lt. Col. Steven Goslin, USMC. The pilot is Comdr. Jeffrey Dieckhaus, USN. The mission specialists are Kelly Gessner, ESA astronaut Donal O'Riordan, and Maj. David Freeh, USAF.

STS-100 will also return astronaut Calvin Stipe to Earth. Stipe is currently in his third week aboard the Mir space station.

Kondratko, 37, is a lieutenant colonel in the Russian air force. He was born in Sergeyev-Posad and attended the Kharkov Higher Air Force School and the Gagarin Air Force Academy. A graduate of the Chkalov test pilot school, he has logged 1,300 hours of flying time. He has been a Russian cosmonaut since 1991.

Koskinen, 33, was born in Marshalltown, Iowa, and attended the University of Arizona. He served with the U.S. Space Command and worked for the Aerospace Corporation prior to his selection as an astronaut candidate in March 1998.

Both Kondratko and Koskinen are astronaut candidates in the final phase of training and evaluation. They will be qualified as Shuttle mission specialists prior to the launch of STS-100.

CHAPTER 49

When Walt Thompson got the call from Kelly Gessner about a casual get-together with her and the other astronaut, Mark Koskinen, his first impulse had been to say he was busy. For one thing, he was back in Dallas at the NTSB field office and wasn't budgeted for any more trips to Houston. For another, his opinion of NASA prior to being assigned to the board investigating the Joe Buerhle crash had not been high: aviation specialists thought of the space agency as a collection of "crybabies" (presumably for their self-pitying annual lobbying efforts) or "Shiites" (because their every act was justified because they and they alone were working for the Human Future). What Thompson had seen of the agency since then had not improved his opinion.

He had briefly considered complaining to his boss, but said boss was off in California on that MD-80 crash, had been for months, and would only have told him to do whatever he wanted.

Well, what Thompson wanted to do was find somebody with authority who would call, say, the administrator of NASA, and chew him out. That wasn't going to happen. NASA had too many friends in Congress—more than the NTSB did, in any case.

Don Drury had made that quite clear to Thompson when it came time to get his signature on the preliminary report. The old bastard had never actually discussed it with him: no, but Thompson had received a phone call out of the blue from some snot-nosed creep on the staff of the House Aviation Committee. "We're all looking forward to putting this accident behind us," the creep had said. Probably a fucking lawyer. "Do you have a specific reason you're refusing to endorse the board's verdict?"

Yes: I think the pilot was drugged. But how could he say that and prove it? If he started with that scrap of Joe Buerhle's liver and the tox tests, he would sound like a sorehead, or a moron, because *nobody else would back him up!* Drury already had the two astronauts' signatures. "I'm here to help," the creep had continued. "What do you need?"

I need a time machine, because these guys ignored procedures from the beginning. "I guess I just needed a little extra time to review the data," he had heard himself saying.

"That means you'll be signing the statement."

"Yes."

"Well, that's outstanding," the creep had said. "You know, if there's ever anything I can do, here's my number." *Yeah, you can find me a spine somewhere. Don't look for one in Washington.*

With a few weeks to cool down, to appreciate that he still had a job and a career, Thompson was more inclined to be forgiving. Or cynical. He even told himself that Gessner and Koskinen had been leaned on.

And what about that weird little newspaper article about Joe Buerhle a week back? What was being done about that?

And what about this fax from Houston that arrived in his Dallas office on Friday?

Going to dinner would be a good way to reconcile this data. Going to dinner would, if nothing else, be a way of getting something out of the experience. (What was the most expensive restaurant in Clear Lake?) Going to dinner with the attractive Kelly Gessner wasn't the worst thing in any case. She didn't even flinch when they spoke a second time to arrange a location.

The dinner was set for seven-thirty on a Monday, and Adriano's, the Italian restaurant near the Baybrook Mall, was already emptying. Well, the clientele was a family and government crowd. Early to eat, then early to bed.

Gessner and Koskinen arrived within seconds of each other, in separate cars. "Are we late?" Gessner asked, smiling pleasantly and looking even more pleasant in a blue suit, a blouse and low heels.

"No, I'm early." It was a habit he'd had to develop. In his brief time at the NTSB he'd been late too many times finding strange addresses in new towns. Just as it was a habit to ask one question too many—hence the folded fax in his jacket pocket. He wasn't sure he was going to haul it out. It all depended. . . .

They sat down and ordered, with Thompson between the two of them at a table for four. He couldn't help but feel that there was some tension between them. Gessner—Kelly—was bright and talkative, but Koskinen seemed quiet, even sullen.

Both, it turned out, had professional news. Kelly was going to fly in space again. "I heard that," Thompson said.

"I was a little surprised," he added, recalling their conversation aboard the *Halverson*.

"Me, too," she said. "You must have caught me on a bad day."

"I *know* I caught you on a bad day."

Kelly then turned and looked at Koskinen for the first time. "And now it turns out that Mark is going to be flying on the same mission."

Thompson hadn't heard that. "Congratulations." Then it occurred to Thompson why Koskinen was so withdrawn. "Oh my God," he said. "I heard about your girlfriend. I guess it's condolences, too."

Koskinen just nodded. The waiter arrived then to take their order. By the time he had finished their conversational momentum had completely dissipated. Fortunately Kelly started things rolling again. "What exactly is going on with the board right now?"

"The various manufacturers are drafting detailed histories of the aircraft and all its systems. I drafted a chronology of the flight, from rollout to, uh, impact, which both of you will have to review at some point. Within a few weeks all these documents will be put together in a final report. And that will be that."

"That will be that," Koskinen repeated.

"Unless you guys have some way to change it. I'm not sure it even matters. It's not as though we're saying Joe Buerhle deliberately screwed up. The verdict simply rules out all mechanical or meteorological causes, leaving pilot error as the most likely cause."

Kelly said, "Which is fine, except that if someone really did drug Joe, he gets away with it."

"Well, yeah, that's the problem," Thompson said, feeling the folded fax paper in his jacket. Why hadn't he taken it off? He was sweating in here.

As Thompson reached for the fax paper, he heard Koskinen say, "Something is being done, you know."

"I don't know. But I'm darned interested."

Thompson saw Kelly's raised eyebrow. Was that a warning to Koskinen or cautious permission? "You saw that article on Buerhle?"

"Yeah. I figured it was related, but . . ." He shrugged.

"We have a good idea who the drugger is. And I think we're going to get him. I can't tell you the details yet, but . . ."

Thompson laughed. It came out unexpectedly and loudly. "Sorry."

"What's so funny?" Kelly asked smoothly.

"This thing! Can't you guys get your act together?"

"I don't know what you're talking about," Koskinen said.

Thompson took out the fax paper and unfolded it. He handed it to Kelly first, who glanced at it, reacted with surprise, then handed it to Mark. "It's a statement of death for Joseph Buerhle," Thompson said. "Signed by the medical examiner. You won't find any mention of drugs or controlled substances."

Kelly glanced around before she spoke. *We're back to that.* "This isn't a death certificate, it's a letter."

"You noticed. It's a letter that's now part of the report. It's as good as a death certificate, because, as I understand it, Joe Buerhle's death in international waters is outside the official jurisdiction of the Harris or Galveston County M.E.s. It really just allows Buerhle's heirs to collect on their insurance."

"And it really makes us look like fucking idiots," Koskinen said.

"Only if your story gets out." Thompson sort of liked these two, but he also felt a little smug. "Neither of you knew anything about this?"

They didn't need to reply. Thompson laughed again. "Well, good luck in running down your murderer. What are they planning to do? Make him disappear?"

Dinner finally arrived. "We might as well eat," Thompson said. He got the clear impression he was the only one at the table who was still hungry.

CHAPTER 50

I think we need to talk,'' Mark said the moment they saw Thompson drive away from Adriano's.

"I was hoping you'd say that."

"My place or yours?"

"Yours. I'll follow you." She needed time to think about several matters. About what Thompson had told them—that now there was some kind of quasi-official death certificate for Joe Buerhle. Where had that come from? Drury? Fehrenkamp?

She also wondered about Mark. Over the weekend she had received a call from Goslin telling her the almost unbelievable news that Mark and Viktor Kondratko were joining the crew of STS-100. She had tried calling Mark immediately and got nothing but a recording, and had never heard from him at all. She had considered just dropping in on him Sunday but had had to run all the way across town to Houston Intercontinental Airport, and looked and felt too dismal by the time she returned. It was only at the pilots' meeting that morning that she had caught up with him, offering congratulations. "Thanks," was all he said. She had managed to tell him about the Thompson dinner before being pulled away to a payload meeting.

Had Fehrenkamp somehow gotten to Mark? The unprecedented assignment to a mission certainly suggested something irregular. But why would Mark have told Thompson that there was a suspect? There was no reason to volunteer that information.

The world had ceased to make sense.

Mark was making some tea when she arrived. He seemed more relaxed than he had at dinner. Could she have been reading him all wrong? No: he had been downright frosty all day.

Was that a problem? What were her intentions here, anyway? Clearly they were both attracted to each other—the last day notwithstanding. She had to admit to herself that Mark was the kind of man she could fall in love with. Unlike Joe Buerhle, he was even the kind of man she could marry.

But there were compelling reasons for both of them to go slowly. Both were bereaved, for God's sake. And now both of them were on the same Shuttle crew!

And Kelly still had no real sense that Mark was as interested in her as she was in him. . . .

"So what did you think of Thompson's little grenade?" Mark said once they were settled in the living room.

"It was a complete surprise."

"Am I just being paranoid or does it really make things difficult for us?"

"Only if we dispute the board's verdict. I think someone has gone to a lot of trouble to make it very easy for us to go along."

"Is that what we should do?"

"Are you asking *me*, Mark? Would you go along if I told you to?" He was squirming a little: good. She preferred to have him off balance at a time like this.

"Probably not."

"Well, I'm not giving up, either. I'm in this until Stipe is punished." She sat back with the teacup in her hand. "So maybe you better tell me why Fehrenkamp put you and Viktor on this crew."

Telling her seemed to relax him. Like a confession. "Basically, it's *Apocalypse Now*. Stipe's methods have become unsound. Viktor and I will be the errand boys sent to collect a bill."

"Why not wait until he comes back?"

"Every day he sits up there, he does more damage. He gets harder to control. Have you heard this? There are some proposals floating around to extend Stipe's stay past Polyakov's record." Polyakov was a Russian physician cosmonaut who had spent fourteen months in orbit aboard Mir. To do that, Stipe would have to remain aboard Mir through 1999, to the very end of its life. Or, as some would say, its afterlife.

"You've got to be kidding."

"The rationale is that we need to get all the biomedical data we can, and why let the Russians have the only real long-term study subject? If Stipe's already up there and willing to press on . . ." Mark shrugged. "Anyway, you can see how Stipe is selling it, because he's clearly the one behind it.''

Kelly's tea had gotten cold. She had hardly drunk any of it, anyway. ''Well, it's going to be interesting when we show up and tell him the party's over.''

''Crew systems is working on a pair of leg irons and shackles.''

Kelly laughed, though the idea wasn't as ridiculous as it sounded. Sooner or later somebody was going to freak out on a mission and need to be hauled back to Earth. She had heard rumors—nothing ever confirmed— about one of the pre-*Challenger* payload specialists, who had gotten so unruly on a mission that the crew had essentially taped him to the floor of the mid-deck until he cooled down.

''I, ah, saw you Friday afternoon. Right after Fehrenkamp told me the news.''

Uh-oh, what was this? ''Where was I?''

''Heading out to the parking lot. It was about six or something.''

''Why didn't you say hello? I would have loved to have known Friday—''

''You weren't alone,'' he said, interrupting her. His tone was definitely more one of sorrow than of anger, but Kelly could still sense a good deal of anger.

''What was I doing?'' she said evenly.

''You had your arms around some guy.''

''Oh my God.''

He sighed. ''Look, this has been a weird time for me. I don't know, we seemed to be moving toward something—''

''Mark.'' It was her turn to interrupt him. ''It was my *brother*.''

''The model collector? Clark?''

''Yes. Clark came to town Thursday. I put him on a plane yesterday.''

He was clearly trying to make sense of this. ''What was he doing at JSC?''

''Visiting me. Collecting autographs.'' Now Mark looked even more puzzled. She realized it was time to tell him: ''Clark is special. He has Downs.''

Mark opened his mouth and closed it. He tried again, and the best he could manage was ''Oh.''

''He's like a big ten-year-old. He can read and write. He has a job back in Orlando. You can put him on a plane and he'll get where he needs to go. But that's about it.'' That was far from it, of course. Kelly used to wonder what it would have been like to grow up with a brother who wasn't special, who could have challenged her, maybe taught her things. But that hadn't happened; Clark had always been the way he was. Besides . . . she had learned things from him, too.

Mark was actually blushing. "I saw him hug you."

"Clark is very affectionate, and I'm one of the things in the world he loves most." She leaned forward and patted Mark's hand. "And you thought I was two-timing you. . . ."

To her great surprise, Mark took her hand. "You're exactly right, and it bothered the hell out of me." And then he kissed her. It was all his idea this time. Not that Kelly considered pulling away.

Momentarily they found themselves lying side by side on the couch. "Are we going to regret this?" he asked her.

"Only if we keep asking ourselves questions," she said. "Let's go upstairs."

"Yes, ma'am."

Kelly saw no reason to make love on a couch when a bed was available. Especially not a first time. Beds were bigger. Dark bedrooms were more forgiving.

They paused in the doorway. "This is all because I wore a skirt tonight, isn't it?"

He grinned and slid his hand up the inside of her thighs. "It sure didn't hurt."

She unbuttoned the blouse. "You'll still find me attractive when I go back to my jeans and polo shirts?"

"You can wear an LES and a helmet and it won't stop me." The thought of that bulky orange pressure suit reminded Kelly of the upcoming mission, and just as quickly, of certain responsibilities of her own.

"Would you happen to have what we single gals call protection?" What would she do if he said no?

"I've got you covered."

"*I'm* not the one who needs it."

Wearing her panties, she slipped under the covers. Mark stood before her, struggling out of his pants. He looked even better naked.

Then he joined her.

How was she ever going to tell him about Joe Buerhle?

It could wait. It could all wait.

PART V
GOING UPHILL

NASA N E W S

National Aeronautics and
Space Administration

Mir-31 Status Report #28 Mission Control Center, Korolev, Friday,
June 4, 1999

NASA astronaut Calvin Stipe, already the U.S. space endurance record-holder, prepares to break the 200-day barrier in his mission aboard the Mir space station. Stipe says that he feels fine. "I miss my friends at JSC," he told reporters this week, "but I have the most challenging work in the world right here, and two good friends." He was referring to Mir-31 commander Yuri Petrenko and flight engineer Vladimir Belokonev.

Stipe's primary activities during the past week involved the Advanced Binary Colloidal Alloy Test (ABCAT) experiment. Based in the Priroda ("Nature") module of the Mir complex, the ABCAT allows researchers to study the long-term behavior of crystal alloys in microgravity.

Stipe continues to use cameras aboard Mir to document seasonal changes on the Earth's surface. He is also conducting oceanographic experiments under the NEREUS-2 program, developed by the Scripps Institution for Oceanography.

On Thursday Stipe took several measurements that will allow researchers to assess changes in his muscle and skeletal mass during his 200-plus-day stay aboard Mir.

Stipe is currently scheduled to return to Earth this month aboard STS-100, though an extension of his mission is currently under review.

CHAPTER 51

Today's crisis aboard the Mir space station, now past the thirteenth anniversary of its launch in March 1986, concerned the peanut supply. Well, there were also problems with the power system. Two weeks back a controller error at Korolev had allowed the station to turn away from the Sun for too long. The solar power panels, which charged the batteries that ran everything aboard the station, including the attitude control systems, were left useless for a little too long.

A bit longer and the station's batteries would have drained themselves of power, and Mir would have had to be abandoned. It had almost happened at least twice before during Mir's lifetime, most recently in 1997, when the Spektr module had been punctured by an errant Progress tanker vehicle.

This time an alarm had sounded, waking Yuri Petrenko and Vladimir Belokonev from their sleeping bags in the core module. They floated to the control panel to find Cal Stipe already at work in the semi-darkness. "I haven't touched anything," he said in Russian to Petrenko, who, as the recently arrived Mir commander, tended to be sensitive. "I found a couple of batteries we can tie into the main bus, if that's what you want to do."

"Thank you, Grandpa," Petrenko said. To Belokonev, the flight engineer and a space rookie, he added, "We don't need to be here, Volodya. Calvin knows more than both of us. He is the ghost of Mir."

They had all laughed in spite of the near emergency, then set to work. By the time they were in communication with Korolev for their morning session, four hours later, the problem had essentially been solved, though a couple of Stipe's energy-eating experiments in the Priroda module would have to be shut off for a couple of days.

But the peanuts were still missing, and Stipe was beginning to get angry.

A whole five-pound bag had been delivered by Progress MU-3 six weeks before; only a couple of pounds were left, and they had to last until the next Progress a month in the future. This had never happened when Sasha-1 and Sasha-2 were the "main" Mir crew, number 30. But they had returned to Earth in March, along with a Chinese fellow who had arrived with the Sashas' replacements, Petrenko and Belokonev, the Mir-31 team.

Stipe had gone through several training sessions with Petrenko and Belokonev during the year prior to his launch, though never as a team. (The Russians were forever swapping commanders and flight engineers around, and not for psychological reasons, either. Belokonev's predecessor, for example, had broken his leg skiing and had had to step aside for several weeks.) He was sure Petrenko, who had already spent two shifts aboard Mir in the past, would never nick someone's private food stash. Belokonev, though, was young . . . he might think it belonged to everyone.

Peanuts and other salty foods were one of the things Stipe had come to cherish during his seven months aboard Mir. Living in microgravity had that effect on the taste buds, dulling them to some flavors while sharpening them for others. There were other effects, of course. Stipe was now a full inch taller than he had been on Earth, and five pounds lighter. Three months back he had been down fifteen pounds, so much that the Russian and NASA doctors were starting to ask questions. But he had changed his diet on his own; the foods he wanted had been shipped up aboard the last Progress vehicle. Now he was thriving. At a mission-elapsed time of 195 days, he was just about halfway to the record set by the Russian doctor cosmonaut Polyakov.

There was no reason he wouldn't tie that record. No reason he wouldn't break it. True, NASA still carried him as a "DOWN" crew member for the next Shuttle mission, STS-100, now scheduled for launch within a week. But Stipe had started the wheels turning long ago, building support within the JSC Life Sciences Directorate, the other centers, even headquarters. He was the last officially scheduled NASA-Mir crew member . . . why not let him stay on? True, it cost the Russians a certain amount of food, oxygen and water. But NASA was paying the Russians so generously for their involvement in the ISS that getting some additional consumables for Stipe should not be a problem.

Even Les Fehrenkamp had sent a message that the matter was still "open," that it would be decided by the time STS-100 docked with Mir. The plans for STS-100 had changed several times since Cal's launch in

November. They had even added those two crew members, Koskinen and Kondratko. Stipe was quite curious to know exactly why they had been added. But as long as he got his mission extended, he really didn't care.

No one could touch him here.

A working day aboard Mir was less structured than one aboard the Shuttle. The Shuttle was in direct communication with the ground—with good bandwidth—90 percent of the time. Shuttle crew members ran experiments with scientists on the ground literally looking over their shoulders.

Mir lacked real-time communications with ground centers, so this sort of thing was largely left to the crew members. Data would eventually be returned, of course, but if Stipe wanted to operate the Forced Flow Flamespread Test at three in the afternoon as opposed to ten in the morning, it did not cause a crisis.

You needed flexibility to live on Mir, anyway, since routine maintenance and housekeeping took up at least a couple of hours a day. Then there were the mandatory exercise sessions—another two hours. There went half your productive workday right there.

Today's problem required more maintenance. In fact, with the batteries recharging, there wouldn't be any major science, manufacturing or photography going on. Stipe, Petrenko and Belokonev did a front-to-back inventory of all the various systems, starting in the Mir base module, then swimming through the blizzard of cables into Kvant, then Kvant-2, then Kristall, then the sealed-off Spektr, and finally Priroda. Stipe even floated into the module used for Shuttle dockings.

It wasn't until late in the afternoon, while Petrenko was off doing his exercises, that Stipe managed to get Belokonev alone. "Did you eat them?" he asked in Russian.

"What are you talking about?" Unlike most cosmonauts, Belokonev was tall, standing six feet even on the ground, a couple of inches more on orbit. He was able to wedge himself into the hatchway leading from the main radial docking unit into Kvant-2.

"My peanuts."

"I didn't eat your peanuts, Calvin." Belokonev forced a smile. "Should we switch to English? Maybe I'm not understanding you."

"You know goddamn well what I'm talking about. My peanuts. They're not where I put them."

"And you think I took them?"

"I know you did."

"They didn't just float off?"

"I know how to stash things on the station, Volodya. I've been living here for seven months."

Belokonev looked at Stipe for a moment, then gently pushed past him, heading for the base module, where Petrenko was sweating up a storm.

Stipe grabbed his leg. "We haven't finished."

Belokonev rotated. "Please keep your hands to yourself."

But Stipe refused to let go. Belokonev chose not to start a fight— there had been actual fistfights between cosmonauts on orbit, including a famous one some twenty years ago that had led to the premature end of a mission. He did not want to let this go any further, which suited Stipe just fine. "We're going to be living together for half a year," Stipe told the cosmonaut. "We will get along better if we all respect each other's property. I wouldn't go in your bedroom." The main crew members, commander and flight engineer, had tiny staterooms the size of closets in the core module. As the researcher Stipe was free to camp out wherever he chose. "I wouldn't tell Korolev about that nice little bottle of vodka you brought up, either."

Booze and cigarettes were the dirty little secrets of life aboard Mir. Alcohol was technically forbidden, yet some always managed to reach the station. And one crew, years back, had included a committed tobacco addict who had actually turned one of the modules into a regular smoker's lounge. You could still smell it.

"I thought they belonged to everyone," Belokonev finally said.

"My peanuts."

The cosmonaut merely closed his eyes, obviously wishing this unpleasant confrontation would just end. "Your peanuts. I didn't know."

"Are there any left?"

"I don't think so."

"What do you have to say?"

"I apologize."

Only then did Stipe release Belokonev. "All right," he told him, sounding fatherly. "Living in such close quarters, just the three of us—we must respect each other's property. That is the single most important lesson I've learned."

"I understand."

"I won't speak of this to Yuri."

"Thank you."

Stipe turned abruptly and floated off, away from the spherical docking module and into Kristall, at the far end of which another spherical docking module was attached. There he found the Shuttle docking unit, his current stateroom.

He looked around the light gray chamber and realized he would have to move. Within a week the orbiter *Atlantis* would float out of the darkness like a winged beast, bringing seven visitors and several hundred pounds of supplies. Everything would be moving through this chamber.

But after four days the visitors would be gone. The supplies would be getting put to use. And Stipe would move back in. Because he was staying. He was not, as Petrenko said, the "ghost" of Mir.

He was the king.

CHAPTER 52

"All right, the next item is booster status." Les Fehrenkamp sat in the conference room in Building 5 listening to the soothing voice of Carl Strahan as he polled the many departments around the country that made a Shuttle launch happen.

You didn't want surprises at the launch readiness review. The whole purpose of this sort of meeting, held within a week or ten days of launch, was to reassure all the offices that things were going as planned, that a firm launch time could be set.

But at the launch readiness review for STS-100, the tenth Shuttle-Mir docking, Les Fehrenkamp felt that there were many open items, too many things left to be decided. It made him nervous.

Item one: here it was, early June, and he was still awaiting the launch of the first ISS incremental crew, which consisted of one of his astronauts and a pair of Russians. They were supposed to dock their Soyuz TM2-1 to a trio of modules, including the Russian-built control module, which had finally reached orbit in February, and the American Node One, which had been up since April. The problem was that the third major module, the Russian service module, was still sitting in its factory! The political and budgetary chaos in Russia had starved the SM and CM builders for cash. Astronauts and other visitors to Moscow kept returning with horror stories about the Russian module team working for free. Until the SM went up, ISS missions were on hold and Mir missions would continue. Or would they? No one seemed to know for sure.

"Clark, trajectory report, please," Strahan said.

Then there was Russia's political situation, with one president dying and the continuing argument over who was to succeed him, and what that would mean for the NASA–Russian Space Agency relationship.

The Shuttle fleet had suffered through its share of hiccups, too. There had been another scare about the solid rocket motors—the third red flag in as many years—and one of the spring missions had had to be destacked and rolled back to its assembly building. Fortunately the next STS-100 stack had passed its review, and the two missions had more or less swapped places in the manifest. But the destacking had depressed the shit out of one crew while forcing another one into some longer training sessions. It had also caused more rumblings around the astronaut office about the solid rocket motors.

The only problems which technically concerned Les Fehrenkamp were the training and morale issues, but there was no way to separate them from the other matters. The political situation directly affected the eight NASA astronauts currently training at the Gagarin Center, not to mention their support people. The wobbly ISS delivery schedule affected everything from current training schedules to Fehrenkamp's plans for a new ASCAN selection—now on hold because of an agency-wide hiring freeze.

"SRB recovery ships? How are we doing there?"

Any moment Strahan was going to turn to Fehrenkamp for his answers. And for the first time he could remember, he didn't know what he was going to tell them.

It had to do with Calvin Stipe, of course. The ancient astronaut, still circling the world sixteen times a day as he had for the past seven months. In that time Fehrenkamp had become convinced that what Koskinen and Gessner had discovered was true: the creepy son of a bitch had killed Joe Buerhle. He had probably killed Allyson Morin, too. And so far he had gotten away with all of it.

So far.

Many times in the past few weeks Fehrenkamp had dreamed of simply leaving Stipe on orbit indefinitely. Mir was in its final days, of course, but there was still talk of shifting a couple of its newer modules over to the new ISS. Maybe they could just move Stipe *with* them! Stipe would be happy: he could set the all-time space endurance record. Life Sciences would be happy.

And Fehrenkamp would not have to face the ugly business of seeing an astronaut arrested. Possibly even tried and convicted.

It was going to be tricky enough to simply compel Stipe to return.

Koskinen and Kondratko had been trained to deal with that, thank God. But what then? The whole business was still the most closely held secret Fehrenkamp had ever known. Koskinen, Gessner, Kondratko, Drury, himself. And Stipe.

Christ, there were more people in the world who knew that Les Fehrenkamp sometimes slept with men. And Fehrenkamp had made *very* sure to keep that quiet over the years.

Not quiet enough, of course. The one person who knew both secrets was Calvin Stipe. And that was Fehrenkamp's secret shame: that one drunken quasi-indiscretion a dozen years in the past could have somehow led to Joe Buerhle's death. That this . . . what could it be called? A discussion? A proposal? A conversation? There had been no contact! But whatever it was, had it encouraged Stipe to think that Les Fehrenkamp would let him do whatever he wanted just so that secret would be kept?

The real horror was that, until now, he had. Les Fehrenkamp had let Cal Stipe run wild—

"Les, flight crew ops. We still have one major piece of business on the table."

Scott McDowell chimed in at that point. "Yeah, like, how many people are coming down?" There was general laughter in the room and even on the speaker phones.

"We're configured to return eight," Fehrenkamp told them. The orbiter could even launch with eight, though it had only happened once. For the first Shuttle-Mir mission three years back a recumbent seat kit had been developed to allow the long-duration crew to go through entry in a prone position, not sitting up. That kit was partially installed on Atlantis. "A final decision as to whether Stipe returns in that configuration won't be made until we've done an on-orbit evaluation of his physical and mental state." He could have added, *And figured out how to wrap him up with bungee cords and drag him back to* Atlantis.

"And that evaluation is going to be done by . . . oh, shit, we forgot to put a doctor in the crew!" McDowell again. He sounded unusually sporty for a guy whose ASCAN application was again on hold.

"In addition to the kit aboard the orbiter, there's a whole suite of medical equipment aboard Mir. Both crews are trained to operate it. The job is simply data *collection* process; the data will be evaluated right here."

He was sounding pedantic, but he didn't care. He had actually drafted these few sentences before the meeting, to be sure he sounded exactly the right note. Strahan stared at him for a beat. "If you had to bet it, Les, would you say we'll be returning with seven or eight?"

"Eight," he heard himself say. "I can't conceive of the circumstances that would allow us to leave Stipe on an open-ended mission." There, he'd said it.

"Well, then," Strahan said, "without further ado, I think we're go for STS-100 on the tenth at two-twenty A.M." Just like that, the review was over. Fehrenkamp could hear speaker phones clicking off all over America.

Like a body shutting down as it freezes to death, he thought. Like his career, his privacy, his reputation. Thanks to Stipe, he was being shut down bit by bit, dying a slow but nevertheless certain death.

NASA N E W S

National Aeronautics and
Space Administration
John F. Kennedy Space Center
Kennedy Space Center, FL 32899
407 867-2468

June 4, 1999
Barry Leudtke
(Phone: 407/867-2468)

SPACE SHUTTLE MISSION STS-100 COUNTDOWN TO BEGIN JUNE 7

NASA will begin the countdown for the launch of the Space Shuttle *Atlantis* on the tenth and final mission to dock with the Russian space station Mir on Monday, June 7, at 1:00 A.M. at the T-43 hour mark. The KSC launch team will conduct the countdown from Firing Room 1 of the Launch Control Center.

The countdown includes 30 hours and 30 minutes of built-in hold time leading to a liftoff at 2:20 A.M. (EST) on June 10. The launch window extends for six to ten minutes. The exact launch time will be determined about 90 minutes before liftoff based on the current location of the Mir space station.

STS-100 is the fourth Space Shuttle mission of 1999. It will be the 24th flight of the orbiter *Atlantis* and the 99th flight overall in the Shuttle program.

STS-100 will carry a crew of seven into orbit, returning with eight, including NASA astronaut Calvin Stipe, now in his seventh month aboard the Mir.

The STS-100 crew are: commander Steven Goslin, pilot Jeffrey Dieckhaus, and mission specialists David Freeh, Kelly Gessner, Donal O'Riordan, Viktor Kondratko and Mark Koskinen.

The STS-100 crew is scheduled to arrive at KSC at 11:00 A.M., Monday, June 7. Their activities prior to launch will include equipment fit checks, medical examinations and opportunities to fly in the Shuttle Training Aircraft.

CHAPTER 53

NASA T-38 tail number 908 taxied up to the waiting knot of people in front of the Vehicle Assembly Building (VAB), which adjoined Runway 33 at the Kennedy Space Center, and pulled to a stop. "We won't get out until the others are parked," Steve Goslin said.

"Understand," Mark Koskinen told him from the backseat. He could already see the second T-38 just touching down on the runway and knew there were two others on approach. The four T-38s carried six of the seven crew members of STS-100, in addition to acting chief astronaut Clint Hurley and weather pilot Ron Kubiak. Donal O'Riordan already waited with the crowd, having flown in the night before with several guests from the European Space Agency, including its director general, and the crew's luggage. In his blue flight suit, O'Riordan was walking toward the two T-38s, waving like a long-lost brother even though they had all been together in the simulator yesterday at JSC.

Mark could not see the Space Shuttle *Atlantis* on Pad 39A—the incredible square bulk of the Vehicle Assembly Building blocked the view. But he knew it was out there, a Space Shuttle that was going to carry him into orbit in exactly sixty-two hours. He let out a breath. What a long strange trip this had been, from the Joe Buerhle accident in October to the taxi apron at the Kennedy Space Center on day L-minus-two. As of last week, he was a year older, thirty-four now. He had 174 hours of flying time in the T-38. He had spent 600 or so hours in mission simulations, including seventy-five hours of underwater EVA work in the Sonny Carter Facility at JSC.

He was also a full-fledged astronaut now. All the Worms had received their silver pins from Les Fehrenkamp at the semiannual astronaut picnic a month back.

Mark also had to admit that he had a real girlfriend. He and Kelly had probably not spent more than five days apart since the middle of November. He had even gone home to Orlando with her for three days over Christmas.

If back at the end of September anyone had told him that any of this would be happening—the accident, the flight, the relationship—much less all of it, he would have laughed. Then, given his inherent suspicions of good fortune, he would have gotten worried. All in all, it had been a very strange six months.

Even the weather had been strange. In addition to making him cautious about seemingly unearned goodies, growing up in the frozen wastes of northern Iowa had taught Mark to look forward to spring. Several years in Arizona and California hadn't changed that.

But spring 1999 never came! Some volcanic eruption in the Philippines last fall had effectively robbed much of the Northern Hemisphere of spring and, apparently, summer. It had been cold and nasty in Houston. Cold and nasty everywhere he had gone, even trips to the Cape. On some level he was glad, because he wasn't missing any lovely spring weather by sitting in simulators. But it only added to the general feeling of weirdness.

And it all seemed to be prelude to the greater weirdness to follow, of course, because Mark and Viktor Kondratko were under orders to bring Calvin Stipe back to Earth. They had gone through an FBI course at Quantico, Virginia, to teach them how to physically restrain an uncooperative suspect. Kondratko had proven to be a quick study at this, causing Mark to wonder again about his relationship with the security organs of the former USSR. Whether any of these techniques would be useful on orbit was another matter.

The lack of a clear reason for their presence in the crew had only come up once. Of course, it had been in a public forum—the preflight press conference in April. A local reporter named Brad Whitsett, the same guy, Mark realized, who had printed the Joe Buerhle memo in November, stood up and asked Steve Goslin whether the MS4 (Mark) and MS5 (Kondratko) had crew functions that were not covered in the seventy-five-page press kit. ''Some sort of intelligence or national security experiments, possibly targeting terrorist camps from low Earth orbit?'' Goslin had summoned up all his Christian righteousness and answered that there were no ''national security'' experiments on his mission. Zero.

Which, as far as Goslin knew, was true. He hadn't been briefed. To this day he still hadn't been briefed, and Mark was beginning to wonder if he would *ever* be briefed.

Mark had not been able to help shooting a glance at Les Fehrenkamp as the reporter pressed Goslin, but Fehrenkamp's face had been a mask.

Then Whitsett had turned to Mark. "I'd like to address that question to Mr. Koskinen directly, then."

"What was the question again?" Mark said to general laughter.

"Have you been assigned to this mission for some secret purpose?"

"I understand—and Mr. Fehrenkamp can correct this if I'm wrong— that it's only to keep me and my secret recipe out of the annual JSC Chili Cook-off. I want to reveal for the first time, right here," he continued, as the reporters laughed, "that the secret ingredient is soybeans from my home state of Iowa."

The *Chronicle* reporter tried to follow up but got interrupted by Fehrenkamp, getting into the swing of things, who broke his own rule of not commenting at crew press conferences by saying, "My team will do anything to win the cook-off." The exchange rated a sentence in the next day's article, and that had been the end of it. In public.

"Showtime," Goslin said, popping open the canopy and climbing out.

All four T-38s were lined up now, a lovely sight. Mark followed Goslin down the ladder, smoothed back his hair, and joined up with Kelly, who had flown with the STS-100 pilot, Dieckhaus. She took his hand and squeezed it.

"Aren't you afraid people will see?"

"Let them see," she said. They hadn't exactly hidden their relationship from their crewmates, and certainly their sim team suspected. But Mark wasn't sure he was ready to have his photo on the front page of *USA Today* holding hands with his crewmate. Not before the launch, in any case.

In moments all seven of them were lined up behind one microphone, a good twenty feet from the reporters and VIP guests. The distance was due to the limited quarantine NASA imposed on the crew during the last week prior to launch. Basically, the idea was to keep them from catching colds.

There was a scattering of applause. Goslin thanked everyone for coming out at ten in the morning and made the standard remarks about how everyone had worked hard to get ready for the mission, how they were looking forward to seeing Cal Stipe on orbit and closing out this chapter of American-Russian space cooperation.

There were a couple of questions for O'Riordan from the European reporters and several for Kondratko from the regular space beat reporters. The rest of them could have gone on to the crew quarters, and within a few moments they were doing exactly that.

Mark had left a small bag inside the cockpit of Number 908. He crawled back up the ladder to retrieve it. Pausing at the top, he glanced over at the crowd, which was starting to disperse. There was one familiar figure, standing back. Don Drury.

They had not communicated directly in months, not since their last somewhat testy conversation about the accident board's report. The final report was still pending. But in the interests of maintaining the relationship, and because aside from his parents, Mark had no real use for the VIP launch passes, Mark had invited Drury to be his guest. And by God, here he was. Mark gave him a wave, which Drury acknowledged with a nod.

Kelly was waiting at the bottom of the ladder. "Did you see your parents?"

"They don't get in until tonight. I was waving to Don Drury."

Kelly looked for him. "He showed up, huh?"

"He left me a message saying he'd never seen a Shuttle launch in person." Mark had found that hard to believe, until he asked around. Lots of old NASA heads had never attended a launch.

"Probably couldn't stand the tension," Kelly said.

"And we can?"

She smiled. That was one of the things Mark liked best about her. "We don't have any choice now. We're committed, baby."

"So what do I do next?"

"You go through your personal kit so the C-squares know what to load on the vehicle. I go fly the STA." Kelly was to join Goslin and Dieckhaus immediately thereafter in the Shuttle Training Aircraft, which was parked just past the T-38s. "We'll get in a couple of landings before bedtime."

Because of Mir's current orbit, and the need to place *Atlantis* in proximity to Mir with proper lighting conditions for docking, the STS-100 launch was to take place in a five-minute "window" that opened at 2:17 A.M., Thursday morning, June 10. For weeks now the crew—and their sim team and flight controllers—had been adjusting their circadian rhythms so that they woke up at ten in the evening after going to sleep about noon. The crew had been living in special quarters at JSC for just this reason.

"How's the steely commander doing?" Kelly asked. Dave Freeh had pinned that title on Goslin after the commander blew up at the sim supervisor halfway through training.

"He didn't say four words to me," Mark said.

"He has a lot of questions for you and Viktor. He can't bring himself to raise them. I actually wish Fehrenkamp would break down and bring him into the loop, because it would be one less thing on his mind."

"Would it? Maybe it would add a few things."

Kelly shrugged. "That's the other way to look at it." She kissed him on the cheek, then slung her bag over her shoulder. "See you in a couple of hours." And she practically ran for the STA.

Mark picked up his bag. Walking around the airplanes, he almost collided with another familiar face. Brad Whitsett, the boy reporter for the *Houston Chronicle*. "Is this a little astro-romance I see before me? Mark and Kelly, sitting a tree, k-i-s-s-i-n-g?"

Mark kept walking. "I'm in quarantine."

"I've had my shots." Whitsett walked with him, keeping a safe distance away. "Do you have any comment?"

"What's the question again?"

"Don't pull that shit on me again, Koskinen."

Mark stopped. He was not one of those astronauts who hated the press—about 75 percent of CB—but he sure wasn't going to take that tone of voice from a reporter. "You could watch the launch from Orlando. I hear they've got TVs there."

"I don't care about your fucking launch. I've seen twenty of them."

"Then what do you want?" Out of the corner of his eye Mark saw one of the local NASA public affairs people scurrying his way, a look of panic on her face. Mark shook his head, indicating that he could handle this. Not that he was really sure he could. "Confirmation of an astro-romance? We're just good friends, Officer."

"I could care less. Gessner's got a history of sleeping with people she works with." He laughed. "I think she did two years with Joe Buerhle alone." Mark's heart stopped so thoroughly that he almost missed what Whitsett said next. "I hear that Stipe doesn't want to come back and that you and your Russian friend have been sent to drag him."

Mark shook his head. Kelly and *Joe Buerhle*? He needed to think clearly here. "What are you talking about?"

"You two were added to the crew just to make sure this guy came home."

"That's crazy. We were put on the crew months ago. Stipe was barely in orbit; he hadn't had time to decide to hang on. And even if you needed a couple of people to be bouncers, you've got Goslin and Dieckhaus and Freeh. I wouldn't mess with any of them in a bar fight."

Whitsett seemed satisfied with the answer. "All right. But there's still something damned weird about this flight."

"All I can do is tell you to watch and see."

"I will."

"Tell me about Kelly and Joe." He felt like an idiot for asking this guy, but he wanted to know.

"A little jealous, are we? Sorry, I probably phrased that poorly. I mean, they had a relationship that apparently started on their mission a couple of years back. It was still going on when he died."

"I don't believe you." He was trying to convince himself.

"Remember that article I did? Joe Buerhle's secret memo? Ask your girlfriend about it." By now the public affairs woman loomed, and Whitsett knew his time was up. "Have a good flight, Koskinen, *whatever* it is you're doing."

Kelly had had an affair with Joe Buerhle. Kelly had leaked Joe's memo to this guy. What else had Kelly neglected to tell him?

What was *her* agenda? Was Mark Koskinen just part of some larger plan?

Suddenly life no longer looked so weird. Now it just looked bad.

CHAPTER 54

I guess I thought you knew."

It was a weak response, but it was all Kelly had to say when Mark took her aside at the beach house the next morning.

The house was a ancient two-story Florida cottage just down the beach from Pad 39A. It was all that was left of a number of similar shacks that had been bought up and disposed of, one by one, as first the Air Force, then NASA expanded up the coast in the 1950s and 1960s. The house was the one refuge a flight crew had from prying eyes; it was even more private than the crew quarters at KSC.

Tonight, with a day and a half to go before launch, the crew of STS-100, in accordance with tradition and superstition, was hosting a meal for its guests and supporters. The guests, of course, were on the same time as the rest of the world, but the crew would be starting its rest period around noon, so the meal was a brunch, complete with omelets cooked by Goslin. (The steely commander had turned out to be quite the amateur chef.) For the crew, of course, it was just an unusual late-night snack.

The guests included most of the people on the crew's VIP lists, in addition to Les Fehrenkamp. Mark's parents made an appearance, still bleary-eyed from some canceled airline connection and a very late arrival at their hotel in Cocoa Beach. To Kelly it appeared that Mark barely exchanged twenty words with them—from what she knew, not an unusually small amount. They did strike her as anything but happy that their son was going to be launched into space in the next day or so. She watched Mark gamely try to cheer them up. "The Shuttle's got the same motto as Grand Canyon Airlines," he said. " 'We don't lose *all* of them.' " It didn't do much to lift their mood. When Kelly last spied the trio Mark was hugging his mother in spite of the quarantine, while his father was awkwardly patting Mark's shoulder.

"Don't worry," Kelly had told him. "My mother came to one launch and won't come to another. Same reason: she doesn't want to see me blow up." Her father wouldn't come if her mother wouldn't. He had only attended Kelly's second launch because Clark wanted to see it. Nobody was here for the third one, and that was proving to be a blessing.

One surprise, for Kelly, had been the presence of Steve Goslin's wife, Diane, and both of their girls, Renee and Hannah. Kelly had met Diane before, at one of the crew barbecues Goslin had thrown over the months, but had only gotten a glimpse of Renee, the little girl whose illness had put Mark into that cockpit with Joe Buerhle. She was a serious little person with long blond hair who wore a T-shirt from some Clear Lake Bible camp. Kelly saw Mark watching Renee carefully, as if he owed her a handshake. Something.

Assuming everything went well.

Kelly had spent most of this second-to-the-last workday at the Cape attending to what people in CB called "the Ultimate Contingency plans"— the Big Contingency being a situation in which everything did not go well. One of the astronauts assigned as family escort was in charge of the grim business of ensuring that life insurance forms, burial plans and wills were signed, filled out, filed and available. Kelly had life insurance, of course, and had drawn up a will and made out burial plans for her first mission three years ago. She was to be cremated, with her remains scattered at sea off the Cape.

There was now a company which, for a fee of a few thousand dollars, would rocket small amounts of human remains into orbit. Winding down after an early-morning sim two weeks back, Dave Freeh had suggested— jokingly, Kelly hoped—that the crew should approach the company and ask for a group rate. Goslin hadn't found it funny, while Kelly's attitude was this: if she got killed during launch she would take that as a sign from God that her mortal remains were to be forever earthbound.

What Kelly had not done, until the brunch guests were making their quick exits (protocol said that they should stay no more than an hour), was have any private time with Mark. There had been an opportunity at breakfast late the previous night, when he seemed to want to talk about something. But both of them knew that Kelly was scheduled to spend the evening flying more approaches in the STA.

In their first moment alone on the deck, Mark had simply said, "How come you never told me about you and Joe Buerhle?"

And there it was. She had been a complete idiot to think she could have kept something like that quiet. Of course, she had been promising herself for months that she would sit Mark down and tell him. The problem was, a good time had never presented itself. Not during training sessions, for example. Not during Christmas. They had spent evenings and weekends together, but Kelly had been convinced Mark would feel so betrayed he would walk out on her. Inviting that sort of action was like picking a day to have the flu.

"Tell me what you've heard," she said.

"Don't you want the chance to deny it?"

"I think I'd be better off admitting everything and taking my punishment." She winced: that had come out way too flip.

Fortunately Mark was being too wounded to notice. He calmly told her what Whitsett had told him. Some of the information was a surprise to her. "He told you that I leaked Joe's memo to him?"

"That's what he seemed to be saying."

"That little bastard." Now she was really in trouble.

"So that's true, too."

"It's all true, all right? Yes, I had a long relationship with Joe Buerhle. Yes, I leaked his memo to the press. Anything else you want to know?" She was suddenly angry. Jesus Christ, they had a mission to fly! Why was Mark picking *now* to have a fight?

Dave Freeh and his wife came out on the deck for a moment. They were laughing and Kelly got the clear idea that Dave had had a beer or three. The happy couple, dangerously close to one another, took one look at Kelly and Mark and retreated. "Later!"

"Why?" Mark repeated. "Why didn't you tell me?"

Kelly weighed her answer. "There was just never a good time. What you don't know because nobody knows is that Joe and I broke up just before the accident. I mean, that morning. So we—Joe and me—were history at that point. Before you and I even met. And by the time we got involved, it seemed pretty goddamn awkward. Given what had happened, I mean."

"Awkward. There's an interesting word."

"It was an interesting situation."

"What about the memo?"

"I wanted to get Fehrenkamp off his fat ass. He wasn't doing anything about what we told him, if you'll recall. And I wanted to do one last thing for Joe.''

''Even though you'd broken up with him.''

''Yeah. Call me sentimental.'' She put her arms around his neck, and damned if he didn't take them away! ''So it's going to be like that.''

''I don't know,'' he said.

''Words failing you?''

''Right now, yeah.''

That was it. ''Fine,'' she said. ''When you feel like communicating, let me know. We've got a mission to fly and I need some rest.''

And she turned and walked off the deck.

CHAPTER 55

Drury didn't get the chance to thank Mark Koskinen at the beach house gathering, and it wasn't until the next morning, Wednesday, June 9, that he caught up with him at the crew quarters building next to the VAB.

He had almost turned back to his motel half a dozen times on the long drive up Highway A1A because he felt so out of place. It was silly of him, he knew: over the thirty-five years he had spent with NASA he had probably spent two of those years at KSC, a week at a time. But in those days he had a job to do. Even ten years ago, during the first years of Shuttle operations, he had come here on business, never as a tourist.

His VIP badges gave him access to everything but the launchpad itself, and he probably could have gotten a tour if he'd asked, but he was damned if was going to do that. He'd seen launch vehicles up close before, feeling the chill breeze blowing off the stages filled with supercold liquid oxygen, hearing the groaning and hissing of the metal literally changing shape. There was nothing he needed or wanted out of such an encounter.

He was here now, early on Wednesday morning, instead of back in his motel room talking on the phone to New Mexico, because of the time difference. The Spacelifter team worked long days, but even they didn't start until 7:00 A.M., and that was still an hour away. He had also slept badly the night before, in a bed that was so soft it left him with a nagging backache that still hadn't gone away.

"Mr. Drury!" Wearing his blue flight suit, Koskinen met him at the downstairs desk. "Thanks for coming." He stopped about five feet away. "Sorry—the quarantine."

"Thank you for the invitation." Drury was too old-fashioned to accept an invitation without thanking the inviter in person. "I suppose I really ought to see one of these babies lift off before I die."

"I hope it's half as exciting as the Spacelifter."

"Well, it'll be a lot bigger." Drury was pleased that Koskinen remembered the Spacelifter. So many astronauts ignored the project, since they weren't going to fly it.

Keeping their distance from each other, they walked outside, heading around the white blister that was the KSC public affairs center, ending up near the bleachers that looked directly across three miles of grassland and water to the two Shuttle launchpads.

"I was a little surprised that you invited me," Drury told Mark. "I had the feeling you were a little upset with me."

"I'm sure the feeling was mutual."

"Well, you and your gal friend were being a bit pigheaded about things."

"Everybody was doing what he had to do. I think we're all on the same side now. Aren't we?"

"I'm not even sure there are sides. That whole Stipe business is out of my hands." He still wasn't sure he believed that Stipe was a murderer, though subsequent conversations with Fehrenkamp had convinced him that the flight crew operations director did. That was the reason the "final" report on Joe Buerhle's accident was still "pending." Fehrenkamp wanted to resolve the Stipe matter first. "I suppose it's still uppermost in your mind, though."

"One of many things right now."

Drury blinked. The June sunlight seemed especially bright here, reflecting as it did off the white press dome and the huge white VAB. "Do you feel ready?"

Koskinen took a moment to answer. "Sometimes. I know what I'm supposed to do inside the orbiter. I even spent two weeks crawling around the Mir mock-up over in Russia, so I should know my way around there.

"But, I mean, what's going to happen? Do I think I can predict it? It scares the shit out of me."

Drury nodded toward Pad 39A. You couldn't actually see the Shuttle stack from here, since the launch support structure blocked it. But the Shuttle was there. "Going on that thing would scare the shit out of me."

"Just because it's got a failure rate of one in sixty-eight, and we're well into the second sixty-eight?" Koskinen was grinning, but it was the same grin Drury had seen on Marines going into landing boats. "I just have to trust the launch team on that. Nobody lives forever."

"I shouldn't have said anything."

"I'm glad you did. It's the one thing on everybody's mind, and nobody wants to be the first to talk about it." Koskinen crossed his arms, looked out at the stack. Then he said, "Can I ask you a question?" Drury nodded. "Why didn't you come to watch a Shuttle launch?"

"Superstition. I just felt it would be—I don't know, bad luck."

"They had bad luck without you being here."

"I wasn't talking about bad luck for the Shuttle." He wanted to change the subject. "I have a question for you: why the hell did you invite me?"

"Because you're one of the people who put me here," he said. "You and Fehrenkamp."

Drury started to laugh. Wonderful! It wasn't just a magnanimous gesture—it was a form of punishment! *If I blow up, you're going to have to watch!* Maybe young Koskinen would come out of this after all.

He held out his hand, then drew it back. "Sorry! I forgot about the quarantine."

Mark took it anyway. "It's been interesting, sir."

Drury was unlocking his car when Les Fehrenkamp caught up with him. "Someone told me you were in the vicinity."

"Just paying my respects."

"I hope we'll be having a conversation in about two weeks."

"I hope so, too. I hate unfinished business."

"You understand that there might be some . . . radical changes in the report."

For the second time that day, Drury found himself laughing. "I'm beyond concern, Les. If you haul that guy down here and charge him with murder, you're going to be the lead on every newscast in the world. No one's going to give two shits about my little accident report."

Now there was an awkward silence. Drury had reminded Fehrenkamp of the awful penalties for getting the truth out. "How much does Goslin know?"

"Very little."

"Tell him the whole shebang and right now. It was fine to keep him out of the loop before, but he's in quarantine, and he's going to be flying your billion-dollar spaceship tonight. You don't want him surprised, and you don't want him wondering what two of his guys are up to."

"I'll think very hard about that."

Drury wedged himself into the front seat. Christ, it was hot! Why had he let the rental agency give him a car with a dark blue interior? "One other thing . . . what happens to your two bounty hunters when this is over?"

"Kondratko goes back to Russia."

"What about Koskinen?"

"Well, I suppose it all depends on how things turn out, doesn't it?"

Drury looked at Fehrenkamp for a moment. He seemed so small, so perfectly pleasant, in his slacks and short-sleeved white dress shirt. Like a high school chemistry teacher or a clerk at City Hall. "Can I give you a ride somewhere?"

Fehrenkamp stared back. "To the admin building." He got in the passenger side as Drury started up the car.

The trip to the admin building was short and silent. Finally Drury said, "Don't take this out on Koskinen, Les. I know you: this business has been so goddamn unpleasant that you're not going to want this kid around. He'll be a constant reminder of the pain. You can stand there right now and tell me the kid's not in trouble, but you were itching to get rid of him the day he punched out of Joe Buerhle's airplane. Let's face it, it would have been better for you if he'd never made it."

"You make me sound like some kind of vindictive monster, Don."

"You are," Drury said. "I am, too. That's why we've been good for this agency." He had never actually said that before—perhaps he'd never quite realized it. He suddenly felt tired. "We're tools, Les. The hammers and chisels you use to knock holes in things. Nice people don't get the job done."

Fehrenkamp blinked. Then he nodded and got out of the car.

Drury watched him go for a moment. Fascinating man; he wondered briefly what other secrets he held.

Then he pulled back into traffic. God, there was a lot of it this morning.

CHAPTER 56

"You're all zipped up, Commander." The suit technician patted Steve Goslin's shoulder before turning to Jeff Dieckhaus, who was still struggling with his launch escape suit (LES).

The orange LES—better known as the Pumpkin Suit—wasn't really a space suit. It was a cousin of the pressure suits worn by pilots flying high-altitude recon missions in birds like the SR-71, a job Goslin would have loved. At least there was a reason for having the suits on an SR-71. Pilots had bailed out of the Mach 3 birds from time to time and lived.

The Pumpkin Suits, on the other hand, were designed to give the crew protection against loss of pressure and toxic fumes in case of a high-altitude bailout, or just as importantly, to allow an astronaut to survive for several hours in the cold waters of the Atlantic.

In Goslin's informed opinion, it was all window dressing. He calculated that the chances of an abort mode that would require—or even allow—use of the Pumpkin Suits was so slight that it didn't justify the discomfort. And they were uncomfortable: stiff, heavy, with limited range of movement and vision. You had to carry your own little air conditioner with you when you went out to the pad. An orbiter cockpit was so cramped during the leadup to ignition, with the crew lying on its collective backs, that Goslin was afraid someday some orange elbow was going to impact the wrong switch. Bad news.

He wondered what Fehrenkamp would do if he just stood up and started peeling the suit off. Just refused to wear it. Considering the extraordinary conversation they'd had an hour ago, right before breakfast, Goslin was tempted to try it.

In fact, he'd been more than half tempted to simply walk off the flight altogether. Hand the keys to Fehrenkamp and tell him to get some other fool.

So Koskinen and Kondratko had trained in secret to do an "extraction" on Cal Stipe! Cal Stipe, a five-time Shuttle veteran, was crazy! Had he not heard it directly from Fehrenkamp, Goslin would have laughed. "Tell me, Les," he had said. "Are they packing heat?" He imagined his two mission specialists carrying James Bond–style Walthers, or maybe those new plastic guns his brother was always talking about. Glocks. Would they stuff them into their personal kits? "Do we need a metal detector in the white room?"

Fehrenkamp clearly hadn't known what to say, and Goslin had been too angry to let him say much, anyway. He had always known that something was up with those two; there were all kinds of rumors floating around, most of them having to do with some kind of national security crap. He had done his own share of speculating with Dieckhaus, in their copious time off training for a complex rendezvous mission. The pilot had even phoned an old buddy of his now working in the National Reconnaissance Office to check out the rumors, but had been told pretty definitely that there was nothing to them. As far as the buddy knew.

Goslin had quickly forced himself to put his anger aside. To be a true Christian warrior. He told himself that Fehrenkamp's deception was just another test. He reminded himself of the pride he had felt when posing for the crew photo, his satisfaction with the last few sims, where the crew demonstrated supreme crystallization, everybody working in sync, almost without conscious thought, like a single organism.

An organism whose head was Steve Goslin.

"Just give me one straight answer," he had said to Fehrenkamp. "Are there any more surprises?"

"One's my limit."

They had talked about who else knew, and naturally Kelly Gessner's name was mentioned. That figured, since it had been clear to Goslin that his flight engineer and Koskinen were spending a lot of personal time together outside the simulator. They were both grown-ups and it hadn't affected their work, so he hadn't said anything. But it did bother him to think that Kelly had sat right behind him on the flight deck, in the cockpit of the STA, all those times knowing something he didn't know. And never told him.

That wasn't the kind of behavior you wanted from your flight engineer.

"Who can I tell?"

"I may regret this," Fehrenkamp said, "but I'm going to trust your discretion. Anybody you think needs to know."

"Dieckhaus."

"Absolutely."

"Freeh and O'Riordan."

"If you think so."

Goslin thought so, but decided to wait until they were on orbit. The fewer distractions they had, the better. "What does the MOD know?" If there was going to be some nasty business aboard Mir, the flight controllers shouldn't be surprised.

"My next set of conversations."

"How about the Russians?"

"Kondratko is the only one who knows anything."

Goslin smiled, not happily. "Good God, Les."

"We play the hand we're dealt, Steve."

Now, forty-five minutes later, with his weather briefing completed, with a breakfast in his belly and time to reflect, Goslin was more understanding of Fehrenkamp's situation. If he had told Goslin too early, he might have walked off the mission—or let the extraction business get in the way of his training.

When was a good time, anyway? So far Goslin hadn't had time to even talk to Dieckhaus!

Now he stood up, accepting a set of abort cue cards from one of the C-squares. He looked them over, confirmed they were his, with his own notes in colored ink, then zipped them into a sleeve pocket, where he fervently hoped they would remain. There were cue cards all over the orbiter cockpit, of course, but these were Goslin's lucky cards: he'd carried them on his two previous ascents and never taken them out of the sleeve.

Gessner and Freeh were the next pair to don their LESs. As he and Dieckhaus lumbered out, Goslin caught Gessner's eye. She was quick on the uptake. "You talked to Les," she said quietly. Goslin nodded.

"Thank God. It's been driving me crazy." And she gave him a hug. The simple touch washed away his anger. Or maybe he was just feeling more charitable this morning.

"It's going to work out fine," he heard himself tell her.

Then the door closed, and Dieckhaus said, "You talked to Les about what?"

*   *   *

It was an astronaut ritual to play a hand of Possum's Fargo prior to leaving for the pad. Everybody gathered around in the suiting room as Dieckhaus dealt. The idea was to play until the crew commander lost. It took exactly one hand.

"Well, that's twice already today," Goslin said as the cards were packed up. Only Gessner and Dieckhaus knew what he meant. He did see Koskinen and Kondratko exchange glances.

The final ritual was to hug Marie, the crew cook. She was a merry woman who had been concocting meals for astronauts for a decade or more.

Only then was it time for the "death march," the walk to the waiting bus past the photographers, just as the poor *Challenger* crew had done. How many times had Goslin seen that tape? Goslin and Dieckhaus led the parade, followed by the pair of Gessner and Freeh, then O'Riordan, Kondratko and Koskinen in a clump. This was roughly how they would board the orbiter, the first four climbing to the flight deck while the other three rode in steerage below.

Clint Hurley, who would start flying approaches in the Shuttle Training Aircraft within the hour, was with them, too. Fehrenkamp brought up the rear; Goslin doubted that one in ten thousand TV viewers could have named him.

Into the bus, then, and down the road to the pad.

Goslin looked down the bus at Koskinen, who was in the last row looking out the window. It was a nice summer evening, just after 8:30 P.M., so there was plenty of light. Still, there wasn't that much to see.

Goslin had sensed a little coldness between Gessner and Koskinen on the ride. Maybe he was silly, but he expected a little more warmth from the happy couple as they rode to what could be a fiery death. Of course, different people reacted to these kinds of situations in different ways. . . .

Thinking about the Koskinen deception got Goslin angry all over again, this time because of what it had cost him as a crew commander. The kid had some kind of trick memory: once he had loosened up in the sims, he had shown that he was a regular damn walking flight data file, as if he had the cards for the various ascent modes burned into his brain. All he needed was the percent of OMS propellant remaining in the tanks and the apogee and perigee of the orbit and he could tell you instantly whether you were in a transatlantic abort or an abort-once-around. You would never depend solely on that kind of data, but it would have been handy to have sat him next to Gessner on the flight deck.

Maybe next time. If there was a next time.

Within moments, it seemed, they were at the base of the launch complex. The Shuttle stack rose above them, blindingly white in the pad lights. A billion-dollar spaceship, Goslin thought, *and they're letting me fly it.* As they all gathered at the elevator, he indulged himself in a moment of pride at the trust NASA and his country had placed in him. Then immediately asked God's forgiveness.

"What about the astronaut prayer?" That was Gessner. The rookies in the crew looked baffled. Kelly had them form a rough circle and join their hands in the middle. "Dear God," she said, "don't let us screw up."

Even Goslin couldn't help laughing.

As he rode up with Dieckhaus—who hadn't said a word since the bus left the crew quarters—he thought about Diane and the kids, sitting there in the VIP area. They had talked about having her stay at home, but this was his command! She had watched him take off hundreds of times in their married life, and she wasn't going to stop now.

They walked across the swing arm to the white room, where the C-squares and the USA insertion team waited. Now the big white helmets went on. The gloves were clipped to the sleeves. Goslin, followed by Dieckhaus, crawled through the side hatch, then wrenched himself to an immediate right through the access. One of the C-squares was on the flight deck to help him turn left and climb up to the commander's seat.

He settled onto his back and got strapped in. Moments later Dieckhaus joined him. He was sweating from the exertion. "At least we don't have to worry about the cold," he said grimly. Cold was what had doomed the *Challenger.*

"We're going to have a great flight, Jeff. No more negative vibes." He got his comm line jacked in and heard, "Comm check, CDR?"

"CDR," Goslin said. "Sounds good." They would hold the checks of the other channels until all the crew members were aboard.

T minus ninety-five minutes. Somewhere over the North Atlantic the Mir complex—and Cal Stipe—waited. *Atlantis* would chase them for two days.

What would they find? Had Stipe gone completely crazy? Shaved his head and painted himself, like Marlon Brando in that movie? Or had he turned into a spacegoing Howard Hughes . . . all long hair and dirty fingernails, barricaded in one of the modules, refusing to come out?

He wished he knew more. But he also knew that you could only train for certain parts of a mission. The rest you had to leave to your team—and Cal Stipe, thank God, was not Goslin's worry.

CHAPTER 57

The problem with being mission specialist number four in a Shuttle crew of seven was that you really didn't have much to do with the launch. You were a passenger. Most pilots referred to the mission specialists as "baggage with mouths," anyway, and in Mark's case, and even Viktor's, it was truer than most. Except for answering "MS4" or "MS5" on the comm checks, they did no talking at all on the loop.

The only one of the three on the mid-deck who had a job was O'Riordan, who was the jump master in case of bailout. Mark shifted in his couch—his ass was falling asleep—and tried to think of more pleasant things than a return-to-launch-site abort and mid-ocean bailout.

He asked himself why he had acted like such a goddamn child with Kelly—right before their flight! Was it just the tension? Or was he really that immature?

Why hadn't he gone to her room this morning when they turned in? He could have apologized then. Of course, she could have come to him, too. But she had a few other things on her mind, such as flying the ascent with Goslin and Dieckhaus from the flight engineer's seat.

Before their blowup, back when they were still speaking to each other, Kelly had told Mark to be ready for the moment of fear. "It'll hit you when you're finally strapped in and all you can do is wait," she had said, and boy was it turning out to be true.

It was as if he were seeing his life flash before his eyes. The time the neighbor lady had caught him and Randy Toutant throwing mud balls at her house. The night Debbie Milhouse let him unhook her bra. Having a ringside seat at Space Command the night Operation Desert Storm began, when the planes went into Baghdad.

He thought about the interviews he had survived to become an astronaut candidate. Facing five strangers—including a veteran astronaut—across a table. Your résumé and school grades and references got you this far. Your medical exam kept you eligible. But the interview was where the decision got made, where NASA the entity asked itself the questions, "Is this the kind of person we can trust with our spacecraft? Is this the kind of person who can take our message to the public? Is this the kind of person we want to work with?" It was probably a lot like auditioning for the Bolshoi Ballet, without the dancing.

And all so he could plant himself on top of five million pounds of highly explosive and toxic material. Now that the white room had folded up and moved back with the access arm, the crew was alone. There wasn't another human being within three miles *because it wasn't safe!*

It was so easy to forget how dangerous this process was, blasting five million pounds of hardware from a standstill to a speed of 17,500 miles an hour, from sea level to an altitude of two hundred miles, all in about the same time it takes to eat a Popsicle. It had gone horribly wrong once. It had come close to going horribly wrong a number of other times—that number depending on how you cared to define *close*. Statistics said it would go horribly wrong about once in sixty-eight tries.

This was the ninety-ninth.

Mark tried to imagine the horror of being strapped into this seat when things went horribly wrong. Like the orbiter breaking up. The whole cabin would roll like a tin can booted down the street. The lights would go out. The fans would stop. Then you would simply fall. You would fall until you hit the water at two hundred miles an hour, like hitting a concrete floor.

He imagined a desperate attempt to get out . . . to somehow unbuckle himself and crawl across Kondratko and O'Riordan, to blow the hatch and fall free. Depending on the nature of the horror, he and his two partners in steerage might have the ghost of a chance of getting out. A ghost.

But for the four upstairs on the flight deck, no way.

So it was possible that he might live and Kelly would die.

"How're you doing?" Viktor said next to him, nudging him.

"Fine," he said, lying.

"Talk to me, because I'm sitting here remembering how Soyuz has a launch escape system."

Mark laughed. He sort of doubted that Kondratko, a veteran pilot, was sweating the launch as much as he was. He had probably noticed Mark's knuckles going white. "Let's call Goslin and tell him we want to change our minds."

"But then who would do the, what do they call them, the tear-down EVAs?"

"That's their problem."

"You boys all right over there?" That was O'Riordan, whose mid-deck seat was mounted in front of the hatch, several feet from Kondratko's. Not entirely out of earshot, apparently.

"Doing fine, Donnie," Kondratko said.

"We've got a visitor."

Mark and Kondratko both turned—not an easy task in their helmets—and saw Kelly's head and shoulders emerging from the access. She hauled herself to her feet, standing on what would, on orbit, become the rear bulkhead of the mid-deck. Mark thought of Fred Astaire sidestepping up a wall in one of those old musicals. "Steve just heard from Mission Control. We're not looking at any further holds. Weather's good up and down the range. So we should be lighting up on schedule in thirty minutes."

Mark knew most of that, of course. He could hear the air-to-ground traffic in his headphones. "Aren't you supposed to be upstairs?" O'Riordan asked.

"Come on, those guys don't listen to me," she said. "Our steely commander just wanted me to look in on our rookies." She tugged at O'Riordan's straps, then turned to Kondratko. That was a more difficult maneuver, like reaching into a top bunk bed. "To make sure everybody was safe and snug."

"We've got the snug part handled," Mark said.

It was impossible for Kelly to reach far enough to check Mark's buckles. But she took hold of his hand. "We'll handle the safe part," she said quietly. She caught Mark's eye—was that a plea for forgiveness? Or an offer of the same?

Then she slapped Kondratko on the shoulder. "I hope that wasn't your hand I just felt on my ass."

"You can't possibly feel anything through the LES," Kondratko protested. It was all in good fun; Kondratko couldn't reach far enough to pat Kelly's ass even if he wanted.

"I'll see you all"—she pointed—"upstairs."

Then she wiggled through the access again.

The next few minutes might as well have been seconds. Mark wondered if he dozed, because suddenly Goslin was shouting down to them from the flight deck, "Five minutes, everyone." Mark pulled on his left glove. He extended his bare right hand to Kondratko. "Good luck to all of us."

"Even Mr. Stipe," Kondratko said. Oh, yeah, Mark thought. Cal Stipe—the reason I'm in this situation.

Then: "Two minutes. Faceplates." The three passengers were already reaching up to close them.

"There goes the cap," Freeh called. The cap for the giant rust-colored external fuel tank swung away in the last minute.

In the outside world, on NASA Select TV, a public affairs officer would be giving a countdown. "T minus thirty-one seconds. Guidance is now internal." But inside there were only the ritual exchanges between Goslin and Arnaldo Rivera, the ascent capcom back at JSC.

Without warning Mark became aware of a roaring somewhere far below him. He felt the whole Shuttle stack sway. "Three good engines!" Goslin said.

WHAM! The solid rocket motors on either side of the tank lit up, and the cabin seemed to shoot upward, like an elevator run by a demented operator.

Mark thought he heard Rivera say "Tower clear" in his headphones. He hoped so, as the Shuttle suddenly rolled over on its back. They were still heading more or less straight up, but were now pointed to the northeast, slightly away from the Florida coast.

The noise was shattering. The entire cabin shook on three different axes, vibrating so hard and so fast and in so many directions at once that Mark thought his fillings were going to fly out.

One of the storage lockers flew open and a wall of plastic food packages cascaded out, a good number of them right into Kondratko's lap. Mark and Kondratko were both startled by it. Then both started laughing.

Only after a minute of this did Mark begin to feel true G forces pressing him into the seat. It wasn't much more than you'd feel on an airliner, except for the fact that you were upside down, on your back, and being shaken in a blender thirty stories tall.

Now the real countdown began . . . to SRB separation at two minutes and forty-five seconds. With the rattling and roaring it was still hard to hear, but everything seemed to be going all right up on the flight deck—

Thirty seconds. "Come *on!*" That was O'Riordan.

Things could still go wrong on the climb to orbit, but they would involve the Shuttle main engines, which could be throttled or shut down. There would be time to think and react—

Shutdown! Just like that the rattling and roaring stopped. Now the ride *was* like a cruising airliner on a clear day . . . bright and smooth. Now came more G forces, as the lighter stack—having dropped the SRBs and burned thousands of pounds of fuel—began to pick up speed.

Mark could hear again. "*Atlantis*, Houston, two-engine TAL." That was one of the abort milestones.

"Roger, Houston." Goslin sounded calm, as if he'd been doing this all his life.

More G forces now, probably near the maximum of three. Mark felt heavy but knew it was nothing like the old days of Mercury and Apollo.

What was that? A warning bell? "Shit," he heard from the flight deck. *Just when he'd started to relax*! It could all still end badly! He wished he was on the flight deck. He wanted to be able to *do* something, not just wait—

"We've got a warning light on an APU," Goslin shouted to the crew, meaning one of the three auxiliary power units that moved the orbiter's flaps and other aerodynamic control surfaces. "It's fine, don't worry." The APUs had to work or there wouldn't be a launch. The problem was, they also had to work for landing.

When Apollo 12 had blasted off in a thunderstorm back in 1969 it had been struck by lightning, which knocked out its electronic systems for several minutes. The spacecraft had limped into orbit, where everything was brought back on-line. No one on the ground or in the spacecraft knew, however, whether the lightning had damaged the parachutes that were needed to bring Apollo safely home. The decision then had been, We might as well let them go to the Moon. That was how Mark felt about the APUs.

Besides, he was seeing that the loose strap ends on his suit were floating. So were some of those food packages that had gotten loose. They were in microgravity now—

"Main engine shutdown," Goslin radioed to Houston. Otherwise Mark would not have known. Then the commander called, "Welcome to space, people!"

On the mid-deck the newest world space travelers started clapping. And they weren't the only ones.

CHAPTER 58

A"*tlantis*, Houston, we can see the DM in the camera."

"Glad we're pointed in the right direction."

"That's a first," McDowell said to Yakubik, off-mike. The capcom laughed.

Scott McDowell stood at his console in Mission Control, Building 30-South, with capcom Greg Yakubik to his right and a TV image of the Mir space station on the big TV screen in front of him, listening to Dave Freeh playing grabass or whatever he was doing on the flight deck of the orbiter *Atlantis*.

Around JSC it was said that astronauts lost about forty I.Q. points when they went uphill. With some astronauts—Freeh was a good example—a loss of forty still left them in the upper tenth percentile of the general population. Still, it was a big difference from the integrated sims, when Freeh and Gessner and Koskinen, in particular, were always right there with the teams, if not several steps ahead. Now they were having to remind the crew—turn off that system, locate page 11 of the checklist, what did you say you lost this time?

There were solid physiological reasons for the apparent on-orbit stupidity. The shift of fluid to the head. The challenge of operating in microgravity, which overloaded the sensory system, as if the brain got so busy worrying about which end was up that it couldn't add two and two.

Astronauts who had flown before usually knew they were going to be stupider for the first few days and made adjustments, the same way a baseball player coming back from an arm injury would warm up slowly and carefully. McDowell felt that Goslin and Gessner had made the adjustment; Dieckhaus had gotten a little sloppy.

The others—well . . . It was only three days into the mission, with seven to go. There was time for improvement.

Besides, astronaut stupidity aside, STS-100 was going well. Right now *Atlantis* was about eight miles behind Mir, coming up on its terminal initiation (TI) burn. During the three days since reaching orbit, Goslin and Dieckhaus had made eight other burns, each one aimed at reshaping *Atlantis*'s orbit and allowing it to catch up to Mir with minimal use of fuel.

Following the TI burn, *Atlantis* would slowly close in on the Russian station, ultimately winding up slightly below the docking module (DM) on the R-Bar, the imaginary line connecting the DM to the center of the earth. Then Goslin would fly *Atlantis* up that line using the orbiter's steering thrusters. They would be in a low-Z mode, meaning that any thrusters that pointed directly at Mir were disabled.

"Tell them 'go' for TI," McDowell said, looking at his screen after hearing the report from the proximity operations team. Yakubik relayed the message to the crew.

McDowell assumed the docking would go well. Nine earlier dockings had succeeded without so much as a hiccup, a real tribute to the training people, to the prox ops teams, and to the hardware itself.

It was what was scheduled to come *after* docking that had him worried.

Les Fehrenkamp had finally come to see him yesterday after the orbit-one shift briefing, to let him know what was really up. He had found it easy to believe that Cal Stipe was in need of extraction; someone should have extracted Stipe out of CB years ago. But to have gone to such elaborate lengths to train Koskinen and Kondratko in secret . . . "Why, Les? If you can't trust the MOD, who can you trust?"

Well, shit, he had known the answer to that before it was out of his mouth: Les Fehrenkamp trusted no one. "If the real reason comes out, you'll understand why we didn't talk about it."

"And that's it? 'Don't be surprised if a couple of the MSs grab hold of Stipe and tape him to his seat in the mid-deck? I'd tell you more but I'd have to kill you'?"

Fehrenkamp had smiled his tight smile. "I'd probably have to kill myself, Scott."

Now what was *that* all about? A cry for help from Les Fehrenkamp? For some reason that statement absolutely chilled McDowell. He had half considered calling one of those suicide-prevention hot lines, but then he remembered who he was dealing with.

"Burn's looking good," prox ops told McDowell. As flight director he was always presumed to be listening and watching. It was not required that he respond. "Shutdown . . . nominal."

"Tell them they did a good job, Greg."

"*Atlantis*, Houston, burn was nominal. Good job."

They heard a curt "Thank you" from Goslin.

It wouldn't be much longer now. The orbiter would be moving so slowly that from inside Mir—they were getting a video feed via the Korolev control center even now—it would barely appear to be moving. That was fine; you had two vehicles each massing about a hundred tons essentially falling free. If one of them bumped into the other it would be enough of a bad day for everyone. There was no rush—

McDowell wondered if Fehrenkamp would come to Mission Control for the docking; he usually did. But he had already missed several STS-100 milestones. Had someone said Fehrenkamp was on a day trip out of town? Out of town somewhere other than the Cape? That made no sense.

Now *Atlantis* was on station about 170 feet directly below Mir. "Korolev says we're go for docking," the MCC rep there reported. McDowell polled his own team, imagining Goslin at the aft control panel, looking through one of the overhead windows. Dieckhaus would be sitting in the commander's seat while Gessner would be operating the rendezvous and prox ops computer.

"Go for docking," McDowell told Yakubik.

The crew would spend the first working day moving cargo from the SpaceHab into Mir. On the second day they would be working in reverse, moving experiments and materials back to the SpaceHab for return to Earth. The third day would see Kondratko and Koskinen's "teardown" EVA, with a little help from the Mir-31 guys.

At what point, and on what secret timeline, did it say "Grab Cal Stipe"? Logically it would be day four, the day before undocking, but logic did not appear to be at work here.

Atlantis stopped about thirty feet from the docking module for a final alignment check, then proceeded. . . .

McDowell suddenly felt depressed. He was never going to be on an orbiter's flight deck. The hiring freeze had been the first bullet in his final application. This business with Stipe would be the second, and the third, even if it all worked out! He would be too notorious. He was looking into the open grave of his astronaut career. Joe Buerhle had been right: he just didn't have it.

"We're docked, Houston," Steve Goslin said.

"Smooth as a baby's butt," McDowell said. Yakubik turned and looked at him. "Say it however you want," he told him.

"Ah, *Atlantis*, Houston. Nothing but silk, Steve."

McDowell felt a hand on his shoulder. He turned—it was Carl Strahan. "Good job."

Did Strahan know? Probably not, given that he wasn't actually working the mission. "Did you hear the news?" Strahan said.

"What news?"

"Something about a high-ranking NASA official being found dead. Heard it in passing out in the hall."

NASA official dead? McDowell remembered Fehrenkamp's comment. "Who?"

"No fucking idea," Strahan said. "All I know is that *I* feel fine."

NASA N E W S

National Aeronautics and
Space Administration
John F. Kennedy Space Center
Kennedy Space Center, FL 32899
407 867-2468

June 12, 1999
Barry Leudtke
(Phone: 407/867-2468)

FORMER NASA OFFICIAL DRURY DIES

Donald Drury, former associate administrator for engineering, and a 35-year veteran of NASA, died at the Kennedy Space Center yesterday afternoon.

Drury, currently serving as a consultant to the Spacelifter program in Las Cruces, New Mexico, was attending the STS-100 launch as a special guest of the crew. He apparently suffered a heart attack while driving. His car left the road and flipped over. Paramedics pronounced him dead at the scene.

Born in Kansas City, Missouri, in 1925, Drury served in the United States Navy during World War II, then attended Purdue University, graduating in 1950. For three years he worked for the Bell Aircraft Company, then joined the staff of the N.A.C.A. in its Piloted Aircraft Research Division. He was one of the original members of the Space Task Group which managed Project Mercury, and held positions in the Gemini, Apollo, Skylab and Space Shuttle programs until his retirement in 1988.

He is survived by his wife, Virginia. Funeral arrangements are pending.

CHAPTER 59

How easy would it be to sabotage a Shuttle launch?'' Les Fehrenkamp asked Walter Thompson.

They were in line at a Starbuck's inside the gigantic main terminal of Dallas–Fort Worth International, a horribly public and noisy place this afternoon. Fehrenkamp realized that he was mentally exhausted, or he would never have allowed himself to think such a question, much less verbalize it.

The young man from the NTSB almost flinched at the words, considered them, then said, ''Your system, Mr. Fehrenkamp, is so marginal that anyone who wanted to destroy it only has to sit back and wait. It would be very difficult to compromise a specific mission. I mean, you have awesome security and, most important of all, a limited number of passengers. I don't think your astronauts are potential terrorists.''

Don't be too sure about that. Fehrenkamp stopped himself before he could utter those words. He really needed a rest.

''But statistics say you're going to, uh, lose one again soon, either on launch or landing. That's if you don't manage to ram one into Mir or the Space Station.'' He paused to order a coffee, some Sumatran boigne, if Fehrenkamp heard correctly. ''The only way you can approach commercial safety rates for your Shuttle is to quit flying it.''

Fehrenkamp ordered a cappuccino, not that he would do more than warm his hands on it, then turned to join Thompson at a table that was slightly larger than a serving plate. ''Is that what you came to see me about? Accident prevention?'' Thompson asked.

Over the last few days, for the briefest of moments, Fehrenkamp had allowed himself to picture *Atlantis* being hit with a sudden crosswind on landing, just enough to kick it off the runway, where it would almost certainly flip over at almost two hundred miles an hour, shattering into a thousand pieces and almost certainly killing the crew. And eliminating all knowledge of the Cal Stipe situation.

Fehrenkamp hated himself for even allowing the image to form in his mind, the way he hated himself for luxuriating in the sight of a handsome young man. He was not that kind of man. The murdering kind of man, that is.

Besides . . . an unfortunate accident that silenced Koskinen and Gessner and Kondratko and Goslin—and Stipe!—still left that mystery man Koskinen had told him about in their first conversation, the man on the board who knew about the tissue.

A little sleuthing by Melinda Pruett at headquarters had pointed at young Mr. Thompson and gotten Les Fehrenkamp on a plane this morning. In a way the news that Thompson was also aware of the "situation" was a relief, since it allowed Fehrenkamp to bring Scott McDowell into the circle as well. McDowell would never tell. Fehrenkamp's purpose here was to make sure Walter Thompson wouldn't, either. "I need your help," he said simply. "I think you know why."

Walter Thompson seemed to be examining his cup of overpriced, overheated coffee. "Your Joe Buerhle mess?" he said, finally, with what seemed to be a bit too much pleasure. "I'm going to find this fascinating."

"I'm not going to bribe you, Mr. Thompson. I'm not going to threaten you, either. I don't frankly know what you know.

"I'm not trying to cover my ass. I'm trying to get the human race into space," Fehrenkamp said, warming to his own sense of purpose, thinking of Mark Koskinen and Kelly Gessner—and Cal Stipe. And poor old battered Mir. And *Atlantis* floating around the Earth. How the hell was that going to end? If Fehrenkamp thought about it, he got tired and frightened at the same time. "I'm perfectly aware that I work in a system that is often arbitrary, corrupt, wrongheaded, whatever you want to call it. I wish it were better. I try to make it better—"

Thompson was holding up a hand. "Stop. Just, please . . . stop. I believe you believe it. You and all your little Boy Scouts and Girl Scouts; I hope you all get a chance to walk on Mars.

"There's nothing you can offer me, Mr. Fehrenkamp. Nothing you can beat me with, either, thank God. I've been out to my bosses for years now. Your world is a hostile one, so don't expect me to defend it. . . ."

Had he said "out"?

"Actually, Walter . . . may I call you Walter? I think we do have something in common."

CHAPTER 60

Welcoming ceremonies for Shuttle crews visiting the Mir space station had, after nine previous dockings over three years, fallen into a routine. There was a brief ceremony when the connecting hatch was opened. Hands had to be clasped more or less in the middle—though never, because of Russian superstition, over the threshold itself—between the commanders, no one else. The Shuttle crew carried a loaf of bread and salt, in deference to another Russian tradition.

Then it was on with the tour, and ultimately the business.

Mark was the last of the STS-100 crew to float into the station. Goslin had been first, of course, with Viktor Kondratko right behind, to provide some translation and cultural interface. Goslin knew some Russian; everyone on the crew had had to go through fifty hours of instruction. Fortunately the current Mir crew, Petrenko and Belokonev, were fluent in English. Well, better in English than the Shuttle guys were in Russian.

And then there was Stipe, of course.

He took up the third place in the receiving line, as the seven visitors floated up from the orbiter's airlock, through the docking adapter into the spherical Russian multiport unit, and finally into the Mir core module itself, shaking hands, offering hugs. With his beard and his face softened by months in microgravity he looked like a distant cousin at a family reunion, not some crazy man.

Not a murderer.

Stipe took Mark's hand firmly and pulled him toward him. "Boy, I have to say I never expected to see *you* here."

"It was a big surprise to me, too."

"Well, welcome to Mir."

Mark found himself struggling to make small talk. "So, where do you bunk around here?"

"Used to be right here in the DM." Stipe said. "I moved to the Soyuz." The Soyuz vehicle was parked at a docking collar at the opposite end of the Mir complex from the Shuttle. It was as far as you could go and still be aboard the station. Mention of Soyuz set off an alarm in Mark's head—there was something ominous about that. Stipe taking it in his head to leave prematurely? No, no, not that.

But what?

"All right, my crew," Goslin was saying from the hatchway, right below the portrait of Yuri Gagarin, "we need to spend a few moments on safety issues." That was certainly true: it took a hundred hours of training before a crew member was considered "safe" on the orbiter, and Mir had probably six times that volume in its various modules, including closed-off Spektr. The 100 crew had gone through the simulator at the Gagarin Center, but that had involved less than an hour in each of the modules, taking notes from one of the uniformed lecturers. It was nothing like floating here in a blizzard of cables, with food bags and papers taped to the walls.

Mark found that he was able to move through the different modules with relative ease. He had been a little worried, because he had been a very sick puppy his first day in orbit.

Having space adaptation syndrome (SAS) wasn't as bad as being seasick, but it was close. Mark's head had felt full, his hands and feet were cold, and he occasionally felt—accurately—that he didn't know up from down. It was a relatively common ailment: half the people who went into space were susceptible, and there was no way to predict who that would be. An astronaut's physical condition was no indicator, nor was a background in, say, gymnastics or aeronautical acrobatics. One of the earliest sufferers, a Skylab astronaut, had flown with the Thunderbirds.

Fortunately SAS was treatable with scop-dex, and virtually certain to clear up within a day, two at most. And Mark was not alone in his suffering. Kondratko was green, too. And to Mark's surprise, so were Goslin and Kelly. "I thought space veterans didn't get sick," he had told her as they tried to keep out of everyone's way.

"You thought wrong."

At least they were talking again, acting as if there hadn't been an argument. In spite of the fact that *Atlantis* carried a SpaceHab module and the docking tunnel, there was no real chance for a private conversation, not with either Freeh or O'Riordan spending all their time in the SpaceHab. In addition to serving as the orbiter's sick bay, the mid-deck was constantly in use for meals, treadmill exercise and attempts at sleep.

There was the flight deck, of course, but with eight burns scheduled and a commander who was still feeling woozy, it was no place for "baggage," not this early in the mission. Mark had floated up there once on the first day to take in the stunning view of Earth flying below them.

Then he had gone below again.

As he and Kondratko felt better, they spent their time practicing the donning of their EVA suits and working with their tools. Their hours in the big water tank had paid off: with a few easy adjustments, working in microgravity, even in the mid-deck or airlock, was a lot like working underwater. Even the addition of the SAFERs—the emergency maneuvering chestpacks Mark and Kondratko were to wear—wasn't nearly the complication Mark had feared.

Now, of course, they were aboard Mir, and the inevitable confrontation loomed.

The whole crew knew about the planned "extraction" by now. Goslin had been briefed by Fehrenkamp before launch; the commander had told his pilot. Sometime during that first day Dieckhaus had broken the news to Freeh and O'Riordan.

Last night before bed Goslin had gathered the crew on the mid-deck to discuss the matter. "As I see this, there are three ways this can go. Stipe can be a professional, and come back as planned. He can pout and carry on, and come back as planned. Or he can make things difficult.

"I feel confident I can handle the first two modes. As to when and how I break the news to him depends on my reading of his mood when we're face-to-face."

"Don't fool yourself, Steven," Kondratko said quietly. "He's going to ask you the moment you arrive. He will force you to deal with him."

If Goslin resented comments from a foreign guest in his crew, he hid it. "I suspect you're right, Viktor. This is Stipe we're dealing with. I think we can assume I'll be having that conversation sooner rather than later."

"And then what?" That was Dave Freeh, who, like Dieckhaus, still seemed to be angry about having been kept out of the loop for so long.

Kelly said, "If he gets pissy, we jolly him along, remind him what a genius he is, how he's the American record-holder, all of that. It's how everyone around CB's been dealing with the son of a bitch for the past ten years, anyway.''

"I can't believe he would refuse to come," Donal O'Riordan said. "It would be *incredibly* unprofessional." To Mark it seemed that O'Riordan was still treating the matter as a joke.

"I find this just as implausible as you do," Jeff Dieckhaus said. "But we've only just been read into this deal." He nodded at Mark and Kondratko. "Other people have been tracking this for a long time. We've got to be ready for—what, a fight?"

"Let's hope it doesn't come to that," Mark said. "But if it does—" He looked at Kondratko.

"We're ready," the Russian said. "I also plan to brief the main crew about a possible problem." He smiled. "I will tell them it's medical. Cosmonauts know that all disciplinary matters are ultimately called 'medical problems.' ''

Following his Mir safety briefing and tour, Mark had to join O'Riordan, Freeh and Dieckhaus back aboard the orbiter. Dieckhaus would man the flight deck while the other three began the process of transferring the food, water and other supplies Petrenko and Belokonev would need for the next few weeks. It was tedious work involving supermarket-like scanners (since the packages were all bar-coded), and especially at first, since none of them had actually moved the packages in microgravity through all the twists and turns. It took, in fact, twenty minutes just to move one item from the SpaceHab to its location aboard Mir.

Which was why Mark lost track of Goslin and Kelly—and of Calvin Stipe.

It was only at the end of his working day, five hours after docking, that he floated back to the mid-deck and found Kelly cooking dinner. "There you are," she said. "Goslin wants to talk."

"Okay."

Just when he thought she was back to being all business, Kelly reached out her hand and squeezed his arm. "How are you feeling?" Like Mark, she was wearing a black polo shirt with the STS-100 logo, and a pair of blue shorts. Her hair floated freely in microgravity. Even though it wasn't long, it still gave her an auburn halo.

She looked so lovely that Mark wondered again why he had doubted her. "I'm over it. How about you?"

"Same here. Good thing, too." She nudged him. "If you were still green, they wouldn't let you do the EVAs."

Here was his chance. He had framed the sentence in his mind—*I'm not mad at you anymore*—but then heard: "Kelly? Mark? Upstairs." It was Goslin on the flight deck.

"Our master's voice," Kelly whispered. She pulled herself through the access. Mark followed at her heels.

Goslin was here with Dieckhaus. "Kondratko was right," he said. "Stipe hit me with the big question the moment he had me alone."

"And then?" Kelly had never shown much patience for Goslin's style of storytelling.

"I told him the visit was over, that no matter what he was hearing from his friends at Life Sciences, when we pulled out, he was going to be with us."

"How did he take it?" Mark asked.

"Surprisingly well. He just nodded once, shook my hand, and said, 'It's been fun. I'll get packed.' "

So that was it. Well, Mark wouldn't be the first astronaut to have devoted hours to training for a contingency that never occurred.

"He did have one idea," Goslin said to Mark. "He wants to use one of the Russian suits and join you guys on your EVAs."

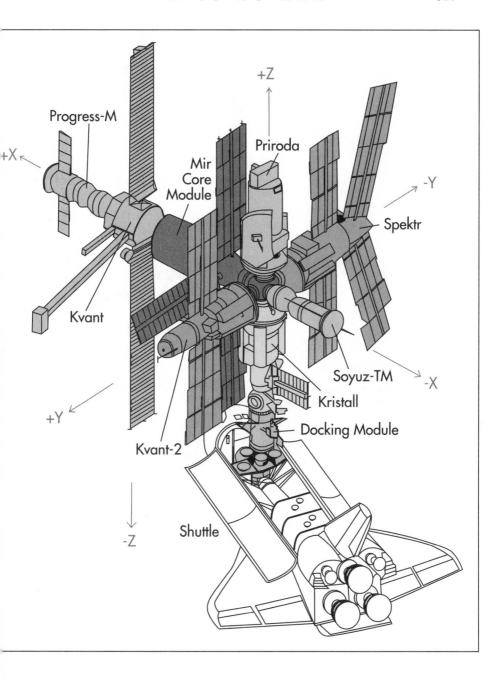

Mir Core Module / Kvant / Kvant-2 / Kristall / Spektr / Priroda / Docking Module /
Soyuz-TM / Progress-M / Shuttle-Mir Missions
Mir Components from Shuttle-Mir Web.

CHAPTER 61

The lone dissenter on the STS-100 crew on the matter of the Cal Stipe EVA was Kelly Gessner. Not that she was able to discuss her reservations with anyone but Mark. "This is what happens when you compartmentalize information," she told him. They were inside the Kristall module, which also contained the Russian Orlan EVA suits and the airlock. It was early the next working day. Kelly and Mark were hard at work moving food bags and water into Mir. Around lunch they would start to reverse the process, taking Stipe's baggage back to the orbiter, along with whatever Petrenko and Belokonev wanted to ship home.

"Why don't you say something to Goslin, then?"

"Is that the best you can do?" This was one of the things she didn't much like about Mark, this passive-aggressive shit. It made it a little easier to stay mad at him. "What's *your* opinion?"

"Stipe might actually be able to help us out there. He's done a Mir EVA already."

"You guys are trained. No one else needed anybody to hold their hands."

"We're minimally trained. Everybody else who did an EVA like this had a hell of a lot more experience."

"You know, you were a perfect selection. You can just lay out that party-line crap like you really believe it." She floated away from him, wondering why she had bothered to say anything at all.

Mark pushed himself along after her, catching her wrist. "You're right. I'm trying to avoid any more problems."

He had to stop when Petrenko floated into view, pushing a container the size of a suitcase. It contained the latest in a series of failed gyros for

312

Mir. "Coming through. Pardon," he said. He smiled over his shoulder, as if he were passing lovers in Gorky Park.

Then Mark said, "I'm just freaked out by the EVA, I think. It's all that's on my mind right now: don't screw it up." And this was one of the things she liked most about Mark—his willingness to admit his weaknesses. Her ex-husband, years past, had never been a champion in that department. And as for Joe Buerhle . . .

Forget Joe Buerhle. What about Kelly Gessner? She'd been doing a lot of thinking as she moved through the modules of Mir about what had gone wrong between her and Mark. Why she hadn't told him about her relationship with Joe Buerhle. Why hadn't she told Mark about the Hundred Mile Club, that very exclusive group of ten or twenty (the number varied) people who had had sex on orbit?

On day ten, two thirds of the way through their mission together, eleven days after their initial bout of lovemaking, Joe had floated up to the mid-deck where Kelly was working the late shift, alone. "Aren't you supposed to be sleeping?" she asked, noting that he was shirtless, wearing only a pair of regulation NASA shorts.

"Too quiet down there."

It was about four in the morning, Houston time. What little air-to-ground communication there was was between Spacelab and payload operations at Marshall. "How are the others?"

"Sacked out and zipped up." He grinned, then floated over and kissed her, grazing her cheek as he moved by. Holding herself in place with her left hand, she grabbed him with her right and hauled him back. "You can do better than that."

"I can try to do better," he said. "That is, if you want to."

"I even shaved my legs. I've got the cuts to prove it."

Joe pulled two bungee cords out of his pocket, hooking them behind him like a telephone man with his safety strap. They were now entwined and relatively motionless. "I get the horrible feeling you've done this before," Kelly said. She hoped not: Joe's first crew had been all male.

"It's all in the sims."

She unzipped her own shorts and pushed them down. He didn't bother to remove her underpants . . . merely tugging them aside as he entered her.

She tried to make sure she didn't hit a switch by mistake, but knew she was in the corner next to the folded, padded chairs. She wondered whether someone at Mission Control would call up for some bit of housekeeping.

But as the sun suddenly burst through the overhead window, she buried her face in Joe's shoulder and quit worrying.

But it had been thrilling. Reckless. Something she and Joe had shared. And yet, he had still dumped her. And she was still afraid to admit that. Even to Mark.

"I'm just trying to make it a little less freaky for you," she said.

He frowned. It was harder to read body language in microgravity than it was on Earth, but the message was clear: for all his willingness to concede Kelly's point, Mark still wasn't ready to fight for it. "Goslin's already made up his mind." He jerked his head in the general direction of the departed Yuri Petrenko. "The Russian's already got his people on board. Stipe in for Petrenko. Belokonev's even going to split his bonus with his buddy." Russian cosmonauts got paid additional chunks of money for doing EVAs. "Changing the plans again is going to be a big problem."

"So you'd rather risk your life than make a few waves?"

Mark burst out laughing. "I think you've not only summed up this particular matter, you've described my entire life."

O'Riordan was coming toward them now. Christ, wasn't there *one* private place on the whole station? "Okay," she said, knowing all too well what he was feeling.

Even if she was too cowardly to be honest, she could still take some kind of action. She could stop this EVA. Couldn't she?

After a session on the treadmill in the orbiter mid-deck, a group meal and a TV broadcast starring Donal O'Riordan for some schools in Ireland, Kelly returned to Mir to help with the off-loading. Whether anybody wanted her to or not, she was also going to have a talk with Cal Stipe.

She found him working in the orbital module of the Soyuz spacecraft. The Russian vehicle was docked at the opposite end of the complex from the orbiter *Atlantis*.

"Welcome," Stipe said when she rapped on the metal wall of the docking port. As she swam inside, Stipe smiled at her. He wore shorts and a gray T-shirt that was damp with sweat.

The spherical module—barely big enough for Kelly to extend both arms—was filled with Stipe's personal gear: clothing, food bags, sleeping gear and books that had been shipped up over the months. There was something odd about the light, as if there was a red filter over everything. Maybe that was the Russian style. Or maybe it was another sign that Stipe was far, far upriver.

Stipe had to wedge himself in the hatch that led from the orbital module into the even smaller bell-shaped descent module. "Amazing, isn't it?" he said. "At least one pair of cosmonauts spent eighteen days in space living in this."

"I'll bet it wasn't much fun."

"Nor very safe. They couldn't walk when they landed. I don't believe they were walking for several days thereafter." He grabbed a floating flight manual. "We still had to spend two days in this thing, between launch and docking."

Kelly shuddered at the idea. The orbiter was cramped enough with seven people, but three people in this! And all because the Russians were still using a rocket design from the 1950s and a spacecraft from the 1960s. They simply couldn't carry enough fuel to make the big burns necessary to make rendezvous any faster. "It's not a bad bedroom for one, though."

"No, it's great. The station's actually quite big by now."

"I've noticed. I think I even got lost."

"Just follow the cables . . . they'll always take you back to the core module." Kelly decided that seven months in space had done nothing to improve Stipe's sense of irony. She realized with a start that one week had dulled some of her senses, too. *Don't forget, this guy is a murderer!* "If you're here to off-load my things, I'm sorry to say I haven't finished packing. It's amazing how much junk I've acquired."

"I'm not here to help," she said, fighting hard to keep from showing how tense she was.

"What's on your mind?" She saw Stipe wedge himself more firmly in the hatchway, as if he expected her to spring at him.

"I don't think your EVA is a very good idea."

Stipe blinked once, twice, then looked at her as if he couldn't quite understand what she had said. "If that's your opinion, I'd be happy to discuss it. If it's—well, what is it, exactly?"

"I guess you'd have to call it my opinion. My professional judgment."

"Based on your EVAs." She had trained for an EVA but never made one, which Stipe knew.

"Based on mission needs."

" 'Mission needs'? What the hell is that? If this was all about 'mission needs' Fehrenkamp would be begging me to stay on for another six months! We need the medical data."

"Which has nothing to do with your EVA—"

"No. The EVA has everything to do with making sure all of the experiments some very dedicated people have put outside get brought inside, and in one piece, too, before Mir is abandoned. Most of these EVAs don't go as scheduled, you know. Even Petrenko and Belokonev had to do an extra one because they just didn't know their way around out there. And the MOD couldn't bring itself to schedule Koskinen and Kondratko for more than one, so why not have an expert along with them? It costs nothing and it might do a lot of good."

He was actually red in the face. Kelly wanted to get out of there but couldn't see how. And there was something about Stipe—her sense that it was all an act, all a simulation of righteous anger—that sent her over the edge. She thought about Joe Buerhle, then Allyson Morin, whom she'd never even met, and said, "You've got a lot of explaining to do, and we're not talking about this mission. I don't think you're mentally fit for an EVA. So stop trying to bullshit me, Cal. I'm not Les Fehrenkamp. You don't have any pictures of me or whatever you've got."

There was a long moment where Stipe actually seemed surprised. Probably one of the few times in his life. Suddenly he pulled Kelly toward him and kissed her. Now it was her turn to be surprised. She struggled, but he didn't let go. With his face right in hers, he said, "I don't need to bullshit you, Kelly, honey. I'm a pioneer, and so are you. Buerhle was bad. Now things are better. If they let me stay up here, they'll be better yet. People will get excited—they'll see that we *can* go to Mars."

Now he let her go. "You're a menace," she said.

"I'm going to do the EVA. And until then you're going to leave me the hell alone."

"What happens when I float out of here and tell Goslin?"

"I don't see you doing that, Kelly. Nobody wants to have an international incident aboard Mir. Think of the damage that would do."

There didn't seem to be anything else to say. She sure wasn't going to throw herself at Stipe.

She pushed herself out of the Soyuz, quickly rotated in the docking port, then swam as quickly as she could down the X-axis. Not for the first time this mission she wished she could take a shower. Or even a decent bath.

She needed time to think. What was she going to tell everybody now? If she told them anything at all?

CHAPTER 62

A problem had developed with Viktor Kondratko's SAFER chestpack. The propulsion unit itself, which would be attached to the life support backpack of Viktor's suit, was fine, but the chest-mounted control unit refused to tighten into place. So Mark, Kondratko and Freeh, who was the "intra-vehicular activity" crew member—the mission specialist assigned to assist the EVA team—literally took the mounting apart.

As with most routine manual tasks, this was a lot more difficult on orbit than on Earth. Mark ultimately wound up trying to hold the housing still so that Freeh could go to work on a stripped screw. Kondratko complained that this could just as easily be Mark's SAFER, not his. "Forget it," Freeh snapped. "Mark's has the red stripe, like his suit." The lead EVA crew member was distinguished from his partner by a red stripe. The marking had less to do with authority than it did with identification, allowing observing crew members and ground controllers to tell one spacewalker from the other.

The work went smoothly, if slowly, allowing Mark to brood about Cal Stipe and Joe Buerhle, and about Cal Stipe and Allyson. He kept picturing Stipe's nest in the Soyuz, using his memory to take a virtual tour of the cramped Russian spacecraft. Here was the spherical orbit module, here was the descent module with its three specially contoured couches. Here was the control panel, with the onboard computer and the Igla docking readouts . . . there was the package of rescue gear—

Suddenly Mark remembered what it was about the Soyuz and Cal Stipe that added up to a bad situation.

"Viktor, can you hold this?"

"We're just about done here," Freeh said.

"I just remembered something important." Without waiting for Freeh's consent, Mark handed the disassembled housing to Kondratko and pulled himself out of the airlock, turning into the docking module and heading up into Mir.

As he swam through the Kristall module he wondered whether he should have told Kondratko about his worry that there was a gun in Soyuz. They had been told all through their "extraction" training to back each other up. And here he was, going solo.

Well, he was backing Kelly up. And part of him didn't really believe that Stipe was crazy enough to go for the gun. . . .

He turned plus-X at the radial docking port and moved through the core module, squeezing past Volodya Belokonev, who was busy talking to controllers at Kaliningrad. *"Gdye Kellem?"* Mark asked, exhausting perhaps 20 percent of his available Russian vocabulary. "Where's Kelly?"

"Soyuz," Belokonev said, looking irritated at the interruption.

The Soyuz wasn't more than twenty feet away, but given the intervening hatchways and the bulk of the Kvant module, it seemed a lot farther.

He hauled himself out of Priroda, then through the core module, past Petrenko again, and into Kvant, just to the threshold of the Soyuz orbital module. He took a breath, hoping that Stipe had managed to get lost in one of the other modules—a surprisingly easy thing to do. "Hey, Cal, it's Koskinen!"

No answer.

Mark floated into the Soyuz orbital module. It was quiet, nothing but that strange red light washing over everything.

Through the spherical orbital module and into the cramped, bell-shaped Soyuz descent module. Maneuvering inside the smaller module was incredibly difficult: it was like the early Mercury spacecraft, the kind you "put on" rather than entered.

Mark's memory was clicking like a CD-ROM right now, thinking back to Voskhod-2, the world's first spacewalking flight back in 1965. The crew, Belyayev and Leonov, had ultimately landed way off in the Urals in the middle of winter. While waiting for rescue teams, they had been chased back inside the Voskhod by wolves. Since that time every Russian space crew had been equipped with a pistol called the TP-82, just in case. It was a three-barreled thing, two of them for flares, but one of them was capable of firing a twelve-millimeter bullet.

Mark found the survival kit wedged in behind the flight engineer's couch and started digging around.

No pistol. He couldn't tell whether the kit had been opened and the pistol removed. For a moment he wondered if he had misremembered; maybe Soyuz crews were no longer equipped with the TP-82. No . . . he could still picture the transparency in his mind, still see the instructor pointing to it in the big hall at the Gagarin Center.

The pistol was loose somewhere, and Cal Stipe probably had it.

Mark hauled himself out of the descent module, and had barely emerged into the Kvant when he saw the smiling face of Cal Stipe. "Hi, Mark," he said smoothly. "Find what you were looking for?"

Mark had not really been alone with Stipe since Allyson's death. He had wondered what he would feel. Would it be pity? Fear? He had his answer now: it was anger. Anger at what Stipe had done to Joe Buerhle. Anger at how Stipe had casually killed Allyson Morin. Anger at how this smug bastard could smile at him.

"As a matter of fact, I think I have." And he launched himself at Stipe.

He was clumsy in microgravity, of course, no match for Stipe. Nevertheless, he managed to bang the other man into the hard metal of the hatch. He skinned his own knuckles as well.

That was all Mark accomplished, because Kelly appeared out of nowhere and grabbed his legs, which allowed Stipe to slip past him toward Soyuz. "Mark, stop it!"

She was strong. She was braced and he wasn't. He literally couldn't get away from her. After a few breaths, he stopped trying.

Rubbing the back of his head, Stipe was watching him from the other hatchway, warily, eyes fearful. "Keep him away from me," he hissed at Kelly. And he disappeared inside Soyuz.

"He can't get away with this."

"He's not getting away with anything," Kelly said. "Quietly, all right?"

"All right." His breathing slowed. But he still wanted to take Stipe and bang his smug face into a hatch.

"Remember, there are nine of us and one of him. He's crazy, but he's not an idiot. He's so worried about his place in space history that he really won't do anything stupid. Well, more stupid. We just have to wait him out."

"I'm tired of waiting. I'm tired of keeping my mouth shut about these things just so I can protect the program. It's wrong. We should have called the cops. Stipe should be *on trial* right now, not sitting on Mir."

"I'm not going to argue with you. You're probably right. But it's too late—we made the choice to handle this quietly. And we have to see it through. That's what astronauts do, you know. We stick to the program even if it hurts.''

He looked into her eyes. They seemed bigger, brighter. Was that a sign of her feelings for him? Or the adrenaline? Or was it the fervor of the true NASA believer? Mark couldn't tell. The fact that he couldn't tell made him angry all over again.

He was tired. He was going to be angry about everything now.

Yuri Petrenko floated into the module. He had obviously been on the treadmill inside the core module. He was still wearing his running shorts and his bare torso glistened with sweat. He immediately began scanning the instrument panels. ''Did either of you hear anything? It sounded as though we got hit by something.''

Mark glanced at Kelly. There was no doubt about what he saw now. ''Not a thing,'' she said. ''Sorry.'' And she tugged Mark back toward the radial docking port, back toward the orbiter.

By design the hatches between Mir and the orbiter *Atlantis* were closed at 8:00 P.M. that evening, just as the STS-100 crew members were bedding down for the night. The exception was Donal O'Riordan, who was going to assist and observe the Russian side of the EVA from inside Mir. Jeff Dieckhaus, who supervised the hatch closing with Mark, didn't like the idea. ''So here we have four guys locked in Mir, and if we have some giant problem and take the orbiter away, they've got more people than they have seats.'' It was true: the Soyuz TM only had room for three, and those three were Petrenko, Belokonev and Stipe. Of course, the odds of a giant problem were remote; O'Riordan had dismissed them during training.

''This is how we're supposed to operate when the station gets running.'' That was one issue that was still to be resolved: Shuttle orbiters could not just be parked at a space station for months at a time. Even in an ideal world they might be parked there for a maximum of sixteen weeks out of the year.

What were the four or five or six or seven crew members—the number changed every time NASA and the Russian Space Agency had a meeting— supposed to do if there was a giant problem that required them to evacuate the station? Even two Soyuz vehicles, which was one more than planned, couldn't handle seven people.

This was old news, of course. The fact that Dieckhaus was even raising the matter showed where he stood on the whole NASA-Russia issue.

"I just hope he remembers to get on the right side of the hatch when we do leave."

The hatches needed to be closed so that the air pressure inside the orbiter could be lowered to 10.2 pounds per square inch without doing the same to the considerably greater volume of the Mir. Not only was it wasteful to dump hundreds of pounds of perfectly good air overboard, the change in pressure meant stress to the aged station and its modules. They were robust enough to survive launch, but essentially they were still rigid metal balloons.

Lowering the orbiter's pressure to 10.2 psi for twelve hours was one of the standard preparations for EVA. It meant that Mark and Kondratko would have to prebreathe pure oxygen for only one hour, not four. Four hours in the EMU suits added to the six hours for the scheduled EVA meant a long, boring, intensely uncomfortable workday.

So it was early to bed for Mark and Kondratko, then early to rise. By 10:00 A.M. of day three Mark, Kondratko and Freeh were hard at work inside the orbiter's airlock, donning their EMUs, a complicated job for three.

Mark knew that a few score feet away Cal Stipe and Volodya Belokonev were getting ready to do the same thing. They would be helped into the Russian Orlan-DMA EVA suits by Petrenko and O'Riordan for their purging and prebreathing. It was a slightly different protocol because the Orlans operated at 5.7 psi. The Russians also had more lax standards about nitrogen bubbles in the bloodstream. What this meant was that Stipe and Belokonev only needed to spend a little more than half an hour inside their suits before exiting.

The thought of even half an hour inside an Orlan made Mark uncomfortable. The Orlans aboard Mir were used for as many as ten EVAs before they were replaced, which meant stuffing the old suits into the Progress supply module, which would burn up on reentry. Given the complexity of the suits—which were, in effect, man-sized spacecraft—Mark was amazed they held up. He was also appalled when he thought about the, uh, hygienic situation. Talk about eau de locker room.

Stay focused, he told himself. Stipe is the enemy. This is space combat.

It was difficult; Mark was feeling tired. It wasn't true fatigue, but something his system did to him in extreme stress. He wanted to go somewhere and lie down. Instead he was wearing water-cooled long john underwear and mask and oxygen pack, and helping Viktor Kondratko to wedge his head and upper torso into the rigid upper body of the first EMU.

Eventually, much more quickly than he would have expected, they were buttoned up. Because of the bulky EMU backpacks and lack of space inside the orbiter's airlock, Mark had a terrific view of Kondratko's legs and feet. "The first sixty-nine in space," Kondratko had said the moment they were alone.

"You're way too late, Viktor," Mark said. "Not even in the top ten."

"I meant the first *International* sixty-nine." Downhill at Mission Control, some NASA public affairs officer was telling her audience that this would be the world's most populous EVA, by four astronauts from two different countries, with each team consisting of a Russian and an American. How it would be a forerunner of future International Space Station EVAs.

And all because Cal Stipe wanted to have his name on another record.

They didn't have much to say for a while. Kondratko dozed. Now that he was in his suit, of course, Mark was wide awake. The Snoopy cap he wore under his helmet helped deaden the droning of the suit's fans. He was able to listen in on some of the air-to-air chatter between the orbiter and Mir.

"Five minutes," Freeh told them at one point. Mark shifted inside the EMU, flexed the gloves and prepared to unhook himself from the wall. He saw that somebody was trying to get his attention at the window—Kelly. She pressed her face up against the glass like a little girl, then held up a hand-lettered note: *Be careful!* she had written. Then she turned it over. *I love you.*

Seeing those words written so plainly, Mark reacted without thinking, thumping his chest and mouthing them back to Kelly. She smiled, then gave way to Freeh.

It was a simple sentence, just three words. But Mark and Kelly had not said them to each other in all their months together.

The EVA no longer mattered as much. Neither did the Cal Stipe situation, or even NASA and the great mission of humans in space. Kelly was what mattered.

Mark had heard about astronauts experiencing epiphanies upon first seeing the Earth round and blue beneath them. He never expected that his own would come while he was floating upside down in the dark.

Goslin came on-line from the flight deck. "All right, guys, Stipe and Belokonev are out. You can open the door."

The first thing that struck Mark was how bright everything was, everything being the orbiter's payload bay, which was filled with the bulky docking system and SpaceHab modules, all wrapped in white thermal blankets. The silvery insides of the payload bay doors shone like mirrors. And then, above them, loomed the towering collection of cylinders and solar panels which was Mir.

To his right was the blue beauty of the Pacific Ocean.

Very quickly Mark began to think of Mir as next to the orbiter, not above it. His stomach had flip-flopped at the idea of this thing hanging overhead, and he mentally reoriented himself.

Step one, hook up the tethers for himself and for Kondratko. "Ready to go?" he radioed the Russian. Kondratko merely gave him a thumbs-up.

Their plan was to spend fifteen minutes or so in the payload bay, unshipping their tools and storage gear while getting used to moving around in microgravity. The suit was working wonderfully: even when Mark found himself in the shadow of the docking unit for several minutes, he never felt any change of temperature. The instructors had been right: it *was* just like working in the tank.

The next item on the agenda was the so-called handshake, scheduled to take place on the outside of the Kristall module. Mark could already see Stipe and Belokonev, who had exited from the Kvant-2 module on the +Y arm of Mir, moving from Mark's feet upward to the radial docking port, then straight toward him on the Kristall handrails, trailing a pair of safety lines each.

That was every EVA astronaut's nightmare—somehow coming unhooked and floating away from the orbiter and the station. Pilots were trained to go after you in some contingencies, but not when the orbiter was docked to Mir. You'd be dead before they could get undocked, assuming they could even begin to maneuver the orbiter to you.

Mark and Kondratko attached their long tethers, then, with about half a dozen checks, released the short ones. Then they, too, started moving hand-over-hand across the side of the Mir docking module to a point right next to the main Kristall solar power panels.

Kondratko went first, shaking hands with Stipe. Then Mark and Belokonev did the same. The EMU gloves were so bulky, especially under pressure, that Mark could just as easily have been picking up a hammer. It probably felt the same to Belokonev.

They turned back to the orbiter, so they could pose for the TV cameras. There was some chat with a deputy director of the Russian Space Agency and Melinda Pruett from NASA HQ, which Mark found distracting and annoying. They'd already used up the better part of an hour, and they hadn't even started to tear down the equipment!

"Back to work," Stipe announced suddenly, as if he were the man in charge. Well, of the four he was clearly the EVA champion.

Kondratko's and Mark's first goal was a package on the +X side of Kristall, essentially below them. Stipe and Belokonev, according to their sketchy and improvised EVA plan, were to back off to the radial docking port and stand by. Once the Shuttle pair had completed the bulk of their teardowns, the Mir team would move over to Priroda to change a battery. There was always a battery that needed to be changed on Mir. In fact, Mark had studied all the documentation on the various Mir service EVAs and had a pretty good idea which panel Stipe and Belokonev would be opening.

There was relatively little chatter on the comm line, a good thing, because the tortured path a UHF signal had to take—from the Shuttle team's radios into the Shuttle, from the Shuttle into Mir, from Mir into the Mir team's radios—meant there was a lot of noise in Mark's ears every time anyone said a word. Even worse, the volume on the Russian suits was cranked up, so they seemed to be shouting.

"Mark, say again." There was Kondratko again. "I'm really having trouble hearing." He tapped his helmet near where his right ear would be.

"Let's try this," Stipe said, his voice so loud he seemed to be sharing Mark's EMU. "Viktor, let Volodya help you here. . . . I'll move back to the battery with Mark for a few moments. Maybe you two will be able to hear each other better."

"Good idea, if it's okay with you guys." That was Freeh, who had to have conferred with Goslin and Petrenko. "We're ahead of the timeline."

Mark gave up his place to Belokonev, then began to follow Stipe toward the radial docking port. "We should probably keep it quiet for a few minutes," Stipe said, sounding as if he were out for a Sunday stroll with an old friend. Yesterday's ugly confrontation might have just been Mark's dream. "Let's get you hooked up here." Stipe smoothly inverted himself and transferred Mark's tether to the same attach point on Priroda he was already using. It was a good thing: Mark had reached the limit of his tether and was starting to find his movements restricted.

"I agree." What did they have to talk about, anyway? Joe Buerhle? Allyson? Wouldn't *that* have made a tasty subject for the folks in Mission Control?

"Too bad we can't just touch helmets." Deep-sea divers were able to communicate by putting one helmet in contact with another: sound waves would travel very easily through the air and metal. But that wouldn't work on an EVA: the helmets weren't all metal, and there were too many layers to allow for clear conduction.

"Got your cuff list?" Stipe said. The cuff list was a thirty-page flip book that an EVA astronaut carried in a pocket on his arm. It was basically the manual for the EVA, not that you really needed to refer to it. Stipe was hauling his out of a pocket on the shin of his Orlan suit. He also hauled out what looked like a big fat artist's pencil.

As Mark watched in astonishment, Stipe opened the manual, turned it over and *wrote something* on the back of one of the pages. Then he held it out to Mark: *First US-Russian EVA comm device, price $1!*

"Don't tell the taxpayers," Mark said. This was a reference to the old story about the difference between the ways NASA and the Russians approached problems. When NASA wanted a writing implement for astronauts, it spent a million dollars designing a special pen that could write in microgravity and was impervious to temperature extremes. The Russians simply bought pencils.

"Cal, this is Yuri—would you open the battery panel for me?"

Stipe acknowledged the call and turned away. Mark had just started to turn back to see how Kondratko and Belokonev were doing when he remembered something about the Priroda attach points, something he had memorized from another set of photos viewed in Russia.

In fact, it made his heart beat faster. One of them had been damaged on a previous EVA! He carefully pulled himself down and moved the tether back to a cleat on the radial docking port. He should move Stipe's, too, but not without telling him.

"Cal," he said, but Stipe, five feet away, merely motioned for silence. Okay.

He felt himself relaxing from the potential disaster. The EVA seemed to be going well. All that remained was the business of the Stipe extraction, and now that he had his EVA, that *should* be easier.

Suddenly Stipe turned to face him. Mark could see a smile on his bearded face as he started reaching into the other pocket. Mark realized what that shape meant. Almost in slow motion, Stipe pulled out the TP-82 pistol as Mark launched himself at Stipe's chest.

There was no feeling of impact—only the startled look on Stipe's face as Mark came flying toward him. Both men went sailing off Mir in opposite directions. Mark saw the surface of the Priroda module falling away from him. Before he could say anything, he reached the end of the tether, and, like a bungee jumper, headed right back at Stipe, whose tether was still slack as it played out behind him.

Stipe still had the three-barreled pistol in his hand. He aimed it in Mark's general direction and fired. Mark waited for the slam of the bullet, the burning pain, the hiss of oxygen escaping from his holed suit, but nothing came. Stipe had missed.

Worse for him, the reaction of the shot had pushed him farther away from the station. As Mark watched in growing horror, the cleat holding Stipe's tether snapped. The cleat and the tether whipped slowly away from Mark and the Priroda. He tried to catch them, but never came close.

Now Mark heard several people shouting, it seemed, all at once. The one that came through loudest was Cal Stipe. "Oh, Jesus; oh Christ. I'm loose...."

Then it was Petrenko and O'Riordan from inside Mir, screaming, "What's going on out there?" while an alarm bell rang.

Someone else was calling, "Mark? Mark? Did you grab him?" And "I see him. He's going end over end...." And "Do something! Somebody fucking *do* something!"

You can't move quickly on an EVA. But you can think. Mark unhooked his own tether, tried to visualize the path he wanted to take, and fired a burst from his SAFER backpack.

The price of the station rotation was that the picture was momentarily lost. But one of the 100 crew aimed a handheld camera out another window. Koskinen seemed farther away from Stipe now.

"Every second that passes makes it less likely the kid is gonna catch him," Strahan said quietly.

"At least he's out there, in the right ballpark if not the right seat." McDowell noted the figures that were appearing on his screen, then said, "Let me talk directly to EVA-1."

"I'm here, Houston." That was Koskinen, sounding far away.

"You're doing good, Mark. The important thing now is to give us a chance to run some of these figures. Your pack only carries three pounds of fuel, about a ten-foot-per-second delta vee. You've used about half of that already."

"I know."

"It's better for everyone if you let us help you from this point on."

"I wish you would."

McDowell ignored that. "Can you talk to Cal?"

"I've been telling him I'm here. But he's doing a slow roll, so I don't know how much he's catching. And I haven't heard from him."

The communications team reported that the crew aboard Mir had heard nothing, either. There was another worry: Stipe's physical condition.

Now that the EVA and prox ops teams had more than a single data point, they were able to form a better picture of Stipe's trajectory, and Mark's, which were close but ultimately diverging. "If we can get him pointed in the right direction for a full one-second burst, we can get an intercept."

"How soon?" McDowell said.

"Within the next ten minutes."

"We'll do it."

Hearing this, Strahan put his hand on McDowell's shoulder. "That won't leave the kid with enough margin to get home."

"We need to send the orbiter after them," McDowell said, and without waiting for Strahan's opinion, sent the order through to *Atlantis*.

"Jeff's already working through the checklist," Goslin reported. "But it's going to take a few minutes."

"Take what you need," McDowell ordered. "We're only gonna do this once."

McDowell took himself out of the loop as the EVA support guys talked directly to Yakubik, and then Mark, on how to orient himself. The station-orbiter complex, and its two human satellites, were in sunlight, so it wasn't going to be easy to find a star to steer by. Landmarks on the Earth's surface were going by so fast that they were useless. Mark had to use the Mir itself as his fixed point.

"Give me Channel B," McDowell said to Yakubik. Channel B was the backup frequency for air-to-ground communications; it was private. "Mark," he said, "this is McDowell. We're set to give this burn in four minutes, thirty seconds. But it's your call—if you want to turn around and come home, do it. Because we're going to eat up the rest of your fuel. You'll have to wait for *Atlantis* to come get you, and that could be a couple of hours."

"My consumables are good for four," Koskinen said. "Let's give it a shot."

Let's give it a shot. McDowell couldn't help smiling. "That's what we're gonna do."

The countdown to the burn was endless, but McDowell's time was filled with the chatter of the *Atlantis* crew preparing to undock the orbiter while getting its own burn and trajectory updates.

"Coming up on thirty seconds," Yakubik radioed.

"I've got Mir just over my left shoulder," Mark said. Twenty. Ten. "Did it."

The picture on the screen didn't change. It wasn't as though the dim white figure that was Mark Koskinen suddenly jetted off in another direction. But within seconds McDowell could see that the slowly tumbling figure of Cal Stipe was closer. Then closer still.

"I've got him."

CHAPTER 64

Mark's statement was a bit premature. Yes, he had Stipe within reach. In fact, he had closed on Cal Stipe so directly that he almost bounced off the other man. But there was a momentary tangle, since Stipe was gently tumbling, until Mark got a firm grip on Stipe's foot.

Now, of course, he was tumbling, too. He fired what he hoped was a fraction-of-a-second burst from the SAFER to stabilize them.

The whole business took several seconds, and the exertion caused Mark to sweat so much inside his EMU that he momentarily overwhelmed the cooling system. He felt cold and wet, and saw clearly just how awfully far he was from the Mir complex and the orbiter *Atlantis*.

"Cal, can you hear me?" The rogue astronaut was clearly conscious: one hand was playing across the valves and connects on the front of the Orlan suit. The other still held the Soyuz rescue pistol.

". . . hear you—" That was all Mark heard. The connection, bouncing from the transmitter on Stipe's suit up to Mir, then through *Atlantis* and back to Mark, was filled with static.

"They're going to come and get us," Mark said. Given his hold on Stipe's boots, he was unable to see the other man's face. He realized they must look like a white letter *T* floating by themselves in orbit. "We just have to hold on."

"Fine." Stipe's voice sounded subdued, very unlike a man who had just been saved from a lingering public death.

The fact that Stipe still held the TP-82 would ordinarily have made Mark a little nervous, but he was too exhausted to care. Besides, with the limited maneuverability, there was no way Stipe could bring the pistol to bear directly on Mark. Better yet, the only thing Stipe had available now were two flares. Even if he did somehow manage to aim the thing at Mark, he would be committing suicide.

Or would he? The capture and stabilization meant that Stipe was essentially motionless, relative to Mir and *Atlantis*. He could be tracked and rescued now. . . .

"Mark, it's Kelly."

Oh my God . . . Kelly. She must have thought he'd lost his mind. "Right here."

"I don't know if you can see, but we're going to back off away from Mir—" At that moment Mark saw *Atlantis* slowly rise from Mir. That was how it looked to him, at least, the white winged beast floating upward, upside down. "It may look like we're going home, but don't worry. We've got to drop below you guys, then come up from underneath."

"I've got the picture."

"Cal, are you there, too?"

"Right here."

"Houston says to just hang on."

"Are we live?" That was Stipe's question, a good one, Mark thought. Had everyone in the world seen his risky maneuver? His *parents*?

"You've been private since Mark started his closing burn."

"Good idea," Mark said, chiming in. "Keep it that way, okay?"

"We're going to lose you as soon as we start juking around here, anyway, but the guys in Mir will still have you on line-of-sight."

Mark started to thank Kelly, but as he did he could hear the signal from *Atlantis* fuzz out. Sure enough, the cutoff coincided with a flash of reaction control motor plumes as the orbiter, now several hundred feet above Mir, rotated its wings and the payload bay toward Mark at the same time the whole vehicle began to drop away behind Mir.

They'll be coming up from below, Mark told himself.

"Koskinen," Stipe said.

"Right here, Cal."

"Let go of me." Stipe seemed to be breathing hard.

"How are your consumables? Is your oxygen mix too light?"

"I said, 'Let go of me'!"

"That's a bad idea, Cal."

"I'm not going back."

"Don't be stupid—"

Stipe started thrashing violently, as violently as anyone could in a pressure suit. Mark found it hard to hang on. "Cool it, Cal! I don't need to get kicked around here!"

Shit, now they were rotating again. Mark saw the surface of the Earth slowly rising to greet him as Mir disappeared. "What the hell is the matter with you?"

"I can't go back."

"Sure you can. You may have some explaining to do, but—"

Stipe succeeded in wrenching his boot free. The two man-shaped Earth satellites, now free to move in their own orbits, bumped into each other. "Give me your hand!" Mark snapped.

The only hand close enough to grab was the one with the pistol. "Point that thing away from you and fire it," Mark said. "The reaction will kick you toward me. . . ."

"I'm not going back to explain anything, Mark. I don't belong there anymore." He pointed the pistol in Mark's direction and fired again.

But not at Mark. By design or accident, he had aimed somewhere over Mark's shoulder. The flare blinded Mark as it streaked off into space, eventually to fall to Earth like any one of a billion specks of space dust.

The reaction kicked Stipe away from Mark for all time.

"Don't do this," Mark said, feeling helpless and stupid, because it was *done*.

"You'll see," Stipe said. He was laughing.

CHAPTER 65

Kelly was wrung out by the time Mark, prodded by Viktor Kondratko, emerged into the airlock of the orbiter *Atlantis*. Part of the strain was due to worry about Mark. Then there was the sheer horror of Stipe's self-inflicted situation. And, finally, just the frustration of having to sit at the window watching two very tired EVA crew members slowly cranking the handle—a turn of 440 degrees was required, not much more than a single turn!—to close the six latches.

There was almost no chatter beyond the basics. Kelly advising Mark and Viktor to watch their heads, watch their backpacks, make sure they brought in their tools. What Kelly heard in return were a series of one-word replies. *Yeah. Okay. Man.*

Then she had to wait for the airlock to pressurize. This took a few minutes, too.

The Shuttle's EMU suits carried sufficient oxygen and water to keep an astronaut alive for seven hours, with a thirty-minute pad for emergencies. They were right up against the seven-hour point. Even if the EVA astronauts weren't in immediate danger of suffocation, they were hungry, tired and in God only knew what kind of mental state. Particularly Mark, who had some-where found the guts to fire himself away from the station and orbiter. It had to have been like making your first dive off a cliff.

Then to have reached Cal Stipe, only to lose him! It had all happened while the orbiter was out of contact with Mark. One moment Mark had hold of Stipe and the two of them were going to wait for rescue. The next time Kelly looked, it was Mark alone, with Stipe drifting away.

She had been on the flight deck at the time. "Oh, my fucking God,"

Jeff Dieckhaus had said, the very phrasing that should have brought a stern warning from Steve Goslin.

But Goslin had been stunned into silence—for a moment. He said, simply, "We're going after Mark first. Make sure Viktor is standing by to grab him." Only then did he tell Houston what he was doing . . . and that Stipe was adrift again.

It was the only decision Goslin could have made. Mark was essentially stationary while Stipe was now headed off in another direction entirely. It had taken all the great minds and computers several minutes to find some way to get the *Atlantis* close to Mark; there was simply no way to then have it go after Stipe, too.

Kelly desperately wanted to know if Stipe was saying anything. If he was talking to Mir, Mir had yet to tell *Atlantis*.

And what was he *thinking*? She would probably never know the answer to that.

She could only imagine what hell had broken loose downhill, in Houston. Every TV network in the world would be covering this live—and NASA had shut down the feed! When would they break in? Who would be stuck making the announcement? And what would they say? "Astronaut Calvin Stipe is adrift in space and not expected to survive. His store of oxygen is expected to run out within the hour." Holy *shit*.

Finally, the inner airlock door opened. Kelly joined Dave Freeh in pulling it aside, and out came pale, sweaty Mark and Viktor wearing their thick white water-cooled undergarments. For a moment the four of them fumbled their way through a group hug. Collision was more like it. Kelly found herself kissing Viktor Kondratko as well as Mark.

Goslin joined them at that point. He literally grabbed Mark's hand. "Welcome back. You did your best." He turned to Kondratko. "You, too, Viktor."

Mark just nodded somberly. No one needed to say what everyone was thinking . . . that somewhere not far from them, perhaps less than a mile or two away, an astronaut was dying the loneliest death imaginable.

What kept Kelly from feeling too emotional about the subject was that this astronaut had killed two other people. But it was still horrible.

"What happened out there?"

"I caught him. I had him in my hands. He just shook me off."

Kelly felt sorry for Goslin. He didn't know about Joe Buerhle and Allyson Morin, so how could he begin to understand the depth of Stipe's insanity? It would never make sense to him until he was told the truth, and possibly not then.

"Dave, why don't you see how Jeff's doing upstairs?" Goslin said to Freeh. "We've got to set up for the redock with Mir. I can help Viktor."

"Aye-aye," Freeh said, pulling himself over to the mid-deck access. That should have been Kelly's job, but Goslin seemed to understand that Kelly and Mark needed a moment together, even though four people on the mid-deck meant there was no real privacy. Kelly was too tired to care. "I was worried shitless," she told Mark.

"So was I."

"It *was* very brave."

"Stop it. I just reacted the way I was trained."

"No one can train you to do something like that."

Mark looked away. For a moment Kelly thought he had tears in his eyes. But then he smiled faintly and shook his head. "You know what it was?" he said, even more quietly. "I lost my temper. I was so mad at Stipe that I wasn't going to let him get away. I went after him because I wanted to kill him."

"Remind me never to get you mad," Kelly said. "Again."

Freeh suddenly appeared in the mid-deck access. "Steve, you might want to come up here. You, too, Kelly."

Kelly didn't like the nervousness she heard in Freeh's voice. Neither did Goslin, who practically dove for the access. Kelly followed.

In the left front seat, the commander's position, Jeff Dieckhaus had his face in his hands. Freeh looked shaken as he held a communications headset for Goslin to listen.

"What is it?" Kelly asked.

"Last words from Cal Stipe, relayed through Mir."

Looking sick, Goslin thrust the headset at Kelly. She couldn't even put it on, because all she heard was a man screaming.

NASA N E W S

National Aeronautics and
Space Administration
Lyndon B. Johnson Space Center
Houston TX 77058
281 481-5111

June 17, 1999
Sam Wirth
Johnson Space Center

STS-100 MISSION CONTROL STATUS REPORT #8

The crew of Space Shuttle *Atlantis* entered its last full day of flight following separation yesterday from the Russian space station Mir. The limited schedule of activities includes closing down the mid-deck and
SpaceHab experiments, and further stowage of materials being returned
from Mir.

At the request of STS-100 commander Steven Goslin, the usual mu-
sical wake-up call from Mission Control was not made. He reports that
the spirits of the crew of seven are "pretty good, given the circumstances."

Program managers here in Mission Control have elected to shorten
STS-100, bringing the orbiter home a day early. This is partly due to
predicted weather problems at the primary landing site at the Kennedy
Space Center in Florida, and also related to the loss of astronaut Calvin
Stipe during Tuesday's EVA. Flight crew operations director Lester Fehrenkamp said, "The crew made a valiant and exhaustive effort to save
their comrade. We think it would be best for all concerned to have them
home as soon as possible."

The Mir-31 crew of Yuri Petrenko and Vladimir Belokonev are continuing their flight. They have expressed condolences to the family and
friends of Calvin Stipe.

CHAPTER 66

A tlantis, Houston, we've got you at ten thousand, heading around the circle.''

"Roger."

The terse exchange between Arnaldo Rivera and Steve Goslin echoed in the surprisingly cool Florida morning. Les Fehrenkamp stepped onto the roof of the crew quarters building and looked to the south. Sure enough, there was the tiny white arrowhead of the orbiter, a spot of brilliance in the sky. A moment later a double *crack!* rolled across the shoreline.

"Space Shuttle *Atlantis* has announced its arrival at the Kennedy Space Center with twin sonic booms." That was the voice of NASA public affairs. It wouldn't be long now.

Another one of Les Fehrenkamp's pleasures was greeting his Shuttle crews when they landed. Occasionally it was out in the high desert at Edwards Air Force Base, but most often it was at the Shuttle landing strip at the Kennedy Space Center in Florida, right next to the Vehicle Assembly Building where the Shuttle stacks were built.

Like launches, landings sent Fehrenkamp through a whole spectrum of emotions, but in a different order. He was never quite as tense about landings as he was about launches, for the simple reason that none of the landings had ever ended in utter disaster. Fehrenkamp knew it was possible. On approach the orbiter was more like a falling stone than an aircraft, in spite of its wings. Mismanage the energy and you simply don't make it to the runway—or you land too long. Either way, the orbiter would flip over just like a crash-landing airliner, with the same results: destruction of the vehicle and fatal injuries to most, if not all, of the crew.

Nevertheless, Fehrenkamp did not feel fear in his bones the way he did at launches.

The other difference was that when the landing was over, he finally relaxed. Even though he tended to relax once the orbiter made it safely uphill, he would still be nagged by his worries about the critical milestones ahead. There was nothing for him to worry about once the orbiter reached wheel stop. True, the bird was still full of toxic fumes. A leak or explosion was always possible. But not likely.

As he watched, the *Atlantis* seemed to fall out of the sky, changing from a white wedge to a large winged cylinder in a matter of moments. Goslin and Dieckhaus expertly flared the orbiter, dropped the gear, and touched down as close to the centerline as you'd ever need. There was a *whoosh!* as the orbiter rolled past, slowing as it went, far down the runway.

"Houston, wheels stopped." Goslin again.

"*Atlantis*, Houston. We copy you wheels stopped. Welcome home." Normally each capcom read a little message composed by the public affairs people: "Welcome home, *Atlantis*, on another successful chapter in international spaceflight." Or some crap like that. There had been no dissent when Fehrenkamp suggested a more subdued approach. Otherwise Arnaldo Rivera's message would have been more along the lines of "Condolences, *Atlantis*, on losing one of your crew members."

Fehrenkamp had called NORAD upon awakening this morning. They were still tracking Cal Stipe's body, which was still slowly tumbling head over heels in its steadily decaying orbit. It would probably reenter and burn up within a month, perhaps sooner, affording Stipe the Viking funeral he so richly deserved.

Still, it was a horrid reminder of what had happened—what the news people called "one of the worst disasters" in the history of manned spaceflight. The *Challenger* accident was number one, of course, and Fehrenkamp guessed you would have to count the 1967 Apollo fire and the 1971 Soyuz 11 accident as tied for second, since both had cost three lives. The 1967 Soyuz 1 crash that killed Russian cosmonaut Vladimir Komarov would have to be fourth, since that disaster had also killed any chance the Russians might have had of beating the United States to the Moon.

Cal Stipe was no better than fifth. That would have bothered him.

Of course, unlike the unlucky souls in the other accidents, Cal Stipe had managed to leave a message—a legacy. As he floated out of Mark Koski-

nen's reach, he had told the world to "keep believing" and "keep explor-
ing." "We all have to work together, because this is a dangerous business—
no one can do it alone."

No one can do it alone. NASA public affairs had told Fehrenkamp that
hits on the Shuttle-Mir web site had skyrocketed. Far from being turned off
by the spectacle of an astronaut's floating off to his doom, the people of the
world had been totally fascinated.

Careful, he reminded himself. Don't start being too cynical about this
"tragedy." He straightened his tie and headed for the steps, and the bus
which would take him to the *Atlantis* and the crew of STS-100.

He was going to pin everything on you," he told Mark Koskinen an hour
later, once the crew had staggered off the orbiter to be driven back to their
quarters. He met Mark alone in his room—the kind of thing he did, briefly,
with all the crew members, beginning with Steve Goslin, who had frankly
done a terrific job, given the circumstances. And who would need all the
Christian forbearance he could summon to face those who would ask him—
for the rest of his life—why he had not simply gone charging off to rescue
poor Cal Stipe.

"I suppose that makes sense, but how?"

"Once the, uh, accident occurred I took steps to secure his residence,
as we say. I found some notes about your movements and actions last fall.
Some of the materials found in his personal gear from the station indicate
that he was ready to make a case that you had somehow caused the Buerhle
accident, that he had confronted you about it, and you had attempted to
harm him during the EVA."

"And my tether came loose—"

"With so much force that even your SAFER pack would not have been
able to get you back to safety. You can see the various scenarios, all bad
for you." Mark seemed to shudder. Fehrenkamp looked forward to the EVA
debrief.

"Do you suppose he was worried that I would start accusing him as
my oxygen ran out? I could have talked for a couple of hours."

"The notes were Stipe's protection against just that contingency. They
would show that he had suspicions about you from the beginning."

Mark looked about as disgusted as a human being could look. "What
about Allyson?"

"The notes say that was probably an accident. If you were dead and unable to defend yourself, of course, I'm sure it would have looked a bit more suspicious.''

"Like I was some kind of psycho killer. Joe Buerhle, Allyson, tried to kill Stipe. He'd have looked like a goddamn hero.''

"I imagine so.'' Fehrenkamp cleared his throat. He was not used to talking about this matter. It made him very uncomfortable. "The notes, of course, are perfectly ambiguous—if you don't know the truth.''

Mark got a strange smile on his face. "Would you have come to my defense, Les? Would you have rushed right out and told the world that it was *really* Stipe who did it?''

"I'm going to assume that was kind of a joke, that you're really not quite recovered from the flight.'' Fehrenkamp was prepared to tolerate a certain amount of attitude from Mark and Kelly, in particular, and the rest of the crew. Getting through a mission was tough enough, much less the first one in history forced to stand by helplessly as a crew member drifted off to certain death.

HQ had shortened the mission by a day in order to simply bring the crew home as soon as possible. A few experimenters would be unhappy, but they were often unhappy with the Shuttle program.

"Well, what happens now?'' Mark said.

"What do you mean? With your career? I probably can't turn you around on another mission right away. You'll probably have to spend a year on a tech assignment, like your classmates, before you go back in the pool—''

"No, Les, with Buerhle and Allyson and Stipe. What do we say?''

"I think we've said all we can.''

"Which means nothing. Buerhle's accident was pilot error, Allyson's was driver error, Stipe's was, hell, an act of God.''

Fehrenkamp did not like what he was seeing and hearing. Mark was close to putting himself in a position he could not easily abandon. "Let's talk about this back in Houston. When we've all had time to rest and think things through.''

Fehrenkamp squeezed Mark's shoulder. For a moment he believed his suggestion had done its work, but then Mark looked up. There were tears in his eyes. "I don't need a rest and I don't need to think, Les. I can't play this game. I can't just put this all out of my mind, pretend it was an accident, just so people will go into space. Just so the goddamn program will be saved. Because if this is what it takes, it doesn't deserve to be saved.''

He could not have made himself any clearer. "Well, then, Mark, you do what you feel is right—and so will I." He turned to walk out of the room, then stopped. "There was one thing," he told Mark. "We found a mountain bike at Stipe's place. I think it belonged to you."

The next room belonged to Dave Freeh, but Fehrenkamp passed it. In a fog of anger and frustration, he walked all the way out of the crew quarters building and into the parking lot. When he got there he just sat down on the curb and put his aching head in his hands.

Why was Mark doing this to him? Hadn't he done everything he could to help him? What did he want?

Presently he raised his head and took out his cell phone. His poor secretary, Valerie, was in for a rough day.

NASA N E W S
National Aeronautics and
Space Administration
Lyndon B. Johnson Space Center
Houston TX 77058
281 481-5111

October 8, 1999
Lou Wekkin
Johnson Space Center, Houston TX
(Phone: 281/483-1511)

KOSKINEN TO SPACELIFTER PROGRAM

Astronaut Mark Koskinen is taking a leave of absence to work on the Spacelifter program, where he will become director of space applications.

Koskinen, a member of the 1998 astronaut class, is a veteran of the STS-100 Shuttle mission (June 1999).

"Mark has made a terrific impression on all of us in the short time he has been at NASA," said flight crew operations director Les Fehrenkamp. The leave of absence is scheduled to last one year, at which point Koskinen could return to the astronaut office.

The Las Cruces, New Mexico–based Spacelifter program is a privately funded reusable launch system funded in part by NASA, the Department of Defense, the Ballistic Missile Defense Organization, and the Federal Express Company.

For a full biography of Koskinen, see the JSC homepage at http://www.jsc.nasa.gov/astro/bios.html

CHAPTER 67

The forecast for this October morning said it would be unseasonably hot, maybe into the low one hundreds. Really too hot to be riding a bike, but Mark decided he would simply carry extra water. It wasn't as though he had errands to run. He would probably be locked up at the test site.

Besides, the car would be blistering, sitting outside in the parking lot. Better to leave it in the garage.

He delayed his departure for a few moments to turn on CNN, fearing that he was already too late. But no: there was the *Endeavour* sitting on the pad at T minus nine minutes and holding. The launch was STS-106, the fourth Space Station assembly flight. The crew of six was commanded by one of the veterans Mark knew only by sight: the pilot, however, was Jason Borders, one of Mark's fellow Worms. Another Worm, Greg Yakubik, was a mission specialist in the crew. He was supposed to do a pair of EVAs.

But there was a weather hold, a problem at Banjul, one of the abort sites across the Atlantic. It didn't look as though it was going to clear, and Mark was just about to leave the house when the phone rang.

"Are you watching?" It was Kelly Gessner.

"Why wouldn't I be?"

"Bitterness. Intelligence. A desire to put that part of your life behind you."

"It's not that far behind yet," he said. Not at all. He had barely been living in this rental in Las Cruces for a month. Virginia Drury, widow of the late NASA veteran, had found it for him. Mark found it strange that his life had become permanently intertwined with Drury's—he was scheduled to have dinner with Virginia and her son tomorrow evening, in fact—since he had grown convinced that Drury thought him immature and unwilling to follow orders. Maybe Drury had wanted to shape him up, to salvage him.

Or maybe this was just one last attempt at having his own way, even in death.

"I thought things moved faster on those little X projects."

"Not that fast. Where are you?"

"The office."

He could picture her, feet up on the desk in the same space they had shared this past year. Goslin had moved to a corner office; he was the new chief astronaut. Dieckhaus was down the hallway, since he had his own crew now. O'Riordan was also in a new crew, and Kondratko was back in Russia, maybe forever. Only Freeh would be around, and Mark seemed to recall that he was heading up the C-squares now, so of course he would have been at the Cape strapping in the 106 crew this morning. "Hold it a sec," she said, setting down the phone. Then she was back. "They're picking up the count."

"Good. Let's see how they do . . ."

He imagined Kelly standing in the doorway now, watching the TV at the secretary's desk. Eight minutes.

It was hard for Mark to believe that five months ago he had been one of the humans hidden inside that white beast, its image shimmering in the Florida heat. It was even harder to believe that it was only a year ago that he had shown up at Ellington Field for a routine training flight with Joe Buerhle.

Thinking about the T-38s made him a little sad. What a lot of fun that had turned out to be. He had eventually gotten up to 186 hours in the little white rocket, a ridiculous number. But if pressed he could remember each flight.

That was gone now. Only active astronauts had access to the T-38s. And Mark Koskinen was no longer active—but on leave to the Spacelifter project. The door was officially open for his return, but he sincerely hoped that no one at JSC was holding his breath waiting for Mark to come knocking. He was committed to the Spacelifter now. With a little luck, the reusable demonstrator would be flying out of Edwards by spring. If that went well, a full-scale unmanned model would be in orbit in the year 2002, long before the International Space Station would be finished. It wouldn't be a giant step from that to a manned flight vehicle, and Mark Koskinen could find himself in orbit again.

There went the main engines . . . then the solids. "We have liftoff on STS-106, the fourth space station assembly mission!"

Mark's heart rate jumped as he watched *Endeavour* rise into the sky on its SRBs. Knowing what it was like made the idea of a Shuttle launch even more terrifying. No wonder it was the rookies who looked exuberant while the veterans were scared to death!

Thinking of death in space made him think about Cal Stipe, who was well on his way to becoming the patron saint of manned spaceflight. He had chosen public death over an equally public humiliation—well, up until the very end, when he had finally realized that it was all over. Until the screaming started, however, he had lobbed one sound bite after another at the world, which listened, horrified and fascinated. *We've got to work as a planet. No one country can afford it. The human race can't put all its eggs in one basket. Even if there isn't life on Mars we could put it there* . . . One enterprising soul had collected and edited the material into a CD, complete with some stirring theme music from a recent Academy Award–winning epic, and had cracked the *Billboard* chart with it. To this day no more than half a dozen people knew that Stipe was a murderous psychopath. Even if Mark wound up on *Larry King* with pictures and proof, he would do nothing to mar Stipe's saintly image. It was all about the message, anyway, not the messenger. And thanks to Stipe's message, people were more enthusiastic about spaceflight now than at any time in the past thirty years.

Fehrenkamp had also prospered. The director of flight crew operations was moving up to become deputy director of the Johnson Space Center. He would have even more power.

Or so it seemed. Kelly had told Mark that Fehrenkamp's promotion was anything but. That the new slot was little more than a holding cell until the space agency could quietly ease him out.

Mark knew he would never figure it out. He knew by now that no matter what was said publicly, or even privately, there would always be another reason, a different sequence of events, or a mysterious motivation. That was NASA.

In spite of that, Mark really didn't hate NASA. That would be like hating a whole country. Or the weather. The organization had been created to put a man into space, then to put one on the Moon. It had done both jobs spectacularly well, on time and pretty much on budget. Then, however, like a drunk at a party, it had simply stuck around, eventually finding the Space Shuttle and ISS to justify its existence. There were good people—great people—all through the agency. But there were bad people, too. Empire builders as arrogant, intelligent and ruthless as the Khmer Rouge. They wanted you to be good in their way—or they'd kill you.

Mark was happier where he was, working with a small team of young people who were building a dream. Like NASA in the old days.

Kelly came back on-line. "The SRBs are gone, so I guess I can relax now."

Oh, yes, Kelly. One of the good people still embedded in NASA. "When are you coming out here?"

"I thought maybe this weekend. If you can promise me that it'll be really hot and dry." He laughed. They were still trying to rebuild their relationship, which had just about ended right before the 100 mission. It was only once they were back in Houston that they had been able to take even baby steps toward a new start.

"Over a hundred today and through the weekend."

"Great. I'll bring two swimming suits."

"Don't forget your résumé." Things wouldn't really start again until they lived in the same town. Until Kelly was out of NASA.

"Maybe I will," she said. "Still love me?"

"More than all the sand between here and Houston."

After they hung up, Mark found himself at the window, looking north and east toward the San Andres Mountains. Beyond them lay the blinding waste of the Tularosa Basin, which was home to the blockhouses and battered old hangars of the White Sands Missile Range.

It didn't look inviting, but neither had the Cape in 1959. Or the area around JSC in 1963. Or the Baikonur Cosmodrome in 1954.

Mark felt that Don Drury had done him a tremendous favor before he died, giving his name to the Spacelifter people. He was already learning to love the little beast the way Drury had. He would never have loved the Shuttle or the Space Station. He was glad he had realized that before giving up ten or more years of his life. And it was just barely possible that the Spacelifter would be a little better because of Mark.

If he got started now, he would be at the site by eight.

ACKNOWLEDGMENTS

Missing Man owes a debt to many people, none of whom should be blamed for my inevitable mistakes. H. E. "Bud" Ream, formerly of the Aircraft Ops Directorate (CC), took me through Ellington Field and got me into a T-38 cockpit. The late Donald K. "Deke" Slayton and Walter C. Williams provided anecdotes and inspiration. Bob Thompson shared his insights into the space business with me. Tom McClure briefed me on some of the challenges of being an astronaut candidate.

The origins of the ASCAN Ten Commandments are, as they say, shrouded in mystery—but Ken Jenks brought them to my attention. Michael Grabois explained Shuttle launch operations. Bernard Harris straightened me out on a number of points. Mark Hess educated me on Shuttle-Mir EVAs. ElizaBeth Gilligan put me in touch with Ray Murphy, to my great benefit. Robert Crais made an offhand suggestion that proved key. Steve "Barracuda" Roberts shared his sailplaning stories. Bert Vis was generous with his knowledge. Catherine Johnson was kind enough to offer advice.

Charles Vick encouraged me to join the Friends and Partners in Space 1997 tour of Russian space centers, directed by Jennifer Green, to my benefit. Boris Yesin of the Gagarin Cosmonaut Training Center gave the tour of a lifetime. My agent, Richard Curtis, found *Missing Man* a home, and Beth Meacham, my editor, made it a happy one.

Thank you all, and my apologies for the liberties I have taken.

Michael Cassutt
Los Angeles, July 1997